RETURNING AS
SHADOWS

RETURNING AS SHADOWS

Paco Ignacio Taibo II

Translated from the Spanish
by
Ezra E. Fitz

THOMAS DUNNE BOOKS
ST. MARTIN'S PRESS ❧ NEW YORK

THOMAS DUNNE BOOKS.
An imprint of St. Martin's Press.

www.stmartins.com

Design by Phil Mazzone

Library of Congress Cataloging-in-Publication Data

Taibo, Paco Ignacio, 1949–
    [Retornamos como sombras. English]
    Returning as shadows / Paco Ignacio Taibo II ; translated from the Spanish by
Ezra E. Fitz.
        p. cm.
    ISBN 0-312-30156-1
    I. Fitz, Ezra E. II. Title

    PQ7298.3.A58 R4813 2003
    863'.64—dc21

                                                                200203588

Originally published in Spain under the title *Retornamos como Sombras* by Editorial Des-
tino, and in Mexico by Editorial Planeta.

First U.S. Edition: January 2003

10   9   8   7   6   5   4   3   2   1

I come, I go, I retreat, I advance madly
All the while seeking to keep clenched in my fist
The shadow of the shadow of oblivion.
—PEDRO GARFIAS

My ignorance, it had been decided long ago, was to be
lessened only through learning by myself.
—ERNEST HEMINGWAY, *True at First Light*

A robust yet tormented soul looks in on itself
And anxious, mortal troubles burden,
Bring down only noble heads.
—FRANCISCO DE QUEVEDO

AUTHOR'S
PRELIMINARY NOTE

Returning as Shadows is the sequel to The Shadow of a Shadow. But if readers are as irreverent as I am, they may read them in whatever order they prefer.

I began this book in 1985 and ran into many roadblocks. I had in mind a Dumasian novel that picks up stories left Twenty Years After: a tribute to our master and a revisiting of old characters. But it was the character of Dumas himself that infected the writing. Nearly ten years passed in which I could write only loose, disparate notes. Soon after picking it up again in 1996, I received word of a terrible accident in which the stage director Guillermo Cabello, who directed the first production of Shadow of a Shadow, was seriously injured. I wrote on, hoping that he would recover quickly and eventually be able to bring back to the stage these characters whom he understood so well and loved so much. But Guillermo did not survive the accident. It is to him, and in his memory, that this book is dedicated, as well as to Javier González Garza, a surprising Hemingway aficionado.

It goes without saying that although a multitude of historical figures (or rather, those who are usually thought of as historical) run throughout this story, it should be treated as a novel and its histories, therefore, belong completely to the realm of fiction.

A note at the end of the book gives informative sources, tricks, and transgressions of the story-history. However, I do have some suspicions that what we call "the truth" is actually something much more subtle and elusive than what can be found in history's record.

PART	I

CHARACTERS AND CROSSES

INTERRUPTIONS
AND INVASIONS

3. There were many birds. Goldfinches, sparrows, and starlings. Doves and turtledoves, swallows and blackbirds. Both free and caged. Masses of canaries fluttered about in tiny cages piled on the backs of vendors; there was even a lazy buzzard circling in the terribly blue sky high above the rooftops. Paradoxically and quite unusually, the birds were sad and silent. Perhaps the end of spring?

4. So it was that in 1941 the embassy of Nazi Germany found itself located at the corner of Hamburgo and Insurgentes streets, in Mexico City, and there was, on one side of the green gates, on the old stone wall, moss-covered and teeming with tiny ants that marched tirelessly over the walls (since when the hell do ants sleep?), a plaque bearing an eagle, aggressive yet distant, dull and coarse, that held in its talons a shield emblazoned with a giant swastika.

4. A corollary (though this is not what's interesting): Fascism is filled to no end with eagles, bronze statues, plaques, and the rest of this sort of paraphernalia; its caustic symbols fill our eyes, its torchlit parades and militarized children burn our pupils. But the truly important thing here is that this plaque was invariably cleaned every morning with a buffer and, sometimes, with polish. The buffer was a "Limcream" brand, while the polish bore no mark.

4. An obliging corollary to the corollary: a story, this story, beginning

when Faustino (a young fellow on the embassy's staff, whose function in the German bureaucracy began morning after morning with the same ritual: polish the plaque) finds it covered in spit. What do we know of this fellow? Not much. Do we want to know something besides the fact that he dresses in dark blue overalls and a cap of silvery-gray cloth? Perhaps. Faustino is a man who leads a double life. While he works mornings in the German embassy as a janitor, in the afternoons he is king of the kings of the dance floor in the Salón Colonial. That's his true world, full of turns and cuts and moves in a space that measures scrupulously up against the bricks where his white patent leather shoes and the stiletto heels of his occasional partner trace tiny, delicate lines to the sound of the trumpet. He's spent the past three months competing in a contest held by XEQ Radio and has won round after round, advancing furiously to the well-deserved final. All of this is essential for understanding later developments. But here, this morning, when he begins to clean the plaque with his cloth, he gets the feeling that someone is watching him.

5. Shifting our point of view (and by that I mean a literary twist rather than a physical change of perspective): a character who would like to call himself Mark Twain is watching from the other side of the sidewalk, his gaze myopic and relentless.

5a. Mark Twain is not Mark Twain. He's someone who's borne two stigmas and an impediment ever since childhood. The two stigmas are (1) a persistent baldness that leaves him stubbornly opposed to the strong April sun of Mexico City and (2) a ridiculous name, Pioquinto Manterola, which spawned, in the most secret chest of his recondite passions, where the little spiders of hidden dreams weave their nests and webs, his desire to name himself after the North American writer. The impediment is that no matter how often he's tried, he's not only unable to write in the mornings, but he's also incapable at any time of day of writing the novel he desires. And he's even more unable still to go to court and change his name.

Well, either Mark Manterola or Pioquinto Twain watched Faustino painstakingly polish the plaque, removing the traitorous, nocturnal saliva that this same journalist had spit just a few hours earlier, since the nightly defacing of the Nazi eagle has become his responsibility.

Manterola is coming off a hard night of drinking and heads toward the offices of the recently created UPI Press Agency (where he doesn't work) without having slept. He comes thinking about trivialities like, for example, the exact weight of a sterling silver ingot.

6. Although Manterola doesn't know it, one of those sterling silver ingots weighs nearly a kilogram, 880 grams to be precise, an arbitrary number resulting from a mold that some Stalinist bureaucrat had decided on as stan-

dard. And silver in changing climates barely varies in weight, or at least this is what they'll continue to think as long as they live. So as far as this business about grams goes, no matter how hard we dwarves try, the units of weights and measures, jealously kept in Paris and now guarded by Hitler's armies, neither grow nor shrink. But somehow, this ingot, almost without wanting to, brings us to Havana:

7. Kowalski has left from one of the informal offices of the Anglo-Caribbean Steamship Company, located on the third floor of the Hotel de Ambos Mundos, in the foothills of the colonial part of the Cuban capital (which the locals call Old Havana), and now at the jetty he meditates, his gaze lost on a distant point beyond the old Morro Lighthouse, on how to better hide the eighty-three ingots of pure sterling silver that he has smuggled into Cuba and which he now keeps carefully piled under his bed after having unloaded them the previous night from the Swedish steamer of the Havanese *Muelle de la Machina*.

8. They call me to eat. I have no choice about the menu that the fat little lady has put together. So I resign myself, though I do think that there can't be much literature without freedom. Hazards of destiny.

But are we in agreement?

Yes. The characters, for now, number three. Let us summarize: Faustino, Manterola, and Stanley Kowalski. A few are still missing. And what's more, a few of those missing will be essential, intense, immense, the only ones: four of those five who will become the poker players. As for the rest of us, damn it all.

A PHONOGRAPH
IN THE JUNGLE

This wall of greens that washes over you is the only truth; it is the death of clogged pores at the hands of emerald greens, ashen greens, burnt greens, damp, eastern greens, loving, apple greens and grass greens, the green of the flag, and the aggressive greens that remind one of the limes that grow near the Gulf and the Caribbean. Tangles of plants that are no longer plants but rather the remains of plants now overrun by other, stronger species; cannibalistic plants that rob you of the sun, that collapse on top of you, tearing at your skin. Warm and rotting. A colorful inferno. Wasn't hell supposed to be black and white, like in the movies? And isn't the one true jungle the one from the movies? A French mestizo poet in Hong Kong once wrote that the Eskimos have eleven words for "white" and a certain Amazon tribe has a thousand thirty-six for "green". This mestizo was left for dead: smiling, looking friendly and kind, with a tiny hole in his forehead where a small-caliber bullet had struck him as he was leaping over a barricade. Just a scratch, really, and a sliver of red blood trickled out from beneath his black beret, an anachronism to remind him that he'd once visited Paris. A wisp of vapor had risen from the wound, as if Death were smoking.

Tomás Wong, a spurious Chinaman born in Mazatlán, urged his bulldozer through this jungle, eagerly razing, devouring, and destroying the vegetation that closed anew behind his track. The swath was wider as the great machine plowed on, burning oil and belching smoke through its little side-ways chimney, wider than it was even moments later, for the jungle constantly sought to reclaim its turf. He wrestled with the enormous tree trunks as if his life were at stake. Angry. Furious. Growling menacingly at each collision with the lush tropical vegetation.

Fifty meters behind the machine, a team of construction workers, machetes in hand, finished clearing out any remaining brush. The afternoon, or some such thing, shadows more or less lengthening in the jungle, had come falling over the group, and the sweat stains on their shirts had grown into a single, uniform stain that soaked the fabric throughout, darkening the drab khaki color. Mosquitoes caught wind of this sour smell and came to feast; there was something especially attractive about Wong's lean body, and they came in droves, searching for exposed skin.

"He's got to be kidding. He wants to do the whole damn thing himself," said one of the workers. "You paying him more, boss?"

The chief engineer smiled. "Drop it, Anselmo. You're always trying to take on the world. Better to just be happy watching the jungle go on by and scratching your balls. We're just here to help the job along." Then he looked up at the enormous yellow bulldozer whose hydraulic blade was plowing its way through the trees. They had found themselves in a small clearing. "Stop here. Half an hour for coffee!" he cried as he let the dossier he had been carrying under his arm fall to the ground.

Tomás Wong pretended he hadn't heard and continued on in low gear, trying to level a giant, tangled mangrove. Most of the workers began unpacking the mules, while the rest morosely began to gather sticks for the fire in which to make the coffee. Now some seventy meters away, Tomás continued driving his machine over the trees and brush. This battle with the jungle seemed to have become a deeply personal issue. The rest of the crewmen, meanwhile, fell to the ground in exhaustion, searching for shade or cover.

Finally Tomás stopped the bulldozer, the motor shutting down with a rumbling echo. Silence suddenly invaded the jungle, though only for an instant before the songs of the birds returned along with the howling of a pair of monkeys hanging high in the branches of a nearby tree. He got out of the cab and jumped to the ground. From the forest floor, he tossed a casual glance toward the workers who were setting up camp, and lit a filterless Águila. The smoke scattered the mosquitoes from around his face. It was a tan and weathered face, for he had worked at one time or another through the sun and snow, in solitude and alongside drunks, through nights full of bad dreams and things that go bump in the dark. The face of a beggar sketched by da Vinci, if the master had ever painted a Chinese man. An angular face crowned by a mop of short, thick, black hair and flanked by a two-week-old beard. His eyes were very black and his gaze rabid.

Tomás walked further into the jungle without stopping to call to his companions, continuing on in the direction laid out by the blunt snout of his yellow bulldozer. He walked a hundred meters, perhaps two hundred. He had entered into another world. Stopping, he took one last drag on his cigarette and began to urinate, directing the stream at the base of a tree, soaking the crusts of moss that clung to the trunk.

The music came to his ears just as he finished pissing. Very soft, and without urgency. Tomás lifted his head, trying to determine what direction it was coming from. He followed it away from the camp, leaving behind the fellow crewmen with whom he'd been working for the past few months.

Gradually, the music began to take shape; it had a military touch, something like a march, that disconcerted him. And as he finally was able to place the chords, the uneasiness which he had felt just a moment before surged into full-blown anguish. The music brought emotions crashing to his face like a tidal wave, a great rush of caustic memories in which there also was fear.

The dense vegetation had opened sharply into a small clearing unquestionably manmade; further up was a long tear in the jungle, some forty meters wide, that opened straightaway into a deep scar 350 meters long.

Tomás dropped to the ground when he saw the source of the hostile music. At the end of the long hollow in the jungle was a smallish cabin. Nearby, a group of some twenty men in dun-brown uniforms marched back and forth in front of a table where a wind-up phonograph was blaring "Deutschland Über Alles." Their clothes were, without a doubt, the same light brown uniforms, replete with decorations and leathers, that he'd seen many times on soldiers in Hamburg and Kiev as they raided the local syndicals and roughed up his friends, the dockhands. He'd seen them, too, in the photos of parades in the illustrated German magazines that were the only permitted reading material on the Dutch cargo ship on which he'd once spent a couple of months. Those same brown, national-socialistic shirts. But hadn't Hitler replaced these soldiers in Germany to make room for the SS?

Tomás felt like a block of ice had just passed down his sweat-drenched back, cutting and scraping. His eyes went glassy. Carefully he got to his feet and retreated, at first cautiously but then breaking into a sprint as he moved through the jungle. He didn't even try to orient himself; he simply lunged blindly ahead, branches and lianas tearing at his face.

Five minutes later, the crewmembers had just begun to serve the coffee when they saw him burst into the camp. Blood ran from a pair of cuts on his forehead; his face was twisted and wild.

"Something happen, Tomás?" asked the engineer as he stood up.

"Someone call the exorcist!" cracked a worker.

Tomás ran right by them without so much as a glance. He stopped at the rear of the bulldozer where he whipped out his knapsack and began to rummage through it. Books of poetry, dirty shirts, a pair of binoculars flew through the air, along with letters written yet never sent.

"He saw a snake."

"Nah, he saw a ghost!"

"Watch you don't get hit! He's got the look of death in his eyes!"

Tomás, as if confirming this last statement, produced a pistol, wrapped in a white linen cloth, from his knapsack. It was an old pistol, but he had kept it clean and well oiled, and it shone brightly as he unwrapped it in the afternoon sun.

"What's this, Tomás? Don't you have enough fighting back at home?" asked the engineer, forcing a smile as he walked toward him. But Tomás stopped him short with a wave of his left hand, while his right hand cocked the pistol.

The other workers had begun to crowd around, trying to cut off his path back into the jungle.

"Easy there, man," one of them said, reaching out so Tomás could hand over his weapon. But Tomás stepped aside and leveled his pistol at him. He froze while the rest of the workers slowly backed away. Smiling, Tomás walked on past them and back into the jungle. For the first time since he had come here weeks ago to build the Pan-American Highway, Tomás was smiling.

INTERRUPTIONS
AND INVASIONS

3. Why didn't life smile upon the Spaniard Bastión Alamedas? It was largely a problem of unfaithful women, women lacking one quality or another of love. Hearts broken years ago still continued to return to his memory and made him cry with rage and brutally bang his head against the walls of his home. I should explain to you that these women didn't deserve so many tears and beatings, so much blood and pain; that no woman in my experience deserves the pain and suffering of hatred. I put my greatest gifts of faith in reason, but he always responds, "Why not?"

2. These things ought to be more or less as I describe them. At times, nonetheless, I forget details. How many newspapers were there in Mexico City in those days? *El Universal, Excélsior,* and *El Popular*. But *El Demócrata* wasn't around, nor was *El Heraldo*. I'd like to include the young dailies *La Prensa* and *Novedades*, and then there was the sad, official *Nacional*. But for what possible reason could an illiterate city such as this one want so many newspapers? To look at the little diagrams and photos? To read into the ads for antibaldness tonics and examine the buttocks of the rhumba dancers?

And there are more questions: What was the name of the mens' clothing store in Mesones? What color eyes did the blond girl have? How would the Chinaman be dressed that afternoon?

The seclusion here makes everything fade away, even memory. Things that happened seconds ago seem distant. Everything past is unreal. Only flashes of childhood things, recollections and evocations, return to you: your first pair of long pants, the amazed looks of Zapata's men riding into the city, students flooding the prep school, the mixture of astonishment and pleasure that you got from seeing a drainpipe gushing out water instead of swallowing it, the kiss you stole from a servant-girl, a gash in the skin that you felt only when the blade was removed and both you and your playmate watched in a stupor as the blood you drew flows out. But events that happen in the final years of life stink up ancient history. The return of eternities and irrealities . . . these are the real ones, aren't they? The barred windows, my mind imprisoned between these padded walls, my false memories, my true memories, this story? Are only these essential truths real? Or are they, perhaps, the greatest lies?

3. But, whatever happened with Kowalski? Probably nothing. Or maybe many things, but these will happen much later. In any case, to satisfy curiosity, it is necessary to point out that Kowalski had a terrible case of the flu, and he was treating it the way any good sailor would: with whores.

We'll leave Kowalski for now, stretched out on the bed in room 202 of the Ambos Mundos, recovering from the unavoidable sex in this hotel full of sailors, smugglers, insurance agents, and salesmen proffering self-protection, magic charms, and love potions.

One last thing: recently I've been meaning to get back to reading one of Ernest Hemingway's novels, *Across the River and Into the Trees*. For certain . . .

THE POET'S WORK

The man with the elegantly wild hair and almond-colored three-piece linen suit left the Hotel del Prado, looked furtively around to make sure no one was following him, and, feeling safe, began to walk. But he was either very sharp or very dumb, because evidently he was being followed.

"Only those with skeletons in their closets check to see if they're being followed," the Poet in pursuit said to himself. He watched the fellow walk briskly away. People didn't used to go out for strolls through Mexico City, he thought, blowing his nose noisily and stepping out from behind the column that had been his cover, making him at once both unseen and ridiculous-looking.

He was thinking as if talking to himself in a low voice. You could almost hear his thoughts. A solitary life leaves you a bit barmy, he thought anew.

A torrent of sneezes was on the verge of exploding, of veritably racking, rupturing his fragile body. It's tough to navigate through a city like this, lopsided from the loss of an arm. You can't steer straight when you're rowing with only one hand. Rowing with one hand, and bitter at that.

The German agent (the Poet was sure that's who this was) continued on down Avenida Juárez, pausing to look in the display window of a lamp shop for the reflection of any pursuers. The Poet halted as well, maintaining the fifty-meter advantage he'd granted his target. After all, if he started to run, he could always just let him get lost.

When nothing is sought is when everything is found.

He crossed the street to assume a more innocuous presence, this one-armed Poet wandering along La Alameda. The girls in the park wore their flowered dresses that played in the breeze; necklines cut generously low, hairstyles flirtatious and chiffon skirts fluttering as they covered up calves that weren't accustomed to the sun. "Everything is theirs, nothing is mine; it's the price for being an impenitent bachelor," the Poet said to himself out of habit, the rhymes mirroring his reality.

The man in the almond suit was walking with a strange gait, the Poet noticed, quickening his pace. What was he doing? Trying to avoid the cracks in the sidewalk? Was that it? Avoiding the seams in this concrete mosaic; evading the steps of his own shadow? A childish game surprising in this elegant adult. Certainly out of character for a secret agent. Absurd, even. The man did a little hop-skip-and-a-jump when he came to Iturbide Street and quickly crossed.

The Poet crossed Avenida Juárez, nearly being run over by a pair of cyclists while noticing a small cloud of butterflies that whirled around a curio dealer.

"That Aztec fortune-teller was right, insects do follow me. Flies follow me; cockroaches patrol my bedposts. And now these damn butterflies are after me," thought the Poet, ducking the swarm of tiny, white-winged insects that had abandoned the curios in favor of following him. He swatted away the more stubborn or foolish ones with a swipe of his hand.

The man in the almond-colored suit went into a toy store called Children's World. The Poet lit the #5 Supremo Extra that he had saved for a moment like this when he might have to slip swiftly away. No stalker, after all, would smoke only the two-peso Dominican brands.

Avoiding the glare that occasionally obscured his man, the Poet watched as, in front of an enormous electric train set (the engine was pulling into the station just at this moment), the man in the almond suit held out his hand to greet another man, dressed in black, who had just removed calfskin gloves. The Poet shifted a bit to get a better look, but more to get away from the rows of dolls stacked neatly in front of him. He didn't even want to think about what his friends would say if a rumor got out that now he had acquired a hobby of collecting dolls.

But who was this new man who dressed all in black? wondered the Poet as he scattered his entourage of stubborn, foolish butterflies, blowing them a cloud of smoke from his #5 Supremo. A few died, but most persisted, stopping to enjoy the smell of the tobacco. It was then that he caught a glimpse of the strange new man's face, just a fleeting vision, actually, that vanished as the man once again turned his back to him.

The Poet brought his one hand up to his forehead in disbelief, a theatrical move that a vigilant spy should have avoided. But it was true: the man in the almond suit was speaking with Georg Nicolaus! For once, his instincts had been correct.

Once again he shifted his position, trying to get a better look at the face of this man, the Chief of Espionage for the German Army in Mexico, Central America, and the United States, but the face of the former member of the Abwehr IV was distorted in the reflections. To make matters worse, the damn butterflies were back, making it even harder to see. Could they be Germans as well . . . ?

INTERRUPTIONS
AND INVASIONS

2. A young Colombian boy named Gabriel García Márquez was buying a train set at a toy store in Mexico City when he was attacked by a flock—an innocent army—of butterflies. I state the facts.

3. Who gave me the assignment of writing this book? God? The devil? (And which one starts with the capital letter?) Or a combination of both? Some cultured, bibliophilic archangel? None of these. From what I know, it's a much more respectable entity: Fate.

I write from my room above the evening promenades. I write madly, without mercy for my fountain pen. I make them think that a novel is a chronicle of facts. That reality is fiction. And fiction, they believe (actually they are completely convinced of this), is innocent. Because everyone knows that Isabel la Católica and Bolívar streets in the viceregal center of Mexico City do not meet. And nearly everyone knows that the attempt to poison General Francisco Múgica never happened; it's common knowledge that the Soconusco region of Chiapas doesn't even remotely resemble the one I've described. And it's also known that the mediocre if greedy politician Miguel Alemán, the first of this new breed of young lawyers who will replace the generals, was forty-two years old at the time of this writing, not forty-four as described here.

So?

All is calm. There are no tragedies. It's only fiction, I say . . .

WHEN YOU'VE GOT NOTHING

T he fact is that you've got nothing that says anything, *amigo*. Because there *is* nothing. They're more quiet than mice, holed up in the Embassy there, all humble-like. Wait for the gringos to start chasing phantoms and the papers will invent nonsense."

"You think?" asked the Poet, lighting a filterless Elegante and letting it hang in the corner of his mouth so that it hid his smile in a way he thought was quite sly.

The chief continued: "Cedillo is already just a memory, the Spanish Falangists are all back home wolfing down hard pork and blood sausage, on their land, their damn ranches, with their damn wine. Italians are good for nothing either, except singing that damn opera. The Germans throw their money away and lose themselves in their perfumed fogeys like that Doctor Atl, or in that magazine *Vasconcelos* with its pamphlets and idiotic articles that no one reads anyway . . . And with the expulsion of Dietrich, they don't even do that anymore. They don't have any influence over the press. What net of German espionage? Well, yes, it exists, I'll grant you that. But we've got it under control and whenever we want, or whenever the president or the minister says, we cut off both the tail and the head, we rough them up, pack them in a ship riddled with holes, and sink them right in front of Veracruz."

"Pardon me for interrupting, but I think it's more serious than that . . .

they're not just the longtime toys of Arthur Dietrich and the Fascist ranchers around there. This is a network of professionals. Nicolaus used to work for the Abwehr IV, the German army's espionage branch, and he's got a nucleus of agents that we've barely even heard about. Did you read my report last week?"

"No. I've got it locked away, Fermín. If I started reading your reports, very strange things could come to pass here. But what I did read was a porno novel that Alegrías published and that León Vaspatrás himself signed. Now if someone told the minister that one of our agents had two jobs, one in this office and one at Editorial Alegrías (which you know, of course, is the parent company of the Botas house that doesn't even have an address, and that was founded solely to make money through pornography), well, I don't even want to tell you what'd happen to his ass."

"But don't you think it would be a good idea to continue to investigate Nicolaus's group?" asked the Poet, deflecting the threat with a smile.

"This is Mexico, Fermín. Go ahead and go through the motions, but don't fuck with me. I'm only letting you do this because General Múgica asked a favor of me a year ago. And one's got to have a heart."

The chief looked up from the Azuela novel he was reading. The Poet returned his gaze with what he thought was fierceness in his eyes. The contest lasted for a few seconds before the chief turned his eyes back to his desk.

"Fine, be a stubborn bastard. Sit down at your typewriter and knock me out a report, and sign it A39, like you always do, just so it seems more mysterious, and when you're done wasting your time banging away with your one arm and the secretary curls up into a ball, that sorry fool . . . then finally the Chinese spies will show up all goddamn day long, just coming and going, the sneaky cowards."

The Poet nodded. Yes, he'd go make his report. Yes, Chinese spies would arrive at the office here, along with a heap of sealed envelopes (that smelled, to suckers, full of bills) from the German embassy. But the chief was right about one thing: he did have a bit of a heart, which is why he charged not only the Germans but also the gringos in the OSS.

He got up from his seat thinking about how much he hated secret agents, that they were the true assholes, that the entire nation would continue to be caught in the grasp of this miserable lot. To Mexicans, counterintelligence was, at most, a mix of releasing and detaining only those who have gone overly soft in the head. It had fingered him in the mysterious lottery that justice in Mexico had become.

"One more thing," said the chief, stifling a yawn. The Poet drew himself up resolutely. "If you ever again use information in your reports that compromises the integrity of this Office, and those reports are made public, I have orders from the minister himself to personally cut off your balls."

"The minister has read my reports?" asked the Poet a bit uneasily. Minister Miguel Alemán was not exactly a friend of his.

"No he hasn't, you lucky fool. If he knew about them, well, let's just say that you and I would not be here speaking to each other," said the chief, pointing to the strongbox marked Robinson that sat in a corner of the office, black and shining, malignant and ominous. Later, Demetrio Fagoaga, Chief of the Reserve Forces, winked at the Poet, a gesture that at first glance seemed a sign of camaraderie, but one that Fermín wisely interpreted as a tic, similar to those that the Butcher of London expressed just before the action went down, according to a prostitute friend of his who'd never actually seen the Thames up close, but who always got her stories from good second sources.

INTERRUPTIONS

AND INVASIONS

6. . . . a good writer does not always create a good character and what's more, characters over the age of fifty don't have the physical agility or the passionate offers and presentations of the soul that they once had. They don't leap over barricades, nor do they devote themselves to pursuing impossible love. Manterola is fifty-eight or fifty-nine, around the time when he'll be considered old within a year. The Chinaman ought to be fifty-one and although he should show through his deceptive, even tough, manner the headaches and echoes of yellow fever, he hides them. The Poet will be fifty-five, but he has lost an arm, throwing off his balance when he runs. I, myself, am around fifty-three.

To fill out this chronological table with dates, we'll say that Adolph Hitler is fifty-two, that Manuel Ávila Camacho, the President of Mexico, is forty-four, that the doctor Argüelles (with whom I occasionally speak) is fifty-eight, and Ernest Hemingway (who was very much in fashion in those days, as everyone went around carrying one of his books) would have been forty-two; he'd turn forty-three on July 21.

To summarize: the characters and other people of whom I speak have rusty joints, aging muscles, and torn-down passions.

7. As is the norm in this world of shit, sensibility's edge is often dulled. Certainly too many people are dying, but Europe is so far away. There's a war going on. We live in its echoes. Echoes have no edges; they draw no

blood. The echoes travel in the name of numerology; the dead die in mere quantities.

8. Kowalski tears open the leather satchel which a mulatto had brought him earlier today and pulls out a slip of fine—exquisite really—paper upon which a series of numbers is written; he carefully opens his Spanish edition of Hemingway and begins to decipher: page 44, line 3, seventh letter from the right . . . *V*. Page 82, line 26, letter 11 . . . *E*. Page 240, line 10, letter 24 . . . *R*.

"Veracruz," it read, and already he knew what to do with the silver.

9. General Francisco Múgica ought to have been president. He was the man who represented the continuation of Cárdenas's progressive line and if the general hadn't smuggled silver and succumbed to the pressures that the bigwigs in the governing party had placed upon him under the logical swinging of the system (just a bit to the left, now just a bit to the right, yes my general?), the foolish Manuel Ávila Camacho would not have been elected.

So, in 1941, Múgica was The President Who Should Have Been. Mexico is a land of misfortune, I seem to recall someone saying . . .

8	

THOSE OF THE OTHER CROSS

Nevertheless, Múgica, with his curly hair, his great white beard, and his short stature disguised by thick boots and a puffed-out chest, had no nostalgia for the presidency he ought to have had. Rather, he missed the time he had spent as director of the prison on the Marias Islands, for that was the only time in his life when he didn't have to worry about wearing a tie and when he had plenty of time to read. Now, as Governor of Baja California, he was forced to travel for three days every month to Mexico City to deal with the Federation, whether he liked it or not, like a pre-French Revolution madame: with a reception room. He received acquaintances, friends, petitioners, gold prospectors, old comrades-in-arms, and Reds who wanted political asylum or respite from persecution by the international spread of Fascism or by the repressive will of the imbecile president. Add to this an entire legion of the downtrodden and dispossessed, for the country's meanderings produced a world of offenses, abuses and insults that above all hurt those who weren't able to defend themselves. All of these folks (plus the crazy ones who don't have to be rude) turned Múgicas's receptions into unexpected fountains of surprises and conflicts. Therefore it did not surprise him in the least when, upon entering the antechamber of his bedroom, in his greenish military uniform stripped of insignias, a cup of coffee in his hand, he ran into a group of Indians from Chiapas. Chiapas being, of course, at the complete opposite end of Mexico, a serious trek for these three men dressed in white pants, embroidered shirts, and pointed sombreros.

"We have a grievance for you to resolve for us."

"Sit down, please," said the general and, with a gesture, he signaled for his assistant to bring coffee to the three men who had cautiously removed their sombreros.

The three Indians let themselves sink down softly, like anxious feathers, onto the edges of their seats; they looked at Múgica as if he ought to know what was going on without their having to say anything. The general decided to invite everyone to eat something, and asked the waiter to bring bread and marmalade, which he did quite ceremoniously.

"Things are very bad down there in the hills," one of the men said finally. He had a scar on his forehead that sprouted a tuft of white hair in an otherwise jet-black mane. He ought to be about the same age as me, though with better teeth, thought Múgica, remembering among other things that he had once again postponed his dental appointment.

"They march on the *pueblos* and kidnap . . . (he paused as he searched for the word in Spanish) our children, they kill our goats and crucify anyone who resists."

Múgica brought a hand up to his face. Why did these atrocities concern him? This was just one more tale of brutality and suffering in a Mexico that continually refused to leave barbarism behind.

"Do you have any disputes with the ranchers, with the Guardias Blancas?"

"No, they are not Castilians. The Castilians we know. They are stupid and very greedy. But these ones are mad."

"Mad from here to here," said another of the men, gesturing from his forehead to his ass just to be precise.

"Mad with evil. Pure evil, General. It is not an innocent madness, General, it's iniquity that they spread over our lands. They'll gut a woman with a knife and leave her sprawled out on the ground so that her blood soaks out into the dust."

"They're not Castilians, and they're not the ranchers. So who are they?" asked Múgica, gently pressing the issue. "You're trying to take other indigenous communities upon yourselves. If you are Tzotziles, then you're taking on Choles. Who, then, are the instigators, the ones causing the problem?"

The envoy shook its collective head. Didn't the general understand anything?

"They're of the cross. The ones doing the killing are of the cross."

"What are we talking about here? Priests? Monks? The damn clergy again? Did the priests go mad? A cassock rebellion . . . I've already told Cárdenas that sooner or later we're going to have to arm a religious uprising in the south. Or are you talking about a religious congregation here? Were you attacked by the church?"

One of the Indians hung his head in his hands. Was there no way to explain this to the general? Could he really understand so little?

"No, it's nothing like that. These ones are of the *other* cross." The other two men began to speak earnestly in Tzotzil to the one with the white streak of hair. He checked them with a wave of his hand and continued to speak, with forced courtesy, to Múgica.

"It's said that they come from Hell, because they wear the crooked cross."

"And what cross is this?" General Múgica asked with forced patience.

The three Indians leaned together with the resolution of making him understand once and for all. The one who was acting as spokesman took a wrinkled piece of paper from his knapsack, leaned over the coffee table, and handed it to the general. Múgica carefully opened the twice-folded paper and saw with a shock that it bore the rough sketching of a swastika.

When the commission had gone, with the governor's firm promise of sending the Federales to investigate, Múgica, with yet another cup of coffee (his third of the morning) in hand and a look of astonishment wrought on his face, went down the third-floor hallway of the Hotel Alameda to meet with his lazy assistant, Corporal Peñaloza, who was currently occupied by trying simultaneously pick his nails and flirt with a waitress in a dapper white cap. Out of the blue, as was his custom, he ordered,

"Call headquarters and find me the secret service agent they call the Poet. Be discreet, Peñalosa. I don't want anyone to find out that I'm going to be meeting with him. You know whom I'm talking about? A short, one-armed man whom we recommend by Cárdenas's instructions. When you find him, set up an appointment, here, in the hotel. It's better that I don't go there myself, since then they'll think I'm conspiring about something . . .

"And Peñaloza!" he added when the diligent corporal had gone down the stairs to the lobby. "Be nice about it; no strong-arm soldier talk. Because if you see a hard look come into this poet's eyes, he's likely to kill you. Either that, or write a verse."

INTERRUPTIONS

AND INVASIONS

It doesn't rain in Mexico City the way it used to. Bit by bit, the city has been destroying the routines of the rain as if it were trying to ruin itself. The rain has become erratic, imprecise; it drizzles on unsuspecting mornings, it comes in torrents during the dry season, vanishes for months, returns in mid-April, and then disappears again in September. Halfway through 1941, the rain has become one hell of an unpredictable bitch. A hostile rain that falls when it wants to and not when it doesn't; now it doesn't, it's absent, and I need that rain to tire my characters, to soak them, make their bones rheumatic. Further:

9. What does this woman have to do with the Minister Miguel Alemán, who certainly has nothing to do with the revolutionary of the same name who died years ago? Because he's one of the lawyers, not one of the *top guys*.

10. What, in turn, do these two have to do with the Mexican pharmaceutical industries and their German capital? Specifically, what do they have to do with I.G. Farben?

11. What role does the brothel in the Colonia Roma play, the one where the girls amuse the clients, as they say, "orientally"?

12. And speaking of Orientals, why will Tomás Wong, almost inaudibly because the line was flooded with other conversations and what sounded

like belches, call from Tapachula in the not-too-distant future, sans the Chinese accent he had developed twenty years earlier?

13. What brand are the animal crackers that they sometimes bring me with a glass of milk? Is it true that they bear the faces of Ortiz Rubio? Of Cárdenas? Of Chamberlain? Of Humphrey Bogart? Of Stalin? Do they really make sweets (or am I just imagining them) that melt instantly when they hit your tongue? The ones topped with red sprinkles? Ah, to be wholly absorbed in a glass of milk, and watch the faces melt away . . .

$$\boxed{1} \; \boxed{0}$$

SEEING YOUR OWN RAGE

On the road back to where he had seen the dun-brown-shirted soldiers marching, Tomás was tempering his rage, or better yet, it was changing into a mixture of rage and interest, fury and curiosity. What was this score of Nazis doing in the jungles of the Mexican southeast? Were they Germans? Was there a larger force further on? Or was it just a bunch of young men playing at Nazism? Weren't the dun-brown shirts an anachronism? Hitler had gotten rid of both the uniforms and his chief, Ernst Roehm, during the Night of the Long Knives, back as far as June of 1934. He tried to remember the faces of the men he had seen marching to the rhythm of that German hymn and only then did he realize that he hadn't seen their faces at all, but only their uniforms. He knew that there had been a German community in Chiapas for some time, but that was, he thought, in the coffee-growing region on the other side of the mountains, some hundred kilometers from here. If these Nazis were part of that community, then what were they doing in uniform so far from home? Were they Mexicans? Had a Mexican Fascist organization using the Nazi's symbol been created? Using the dun-brown shirts, the *Sinarquistas*, the Aztec eagles, the anti-Semitic committees, and the rest of the trash that had risen from the depths of the country, provoked by the social transformations of the Cardenista reign? Was he such a stranger to his own country that he no longer knew what was going on? Had he become completely Chinese?

The rage continued to roil inside him, and Tomás Wong, with his five human senses plus a sixth that had sustained him through two stifled revolutions, a long march, and thousands of persecutions, returned the way he had come, following the breach that he had opened just a few hours earlier with the bulldozer.

What was he going to do? Kill them? His pistol was an eight-shot Tokarev 7.62mm, and he thought he'd seen a hair under two dozen men. How many could he take down? He tried to remember as best he could . . . they were armed with Remingtons and Mauser carbines, and at least one of them had two pistols strapped to his gunbelt.

So I'm a chink and I'm deluded, Tomás said to himself, and he smiled. He smiled for the first time in the six months that he'd been exiled from the world, building that highway that, say what the engineers might, led to nowhere.

Back at the camp, he had apologized to the engineer, packed two canteens of water and a change of clothes in a small duffel, and then topped it off with his ever-blank notebook, a couple of books, his new reading glasses. Lastly, he'd hung a machete on his belt and took leave of the group, accepting the half-week's pay that the cashier gave to him. Now, with the last of the afternoon light, he was tracking back through the open swath in the jungle in search of the dun-brown shirts.

That night he slept some two hundred meters from the bonfire around which they had set up camp.

The Chinaman followed the group of Nazis for three days through the thick jungle tracks, heading always in the direction of the coast. They had ditched their uniforms in favor of civilian clothes, and their rifles had been replaced by shotguns. He followed them closely and crept even closer at night to fish for bits of conversation; during the day he lagged just one ridge back, listening for the direction of their movement and then pressing on. They were Germans. That was what they spoke, but at times they also spoke Spanish. They were fast hikers, but they scorned the jungle: they didn't bury their shit, they hacked at young shrubs for no reason, they shot birds and jackrabbits for sport, and they stripped the bark from trees.

Almost all of them were young; many spoke of Germany without really knowing it, without ever having set foot upon it. Others, at least, had been in Berlin and Munich, had participated in the last Hitlerite thumpings, the annexation of the Sudetens, the Anschluss against Austria . . . one had even been in Spain with the Condor Legion. This much Tomás was able to reconstruct from eavesdropping with his spotty sailor's German.

They were Germans and they were Mexicans, they knew of tamales and hammocks, of coffee plantations, and they joked about the time Herr

Schmidt had struggled to move a piano into his second-floor apartment and, in the end, his wife decided to take up the marimba. Christ, he thought, they're domestic Nazis.

One night on their phonograph they played the "Ride of the Valkyries" and the Chinaman, who was a passionate Wagnerite, was on the verge of forgiving them and leaving them to their fates. But around and among the overture's notes that rose through the tops of the trees as if trying to shake loose the highest leaves came the voices of the men as they recalled how they had, not too long ago, clubbed an uppity worker on some hacienda to death and how they had then left his body to rot in the sun and heat. And the Chinaman suddenly felt in Wagner those emotions that he had always harbored inside of himself: those of war and vengeance.

He was beginning to form a concrete objective out of his rage. He chose his victims: the fat one who patted his belly when he wanted to emphasize something, the one who chuckled furtively when he told of how he had raped an Indian woman, and the sickly, skinny one who looked at the sky with the face of a dreamer when he described to his companions the fervor of Berlin's torchlit parades.

The fact that he had no rifle left a close-quarters strike under the cover of darkness as his only option. After the initial attack, he'd fall back into the jungle, drawing them in after him, and then dispatch them one by one, hunting his hunters. He had nearly finalized this plan when, at dawn of the sixth day, the Nazis walked up an access road to where two cars and one truck stood waiting. They climbed in and disappeared.

INTERRUPTIONS

AND INVASIONS

1. A man accompanies me when I take my evening walks through the back garden. I walk beneath two laurels in which at least a thousand birds are hidden. Someone ought to have told my companion that conversing with me is rather difficult, as I rarely offer up a word. Perhaps I am guilty of the sins of harshness and evil-mindedness and simply thinking myself a mute.

In the back patio there is, hidden high in the wall, in the middle of the flagstones and ivy, a little nest of spiders. I contemplate the fact that they develop no sense of me, and the silence there brings me peace.

2. And Kowalski? I ask myself. How will his health be? Kowalski does not exist, I decide. . . .

FOR NOT KNOWING
HOW TO DANCE

He had decided to call himself Brüning, since after all it was the name that appeared on his passport, an Austrian passport, issued before its annexation by the Germans, approved by the Mexican consulate in Lisbon, and notarized as stateless.

Brüning, the man in the almond-colored suit, of average height, sharp nose, and delicate features (so fine, in fact, that he looked like an aristocrat carved from stone), was dancing. He was dancing with a brunette who, from time to time, let her leg slip out from under her skirt slit like a wound, offering just a glimmer of lasciviousness. Where had this asshole learned to dance?

The Poet feigned reading the paper while he watched the couple out of the corner of his eye, leaning upon the bar in El Salón Ventura and drinking an ice-cold beer. It was an enormous bar; not quite as nice as the best in Mexico (that would be La Ballena in Tijuana, which stretched a full 241 feet), but it was quite spectacular indeed. He realized then that it was already afternoon. Brüning walked past him and smiled. A sweet, tender smile. Had he just been marked?

Two men approached from either side. Fermín shrank back against the bar, gripping his beer, his paper, and his fear.

"What are you drinking?" He asked with forced friendliness.

"If you're paying, then nothing," the taller of the two men said in a hoarse voice. "Here, my *compadre* has a question for you."

"Excuse me, but do we know each other?"

The second man, with hollow, pitted cheeks, scattered saliva as he spoke: "They tell me you were seen last night dancing with Elena."

Brüning continued to move slowly through the crowd, working toward the exit. The band had begun to play "Magnolias." The Poet made a move toward the door himself, but the two men barred his path.

"I'm sorry, I'm at a bit of a loss. I don't dance. In fact, I've never danced; I haven't got the skill . . . Who's this Elena, anyway?"

The taller man planted a hand solidly on his chest. The man with the pitted face caught hold of the sleeve to the Poet's missing left arm. He drew a switchblade, and snapped it open.

The band continued to play, but the knife drew a certain amount of attention, and half a dozen dancers stopped to see what would happen. A couple passed by the three men, keeping with the beat but without averting their eyes from the scene.

"You don't know what you're getting yourselves into . . ."

The pitted man lashed out with a sideways stroke, which the Poet managed to parry with his rolled-up paper. But the blade deflected downward and caught his thigh, blood spurting flagrantly.

The thugs watched, pleased, as the Poet staggered back. "Fuck," he breathed as he watched the blood pouring from the slash in his pants. He reached for the small of his back and, in a single, smooth motion, drew and fired his pistol at the leg of the pitted man. A leg for a leg; poetic justice. The shot did what the knife hadn't been able to do: stop the music and scatter the crowd. The tall man fled while his companion fell groaning to the floor. The Poet continued to retreat, stumbling, until his balance gave out. As he fell he dropped his pistol and grabbed wildly at the black, flouncy dress of a screaming woman. He couldn't fully appreciate the leg that bared itself to him, complete and marvelous, covered in a black stocking and crowned with a garter belt that somehow reminded him of a bishop's cloak, but it was without a doubt the same leg he had seen earlier during the dance. A leg for a leg for a leg; triple poetic justice.

INTERRUPTIONS

AND INVASIONS

10. Writing a novel is fundamentally an act of shamelessness. Combing one's hair is also an act of shamelessness, if only because you're trying to cover up deep scars with a thick head of hair. But this is only a minor act, whereas writing is something much more grave. It's a masking of reality, an obscuring of fears, a reinvention of things said and, ultimately, of those who said them.

There is a certain perverseness in writing a novel, I tell myself. It's something that can't be done with a tortoiseshell comb. And perhaps this is what gives pause to my fountain pen at night: not, as they say, to stop me from choking as I chew on it in thought (how absurd! The worst that could come of that would be a chronic hoarseness), but rather so that it does not kill anyone by revealing the darkness of his fears, his heavy secrets, his sick prides, the violations of his honor, his lack of a motherland, of common sense. So that it does not bring them to the absurd depths of sand in the ass and nocturnal droolings.

And of course I put down the comb, for I feel that no one can kill himself with tortoiseshell.

11. For certain, dear reader, I would like to have mariachis at my funeral. . . .

CITIZEN BY CHOICE

Manterola observed, narrated in his head, described what he saw in words. It was an old journalistic trick, verbalizing in order to remember: a parade of mounted police, a horse shitting on the pavement, a woman checking herself in the reflection of a haberdasher's shop window, totally oblivious to what was happening. It started to rain.

The protesters carried only a single small banner that read: IN GERMANY THEY KILL YOU—JUST FOR BEING JEWISH. There were no more than a dozen of them. Near to where they were flying the banner, at the Club Heinrich Heine, Manterola recognized a group of writers . . . funny, he thought to himself, Kisch is Jewish but not practicing, and the rest, Bodo Uhse, Ludwig Renn, and Anna Seghers, aren't even that.

At the center of the silent protesters was a group of children. They all wore yellow Stars of David pinned to their lapels: the mark the Nazis had forced Jews to wear throughout all of occupied Europe.

Manterola looked at the offices in the small palace across the garden that held the German embassy. There was movement inside: faces that came and went behind the windows. He walked toward the head of the mounted police division and presented himself:

"Manterola, from *El Popular*. What are your orders here, Sargeant?"

"To quell any disturbance. If the people out here start throwing rocks, I run them through. If the people inside the embassy come out swinging, I cut up their mothers. But if everything is peaceful, I go peacefully," he responded with great clarity and without altering his staunch gaze.

"And if the reporters come through here?"

"No, the press is fine. You've identified yourself."

Manterola approached a pair of small boys, blond and freckled, who seemed like brothers. They were handing out flyers that read, "Hundreds of thousands of Jews have been deported to Eastern Europe and imprisoned in concentration camps where they die from hunger and torture."

A woman marching alongside the banner waved to him. Very few onlookers were in the street, perhaps a car or two that passed once in a while, and barely two or three journalists. Not even his photographer was there. The woman wore a yellow star. Manterola watched her, fascinated, before accepting the pin she offered him. She spoke to him in a language he did not understand. He looked at her with affection, and it began again to rain. Great scattered drops began to dampen the pavement.

"Are you Jewish, *señor?*" asked one of the boys in a Mexico City accent.

"No. I don't know." Perhaps he was a new breed of Jew, of the seventh and lost tribe of Israel, born in Pachuca, a city forever hounded by the winds.

The woman looked back at him. A sweet look; a smile that remained in the eyes even after it had left the lips.

"*Shalom.* Welcome."

As the journalist turned to follow the ample path cleared out by a healthy secretary as she headed for shelter from the rain, a boy of no more than twelve pressed a slip of paper into his hand and squeezed it in a hopelessly enthusiastic salute.

Manterola, who had come to regard life as an endless conspiracy, took his ragged handkerchief from his pants pocket, deftly tucked the paper inside, and wiped away the greasy sweat that had been accumulating on the back of his neck. He would read this note later. He wiped away the sweat again and smiled, bringing a sheen to the scar that ran across his neck: the fruit of a certain dark past experience. He smiled in knowing that there is nothing better than a good story and, cheered by the ample buttocks of the secretary who walked in front of him and despite lacking a definite destination, he decided that today he had gotten two such stories.

Later, in the solitude of dawn, the time for diary-writing, he read the note and did not feel deceived: "There are certain persons who wish to ask of you a very important favor. They will approach you shortly. Please comply with what is about to happen." The note was not signed.

INTERRUPTIONS

AND INVASIONS

16. This city excites me, makes me happy. More than I thought possible at first. Three years of seclusion—five, eleven, three hundred—have caused my love for it to grow. Closing one's eyes elicits the pleasant experience of foresight. Love grows in ignorance, in intuition, in false memories, in oblivion.

Blindness is an efficient and exact way to see. Nothing is more precise than memory when fantasy is stirred in. This is an unfinished city, but what city isn't? What city that boasts of being complete doesn't show an indeterminate face? The sense that something is missing from the register?

It is because of this that I find it easy to invent other, new cities, because without pursuing them, I always return to the original.

17. Tomás Wong was a good hiker when we knew each other back in the twenties; he'd walk for miles as you or I do city blocks. But the march in China had forged him into the strongest of wayfarers. He steps surely, assertively, his weight moving swiftly over his feet so as not to tire, he dances, slides, floats even. All in the art of walking. His feet have logged thousands of miles, the cat of a thousand leagues, gifted with winged shoes . . .

ISN'T THE COUNTRY
A BIT ODD?

The hotel bar was situated in a pleasant, solitary penumbra. It wasn't a bar for coffee drinking and it was too early for the winos and confused tourists. A sleepy waiter patrolled one end of the room. The Poet was slumped in a black leather chair in front of a low table, wishing that life would return to the pace of simpler times. He felt old and afraid. When General Múgica entered the room, he tried to get to his feet, but his newly injured leg quit on him and he fell back into the seat.

"How are you, Fermín?" asked Múgica, with genuine concern.

"I caught a knife in the leg. Occupational hazard. I'm afraid I may be out of commission for a day or two."

Múgica tossed his head at the sky and then looked attentively at the Poet. He wasn't as he remembered him. In the past two years he had . . . aged? Fermín seemed deteriorated, run-down. He still had just one arm, but his once jet-black hair was now streaked with gray, his leg was in obvious pain, and his eyes showed the sickly sheen of an insomniac going through the motions of the waking day.

The waiter, startled out of his apathy by the general's presence, fetched a pot of coffee.

While Múgica parsimoniously stirred in his sugar and inhaled the strong aroma, a custom from nights spent in camps and barracks, the Poet spoke sharply:

"Strange things are afoot, eh General?"

"It doesn't seem that way if you read the papers."

"The papers, save two or three real talents and two or three honest intentions, my General, are a disaster. Even just a few days ago there were Nazi parades, supposedly for economic reasons, German machinery and Swedish money are being imported by Germans, and Dietrich himself has invested a good amount of money in the papers. During the war in Spain, they were masquerading as Franco supporters by leading the opposition to Cárdenas's ideology and by flirting with Spanish advertisers. Now with the Americans' about-face and under pressure from the big advertising conglomerates, they've gone to lick the gringos' boots. You ought to know that Lanz Duret of *El Universal*, Herrerías of *Novedades*, De Llano of *Excélsior*, and Novaro of *La Prensa* spoke with the American government to ask for loans, repairs, machinery, paper . . . all in exchange for their servility. Only the magazine *Hoy* seems to be steering a straight course. They were all Fascist toilet papers before and they're all Fascist toilet papers now. Pagés was on Dietrich's payroll and since '39 he's been all over the place interviewing the ultraright-wing dictators. He's already met with Hitler and Mussolini, and now he's playing Hirohito. Do you see what I'm saying?"

With a wave toward Múgica's cup, the Poet ordered another coffee.

"A man in your situation must be pretty well informed."

Fermín laughed a short, sarcastic snicker. "I don't know exactly how you feel about the government, General, but I get the distinct impression that they don't want to be very well informed."

"About the war. The Nazis."

"As my secretary likes to say, 'What war? What Nazis?' "

"For economic reasons?"

"That's what I suspect."

"It's a shame," said Múgica, and he cocked his head in a gesture all his own, as if balancing it. The Poet nodded. They drank their coffees in silence, until Múgica suddenly asked, "What do you know about Nazi organizations in Chiapas?"

INTERRUPTIONS

AND INVASIONS

6. Friday: calabash soup.

7. What do I see through the Galileico telescope fitted with 300× Zeiss lenses which they let me keep in my cell?

I can always see a bed of hydrangea on a balcony. It looks like it's on a third story. It's a lively plot that grows throughout the spring and is maintained well into the winter. There are a few other things on the balcony besides the flowers: an empty birdcage and a broken chair that was likely tossed out to make for more room inside.

I look often at the flowers. With the turning of the years, I have witnessed their births and deaths, their perennial resurrections. And I have also often seen the woman who cares for them.

This woman goes out on the balcony very early in the mornings, when the light of dawn still looks unsure as to whether or not it will break, with two glasses of water. She usually dresses in a skirt and belt, but invariably bares her breasts to the morning air. Thanks to the magic of the telescope's optics, I know these breasts well: at once round and pointed, like teardrops, with a gentle heft. Her hair is very dark, and when she finishes watering her flowers she gently massages them in the expansive dawn. She lives alone, without men and without visitors. I only see her in the mornings and for a minute or two at night when she turns out the lights before—I suppose— going to bed.

I care for her breasts the way she cares for her flowers. Will she ever know of our mutual affection?

But the woman's morning ritual does not dominate my days. At times I dwell on her; other times I let the working days pass by without a thought. The hydrangeas and she go on . . .

DELUSIONS OF ONESELF

Fermín Valencia Taivo, known to all (including himself) as the Poet despite the fact that he had yet to publish a single poem, went over his life in the uncertain light of dusk. It's one of those things that you can only do alone, and you may even find that one day a song will have to be written and make you famous, and for enough money Negrete might cover it and perhaps an English version will be done by Cole Porter who, incidentally, wrote the greatest song in history, "Begin the Beguine." "To live it again," that was the Poet's sacred motto.

His examination began with the work aspect: he was a pessimistic secret agent. He went around like a Pancho Villa supporter, always drawing attention to himself, and if his diminutive frame sustained any more injuries it would be left twisted like a grin and stiff like hair that has been too thickly combed with gel. He'd been hit by a bullet that had ricocheted off a wall and left shrapnel near his liver, his arm had been amputated just below the shoulder, taken, they say, by a cannonball on the outskirts of Madrid's Ciudad Universitaria, and now this knife wound; superficial, it's true, though if it had been an inch to the left it would have left him like the famous bullfighter gored to the femur. Ultimately, he was a walking curse that creaked when it rained and cracked when it was cold.

Moving past my worthless physical condition, the Poet said to himself, to my economic state: a disaster. Shit for a salary. But mentally? There's where I'm perfect, he noted with a smile. Fifty-five years old: a dark pal-indrome of an age. Five more and I'll be ready for the old chicken coop.

Or better yet, the cock coop, he thought to himself, amused with the phonetics.

Clandestine creative activity, said Fermín, syllable by syllable, in silence. No glory will come to pass under my name there. Though I have reached the peak of literary titillation, for how many teenagers have jerked off thanks to my feverish, pornographic prose?

The Poet had indeed enjoyed a tremendous publishing success with his *The Mysteries of Lupe Reyes* and, though his publisher declined to pay him any more, his second book, *The Sexual Life of a Benedictine*, sold even better. These two books appeared under the pseudonyms León Vaspatrás and Doc-tor Leandro Voyivengo, respectively, and were apparently dedicated to the study of sexual diseases. The Poet currently had his alter egos working on a pair of new novels: *The Erotic Life of a Young Cristero* and *The Gay Boy Scout*, both of which promised to hold a good deal of intellectual misery and sales potential.

But should he spend his royalties? Clearly, the rules he had fixed for himself to live by precluded that. But I'm no Puritan; I'm a half-cynical, insolent whoremonger. So why be so stingy with money? he asked himself. But money from books burns in mysterious ways. Illicitly, even amorally. The fact is that it rests, never having been counted, under mattresses and inside coffee cans, the kinds of hiding places where it is usually ultimately forgotten.

Questions come and questions go. Stretched out on the cot, when the afternoon light had begun to dissolve, in the pathetic loft painted lime green and without electricity, the Poet felt the smells of incense and copal wash up the stairs, invigorating him and reminding him of his commitments. His leg ached. He dropped his trousers to inspect the wound, and took the opportunity also to contemplate his flaccid penis. The third cock reference of the night. He would soon finish his latest pornographic novel with the autobiographical character. He clambered out of bed, more for want of food than company, and thanked his one-armed state that he never had to, nor wanted to, nor even could put on a tie.

The Poet wasn't fond of solitary life. He wasn't much for cohabitation, either, though he never had much choice among the women who divvied up his life; perhaps because in the great majority of cases, it was the women who decided for him when it came to the divvying. For the past year he had lived with Marcela de Tula, a woman who proclaimed herself the ethe-real and karmic representative of an Aztec princess. He lived with her be-cause she was willing to rent him the green-walled room, because she adored his poems, and because she had a mole just above the line of her pubic hair that drove the Poet wild and constantly reminded him that that was the karmic center of the universe and its sexual revolutions. He also lived with her out of idleness, indolence, vagrancy, neglect, apathy, indecency, sinfulness, and finally because Marcela's housekeeper ironed his clothes.

Marcela was holding one of her seances. She was dressed like a Mexican who was dressed like a prewar Viennese countess who, in turn, thought the Poet, trying to be precise, was dressed as the Maximilian empire's version of an Aztec princess. There was a great fountain of cornstalks in the center of the room for the purposes of animating this ceremony. Besides the Viennese Aztec, the members of the usual tribe that patrolled the house were all there: Melesio, the newsstand owner, whom they had dressed in an eagle headdress and loincloth; the two gypsies from the Merced neighborhood, dressed in black; and a fellow playing the hornpipes, who seemed genuinely Indian for the simple fact that he never spoke. And later, of course, always later, the invited guests, that curious lot of useless folk whom Marcela rounded up in the bars and cafés of the renovated and reborn post-Porfirio society. This society had begun to lift its collective head above the ephemeral intrusion of the generals and had recently converted from the gods Ingot and Centennial and, in the end, liberated itself from what it called the "rowdy, popular Cardenista party."

"Fermín, such a fierce look in your eyes will ruin my sense of spirit," said Marcela, swatting at the Poet's hand as he reached for a peanut.

"Spirits don't exist. They're just a more subtle form of matter. Well, subtle most of the time, but in your case it's damn well blatant, as they say."

"Ah, how prosaic you are, Fermín!"

The man with the hornpipes began to play his instrument while Marcela and her friends the gypsies half-closed their eyes and drifted into a canticle ritual. The lights faded.

In the corner of the room, an exquisitely beautiful woman piqued the Poet's interest. She seemed as bored as he with all the goings-on. Fermín approached her cautiously, trying to conceal his missing arm and newly acquired limp. If she noticed before he'd had a chance to display his charm, she might think he was a beggar.

The woman, wearing a waisted, sky-blue dress, looked at him and smiled.

"Aren't you a bit out of place at an Aztec spirituality session?" he asked.

"You smoke cigars, right?" she replied with a smooth drag on her *R*'s that was unmistakably French.

"On occasion," he said as he shook out the last of his #5 Supremos and gallantly offered it to her.

"No, you have it. I just like being near the smoke." The woman produced a box of matches and struck one, an act of kindness that the Poet enormously appreciated. An amputee going around scuffing out matches with his boots has a certain amount of style, but since maybe only one amputee out of three comes across well, and since this particular one now walked with a limp, his average had dropped dramatically. He thought he'd go for conversation.

"So what's your opinion of reincarnation?"

"I've never tried it. But if I was a rat in another life, then I'm really cashing in on this one."

"Aren't you the rational one! I suppose that makes you and me the only two rational people in this entire room?"

The woman laughed, her exceedingly white teeth sparkling in the midst of her dark mahogany complexion, for which the Poet felt even the word "perfect" to be an insult.

"Such a gentleman! But I've got other explanations for why I am. You are a cynic, a disbeliever, whereas I believe in a pair of certainties."

"Which are?" asked the Poet, thinking that perhaps she wasn't Caribbean but African. This realization, arrived at via some path of intuition, was confirmed when the woman said, without having been asked:

"In the coast of Senegal . . . and in Evil."

"I happen to believe in the latter myself," said the Poet, wondering if she had read his mind.

"I don't think you understand. I believe in absolute Evil. In destruction, in torture, in those who relish suffering."

The Aztec incantations in the opposite corner of the room rose to a crescendo, and a woman broke out into a hysterical fit of screaming.

The Poet looked, transfixed, at this beautiful African woman: hair, combed with a grand simplicity in a lateral part á la Veronica Lake, falling lightly, covering one of her eyes and affording her a veil of mystery that belied her full lips and limpid eyes. A Senegalese fortune-teller who could pass for a Hollywood actress.

"*Caramba*," thought the Poet, "if you really can read my thoughts, then tell me why I'm in such a depressed state."

"Because the same forces of Evil that I'm talking about have been tormenting you. Years ago, in Spain, and even a few days ago here, at the dance hall. So do you still doubt that I can converse without speaking a single word?" She laughed again. "I like the theater too. And I also was in Spain."

"If you don't mind, I think I'll sit down," said Fermín, supporting himself against the wall. This was all too much. The woman stood and offered him the chair. She was a good three inches taller that he. They looked at each other in silence, the Poet trying not to think of a question. But the mind is so often uncontrollable, and he couldn't stop the thought. "And so what is all this prattle about evil?"

"It's absolute evil, believe me!" said the woman, smiling.

"Of course I believe you. Only too well, *amiga*. That's why I went to Spain, and that's why I'm in the world of shit that I'm in now."

The woman looked at him deeply, brushing her hair aside so that she could concentrate with both eyes on the pallid countenance of the Poet. Fermín felt her dark eyes sinking into his flesh, consuming him. He knew then that it wasn't just the firing squads, the exploited civilians, the working-class neighborhoods razed to the ground . . . that it was more than the barbarism of the battle waged by war hawks sick with power, that the rumors harkening from Nazi-occupied Europe were true, that genocide was indeed taking place. It wasn't a metaphor. He, who had always said that Fascism was the epitome of all evil, now felt, without being able to name them, numbers, streets, and faces being devoured by a thick wave of horror.

The force of this revelation shook him in his chair. He grabbed the shelf of a bookcase, empty save for two bottles of tequila. The woman offered her hand.

"I see you are beginning to understand. And it's closer. Things are afoot. Be careful, Fermín."

The Poet gained a new certainty: "You . . . you all . . . you're all in Mexico then, right?"

"I'm sorry, but I'm here by way of an accident. I was born in Senegal, the granddaughter of slaves, and I wanted to try my luck in Hollywood, so I made my pilgrimage to Los Angeles. But the only parts I ever got were Black maids and I had to learn to speak like I was from the American South. So I traveled to Mexico, and ran into all this trouble. Now I'm a translator for the Soustelle group, part of the Free France Committee. Fitting, for a gypsy, to represent a nonexistent country that, if it did exist, would be sold back into slavery."

"So where did you pick up such good Spanish? You barely have an accent."

"My *R*'s still resound," she said, and her voice seemed like a tropical sing-song that caused her vowels to lengthen. The nasal *R*'s and the French vestiges had evaporated.

The Poet looked up, slowly rose from his chair, and limped across the room to catch a waiter proffering glasses of champagne. Fittingly, when he returned with two glasses in his hands, the woman had disappeared. In her place, Marcela had begun a striptease of dubious choreographic virtue in the middle of a cloud of copal. Fermín crisscrossed the house, checking all the bathrooms and the kitchen, to confirm that the woman had gone. She hadn't even left her name.

The Poet, disconsolate, took advantage of his trip through the kitchen to organize a nutritional raid, a blitzkrieg that resulted in two chicken thighs and a caramel sandwich. Later, on the verge of tears and madness at his loss, he went to the cinema; it was the only place where he could fall asleep without his usual ration of sex, either oral or verbal. It was the only place where both ghosts and irrationality disappeared. He had his choice between the Chinese Palace, which was showing a film called *Gift of Kings* starring a good-looking woman named Sara García, and the Olympic Theater, where an American film was playing, suggestively titled *Tainted Whores*. He settled on the latter, though he couldn't stay awake past the opening credits.

INTERRUPTIONS
AND INVASIONS

10. Casavieja relates films to me. He understands that the iron seclusion of prison deprives a man of his most important approximation of reality: the dark theater and its magical silver screen. He's told me, with a surgeon's detail, of two films that I can only describe as being superficial and nearly illiterate: the final two films of Veronica Lake.

He also knows that I like the novels of Hammett, and so he narrates the film versions of *The Glass Key* and, above all, *I Married a Witch*. He even gave me a postcard with Lake's picture on it. Insisting on that haircut, that half-glance that carries a potent hint of eros, will make her the woman of the forties.

I look at her picture every day. Casavieja hopes that I will fall in love with her, that I will eventually lose myself in the suggestions of her portrait. He's committed himself to liberating me from sin through love, but I am a fugitive from such artificial dreams as that. I live in my own dream, I need no dreams of others, and I have my own nightmares about women. Nevertheless, I like her cascading hair, at once casual and kempt about her face. It's not a witch's look.

Casavieja does not know that I knew this woman back when she was known as Constance Frances Marie Ockleman and she was a Brooklynite who appreciated Mexican lawyers. An avid reader of Mark Twain and a lover of strawberry milkshakes and walks along the banks of the Hudson.

A white witch of Hollywood; a black witch of Hollywood. Both comb their hair the same way, and my obsessions compound themselves. . . .

TO KILL A MAN

Tortuous streets that never quite formed nice angles, that searched for a destination that no longer exists, that followed a river no longer there, a path that someone long since dead once enjoyed walking. Gaslights every two hundred meters were sufficient for creating a phantasmagoria, but not for light by which to see. The dogs had been barking at Tomás Wong all night, as if announcing that he was on his way to kill a man. They had followed him from afar through the darkened streets of this rough city, full of fear, fleeing, yet in pursuit.

A fitting epilogue to a strange week, he thought. Probably the strangest of his entire life. And Tomás Wong was no stranger to extremes. To those blessed with normal lives, his seemed generally uncommon and, in times such as these, downright rare. A man of paradoxes: he was a Chinaman who became a Mexican who then decided to return again to his roots. He had a son whose name he did not know and whom he had seen only once. He enjoyed dawn in foreign lands, and these days all lands seemed foreign to him. He was a man of the sea, ships were his home, and yet he had no desire to embark on a voyage. He was trying in some way to recover something that he'd lost, and he felt—not thought, just felt—that he would find it on terra firma, if these Mexican lands could be called "firm."

Tomás Wong clocked through the streets, listening to the distant music of clinking glasses in a cantina, probably the only one in town. Looking for someone so he could find out what they did in these parts to erase people, to kill them, like poisonous plants growing in the middle of the road. Because between the Chinaman and Fascism, there will be death. This was what he knew, for they had tried to kill him not once but several times. This was what he understood, this sluggish assassin, hounded by dogs and ignored by people, as he stole like a drunk through the streets of Tapachula.

He had tracked the Germans' car and pair of trucks to this town and was now searching for more signs: empty beer bottles, urine stains, and haughty glances cast at Indians and mestizos. He had followed their faint scent down through the outskirts of town to this, the last brothel in Tapachula. A rotten, two-story shack, painted sky blue, that hid its filthiness in the night. The dogs continued to bark. Tomás Wong climbed up the fire escape and sat down on the steel steps to smoke and listen. The sounds of sex amplified by drunkenness—moans, yelps, belches, farts, gurgles, and warbles—wafted down and mingled with the sobs of broken hearts and nightstands knocked to the ground in awkward coitus. He was moved. He lost, in this moment of truth, the desire to kill the Germans. The blindness of hate was turned, thanks to the sounds of sex, into curiosity. He finished smoking and let the butt of the filterless cigarette, no bigger than a thumbnail, burn itself out between his fingers and fall, bouncing, between the steps, finally coming to rest on the ground.

One of the rooms on the first floor was silent; on the windowsill sat a pair of tooled leather boots that he hadn't remembered seeing on the feet of the Germans, who generally wore smooth, brown leather military-style boots. This room wasn't it. He moved silently along the terrace. Through a half-open window, he saw the bare ass of a very white man mounting a woman. This white ass wasn't proof in and of itself as it worked in a rhythmic, up-and-down motion, but when he heard the insipid words "gimme more, let's go, oh, oh, fuck me, you cunt" spoken in a strong Spanish accent, he knew to keep moving on.

Using the fire escape again, the Chinaman climbed up another floor. This was it. From within the first, dark room came a steady stream of words, muted but unmistakably German: *"Blumen. Gunther's hund. Komm her."* Tomás cocked his pistol, put a foot up on the windowsill, held his breath, and tumbled into the room. The talking stopped; with his free hand, Tomás searched for a nonexistent lightswitch.

From across the room, another hand struck a match and lit a kerosene lamp. The Chinaman saw and leveled his gun at a pair of naked men, seated on a bed, who blinked at him in disbelief. Hadn't that been one of the pretexts for dismantling the SA? Roehm's homosexuality and those boys in suspenders with knife sheaths and leather boots?

Tomás spoke in German. That ought to freak them out, he thought, this German-speaking Chinaman who was showing them the black hole of a Russian pistol's barrel.

"If Himmler saw you, he'd cut off your cocks, *muchachos*. Cut off your cocks and make cock sausage."

The fat one jumped up and knocked the lamp against the wall, but just before the room went dark again, Tomás saw the other make a move for the chair that held their clothes and, presumably, their weapons. He fired twice. In the muzzle flash of the second shot, he caught a glimpse of a naked body, bloody and twisted on the ground. He backed up to the window and ducked out just as two more shots crashed through the glass and sung past him. His face was cut, but he didn't falter. From the landing he emptied his pistol in the direction from which the shots had come. A short gasp was the only response: a death rattle. He grabbed the railing and leapt down the fire escape while inside the brothel, lights and voices jumped to life.

He was bleeding. Must have been a shard of glass, or a splinter of wood from the windowframe. He ran toward a coppice. Are they dead or wounded? he thought. If they're still alive, they at least know that I'm Chinese. Things could get hairy then. But if they're dead, then the rest should be fairly simple. Even the dead leave trails. Someone will find them and bury them. They had names, and those names will be in all the papers, in the hospitals and morgues. Relatives will come.

Tomás ran through the night, chased by the barks of dogs. He had killed a man, or maybe two, and the dogs knew it.

INTERRUPTIONS
AND INVASIONS

8. The records of dying men's words are usually inaccurate, but they have value in that whoever pronounces them moves in a temporal space and does not have the luxury of time to play around with words. Words are his final grip on reality, his last chance to leave a piece of his soul anchored to the ground.

9. Kowalski sails under both the Cuban flag and the premise of fishing for sawfish and sharks to meet the demands of certain Chinese restaurants in Havana. To the other fishermen, Kowalski, who had joined the crew at the last minute, is a disconcerting man, never smiling, with hair that is more ash-white than blond and a right hand covered in scars. When it's his turn to prepare the food, he uses that hand to dress the fish as if it were a knife.

Kowalski is not well: he suffers from a nervousness, that form of herpes that irritates the axons of nerves in the thorax and that, in Cuba, is known as *culebrilla* because it slips like a serpent around the waist of the affected and once the fangs reach the tail, then the pain becomes unbearable. It's a disease that induces deep feelings of anguish alternated with periods of apathy brought on by the massive amounts of painkillers one must take. Kowalski deals with this pain, tries to push it away, but he cannot help but seem even more mysterious. Further, the men have frequently seen him turning to his flask for relief, downing generous doses of laudanum. They have tried speaking to him, but have seldom gotten more than two words in response. During the daytime he wanders fore and aft like a phantom; at night he sleeps fitfully over his stacks of silver ingots.

10. Amateur historians don't have the opportunity to tell certain stories, dealing all too often with the incredible and therefore fragments of the one true history, the collective memory of those who don't read the history books. . . .

GOD DOES NOT EXIST,

BUT THE DEVIL DOES

And to what do I owe this honor?" Pioquinto Manterola asked the three men who sat smoking and speaking in French, the standard language of exiles.

An honor indeed, he thought, to have Egon Erwin Kisch, Bodo Uhse, and Ludwig Renn seated around his usually empty coffee table. Kisch was a jolly man with a fine beard, curly hair, and a pipe between his lips. He was one of the brightest journalists of the day, and was fond of often stating his amazement that the twentieth century had somehow actually managed to reach this day. He'd first made a name for himself by breaking the Redl story, which was much like the Dreyfus story back in the Great War. Prematurely anti-Fascist, he had, since 1933, begun to see the true nature of the monster that had been hibernating in Germany since the Depression. Now in his sixties, he carried his years with a casual and portly grace. Renn, on the other hand, had a sharp, almost skeletal countenance, a bald head, and a pair of inquisitive eyes set behind elegant, wire-rimmed glasses. There was something sharp inside of him, despite the elegance of his light, double-breasted suit, the vestiges of the aristocrat he once was. To the Mexican left, he was considered a hero for the work he did during the German Revolution and the war in Spain, considered a prototype of the "renegade intellectual." Uhse, in his more casual suit, seemed like a good-natured man, but his eyes bore the unmistakable look of a man who had been through hell and yet had retained some measure of lucidity through it all. They showed it clearly.

For Manterola, each of these three writers held a particular virtue, a particular interest. He, who admired virtually no man on earth, now felt a bit hesitant, as if he were being appraised by these Germans. Renn, a former aristocrat now converted to Communism, had survived the Nazi prisons and miraculously arrived in Spain where he was made chief of one of the major International Brigades. Uhse was a somewhat strange man, of Fascist origins, who had actually grown up inside the German monster before breaking out and turning to Communism, if a skeptical brand. And he was also a poet.

Manterola had interviewed each of them separately on previous occasions and also attended a conference where Kisch, in his Czech-German way, had torn down the principles of traditional journalism and established a purely literary theory of reportage where narrative elements perfect and hone the information.

Usually, Manterola would have taken the head off of anyone who dared to interrupt his morning coffee, which he took every morning at La Aurora. The waiters all knew him, knew his friends and colleagues, and the shoeshine boys who worked the sidewalk and the Cinema Rialto employees who, for years, sat at a table across from his all knew him as well. He'd become quite a short-tempered man, and dedicated that quarter-hour to disturbance-free silence and coffee as he watched the street, the passers-by, and stared blankly through the rain and commotion.

But whoever had chosen these three writers as his envoys knew Manterola's weaknesses well. He knew also that he was a journalist, a writer of ephemeral newspapers who had always wanted to write something with the endurance of a novel.

"We're here to ask a very special favor of you. We know that you have government connections, and so there is something that you might be able to do for us," Renn said in Spanish.

"I have political friends, yes, though not as many these days."

"The same has happened to us," said Kisch.

"It's happened to everybody. Nowadays the government's only friends are somehow connected to it."

"Here's the situation: a ship flying the Portuguese flag, the *Santo Tomé*, is about to arrive in Veracruz. It's carrying some eighty Central and Eastern European Jews, and even a few French. Most have visas for entering Mexico, but there are twelve or thirteen—I can't say for certain—who are traveling illegally. It is vital that one of these men in particular reaches Mexico City safely. There is another, a friend of ours from Spain and a great photographer, who might be of some use to you at your paper, named Walter Reuter. We would very much like for him to be able to disembark without trouble, but the first man I mentioned is essential. He absolutely must reach the capital safely," Renn said in a Spanish laced with a Madrid accent, presumably picked up from his time with the International Brigades.

"Might I inquire as to your particular interest in this individual?"

"Perhaps later," said Kisch, offering Manterola a pinch of pipe tobacco.

"He was smuggled out of Vichy's France. Migration officials in Casablanca were bribed and he boarded the ship there. Now we need for him to reunite safely with us."

"Why?"

The three writers looked at each other. Bodo took the initiative of speaking.

"Because he has in his head a story that nobody wants to hear, but the Nazis have tried at least a dozen times to kill him to ensure that he doesn't tell it anyway. A story that even we can't entirely believe, but . . . believe you me, it is vital that he arrive safely."

Kisch finished the thought: "Our friends in the Jewish community have informed us that the government may change its position and send all refugees without proper documentation back to Europe."

"They have been saying that, yes, but up until now Ávila Camacho doesn't dare break the Evián Treaty that Cárdenas signed."

"You and I both know that that will soon happen."

"Son of a bitch," said Manterola, suddenly ashamed to be Mexican.

"All you have to do is get him off the ship. Our friends will do the rest."

"I've got a card I can play . . . you've always got to have one up your sleeve. But is this really that important?" asked Manterola, draining his cup.

"You have our word. What do you propose to do?"

"What do you do in this country when nothing's working right, when you've got grievances, when someone's life is at stake? You go see General Cárdenas. What's your man's name?"

"He goes by Simón Peres. He's got a Portuguese passport, but it won't hold up under scrutiny, and he can't speak the language. He's a religious man, a rabbi. We call him Doctor S."

"A rabbi? You're not all Marxists and atheists?"

"Hitler's managed to arrange some pretty strange marriages, believe me," said Kisch as he exhaled a cloud of smoke. He chuckled, and then fell silent.

"I have the feeling that God has bowed out of existence, but that the Devil has taken shape and now walks among us. He has pervaded everyday life. Are these the beliefs of a traditional atheist? Can we go on calling these things 'reason' and 'sanity' and 'tables' and 'cups of coffee'? Or do we no longer know them as such?" asked Uhse.

INTERRUPTIONS
AND INVASIONS

1. Doctor Casavieja asks me if we can share the room with a Spanish friend of his who is recovering from a severe case of alcoholism.

He's a man just over forty years old with thick eyebrows, a smooth Andalusian accent, an unbuttoned vest, and a shirt dirty in a way that suggests an indifference toward life, the pessimism of those who don't want to go on dancing in this world.

During the night, he tosses in his bunk like a leaf in a storm, sweating through two sheets. I have no idea what they gave him to purge the rum from his brain, but I know that it's painful to sweat out alcohol. It evaporates from your body, scraping against every nerve along the way; it dissolves, rasps away at sensibility, leaving only the absence of water behind. I know. I know only too well. This man shakes uncontrollably, he babbles, he bears unknown burdens, his eyes thrash in their sockets even as he sleeps. His fingers crisp like claws. When the fever finally broke, he recited, in his sleep, in a voice not without sweetness, the following quatrain:

> My eyes are the guides of a secure ideal;
> My steps an uncertain road do trace

And this dark and tireless river
With its lurking dog, ever awake.

This poem seems to liberate him. He repeats it like a spell or charm. In some way, and although he does not want him to, the god of atheists protects this man. Makes him spout like an ejaculation this quatrain in defense of his burdens.

He sleeps peacefully at last, while I hold his hand.

Nothing mitigates your own pain like witnessing the pain of another. Holding this man's hand, so that he might slip quietly into dream, is like drawing up a bridge so that my own demons cannot wander into him.

In the morning, he awoke and asked me, "Have you ever lost a civil war?" And then without waiting for my answer, he finished: "I have. All of them."

I likely would have said something similar. I, too, have lost civil wars. Even one in my mind.

From then on, I watched him only from a distance, eating a bowl of lentil soup in the cafeteria.

Much later, Casavieja told me that Garfias, the Spaniard, was a great poet and that he had left me the quatrain written on the back of a playbill. I keep it in my bureau and in my memory, this poem that for some reason haunts me. That for some reason desires me, serves me . . .

My eyes are the guides of a secure ideal;
My steps an uncertain road do trace
And this dark and tireless river
With its lurking dog, ever awake.

JOURNAL

From the journal of General Lázaro Cárdenas, former President of the Republic:

June 1941

Jiquilpan. I have just met with the journalist Pioquinto Manterola, a man with whom I feel sincere bonds of friendship and affection. He asked me to intercede with the Immigration Authorities in order to facilitate the entry into Mexico of a Portuguese Jew wanted by the Nazis. Later I will get in touch with the lawyer Demetrio Liévanos to pass along this request. Manterola assures me that he will keep me in the loop regarding this man in whom run such important currents.

In the afternoon we endow the Jiquilpan's secondary school with a new library. Amalia and Cuauhtémoc will accompany me to the event.

INTERRUPTIONS
AND INVASIONS

5. We assume that this is all a *ficción*. That I have voluntarily decided to shut myself away, feigning a madness that exists only as a series of theatrical acts I put on out of habit. We assume that I prefer the apathy of these walls to the absurd obligations of the outside world. In here, no one has to triumph, there are no offices, there are no workdays, wardrobes have been reduced to their bare essentials, you don't have to dust the furniture or cover your debts, nor do you have to make amicable compromises. It's not necessary to have a past, and even less necessary to have a comfortable one. By not having, you eliminate the need to have. Here, passions are boiled down and we ask ourselves to grow. We complete ourselves.

There are no mirrors.

And somehow my family, to escape from my persona, pays with thanks the costs of my maintenance. So I assume.

The library is poor yet extensive, there is a great bougainvillea tree in the garden that blossoms twice a year, the food is horrible, but they say that the nurses—and here is where I find out just how contaminated my reality is by dream—engage in the arts of love with a delicious mix of irreverence and sin.

6. Arsenic can be bought in the pharmacies; strychnine on the black market, *matasana* root can be found in the tea shop near the Cathedral. In Mexico, purveyors of fine poisons are in love with life. . . .

IF GOD ONLY KNEW . . .

Pioquinto Manterola reviewed the various idiosyncrasies that gave weight to his fame: he was the only Mexican journalist to have interviewed Stalin; he was the only Latin American to have crossed swords with a Hungarian count (who now has two less fingers because of it), and he was the only Mexican of the post-Revolutionary era to have slept with the wife of the all-powerful minister and lived to tell about it, though he wasn't in the habit of discussing it.

Stalin had seemed to him more squat than he is usually thought of as being, and he seemed constantly tired. He had surprised Manterola when he emitted a note of admiration for Hitler's restructuring of the German armies and for his allocation of work in the occupied zone. That had dropped him down several moral notches in the minds of most journalists. Lastly, Manterola was appalled by his choice of colors for his fatigues: light green and pale pink for the jacket; blue and hazelnut-brown for the pants.

What's more, nothing of what Stalin said in the interview strayed from the standard Soviet rhetoric, not his inexplicably rational interpretation of the Non-Aggression Treaty with the Nazis, not his declining to comment on the military collaboration that the Soviets had formed with them, or to admit having provided training and permitted the free transportation of petrol and luxury items while Hitler was having Polish Communists face German and Austrian hangmen and firing squads.

All told, Stalin was a shit, and the interview a fiasco. But it was the only fiasco. Manterola didn't overly concern himself with the matter. Of his encounter with the Hungarian count, he kept only the mental image of the saber as it flashed out and nearly took off his head just before he returned the stroke with all the military technique of two children fighting with broomsticks, and he had ended the duel by relieving the count of two of his fingers . . . something the count doubtlessly took quite seriously. Of the minister's wife, he remembered only her name and the little-known fact that she wore pants for horseback riding.

These things that may have seemed so serious to others (the count's fingers and the minister's equestrian wife) just weren't important to the fifty-eight-year-old Manterola. Looming much larger in the arsenal of his precious journalistic memories were things like his interview with the Cuban revolutionary Tony Guiteras just hours before he was assassinated, and a chronicle of the flooding in Tabasco that he had written while standing on an operating table with the water rising past his ankles.

And if these were his professional memories, then compared to them his personal memories were vague images that had been dissolving with time: a brother who had died in infancy, and the face of a woman with the curious habit of poisoning her husbands, with whom he had once been very much in love.

For whatever reason, Manterola had discovered in the past year that he was losing his characteristic rancor and that his hatreds were fading away. Memories became vague, hazy, and, like all journalists to whom the profession had been kind, he found that the stories of those memories remained even after the memories themselves had gone. Now, he looked at the past with less and less rage and interest, and the past that he saw was, without a doubt, becoming frayed and foggy. The present ran the risk of softening too, but fortunately it was reinforced by the steady stream of impossible characters that the country continued to produce. Mexico had him quite angry indeed.

It was because of this anger that he strode through the editing room with a fierce look on his face and an aura of professional divinity about him. He unenthusiastically accepted the greetings the younger journalists offered as a sign of recognition and respect, and their whisperings accompanied him as he sat down at his desk. On that old "front page mission," as they say. Such is the path to old glory or, as its equivalent journalistic idiom goes, such is the way to an early grave.

He took out his notebook and flipped quickly through it, skimming over the pages to refresh his memory and then putting his notes away and immediately beginning to type.

El Popular was able to maintain its status as a redoubt of moderate Stalinists by employing widely known opponents of the government and unhappy bohemians who usually died of cirrhosis before reaching the age of forty, though sometimes too much leftist journalism could do that, too. Or perhaps it was Manterola's sense of justice that kept *El Popular* (albeit precariously) a newspaper and not a girls' school.

Pepe Revueltas came up to his desk, hoping, perhaps, to get a bit of pipe tobacco out of him. Manterola liked this young journalist. They both had something in common with shipwrecked sailors: they were both survivors. Perhaps that was why Revueltas was still on speaking terms with Manterola.

"Do you know where I can get a typewriter ribbon? I need a new one."

"Black, or one of those colored ones?"

"Either way, it doesn't matter. I ought to be writing in invisible ink, actually, so bad is this story."

"Working on another novel at home?"

"Something like that."

Manterola fished around in his desk and pulled out a couple of ribbons. He handed them to Revueltas, who stowed them in his pocket. Revueltas was twenty-seven well-worn years old, having been a political prisoner from age fifteen to age twenty, and he maintained some contentious relationships with the Communist party, of whom he was usually critical and which had subsequently expelled and readmitted him on several occasions. As far as Manterola knew, he was currently a member, but he wouldn't swear to it. What he did know for certain was that Revueltas's imprisonment at the Marías Islands had given him the material from which he wrote his first book, just recently published: *Walls of Water*

"Got a title?" asked Manterola, who had enjoyed the first one.

"I'm thinking of calling it *Human Mourning.*"

"Well, I'll be the first to read it, especially since I'll know that you finished it using my ribbons!"

The combination of Revueltas's thick, peaked eyebrows, his small, sharp nose, and his disheveled jacket and tie had him, looking vaguely wolflike. He smirked. Manterola took advantage of the brief pause to prod him a bit.

"I'm reading a book right now that your party doesn't think too highly of . . . Ernest Hemingway's *For Whom the Bell Tolls*. It's set during the war in Spain. The Russians allowed its publication in the beginning, but then they pulled it off the shelves. The American Communists have squared off with Hemingway too. I don't like them already: pretty uncomfortable bedfellows. The book critic for the *Daily Worker* is accusing him of having participated in the war for personal profit. So now the purging has even reached literature . . ."

"I don't like it much. Too simplistic. To me, Hemingway seems to be a tin-horn liberal who went to Spain to get his rocks off, live an adventure or two, and when the shit hit the fan, when it got really dangerous, then he packed up his bags and left."

"And that's reason enough to burn his books?"

"In some places, Señor Manterola, the class struggle is quite a terrible thing indeed."

"A newly formed society, based on censorship, has few if any new things to fill itself with," said Manterola, who hadn't lost a political debate in thirty years, partly because he was so used to losing at other things.

"Strange, dark, and certainly winding is the proletariat's path. You, who are a populist romantic liberal and even a bit of a libertarian . . . you have to prefer the straight and narrow, right?"

"If it weren't for the fact that I like how you write, Pepe, I'd tell you to go fuck yourself. Listening to you makes me think that maybe Marxism is a step backwards in terms of political thought, a breakdown of intelligence."

"I'd better go before you decide to take your ribbons back."

"Yes, go finish your book, but don't show it to any of your Commie friends, or else you'll never get it published!"

Manterola and Revueltas exchanged a good-natured hug and a laugh. The younger journalist turned and left, while the elder sat heavily on his desk and lit his pipe. Life at the newspaper was certainly interesting, he thought. Even in the past week, some pretty unusual characters had passed through this editors' room: from an assassin with blood-stained hands who begged for mercy from the reporters about to break his story, to a man hawking pots and pans. Revueltas was a tragic figure; he came from a family of geniuses who had all died young. Manterola remembered Silvestre the musician and especially Fermín the painter, one of Mexico's greatest muralists, creator of Virgins of Guadelupe surrounded by golden veils, prostitutes, and mantles of lilacs. Pepe always said that his siblings had died of solitude. And there was a connection: Revueltas was the one who had introduced him to Egon Erwin Kisch and the rest of the German intellectuals at the Club Heinrich Heine, and once he had even introduced him to Carlos Contreras, the famous Comandante Carlos from the war in Spain, and Vitorio Vidal, a retired journalist who had been involved in the first attempt on Trotsky's life, and probably in the actual assassination that happened a few months later. Manterola, with a single wave of his hand, fanned away both the smoke hanging in front of his face and his scattered memories and began to organize his notes. The rest of the room had moved over to the windows to watch a squadron of Douglas and Corsair planes twisting awkwardly through the impossibly blue Mexico City sky.

Manterola looked up briefly. He'd write about that: the disaster that was the supposed modernization of Mexican aviation. A load of scrap iron. On more than one occasion, firemen had had to recover a propeller that had flown off near the Balbuena plain while the rest of the plane had crashed in the countess's old racetrack.

Just as he had started typing again, the Poet appeared and limped into the room. Manterola, not wanting to look up from his page, pretended that he was really struggling with the story, that it needed adjectives and exclamation points and such. The Poet, as patient as ever, crossed the room and stood in front of the desk, lightly tapping one of his boots on the wood floor.

"Did you just appear out of nowhere? Out of the goddamn blue?" The journalist said at last without looking up.

"From the same nowhere as you. Nine years. And I don't see why your nowheres have to be any better than mine," said the Poet as he drew a knife from his boot and began to dig at the edge of his peevish friend's desk.

Manterola still didn't look up from his typewriter. Occasionally he poked away at a few of the keys with alternating index fingers.

"They tell me you work for the government now, Fermín, that you're some sort of cop, a 'reserve' cop, whatever the hell that means. They say that you've turned your coat and work for the bad guys, that nowadays you even speak fondly of Calles and Obregón and refer to that new ape as *señor presidente.*"

"Whoever told you that obviously doesn't have the balls to tell me that to my face. Aren't you ashamed to be going around spreading calumny about your old friends?"

"And aren't you ashamed to be working in that rats' nest?"

"Yes, but at least I'm dealing with it. Someone's got to do what I do, and it's better that it's someone untouchable, someone with the heart of a poet. Have you become such a bastard that you've even forgotten your old *compadres*? I work for them, yes, but I haven't put my ass in a sling. No sentimental *Villista* would ever surrender, anyway."

"Good to know." Manterola looked up from his page and stifled a grin that had worked its way onto the lips sealed around the stem of his pipe. The Poet flung his knife at the floor where it stuck fast and jumped up on the desk in a gymnastic act that belied his lack of an arm, his wounded leg, and his small stature. He jumped down on the other side of the desk and wrapped his arm around his surprised friend.

"Get a hold of yourself, Poet! They'll start to think we're fairies! In this

sacred room there are worse folks than me when it comes to the maledic-
tions, calumny, slander, defamations, gossip, and vilifications that are the
order of the day."

   "If God only knew what the world knows," said the Poet, and he planted
a fat kiss on the bald head of his old friend.

INTERRUPTIONS

AND INVASIONS

1. Today I've decided to write in my pajamas.

2. My neighbor, the man in 33B, is a young sketch artist. Yesterday he told me that he's coauthoring a novel with one Edgar Rice Burroughs. The novel begins, "My mother is a bitch and she's never known my father." I like this opening; it's promising, and these tales of practical orphanhood speak to me. As I said, Angel de la Calle (my neighbor) is also an artist, and he's filled his room with sketches of palms done in India ink. No two are alike; each one has its own uniquely curving trunk and is rooted in its own reality. He draws them as if in homage. From time to time, I've heard him say that the shortest distance between two points is one that circles ever along a palm-lined street. Palms fill an emotional need. Our garden is dotted with perhaps a dozen beautiful laurels, two *ahuehuetes* each a hundred years old, and one damn oak tree, covered with scars. But not one palm.

3. Enough with palms. This is how it will be . . .

WHAT THE WORLD KNOWS

You realize, keyhack, that the last time we were united by circumstances like this was twenty years ago."

The Poet looked into the past with a dense nostalgia, full of caring and longing, eyes wandering about the room until they finally settled on the window. He didn't know why, but the past always seemed to be out there, beyond the windows.

"What do you know about the rest of our old *compañeros*? I saw the Chinaman Tomás in New York. I had just gotten back from Spain with a group of wounded men from the Brigades, and he was either on his way to or coming back from China. Or maybe both. We met for a couple of hours at the wharf. He'd done it. Renounced China. Strange, though, for at that moment he seemed truly Chinese, and I don't mean that in the apocryphal sense. He was working for an international shipowner as a sailor or mechanic or some such thing again. With Tomás, I always got the feeling that, after having been separated from each other, all questions remain, to be answered or not."

"You don't think he'd have gone back to China? There are some surprising stories of what the Communists are doing to resist the Japanese. They've amassed an army on the interior that marches from one side of the country to the other. They raise crops, traverse hills, they disappear and then pop up again five hundred kilometers away, they fight like guerillas out of their mountain bases."

"I doubt that. Tomás was too much of an anarchist to ever sign on with the Communist party."

There is a curious symmetry in recollections, in memories. You are and are not the same, the characters are who they were, and yet in some way they are not. You recall others and you recall yourself. And in speaking of the Chinaman, both the Poet and the journalist had been reminiscing with a part of their minds focused on themselves.

"There was that time I jumped out that window," said the Poet, suddenly homesick.

"Yes, and that marvelous woman who tried to poison me," replied Manterola, his love lingering for the woman but not the poison. The Poet fell silent; he wasn't about to ruin his friend's memories by telling him that that marvelous woman was actually a whore who lived out of a cardboard box.

"Have you read any Dumas lately? Who wrote *Twenty Years After* and *The Return of the Three Musketeers*?" said Manterola, suddenly snapping out of his nostalgia.

"I probably did. Many years ago. Is it the one where the Musketeers go after Milady? No, that was the first one. My father always bought me Dumas's books, and Verne's. Why do you ask?"

"No reason. Dumas was quite benevolent toward his characters," answered Manterola as he began the laborious process of filling his pipe. The airplanes continued to circle in the sky, the sounds of their engines roaring in through the windows of the office.

"Verdugo disappeared. After that whole thing with his wife, he just up and vanished. Maybe five years ago."

"I read what you wrote about that. What a story."

"Verdugo was always close to tragedy. Flirting with it."

"But he's not in prison, is he?"

"Frankly, I don't know. One day I asked about him, and nobody knew anything. No word about prisons, about morgues, nothing."

The two friends sat in silence for a while. Finally the journalist broke it.

"And so to what do we owe our reunion this time?"

"To the fact that some very strange things have been happening to me of late."

"It's the country, my friend, it's the times. Don't think too much of it. The powers that be have been affecting the wheel of fortune, turning it in the other direction, toward modernity. And speaking of which, have you ever stopped to think that we're actually getting pretty old ourselves?"

"It's not that. This is something more specific," said the Poet, scratching the top of his head. "It has to do with the government, with the war in Europe, with spies, with Nazis."

Manterola looked up from his pipe and at his friend. The armless sleeve hung, limp and twisted, with a sense of tragedy that hadn't been there before. Gray hairs had appeared in his beard and at his temples. The two of them had been joined in the past through an impossible combination of chance events. Was the game now about to repeat itself?

"I'm going to try and put some things in order, but I'd like for us to meet calmly sometime soon, in some place more private than this."

"Does this all have to do with where you work?"

"It does, and what's more it has to do with something very strange going on in Chiapas." The allusion to Chiapas seemed to have invited a slight breeze, curiously chilly, into the office. Manterola noticed an open window, and moved to close it. But the breeze must have entered from somewhere else, for it continued to circulate through the editors' room.

INTERRUPTIONS

AND INVASIONS

11. And Kowalski? No, Kowalski doesn't exist, he is merely another of my feverish imaginations. But if he doesn't exist, how can one explain the fact that this man with the silver hair and the silver ingots has arrived in Veracruz? How can we explain that? Or did they arrive . . . ?

PART | II

COFFEE

On a strip of land 140 kilometers long and from 15 to 35 kilometers wide, between the Pacific and the Sierra Madre del Sur, in the humid tropics of the southeasternmost point in Mexico, in a region that is technically a part of the country (even though some say that it's the ass of the world while others say that it doesn't exist at all), in the corner of the state of Chiapas and on the border with Guatemala, lies the region of Soconusco, isolated and unpopulated, devoid of roads and ports, forever condemned to be the periphery of the periphery.

Here a simple virus, a flu, brought unknowingly by the conquistadors, devastated the indigenous population. Guatemalans and Mexicans fought each other with a singular fury over the region, which neither truly wanted, for a thousand reasons, all of them sinister. For cheap patriotism, obscure commercial interests, barbaric exploitation, boundless greed, they assassinated, enslaved, and exploited the region.

There is a certain malignance on earth that can explain the savagery men have waged upon her. Matías Romero, the former minister of the Juárez hacienda, attempted to colonize this region, though he never found the right means. He introduced coffee, but didn't know how to capitalize on it. He made an obsession out of it, and failed. In the end, his plantation was burned to the ground on orders from the President of Guatemala.

But coffee lingered like a rumor both in the land and in the hearts of the few men who had been filtering into the region since the latter stages of the nineteenth century.

They planted both the eastern and western slopes of the mountains with the little trees with the dark leaves, white flowers, and little red beads of fruit. Trees that required shade and a humid climate, and whose fruit, after being sun-dried and roasted, would finally be ground, infused, and drunk across the globe.

The gringos of the Land Corporation looked to take over the region, bringing some three hundred kiribati in chains from the Gilbert Islands. They imported humans to the region like animals, both forcefully and deceitfully, and soon after their arrival, an outbreak of smallpox killed the islanders off to the man. Their sad phantoms now haunt Soconusco.

In 1896, Gissemann appeared in the region, employed by a commercial Hamburg house with its headquarters in Guatemala. He arrived alone, preferring a sense of adventure to the comforts of bureaucracy. Later came his wife, German as well, a servant who knew something both of milking cows and classical piano. Their alliance in 1902 with Wilhem Sticker enabled German capital to begin to flow into the burgeoning coffee plantations. The bosses then included Luttmann, Pohlenz, Edelmann, Kahle, Henkel, Ziegler, Schlotefeldt, Langhoff, Furbach, Dietze, and Widemaier.

But simply growing the coffee wasn't enough. The German ranchers formed partnerships with the commercial Hamburg, Bremen, and Lubeck houses and made the town of Tapachula their new capital. Soon, three distinct landscapes had appeared in the region: the jungle, acrid and mysterious, full of specters and serpents; an ordered, symmetrical zone, the regular geometry of the terraced fields and interminable rows of coffee plants; and the alluvial town, full of adventurers and pariahs, with its Chinese laundromat, a house that would later belong to a British ex-con, a Ukrainian bank, a Catalan tailor, and six cantinas.

Chiapas coffee began to move throughout the world along some strange routes that somehow never intersected with Mexican money. And with it moved a series of rumors, of the sort that usually accompany a newly fashionable food: it boosted energy, it improved digestion, it calmed the nerves, prompted conversations, perked up the sleepy, and made insomniacs coherent. It was transported on the backs of mules from the German haciendas to the small Guatemalan ports of Ocós, San José, or Champerico, where German steamers shipped it back to Hamburg or Bremen.

While Tapachula grew and prospered, with its air heavy from mining camps and its shores red with the fortunes of coffee beans, so did Bremen, with its art deco brick neighborhoods owing to the genial architect Hoetger, the money of the founder of the Hag Corporation, and the inventor of decaffeinated coffee, Ludwig Roselius, who controlled the Mexican coffee network in Germany.

Thanks to Roselius's commercial hierarchy, Chiapas coffee gained fame throughout Europe. It was considered to be finer, smoother, more exotic, and more delicate than the Colombian or Brazilian strains, and far superior to its Abyssinian and Turkish predecessors. Fashion is fashion, after all, and it has hundreds of inexplicable components that the aroma of Soconusco, transported via its coffee, could never explain.

Soon, more than half the coffee produced in Mexico came from the 30,000 hectares that the German plantations occupied. Since 1900, Chiapas had become the primary coffee-producing state in the country. A coffee that became even more valuable because Mexicans didn't drink it. Behind this miracle of coffee were thirty-two German plantations on which lived no more than three hundred German citizens and their families, the twenty-five haciendas, property of their Mexican partners, but above all the hundreds of ill-fated farmhands who lived in slavelike conditions and the thirty or forty thousand contract laborers paid in slave wages.

The Mexican Revolution never reached this region, whose agrarian order remained intact. As far as ranch towns go, Tapachula was cosmopolitan, even European: the Castillian and French languages were used to transmit orders, originally in German, to workers who spoke the various Mayan dialects. And these differing languages went on compounding as if at Babel: Japanese investors who had come to the game late; Americans who came looking for the scraps from the red fruit's feast; Spanish moneylenders, ingenious microindustrialists who created a brand of soda and a company that produced ice; Englishmen dedicated to monopolizing and selling the land.

At the beginning of the war, in 1939, the structure created by Roselius and the ranchowners went on booming, shipping Mexican coffee beans back to Germany on steamers flying neutral colors.

Adolf Hitler didn't drink coffee. He never drank it; he'd completely excluded it from his exceedingly odd diet that included large amounts of cole slaw and Viennese pastries. He thought of coffee as he did of alcohol and tobacco: as a poison that could harm his battered being. His was a staunchly puritanical idea of health and the sanctity of the body.

To boost his health, he took anti-impotence drugs, antidepressants, and remedies for heartburn, indigestion, and flatulence, that elegant digestive degradation that made the once-strong German man fart chronically. He loaded himself with "copramine" and "cortiron" to tone his muscles, "euflat" to void stomach gasses, "torozone" (which was made from bull semen) to combat impotence, "multiflor" (a derivative of Bulgarian yogurts) and "op-thadon" for headaches, "postrophantine" for depression, and "sympathol" and "cardiazol" to bring more blood to his brain, if such a thing were possible.

Karl Brandt had been his chief physician for years, but since 1939 he had taken on an additional, top-secret task with the full powers of a state official: direct, in the many concentration camps, a program of euthanasia for the terminally and the mentally ill. The doctor-assassin's position had previously been occupied by a charlatan named Theodor Morell who had once partially cured the Führer of a venereal disease.

Partway through 1941, Hitler's health took a turn for the worse. He spent many fitful nights tossing and turning, unable to sleep, his breathing raspy, soaking his pajamas in a thick, acrid sweat, pissing himself. He would finally get to sleep near dawn, though he never dreamed, despite (or because of) having loaded his system with sleep agents.

Morell prescribed various drugs of his own manufacturing, as well as copious amounts of lime tea. But this new slew of medication made Hitler apathetic and distracted in the mornings, left him absent-minded and unable to concentrate. And so Morell, faced with the increasing complaints of his patient, began administering two caffeine tablets each morning with a glass of milk and two marmalade rolls.

Later, as the definitive battles on the Russian border began, Hitler demanded stronger and stronger doses, and so Morell began injecting him with a saturated caffeine solution developed in German laboratories. This cocktail seemed to have the desired effect. Hitler sans caffeine was not Hitler . . . not until the syringe entered his vein every morning and deposited its black liquid into his blood.

They say the caffeine that ran day after day through the veins of the German dictator, that allowed him to emerge from his fog and gave him the strength to fight, had originally been a small red fruit, grown in the dense and steaming jungles of the Mexican southeast: coffee beans.

PART	III

CONVERSATION

M any years later, when Pioquinto Manterola recalled the conversation in detail, rummaging through the attic of his mind and the little mouseholes of his memories, fighting amnesia down to the last detail so that no one would ever forget, he saw himself, the scar on his neck half hidden by wrinkles and covered by a kerchief, his aquiline nose leading the way to his curiosity like a promenade, entering the back room of the hardware store La Nación on Donceles Street.

Smells returned to him as well—the stale grease and acetone, the paint and 90-proof alcohol—as he passed the counter. The boss, a retired oil man and a fervent supporter of Cárdenas, smiled at him, as did his assistant, a young man who was a member of the Young Spanish Communists and who was often seen at anti-Franco rallies. And with me, he thought, a journalist, born on Guerreo Street in the elegant city of Pachuca, called here by a group of genteel German intellectuals to speak with a Jew carrying a false Portuguese passport, we have a fairly strange, harlequin congregation. An international conspiracy.

He remembered crossing the back patio where a child was playing with a model airplane beside a koi pond. Manterola recognized it as a Spitfire, and wondered if the British would also be somehow involved. Then the walls peeled away and revealed a warehouse, and when his eyes adjusted to the meager light he saw the people sitting in a circle using a tool chest as a table.

There were three. Manterola knew two of them, knew them well enough to recognize the novelist Ludwig Renn as he stuck his thumbs in his vest pockets and puffed out his chest, like a sailor, he would sometimes say, laughing at himself. In the half-light he also recognized Bodo Uhse, his face illuminated by a cigarillo. And in a corner of the room, warmed by a musty ray of sun that entered through a skylight, was an elder, deathly pale man wrapped in a cloak and hat who smiled at him from behind a pair of thick glasses.

Renn offered him the vacant seat facing the elder man. The privileged spot. But before he could sit, Renn asked, "Have you ever heard of Otto Rahn? Do the words 'Black Order' mean anything to you? I hope this doesn't come as a complete surprise, remembering that this is quite an unusual gathering, and the conversation will be even more so."

Manterola took out a little notebook he knew he wouldn't use, set it on his knees, and began to fill his pipe. Long ago, journalists had discovered that the vice of tobacco obscures ignorance.

"I'm not sure where to begin, *señor*," said the elder man. His Spanish was clear, though colored with something. Portuguese? Galician? No. It was a Spanish tinged with something archaic, something harsh like the German palette. Something like the medieval Spanish of the Sephardic Jews who shut up their houses and left, packing only the keys to their homes in Toledo, in Córdoba, in Jaén, in Zaragoza.

"Do you know anything about European mythology? Have you ever heard of Thule?" he asked quickly.

"You mean the Nordic myth? It's that city that never existed, right?" answered the journalist mechanically.

"In the fourth century (obviously of the Christian calendar, before your messiahs), a Greek by the name of Pytheas from Phocea, the city that would later be known as Marsella, organized a series of expeditions to the north, cheating and deceiving the Carthaginians. He reached the amber lands that would later become Prussia and advanced farther and farther into the foggy region, fighting the ice and storms until he reached an island he called Thule. It's one of mankind's greatest geographic mysteries: the true location of the island, if it even exists, has never been identified. However, its name endures, and a legend has grown around it: a magical land, and the birthplace of the German people."

Manterola could not stop the feelings of uneasiness from surging to his face. To hide it, he busied himself with repacking the pipe that he hadn't yet dared to light. He looked at Renn and Uhse out of the corner of his eye.

They smiled weakly back at him. Were they really descendants of that strange class?

"It's reproduced in various legends; they call it 'Asgard.' A city in the icy fogs of the north. One of the many mythological mysteries. Chimeras, wraiths, wisps . . . the Germans are a primitive people, sir."

Renn weighed in: "Perhaps we should give the journalist some background, rabbi." And then to Manterola: "The story will be too absurd if not tinged with blood."

The voice of the child playing with the toy plane filtered in through a window, along with "Cielito Lindo," which some neighbor was singing. Uhse tried to set Manterola at ease.

"Don't worry . . . it's not Thule that we want to speak to you about. As you can see, we're a rather patchwork group. The rabbi," and he nodded toward the elder man who had spoken of Thule, "Simón Sacal, a divinity student of Sephardic roots, is the man you helped to save by obtaining the Mexican immigration papers. And then we two atheist writers."

The characters nodded as each was introduced, as if wanting to confirm his existence.

"A rabbi and two Marxist, atheist writers. But we all have something in common: we all were German, two of us Jews, who have been forced to abandon our homeland, if such a thing exists, to save our lives. But a death sentence still hangs over us." Here he tried to smile, but managed only a grimace. "I speak a mediocre, literary Spanish. Doctor Sacal here speaks a Spanish tinted with his original, ancient language. And Uhse has taken enough classes here in Mexico to be able to understand what is said here. Also, we have French as a recourse. Do you speak French, *señor?*"

Manterola nodded, and finally lit his pipe. Renn had made him feel safe, even confident; he had read one of his novels and a collection of stories in which nothing good ever happens to the characters, and they end up with nothing save for the sympathy of the reader. He also knew Renn to be one of the most prominent members of the Club Heinrich Heine, formed in Mexico by veterans of the war in Spain and German Marxist intellectuals after the arrival of the Spanish Republicans: the new exiles.

Renn made a gesture with his hand, cutting the air in front of him as if stirring it to keep it from getting too thick, and asked for patience.

"I'm going to try to give some order to what we know, though I expect that my companions will want to cut in from time to time to add dates and historical details. It's not going to be simple."

Why this abundance of prologues? What could they want to tell me? wondered Manterola silently.

"I assume you know a bit about the origins of Nazism. It's a singular

political movement. We Marxists have been defining it very vaguely. Barbaric capitalism? Underprivileged capitalism? Imperialism by Lenin's definition, but with delirium tremens? The alliance of the subproletariat with
the industrial aristocracy, using demagogue-wizards as mediators? Nazism
grows by recruiting all the social scum that rises to the surface of the sea
after a storm: resentfuls, fanatics, opportunists, victims of delusions of grandeur, killers, sadists, the mentally ill, those too extreme for the traditional
parties, underprivileged intellectuals. They took every outcast that a society,
suffering from fifteen years of runaway crisis, could generate, and formed a
party of morbid, racist nationalists."

"That is the known history," the rabbi pointed out, stirring the air with
two fingers as if extracting new information from it. Renn continued without
a pause.

"It's true, there is another side to the story. A completely different story,
in fact. It's not easy to tell it. The record is spotty, like raindrops on a
sidewalk; there is much unconnected material. Ironic, in a society full of
staunchly hierarchical charlatans, that it's so difficult to extract information.
More ironic, even, if we are talking about a secret society, not only in the
sense that its members don't advertise their membership but also in the
sense that they actually enjoy their sense of secrecy, their cultishness, their
ambiguity, their double entendres, their metaphysical games."

"Are you telling me that Hitler . . ." Manterola started to ask without
fully realizing what his question insinuated. Hitler what? Renn ignored the
question and went on.

"We saw him, and we had to laugh. It was like discovering that the
minister's wife was cuckolding her husband, while her husband was off
sleeping with the butler. But there was nothing laughable about it. He was
stirring up a movement comprised of hunters of Solomon's seals, bureaucrats
with salaries devalued by inflation, seekers of Atlantis, reborn Teutonic
knights, rune-readers, wounded veterans whose pensions evaporated in their
hands, followers of an absurd racial purity in one of the planetary societies
rife with halfbreeds, bank-hating bakers, philosophers who created an entire
cosmology based on ice and who now make the real Ph.D.'s bow since they
are in power, fanatics of all forms of racism and exclusion, pimps like Horst
Wessel, euthanasists, imperial astrologers, apocryphal Tibetans who divine
the number of representatives that the National Socialists will obtain in
parliament in future elections, magicians of operetta like Hannusen, whose
opus foreshadowed the burning of the Reichstag because of connections
with Goebbels' bands. And all are united under this meticulous organization, this technique, this surrendering to the insanity of the military and the
industries. United, above all, in devotion to the failure of the revolution."

"I myself was once a part of this madness. A young man who believed in the purity," Uhse said.

"But the madness was articulated strangely. There were beliefs. There was an underground ideology," said the rabbi Sacal said.

"Do you all believe in this?" asked Manterola, thinking that these miserable wretches of which they spoke made up the conspiracy of history, hidden, like a poisonous fetus.

"And later, when the Nazis took power, how could we distinguish among the thousands of harmless charlatans and the dangerous ones, those who flocked to Hitler's court like pigeons, whose madness would have such monstrous consequences?" Renn wondered.

The rabbi nodded and said, "In the past few years, Hitler has been suffering from delirium; he tosses and turns in bed, not dreaming but hallucinating, and in these hallucinations he sees himself altering the course of time, changing the climate, staving off the winter. He put together a team of astrologers to help him interpret these visions. He particularly listens to one called Kerneiz, who told him that his birthday corresponds to a lunar position of six degrees thirty-seven minutes Capricorn which, according to the Hindu zodiac, is equivalent to the Sravana star sign, the one that marks the founders of the world's great religious sects."

"And that's what gave him the right? To piss sitting down?" asked Manterola, smiling.

"To place himself, in his mind, alongside Mohammed, Buddha, and Christ."

"And?"

"And it gave him the right of madness, the irrationality of a deity. For example, he approved, under the September 1939 decree, the euthanasia of 300,000 mentally ill, mentally deficient, or terminally ill patients. He justified state-sanctioned murder. You can't laugh at such things, not at the murder of 300,000 people," said Uhse.

"I, in particular, am a skeptic, but for this meeting . . ." offered Renn.

"*Sprich nicht von Sachen, die Du nicht kennst Ludwig,*" said the rabbi Sacal.

"What did you say?" asked Manterola, unsettled by the tone of the elder man's voice, coming from the shadowy corners of the room.

"Don't speak of unknown things," Renn slowly translated.

"All right, the fact is that it doesn't matter much whether we believe or not; the important thing is that the Nazis believe it," said Uhse.

"And that means . . . ?" asked Manterola.

"It brings us back to the beginning of the conversation. To the myth of Thule."

The child with the toy Spitfire entered the room, carrying a wooden tray of coffee. So even he's in on it, thought Manterola, smiling.

The ever-cold rabbi with stained hands began again: "In the beginning, two lunatic Austrians met, Jorg Lanz von Liebenfels and Guido von List. Proto-Templars, admirers of runes, occultists, holders of castles. Hitler met the former in 1909, when he had formed a neopagan organization to practice magic, promote anti-Semitism, defend racial purity, and dabble in esoteric cults. There was a magazine called *Ad Astra* which Hitler subscribed to."

Renn interrupted: "In the Vienna of Hitler's formative years, it wasn't just Mahler who stood out, it wasn't just Sigmund Freud with his inquiries in Bergasse and Wittgenstein that drove the metaphysicists mad, and it wasn't just the Austrian socialists who designed the working-class housing cooperatives that were more important than anyone could have known . . ."

"Also," the rabbi took over, "their organization managed to sell 100,000 copies of Theodor Fritsch's anti-Semitic catechism, the abridged version of which sold another 140,000. And Guido von List's secret society prospered too, spreading through the military, businesses, banks . . . a society that preached the religion of the ancient Aryans, that proclaimed the secret of the runes and black magic, and unveiled a profoundly anti-Semitic agenda. This was Hitler's breeding ground."

"So at what point were racist nationalism and this crazy occultism officially wed?" Renn wondered.

The rabbi Sacal, ignoring the question, went on. "The key lies with a single person, Rudolf Glauer, of unknown origins, allegedly the son of a railroad engineer who later was adopted by a nobleman, taking his name: Baron Von Sebottendorff. This man, at forty-three years old, after having served in the Great War and having taken it upon himself, in the alliance the Germans had with the Turks, to work for the Red Half Moon (akin to the Red Cross), in August of 1918 founded the Thule Society, Thulegesellschaft. It appeared as if cast off from another mystic organization called the Germanic Society, a racist, anti-Semitic society. Von Sebottendorff, expelled from Germany, went back to Turkey and then traveled around the world, ending up, curiously incognito, in Mexico."

"What did he do in Mexico?" asked Manterola.

"We don't quite know."

It was silent for a moment. Not knowing something lent them a certain amount of credibility, thought Manterola, appealing to his journalistic sense. Always be wary of those who claim to know everything.

"Anything that attempts to explain a madman is pretty maddening itself, eh?" Renn asked Manterola.

"Frankly, I'm quite interested in seeing where you're going with all this," he answered, taking a sip of coffee.

"All right, we have this secret society whose objective is to redraw Germany along racially pure, Aryan lines. From it, Nazism would take many of its signature elements: the *'sieg heil'* salute came from the Thule group; a dentist named Friedrich Krohn designed the hooked cross, which originally included a pair of crossed spears, that decorates the sect's meetings like a banner. All the rhetoric on racial purity, the myth of racial superiority, the torchlit parades, come from this."

"Have you got all that? A dentist, a false baron, and a bunch of rookie magicians," said Renn.

The rabbi went on: "But that's all just a façade. What's interesting is seeing how it links up to a growing social movement: in the beginning of Fascism, Thule seemed more like a financial backer, a hidden accomplice to the plan. Von Sebottendorff, acting as the middleman of the Thule Society, bought the *Volkischer Beovachter* that later, with the help of Rosenberg, became the leading Nazi newspaper. Dietrich Eckart intervened in the operation; he was a strange journalist, an admitted Satanist who, at the end of the war, edited a weekly magazine in Munich where he argued, among other things, that any Jew who tainted German blood through marriage should be sentenced to three years in prison and that any Jew convicted of a second offense should be executed. He was also a theater critic and would later go on to produce some of his own works, including *In Old Bavaria* and *Springtime for Hitler*."

"Have you seen any of them performed?" asked Manterola, just for the sake of asking something. Uhse laughed.

"It would never have occurred to me. Nevertheless, seen with the perspective time offers us, this little hobgoblin was no small-time player."

"Eckart," said Doctor Sacal, "a man of Thule, became one of Hitler's closest counsels and probably the one who introduced the sect. When he died in 1923, Hitler felt abandoned. In *Mein Kampf* he pays him a special tribute: 'He was one of the best, a man who dedicated his life to awakening his people through his poetry.' But other members of the sect would greatly influence Hitler as well. Men like Anton Drexler, director of a small, nationalistic labor party, the German Labor Party, that Hitler assimilated on his way to forming the Nazi Party; Karl Friehler, who would accompany him in the coup of 1923; Gottfried Feder . . ."

"Do those names sound familiar to you?" asked Renn. "Today one is a commerce minister, one's a syndical director, and one is a Reichsleiter."

The elder man continued with the story: "Eckart later worked with Hitler, Röhm and Von Epp on the Freicorps, the White Guards, and the reserves. This gave the new party the military power that it needed. From across the sect, two other cultists emerged during Fascism's peak in 1925: Alfred Rosenberg, who would become a prominent Nazi spokesman, and Rudolf Hess, born in 1894 in Alexandria, who declared himself the trustee of Pharaonic wisdom, who accompanied Hitler on the Bavarian putsch, and who would later be his cellmate in Lansburg. He was the man who was considered Hitler's official emissary on his strange trip to Scotland, which we'll get to later."

"They weren't the only cultists who joined up in those days," said Renn. "There was also Max Aman, an old friend of Hitler's and later one of the party's financial backers. And Karl Harrer, who would later become president of the first National Socialist Workers' Association. Groups loosely connected to the Thule sect, like the Martillo Organization and the Germanic Order, were also dedicated to propagating racism and other iniquities, and they rallied people whose names have become sadly well known in recent years. Names like Hans Frank, the Butcher of Poland."

"Doesn't it seem just a bit intriguing that so many of these men, the founders of Nazism, had previously been members of secret sects and cults?" asked Uhse. Manterola shrugged his shoulders.

"The other key figure in this second stage was Karl Haushofer. He was a brilliant general during the Great War, he had the uncanny ability to predict future events, he was a member of the Vril sect (another runt of a cult), and he lived for a time in India and Japan. He began visiting Hitler and Hess, who was his disciple, when they were detained after the failure of the first putsch."

"It seems obvious that Hitler's a bit of a pragmatist, that during his rise to power he made good use of this whole structure of secret societies, of racist, nationalistic groups," said Manterola.

"Ah, but who used whom?" asked Renn. "Young people, upstarts with good political intuition and a touch of fanaticism, sensitive to the disempowerment of the German working class, equipped with an arsenal of conspiracy theories, with a suitcase full of guilty parties: the Jews, the Communists, gays, gypsies, intellectuals, and professors? People with a philosophy of hate, offering grandeur to all that want their crumbs from an exhausted, apathetic society? I think it's better that they were mutually used. And Hitler's paper isn't that of a delirious opportunist, but rather the reverse. The Thule gave birth to the Nazi crucible, where power politics, esoteric cults, black magic, modern diplomacy, industrialization, and mass murder are all stirred together."

"We think that the Thule was the key that formed public ideology and furthered the secret projects of the Nazis, who continued to arm themselves as they rose to power. And an interesting result is to analyze why, in 1934, the Nazis banned a book by von Sebottendorff, *Before the Arrival of Hitler*, which included a list of Nazi leaders who had connections with the Thule and other secret groups. Why would they not have wanted that information to be made public? What we do know is that von Sebottendorff has disappeared. Possibly assassinated."

It was at this point, Manterola remembered, that silence blanketed the patio. Uhse was the first to break it.

"A great wave of madness has swept through German society. Racism has become a national policy. Already hundreds of thousands—perhaps millions—of Jews from Germany, Austria, and the occupied countries have been confined to ghettos or shipped to concentration camps to be executed."

Again, for a few moments, nobody spoke. Manterola scanned the room: the empty bottles, broken-down cardboard boxes, old lumber stacked in a corner, the dust, the humidity, the single ray of light. He focused on the sunbeam. There's a war going on outside that no man is safe from, he thought. And inside the war is . . . this?

The others were also still, as if the revelation that struck Manterola had somehow affected them, made them retreat, made them sink back into themselves. Only the rabbi looked sadly back at him as if challenging him to admit that he had actually lied, begging him to negate his terrible premonition and the certainty of fate. Finally, it was Renn who broke the tension and the silence.

"In this age of powerful lunatics, science has been controlled by men like Hans Horbiger, a minor inventor of compressors and other bomb parts. A man who has built his entire scientific career on absolutely absurd theories, like the idea that our planet once had four moons and that three of them have since crashed to earth, or the idea that the ancestors of human beings were a race of giants whose traces the Nazis are searching for. A man who came up with something as imbecilic as the theory of eternal fire. Horbiger became one of the system's most prominent scientists. Between 1928 and 1937, one of his disciples, the archaeologist Kiss, organized a series of expeditions to Tiahuanaco, in the Andes. From them he concluded that he had discovered the lost city of Atlantis, and that he had also found the remains of what he claimed were a series of ports for the movement of ships between the other great cities of giants, located in modern-day Mexico, New Guinea, Tibet, and Abyssinia. Of course, all these explorations had military implications."

The rabbi then cut in with more details. "The Nazis have been very interested in Tibet, have been conducting supposedly scientific research there in recent years. On the eve of war, a fourteen-month expedition was organized under the command of Ernest Shafer to search the region for remains of German ancestors. And how did they go about conducting their research? Well, their approach was varied. On the one hand, they searched archaeological sites for maps of the firmament, while on the other hand they took anthropomorphic measurements of the Tibetan people, trying to establish the Aryan origins of the Germanic tribes. What's more, they doubtless sought the help of a shamanic sect of warlocks known as the 'green caps,' who practiced necrophagia and human sacrifice. This is an old story, and investigating it nearly cost me my life. The relationship between the Nazis and this sect dates back to 1925, when a Tibetan colony was established in Berlin. This same year a monk—or a pseudo monk, as the case may be—known as 'the man with the green gloves' prognosticated with certainty the number of Nazi representatives that Hitler would gain in Parliament. Hitler visited this man often."

"And what's the significance of this 'Tibetan relative' of the Nazis?" asked the journalist, sensing that it was up to him to inject a dose of reason into this strange rigmarole. "Pardon me if I seem cynical, but up to now I've been simply crammed with all this maddening, terrifying information. And carrying all this further, such cults seem to me like Judaic rites or, if I may be so bold, like the apparition of the Virgin of Guadalupe."

The old rabbi looked at him through his thick glasses with compassion and pronounced a few words that sounded like medieval Spanish.

"Doctor Sacal says that he's not trying to convert you to Judaism, but rather to show you the paths along which evil so freely flows," said Renn in a conciliatory tone. "I'm as much of an atheist as you, *amigo*, but in order to obtain and organize this information, many people have risked—and lost—their lives. Our good doctor here has been viciously pursued across half the globe because of what he knows. There is no place in this world where he can rest safely. They even killed his two children . . . a seventeen-year-old daughter and a twenty-two-year-old son. And do you know how? They crucified them."

Manterola looked toward the old man but couldn't meet his gaze, his face lost in the shadows of the room's corner. The rabbi let a few moments go by undisturbed and then took a scrap of paper from his pocket, unfolded it, and slowly began to read:

　　　My father broke the seal;
　　　He felt not the breath of malignance
　　　And loosed the demon upon the earth.

"It's a poem by Albert, Haushofer's son, who converted to the resistance movement."

"It's also a metaphor," said Manterola.

"That's one way to interpret it. But what we believe is that there is much more than metaphor in all that's happening. We believe that Nazism is guided by these satanic visions and that its actions correspond to this new ideology. And that many of their actions, which at first may seem inexplicable, can be interpreted in esoteric ways.

"You see the malignant history that has infected the world. So answer me this: why would the second highest Nazi official, Rudolf Hess, board a plane and fly alone to Scotland to be captured? It happened a few months ago, and nobody has been able to explain it. Not in political terms, anyway. Haushofer was the last man to speak with Hess before he left, and doubtlessly was the catalyst for this strange operation. We know that Hess went to Scotland because he was convinced that the 'Golden Dawn' group had a good deal of influence over certain British circles, predominently the nobility, and because this group propagated the Nazis' racist vision. But it fell through because it turned out that Hess had overestimated the power of the group and when he was captured, there was no way of contacting him. Churchill, instead of trying him, simply placed him in solitary confinement in a maximum-security prison. Apparently, the British premier didn't want the world to find out about the fissures that exist in the British aristocracy and its occasionally pro-Fascist whims. The Duke of Hamilton, the Duke of Bedford, and Sir Ivone Kirkpatrick solicited an interview with Hess, who, being locked away, readily agreed to it. However, the press has kept it well covered up.

"Hundreds of events related in some way to Nazism in the past few years permit this interpretation. There are simply too many connections for them to be treated as simple coincidences. For example, there is the number seven Hitler received for adhering to the Workers of Germany party, the prevailing logic turning on the swastika's axis, the right angle twist that animated the designs of the Nazi's military campaigns and fixed their objectives. And there was the SS brigade's mysterious visit to Mount Elbruz in the Caucacus Mountains to meet there with the magic sect known as the Friends of Lucifer and plant there their banner bearing their new symbol, the hooked cross. And the strange phrases Hitler sometimes slipped into interviews, like when he told a North American newspaper that 'we don't necessarily need a coherent concept of the world.' And what can you say about the Luftwaffe's experiments and the waves of radar they sent into the atmosphere that returned who knows what?

"The Thule has become a veritable state in and of itself. It has created not only the strongest military machine the world has ever known, but also a series of monstrous structures as its instruments of destruction. The SS governs Germany through fear. Within this organization, not only the youth recreation centers and the sexual experiments in search of Aryan perfection are controlled, but also the police and the concentration camps and the various armored divisions. And they spawned a new brainchild—the Ahnenerbe Society—a group of geneticists with a pseudo-scientific façade for promoting racism. The Center for the Study of Ancestral Heredity was assimilated by Himmler and the SS in 1935 and finally, at the beginning of the war, it was converted into the grand machinery of investigations into the dark underbelly of Nazism, with thousands of men in fifty institutes spread across Germany.

"We know that the organization has initiated studies and organized movements whose aims include the recovery of the Arthurian Holy Grail and the search that inspired the expedition to Tibet we just spoke of. They conducted genetic experiments on horses and 'Aryan bees.' But it didn't stop there. The animal studies didn't produce enough results for them, so they began to work on human beings, beginning with the sick and mentally disabled, and now, we are convinced, with Russian prisoners of war. Then there was even a secret Ahnenerbe study on the craniums of Russian political chiefs captured on the eastern front . . . after the earlier subjects had all been killed.

"We have tried to put all these seemingly disparate elements in some sort of order, but something still seems amiss. There doesn't seem to be any method, a master plan if you will, just a series of mad searches in the foggy margins of mythology," Sacal finished.

Manterola sighed. The kerchief he had around his neck had become damp with sweat. He took it off and stuffed it in his pocket.

"Why are you telling me all this? What do you want me to do for you?"

"Somehow these forces of iniquity have now been set in motion in Mexico."

"By whom? How do you know?"

"Remember how the conversation began?" Renn asked. "Remember the name Otto Rahn? Have you ever heard of the Black Order?"

"This is the first. I've never heard of Otto Rahn before, and I don't know anything about a Black Order."

"The Black Order encompasses many things. It is the SS, the Shutzstaffel, the backbone of the clashing forces of Nazism. It's a giant net that gathers, as we've told you, everything from armored divisions, centers of investigation, summer schools, castles, concentration camps, the Gestapo, and even Hitler's personal bodyguards."

"Doctor Sacal," said Renn, "carries much key information for the German anti-Fascist exiles and for the very destiny of this war. But two pieces in particular pertain directly to Mexico. One was barely a rumor, a whisper in the mist, but it has had explosive consequences: *Otto Rahn is in Mexico*. But that is impossible."

"Yes. Impossible," asserted the rabbi.

"Who is Rahn and why is he so important to you? Why is it so impossible for him to be here?"

"It's simple. Because he was dead. And every time a dead man comes back to life, it's for a very important reason," said Uhse.

"Rahn was a young intellectual, born in 1904, and he grew up in the crisis of postwar Germany. He was a brilliant student of literature, an expert in Gothism, and always interested in myths and legends. He ended up specializing in *catarismo*, the heresy of gnostic Christians who returned to purity. That great social movement provoked the popes to interrupt a crusade against Palestine in favor of burning Christians at the stake. In 1931 Rahn traveled to France, to the ruins at Montsegur, to study the history of the sect that was destroyed in one of the most barbaric acts of the Middle Ages. He was a singular character of dubious morality. His colleagues accused him of having written false inscriptions on the walls of caves so that he could photograph them and claim himself as their discoverer. But he wasn't just a fraudulent scientist, he was also a small-time crook: he had to flee France on account of his economic problems, and he left a mountain of debt behind him. He wrote a book entitled *The Crusade Against the Grail* in 1933. He was always fascinated by the legend of the Grail, that sacred cup of Arthurian fame that cropped up in legends throughout the Christian world, reaching even the Cathars and later the Templars.

"Rahn returned to France in 1937. But he had changed. He was no longer the insignificant, novice student of false history. Now, he was an insignificant, novice student of black magic. He arrived in France this time as a Nazi, as a ranking member of the SS. We know that he had joined the SA's shock troops in 1933, and that he had passed through Himmler's SS where he quickly rose to become Obersturmführer with the rank of captain. An unusual case for our so staunchly rigid German."

"All we have of him is a photo from his book," said Uhse.

Doctor Sacal took a small snapshot out from under his cloak. Manterola studied it closely. Against the light and inside a cave he discerned a man standing in a strange position: his neck craning and his legs spread wide, in nearly a sixty-degree angle, as he balanced on two arêtes of rock. It looked to have come originally from some sort of alpine magazine. It was impossible to distinguish the man's face or clothes, not their color nor the color of his hair. He had, perhaps, a regular complexion and an average height. Nothing more could be discerned.

"It's Rahn, in the Ornolac caverns in France, searching for evidence of the Templars some ten years ago. It's said that he committed suicide on Mount Kufstein in Germany by swallowing cyanide. That was supposedly in 1939, a couple years after his return to France. But there are other versions of his death too; one, for example, is that he died in a blizzard while climbing Mount Ruffheim. But in all accounts, his body was never recovered. How, then, can we be sure?

"One of the paradoxes is that the official reason for his 'suicide' was the discovery of the fact that he was actually part Jewish. His mother, Clara Margaret, had a half-Jewish father, Simeón Hamburg, whose mother, Lea Cucer, was also a Jew."

"He couldn't bear his burden, so the little Nazi Jew killed himself," remarked Renn with a bitter smile.

"But that's not all," said Uhse. "We also have information that six months ago, an obscure Ahnenerbe office in Stuttgart began a big project with some pretty unusual goals. Why would an investigation on race convene experts on pre-Colombian history, a pair of notorious SS gunmen, a geologist and geographer who had done his dissertation on Mexican volcanoes, a few professors of the Spanish language, and a strange Mexican national named Mendoza who had once taught a few courses? Halfway through the war, and this office is getting attention and resources? Amazing."

"There is no doubt: the focus of that office is Mexico."

"Which means what?"

"We no longer believe in accidents, in chance. We don't know what these developments can mean, but we do know that Mexico has entered into the plans of the heirs of Thule and therefore of Hitler and the Third Reich."

"And what are you suggesting I do with this information?"

"Well, Manterola, you are a man of some influence," said the novelist Renn, lighting his pipe.

The journalist dared not smile. Rather, he felt as if the full weight of the world had just been placed squarely upon his shoulders.

And now, two days later, as he reviewed his notes and reconstructed that long conversation in his memory, he was still unable to smile.

PART IV

THE A39 REPORTS, AND/OR THE TRIBULATIONS OF A WRITER

FROM THE NOTES OF
FERMÍN VALENCIA:

First parenthesis: Many years after this history plays itself out, in a political operation conducted by the followers of President Ávila Camacho, the official records of the government's history will (after having been expurgated and cleared of rats) be stored in this depository of lies and fraud where today the Palacio Negro, the Lecumberri Prison, stands.

In this depository that today I can see only as a prison, there will be, among innumerable others, two dusty books pertaining specifically to the Camacho period. In one of these will be found a case record bearing the formal if uninteresting title of GN-6681-6687, including three appendixes. Here will be the reports that I wrote under the pseudonym A39, with one exception: the one dedicated to Hilda Krüger that I have here. It was never handed over to the authorities.

Second parenthesis: The letters of Ernest Hemingway referred to here will, like so many of his other unedited materials, be stored in the strongbox of his New York publisher, Charles Scribner, after his suicide and by his own request. It is possible that these letters form part of the notes and outline for a novel with strong autobiographical tinges that would have been titled *Lives and Death*. Hemingway sometimes spoke with me about this novel, which I suppose his estate may one day decide to resurrect, edit, and publish.

ATTENTIVELY, A39

At the request of my superiors, I have resumed my investigations into the pro-Nazi activities of one Gerardo Murillo, alias Doctor Atl, the very popular and famous painter and intellectual.

His past in the Revolutionary Committee of National Reconstruction (see: Atl, 1239) is already well known. The organization was formed in 1939 with the intention of challenging Cárdenas and promoting conservative thought, and Atl was (and continues to be?) its spokesman.

His relationship with Arthur Dietrich, press secretary of the Nazi embassy in Mexico (see: Dietrich, 2214–2218), is also documented by various reports previously referred to here. His having been arrested on charges of fraud certainly implicates him in the recent corruption of journalists.

Atl has frequently received money from Dietrich (in notes issued by the Bank of London and Mexico or in plain manila envelopes containing cash) for acting as an intermediary between the embassy and various conservative Mexican political parties.

Atl's pro-Fascist and pro-Nazi tendencies often go beyond the realm of simple theory and ideology. For example, consider the "Italian Pamphlets," paid for by Mussolini's embassy: in their prologue, it states that Atl would be elected President of the Republic to much acclaim if, in return, Atl would laud Mussolini as "the defender of the Italian model of civilization."

Beginning with the onset of the war in Europe, Atl has authored numerous pamphlets by order of the German embassy. There is one, entitled "A German Peace Or a British-Jewish Peace," that not even this scrupulous investigator, functioning now as a writer, could read without lapsing into moral nausea, for it speaks of Hitler as a man of "superior biological strengths who, as history will show, saved Germany from disaster" (author's note: suck on that fiery prose). Among that and other drivel in the pamphlet is a definition of Nazism as a new form of "aristocracy," comparable, it seems, to Atl's own "aristocratic calling."

Ultimately, Atl's obsessions, fed economically and egoistically by Dietrich, center on a virulent anti-Semitism which, as I have stated, disgusts me.

In furthering my investigation, I traveled to that part of the city sadly called De Los Doctores where, despite its name, there isn't medicine enough to cure a horse, much less a man. There is, however, the small press Sole ironically run by an illiterate Galician man who, from what I could tell, is currently printing a new pamphlet titled "Jews Over America." I managed to acquire one of the galleys, which reads like an anthology of the absurd. Consider the following paragraph:

> Unzip a Jew and a Communist steps out. To put it another
> way, all Jews are Communists, from the wealthiest bank
> presidents to industry moguls, rabbis and politicians, to
> those who occupy the most modest of workers' positions.

Gerardo Murillo, alias Doctor Atl, is currently sixty-seven years old, a painter of considerable talent, has published a few collections of essays, some scientific articles of dubious quality, and, in recent years, has become interested in volcanoes. His writings, on Popocatepetl in particular, have appeared in Germany in the magazine *Zeitschrift für Vulkanologie*, published out of Berlin.

Ultimately, and despite the fact that I am profoundly disgusted by this man (and I am disgusted also by recommending this course of action), it is not worth spending any more time investigating this subject. His activities, even the most outlandish of his propaganda, are innocuous, and I must admit that, during a nocturnal incursion into his study at 123 Artículo Street, I realized I still greatly admire his painting (author's note: damn! Such a waste of talent), in particular his portraits of Nahui and especially his landscapes of volcanoes, mountains, and clouds. In the opinion of this humble poet-turned-investigator and report-writer, the aforementioned and investigated Atl knows how to paint.

Understanding that the readers of this report couldn't care less about my artistic appraisals I will, for the rest of this report, retreat from aesthetic issues and return to the central investigation.

Following instructions and my own personal instincts, on Thursday of the past week, the hunchbacked, limping figure of this investigator followed the even more hunchbacked and limping figure of the painter on one of his maniacal errands. For two and a half hours, Murillo dedicated himself to wandering Tacuba, Cinco de Mayo, 16 de Septiembre, and Madero streets on the outskirts of our city. There he gathered information on store and business owners, emphasizing in his study questions on their dealings with Jews (What is your religion and nationality? How many years have you resided in Mexico?), probably in the case of an opportunity for a purge, a pogrom, or whatever other act of racism.

On the verge of astonishment in the face of such dubious morality, I followed even more closely, and was able to definitively confirm his offensive questions and notes.

Admittedly this investigator is a native of Gijón, Spain, raised in Chihuahua, and a nationalized Mexican citizen; however, he would have been quite happy to have been in the position of a Polish Jew boxer, if just for the opportunity to bust this doctor's jaw.

Further investigations brought me into contact with the distributors of the aforementioned pamphlet and other similar ones, but I emphasize that they participate in the distribution for purely economic reasons. They would distribute Protestant bibles, pharmaceutical orders, or the novels of Alexandre Dumas if it were sufficiently profitable.

I once again recommend that, in my opinion, we ought not to proceed against Gerardo Murillo, based on the recently passed anticounterintelligence bill, the fact that his arrest would simply bolster his egoistic personality, and that his activities, if insidious, are harmless. Dietrich, on the other hand, is the driving force behind this and many other such louts, and is a much more interesting and dangerous figure. Atl can go on playing the clown without prosecution.

Attentively,
A39

HEMINGWAY SPEAKS
TO HIS CAT

You would give me a precise task and then I would complete it. But please, don't send me to the Pacific. All those tiny islands full of Japs and those golden mosquitoes with the big eyes don't appeal to me in the least. Make it a specific task, but keep it grounded in reality. And neither do I want to go, for example, to England, where all the knights drink tea and die with that melancholic grin on their lips. I'd much rather be with the New Zealanders or the Australians, and clearly I'd seize upon the first chance I got to make an incursion into occupied France and then later, with a little luck, join an armored division and roll in through the Spanish Pyrenees, or some such thing."

The cat contemplated the man with a lack of interest. She was conscious of the fact that although the man seemed to be speaking to her, he was actually talking to himself, and so she did not pretend to answer. If the man wanted her opinion, he would have proposed something more sensible: "Two meows if you think I should go to Burma; one if it's Malta, being bombarded by the Stukas."

She wasn't the only cat. At least a half dozen more kept her company, three housecats and three alleycats who came and went as they pleased, all of them keeping watch, despite the fact that they had little patience with auditory concentration. At times, an insect's winding flight, a tempting shoelace, or the fluff emerging from a rip in a chair's leather seat was more interesting than this man's monologue.

"Someone ought to have figured out by now that my place is in Europe. It's the perfect place for a man like me. After all, only an American can truly describe that place." He laughed. He could easily be drunk, but on the other hand it was only eight in the morning. "I am the man of the moment. It's up to me to describe Europe so that those fools can understand it. I don't see how they can't realize that. In order to describe it, I have to see it. It's as simple as that . . . you just can't describe what you haven't seen."

The man staggered over toward the cat. Then he dropped to the floor so that he could see the cat face to face. The cat drew back, smelling the alcohol on the man's breath. She had never liked rum. All over the walls and floor of the flat were empty bottles, books, posters of bulls, conch shells, shotgun shells, and muddy boots. And of course the cats, who made up the ever-growing audience.

"Boise, do you know Quevedo?" The man asked the cat, who seemed to be looking at him with the most interest (or amusement). The cat ignored him.

The man, who was dressed only in a T-shirt and shorts, got to his feet and picked his way over to a row of shelves. He searched through them earnestly, tossing any unwanted volumes to the floor. Eventually, he found the one he wanted, opened it to a particular dog-eared page, and began to read in Spanish:

> A robust yet tormented soul looks in on itself
> And anxious, mortal troubles burden,
> Bring down only noble heads.

He stopped pronouncing the sonorous, guttural Spanish verses and returned to English to ask the cat, "Isn't it all quite clear?"

The cat, a bit disconcerted, turned and left Ernest Hemingway without an interlocutor. At least one of us knows how to take care of himself, she thought quietly.

ATTENTIVELY, A39

A brief report summarizing the Dietrich case history, a desirable solution, and possible repercussions:

Arthur Dietrich first arrived in Mexico in 1924. He had a brusque personality that sometimes bordered on despotic, he kept a downcast gaze because he had lost an eye, and he never achieved a native command of Spanish. In this agent's experience, he has been the easiest subject to tail; when his ostentatious character wasn't in plain view, he left a clear trail of clues and rumors behind him.

He spoke very derisively of Mexico in general and of our politics in particular. Once I heard him say, with regard to Lázaro Cárdenas, that the general couldn't wear shoes, since all he had ever known were *huaraches* and riding boots. He was also fond of describing this as a nation populated entirely by slaves, vagrants, and thieves.

After his arrival in Mexico, he worked as a ranch foreman for a countryman of his in Hidalgo. It was either there or before that time that he married a German woman named Felicia, and it was also around then that he did time in prison on a fraud conviction.

Dietrich had quite a notorious reputation in the region, as is evidenced by this agent's confirmation of the rumors that Felicia was not very felicitous, as Dietrich would often come home drunk and beat her.

In 1933 he founded the German National Socialist Party with a group
of German nationals residing in Mexico at the time. Then, in 1935, after
the Nazis came to power in Germany, Dietrich became a diplomat. In April
of that year, he was named press attaché for the German embassy in Mexico
City, and he bought a house in the city's Mixcoac neighborhood. His ascent
to this important office allegedly owes itself to his relative, Otto Dietrich,
the Nazi party's chief of propaganda and also Goebbels' right-hand man.

In the first few months of his office, he maintained relations with the
reactionary general Nicolás Rodríguez and his Gold Shirts, and they owe a
good deal of their anti-Semitic and anti-Communist rhetoric to Dietrich's
influence.

He moved his offices to 17 Viena Street and immediately began to influence Mexican news broadcasts. He founded the periodical *La Noticia* in
1935, which he ran through aliases. This periodical, which didn't amount
to much more than a poster, didn't have much in the way of influence or
readers, but it served to get Dietrich's name known by other, more established journalists.

Dietrich left Mexico for two years during the war in Spain. Taking advantage of his knowledge of our language, the Nazi government assigned
him to drum up support among the local German community and from the
various Condor Legions who sided with Franco and his quarrels with the
Falange.

Upon his return Dietrich stepped up his work in journalism. This agent
found conclusive proof that he gave money to Atl for the publication of
anti-Semitic pamphlets, that he also gave economic support to Vasconcelos's
journal *Timón*, and that he financed the journal *Hoy* both directly and in-
directly through the reporter José Pagés. Dietrich sent Pagés around the
globe to interview international Fascist figures, buying him plane tickets,
restaurant vouchers, and booking him in first-class hotels.

There is no doubt that his hands were sunk deep into the second edition
of *Ultimas Noticias*, and although this agent has not been able to determine
if his connection was through Rodrigo de Llano (whom Dietrich often took
to dinner at such restaurants as La Calesa and Los Tres Barones), the
German embassy has noted clear tendencies in that daily paper and the focus
of its reporting. One has only to look at its coverage of the annexation of
Austria or of Mexico's interventions in the Evian Conference to see the
connections. And no less noticeable has been his influence over Novaro,
editor-in-chief of *La Prensa*.

All told, Dietrich managed to turn the Mexican media into a mass of
Germanophiles for nearly five years. And it wasn't just through the bribes
he generously doled out; it was also in such things as his importation of

Swedish paper via Germany or the sale of German printing presses to Mexican newspapers.

On June 11, on the eve of the election, I received a dispatch from my superiors. The Minister of the Interior had been ordered by the president himself, General Cárdenas, to have Arthur Dietrich arrested and deported, classifying him as an "undesirable alien." This was coupled with another order to formally close down the journal *Timón*.

So I deprived myself of the chance to see Vasconcelos's mug in favor of going after Dietrich.

I personally brought the expulsion orders to two reserve agents, and we then proceeded to the 13th precinct, in the Mixcoac neighborhood. The next morning, with backup, we staked out Dietrich's house. At 7:12 a.m. he emerged from his front door and went over to open his garage. I had set up the police in what seemed to me to be the most secure positions, given that I wanted to preserve my anonymity (an agent who is in the least bit careless can easily blow his cover), and gave the signal to move in. The target saw our movements, but was apprehended before he could get back inside his house. I had been hanging back in a group of journalists and passers-by and, during the commotion of the arrest, I slipped into the house. In the living room I saw his desk littered with letters, and was able to pocket many of them before being interrupted by Felicia. Those are the same letters that I turned over to my superiors, in a bread wrapper (for that was all that was available at the time) but still perfectly sealed.

I rode to Veracruz in the same car of the train as the detained and his two dimwitted guards (author's note: I beg my superiors never again to give such important assignments to agents Domínguez and Sombrerete, who consider the taco to be a great invention and who spent more time in the bathroom than they did watching the detained). Despite my many attempts at conversation with Dietrich, he remained steadfastly mute. A few days later, he was placed on board a ship bound for Germany via Havana.

All that I have reported so far serves as a preface.

In September of this same year (1940) I heard rumors that Arthur Dietrich had returned to Mexico and was living underground and under an assumed name. I traced said rumor back to its origins and found that an extremely myopic American SIS agent had falsely identified a minor official in the Germany embassy, Heyer, as Dietrich. Apparently the screening process for the SIS leaves much to be desired.

In this agent's opinion, the rumor is therefore unsubstantiated. Dietrich worked for whom he worked with German advertisers in his exceedingly deep pockets. His work was highly visible, and he himself was so well known that waiters at four-star restaurants would bow to him when he ate there.

Underground, in Mexico, he would have only the cantinas.

It seems more likely that, with regard to propaganda, the German embassy has, after Dietrich's deportation, gone out of business.

Attentively,
A39

HEMINGWAY LAUNCHES
A ROCKET ATTACK

W hile dining alone, a curious sentence came to Hemingway:

> Thomas Hudson wanted to write a novel but he did not
> know if he had it in him, did not know if he had within him
> enough stories and truths to set to words.

For a few moments, he continued drinking his red wine and toying with his scrambled eggs and sausage, which he had barely touched, and nibbled at a tomato. Then he quickly got up, arranged his napkin on his plate as if to cover up his waste, and walked into his library. He rolled a fresh sheet of paper into his tiny, portable Underwood typewriter that sat on one of the bookcase's upper shelves, and began to type, as always, standing up:

> Thomas Hudson wanted to write a novel

He stopped, reread the line he had written, and returned to the dining room.

Without sitting down, he tipped up the last of his wine and went out toward the garden. The pool was empty.

"Don't wait for me, I'll be back later," he called toward the house, but nobody was listening. He liked to think here, under the low ridge where La Finca was situated like a barque heading to seaward, and he started tacking on down the road toward the town of San Francisco de Paula. Presently he came to the local bodega and went inside. He bought two strings of rockets and an assortment of spitfires, cherry bombs, and those little thundering things that children call lady's fingers.

Rumors of the gringo's presence always worked wonders. When he left the bodega dusk had fallen and he found, assembled in front of him, his complete army, sans deserters and Cacciatos: some twenty smiling children. Some of them, those nearing adolescence, had lit cigarettes. Shooting off rockets with the gringo was evidently a pretext for smoking.

Hemingway arranged the two strings of rockets across his chest like a bandoleer, meted out a portion of his arsenal, brought a finger up to his lips asking for silence, and the group stole off down the alleyways.

Their first objective was the barber's shop. They silently arranged a dozen or so of the rockets underneath the large front window before retreating to the cover and shadows of the palms across the road. It was warm and humid, with scarcely a breath of ocean breeze.

The first volley sounded like a machine gun burst, and the customers inside leapt, half shaven, from their chairs as a barber knocked over a basin of soapy water.

"It's that damn old gringo and those kids," said one of the customers who had gone over to the window to look.

"Christ, you'd think that big American would have outgrown that by now," said another, while Hemingway and his troops ran laughing through the streets on their way to their next assault: cherry bombs down the chimney of the local Holy Joe's house.

While the rockets flew and the black powder crackled, a new paragraph for his novel came to him:

> Thomas Hudson wanted to blow up the world but he
> wanted the explosion to be a craft, a harmless work of art
> with no casualties but all the fire and smoke of a
> magician's act.

He took leave of his *compadres* and walked back to his house to write it. They were the last three lines that he would write that night.

DOUBLY ATTENTIVELY, A39

This agent has absolute confidence in the quality of information that comes from a drunken gringo. It is common knowledge that Mexicans lie when drunk and that the French and Spanish will exaggerate but, for some strange geographic reason, when gringos drink themselves to death, they always tell the truth.

Based on these considerations, the conversation with the man we will call Gringo R., when added to information already in our possession, gives us the following history:

In July of this year (1940), the SIS (Secret Intelligence Service) was created as an arm of the FBI to operate in Latin America. Even then, the nets of American espionage were being cast by the State Department via embassies and consulates. The SIS was first conceived by J. Edgar Hoover who, my informant says, is an incredible closet gay and who likes to dress up as a Turkish odalisque in hotel rooms. Without getting any deeper into that matter (author's note: and knowing my own personal sexual attitudes), it is notable that FBI agents had been stumbling around blindly in order to obtain solid sources of information in Mexico since May of that year, but without a serious dedication.

Other recent additions to the team have brought the total number of agents to twenty-seven (27), and there is some conflict with seasoned FBI veterans who were passed over in favor of recruiting junior agents who had dedicated their careers to the new chief Gus T. Jones from the start.

This office is focused almost entirely on the German embassy and its activities, though recently, to some extent, they have begun to take an interest in the Japanese and the Italian presence, as well as the Falangists in the older Spanish neighborhoods.

Given that they do not have much interest in internal Mexican politics, it is the recommendation of this agent that we consider entering into a formal relationship with the SIS, something that my superiors may well already have considered.

Attentively,
A39

P.S. My informant assures me that our department is on the SIS's payroll. As I do not recall having received overtime or extra pay from the treasurer's office in the past few months, I would like to here register my concerns about such insidious dealings.

Attentively,
A39

HEMINGWAY WRITES A NOVEL

He contemplated the rear part of La Finca from the window. Someone was working in the garden. After a few minutes, he went back to his typewriter and wrote:

> Thomas Hudson was writing a novel using ambiguous
> words. With ambiguous language in general. He knew
> this, which is why

He turned quickly from the typewriter and strode off through the room. He walked back past the window and over to the bar where he poured himself a glass of whiskey with two ice cubes. He swirled the brown liquid around and listened to the ice clinking against the glass. He returned to the typewriter, tore out the page, rolled in a clean sheet, and wrote:

> Thomas Hudson was writing the novel ambiguously and he
> knew it. He could not write it clearly because that was not
> how he had it in his head. It was hell inside his head. Not

the hell that Dante described, but the hell of a war that was and was not his and a woman who did not belong to him.

He looked up. A sudden noise had jerked him out of his concentration: a pair of books that had been sitting precariously on top of a magazine rack had fallen to the floor. Hemingway got up and went back over to the window.

"Don't throw rocks at the mangos!" He yelled at two children running through the garden. La Finca was always full of young invaders. That did not bother him. What bothered him was that they knocked mangos out of his trees with stones. But the matter was more complicated than what it seemed at first glance. Someone, Mario or another of the servants, had once asked him, "How are they ever going to become great baseball players if they don't practice?" Hemingway supposed that he would end up having to buy balls and gloves for all the children of Cojimar if he ever wanted to protect his mango trees.

ATTENTIVELY, A39

Katerina Matilda Krüger, born near Berlin in 1912, goes by her stage name of Hilda Krüger. She is a tall, attractive, blond woman, stylish and able to speak English and a bit of Spanish in addition to her native German. Far from being a spectacular beauty (author's note: I prefer my women less plump and more brunette), she nonetheless catches the attention of many men, turning many heads.

A stage and film actress in Nazi Germany (this agent has been unable to locate a single one of her films here in Mexico), she was rumored to have been romantically involved with Chancellor Goebbels despite the fact that she was married at the time. Her ex-husband had some Jewish ancestors whose discovery supposedly brought about her fall from grace in the German theater. However, this agent suspects that she merely used that as an excuse in order to relocate to a foreign country as a secret agent.

In 1939 she abandoned her husband and emigrated to England. When war broke out, she moved again, this time to the United States, where she apparently resumed pursuing a film career.

After a brief stint in New York, she flew to Los Angeles and, in January of 1940, she moved into Hollywood's Beverly Wilshire Hotel. She remained there for several months while trying to get parts, though apparently without any success. So what did she live on during this period of time? It remains a mystery.

Later she became involved with a St. Louis businessman of German descent named Von Gontard, but suddenly, in February of 1941, she flew to Mexico saying that she was going to obtain Mexican residency so that she could formalize her divorce before returning to the U.S. to marry him.

This agent first came into contact with Krüger through her relationships with her German countrymen Friedrich Von Schleebrugge, Paul Max Weber, and Georg Nicolaus, all of them agents with the Abwehr IV (see: Abwehr, 2-02, reports from May and June). She began to show up regularly at political fundraisers and other social events here in Mexico, apparently having forgotten about her friend in St. Louis.

She attended parties and talked of writing a biography of Malinche. She took trips to Teotihuacán, visited movie producers, and, in the spring of 1941, fell in love with one Ramón Beteta, the Undersecretary of the Treasury and a board member of the National Bank of Mexico.

It was during this period of time that this agent investigated the subject "unofficially," given the expressed prohibitions of his superiors.

The fact that this woman maintained relationships with Mexican politicians as well as members of the Abwehr IV aroused the suspicions not only of this agent, but her activities were also closely monitored by what could only have been Allied agents, most likely the SIS.

Her maid, with whom this agent has, for professional reasons, often met, says that Krüger often writes "notes that no one can read" and then places them in a book which she then returns to the National Library.

For the past three weeks, Krüger has lived in a large, two-story house in the Colonia Roma. If we assume that she has no income in Mexico, then it necessarily follows that someone else is paying her rent. This agent was able to make a successful entry into the house and search of her bedroom on the second floor. In her dresser, along with a plentiful supply of underwear, was found a well-worn copy of Hemingway's *Across the River and Into the Trees*, published by Editorial Sopena and full of underlinings and dog-eared pages. This agent believes this book to be some sort of decoding key to the aforementioned communiqués. Also found was a bankbook in Krüger's name, with regular monthly deposits of U.S. $600 in addition to assorted deposits of Mexican pesos, all in amounts less than 1000.

Prompted by the gardener's information that the subject has a regular male visitor and that this is his maid's house, this agent staked out a permanent watch, alternating between the Hotel Liguria on the corner, the Roxy soda shop, and a loan office on the second floor of a building on Colima Street. After eleven days of observation, this agent was able to confirm that the person who supports Hilda Krüger is the Minister of the Interior, Miguel Alemán, head of the office to which I am assigned, and not only this agent's superior but the superior of the official who reads these reports. His tiny mustache, his hairstyle, and his double-breasted suits are unmistakable, as is the fact that he comes regularly at 2300 hours and leaves just as regularly at 0400.

With nothing further at this time and a burnt stench in my nostrils, I remain

Attentively,
A39

P.S. Given the fact that this report will not pass through the usual paths of bureaucracy (in fact, this agent will seal and bury it), the above-signed would like to add an epilogue affirming that his preliminary opinion was incorrect: the German national referred to throughout these pages is quite a fox indeed.

P.P.S. Does Miguel Alemán know that Krüger works for the German SS? How could he not? If he truly does not realize it, this agent could do well to inform him. Is she using him for something? Does he want to be made a fool? Or is he an agent himself and/or involved in some sort of collusion that this relationship furthers? Or, finally, is he simply sleeping with the enemy?

Attentively,
A39

HEMINGWAY WRITES A NOVEL

The writer was stretched out face down on a couch in the living room, his right index finger slowly stirring the contents of a martini glass that he had set on the coffee table. When it had been sufficiently mixed, he licked off his finger appreciatively. Then he got up and, stumbling into a magazine rack, fell awkwardly and ended up with his hand caught in the teeth of a lion-skin rug that lay at the side of his bed. He took a deep breath, got to his feet once again, and carefully picked his way over to his typewriter to write:

> Thomas Hudson was trying to write a novel. But what he wrote was not true because in those days there were few truths left to him and he had only dreams and delusions of grandeur and fears and idleness. But he went on writing that untrue novel because . . .

PART V

GRAY, BLACK, AND BROWN

INTERRUPTIONS

AND INVASIONS

6. A fine, light gray rain is falling, tinged with the dross of a fire that recently burned through these hills. The nurses have given up any hope of keeping their uniforms white, and the collars of my shirts leave much to be desired.

7. I once knew a witch. I defended her in court, but not for practicing magic. After the Revolution, no one was ever charged with that. No, she was accused of having stolen a mahogany radio console. I couldn't be certain. But she was certainly intriguing, and perhaps the time has come to bring her into this story. Her name was Amalia or Amelia, or something like that.

She was well-known in her neighborhood for both good and bad reasons. The good ones had to do with justice, while the bad ones (as is always the case in Mexico) with provincialism and abuse. One of the good things that was said of her was that she had murdered her brother, a farmhand who kicked cats, raped adolescent girls, and assaulted old women. On the other hand, she was generally blamed for the fact that it rained so much less in the neighborhood of Tacubaya than in the rest of the Federal District, even though it lay at the edge of the Chapultepec forest and, as we all know, forests draw the rain. At forty-nine years old, she was a quiet and even-tempered woman, though she was known to look daggers at those who made her cross. She rarely spoke unless spoken to, and when she did, it was in her own, picturesquely obscene language. To earn a living, she sold lottery tickets over the counter while under the table she performed exorcisms and ran cons.

I lost my judgment. I felt obligated to obtain another RCA console to prevent the woman from going to jail. I got one cheaply from a burglar whom I also once defended, a Cuban named Mariano Rodríguez who was friendly to a fault. He stole gramophones and liked the music of Mozart.

8. The rain and ash remind me of the story of another fire. Ten years ago, the Reichstag, the German congress building, burned. It was one of the cheapest and roughest transgressions in modern history, and it was orchestrated by the Nazi party. They moved into the city, and when the chief of police first learned of the blaze, he calmly took a siesta. They briefly considered arresting Dimitrov, one of the directors of the *International Communist*, but soon they settled on a mad Dutchman, who was, if anything, merely a pawn, and then hand-picked a jury just as they did during the Moscú trials. What resulted was absurd, even farcical. Communists were hung out to dry, and the doors were open to Nazi dictatorship. I was not there; I wasn't in Europe at the time, as I had returned from Berlin some years earlier. The Attorney of the Process didn't go, and so of course it didn't seem very important to me. It scarcely piqued my interest, and I didn't even follow the story in the Mexican papers. I don't know why I am now able to see the flames with such clarity, such intensity, and neither do I know why the light of that fire has come to burn so brightly.

9. The man with the ash-blond hair disembarks in Veracruz and disappears. Exchanges his identity for a new one. People often vanish in Veracruz; the rough climate, the never-ending games of dominoes in the plaza archways, the sweat and lethargy, the smell of freshly roasted coffee beans, the music of the marimbas, and the warmth of the breeze produce such effects.

And the silver disappears with him . . .

MISUNDERSTANDINGS

I t was a somewhat complicated situation. The woman knew that men liked to watch while she put on her stockings, and so she did it slowly, relishing every tug. The minister watching her was from Veracruz, though he had long since lost his accent, and while he was enjoying the show, that was not the reason why he was there. The woman smoothed the nylon over her skin, adjusted the clasp of her garter belt, turned her slender white calves out a bit, and exposed the delicate designs of her underwear.

The minister was simply killing time before meeting with the two Germans that she had identified. They were waiting in the small adjacent room coquettishly done up in the Swiss mode, or rather in that hybrid mode of a German who has never set foot in Switzerland but who has done up a room that might look Swiss to pretentious Mexican eyes. The two men were seated in excessively low chairs brocaded in blue, surrounded by tiny wooden carvings and cuckoo clocks, and were fairly uncomfortable. To make matters worse, these two Germans were not truly German, and this, to the smarter of the two, presented a problem. Because having been born in Pachuca to Prussian and Colognese parents, he was now being blackmailed for being German by a native of Torreón now living in the Federal District who sprayed tiny bread crumbs when he spoke: Minister Alemán.

Two clocks chimed out five o'clock within a few seconds of each other.

A pointy, red-feathered bird popped in and out of its door.

"And how can we be sure of equal treatment? What guarantees is he offering us?" asked one of the pseudo-Germans, called Müller.

"If they accept them, a gentleman in the next room will come in to greet us in a few minutes," said the other, who called himself Henriques because his father had married a Portuguese woman.

"I think we could consider it," said the first.

In the other room, Alemán's secretary entered unannounced, and surprised Hilda as she was taking off her skirt. The minister shot him a withering glance. The soft afternoon light filtered in through the half-closed blinds.

"They are ready, *señor*."

The minister got up, straightened his tie, and sharply opened the door to the little Swiss waiting room. The Germans were not prepared for this rather theatrical entrance and stood up awkwardly from their brocaded chairs. Alemán did not give them the chance to collect themselves.

"Gentlemen, I understand that you need some form of guarantee, but it is clear that we cannot put these things down on paper. So consider well the words of my secretary, and my future actions."

And without waiting for them to respond, he nodded smartly to each of them, turned, and made his way down to the lower part of the house where a servant was hanging up his pearl-gray sombrero.

3

INTERRUPTIONS
AND INVASIONS

6. The chief of the SS, Reichsführer Heinrich Himmler, asks his doctors for a precise method for ensuring the gender of his offspring. He had heard of a man in the Bavarian Alps who wanted a son, and so he abstained from alcohol for a week, went on a twenty-kilometer walk at the start of each day, and copulated with his wife immediately upon returning. Himmler wants to know the scientific basis for such behavior, but the doctors have none for him.

7. But the linchpin of the history is a city that has risen above the fear which the stone Aztec skulls had loosed on the plateau's countrymen. The same fear that the Aztec holders of power had toward the nearby phantom city of Teotihuacán. A city that had ripened in Extremaduran barbarism that destroyed pyramids and filled in canals, drowning them forever with stones from the walls of marvelous houses so that the teams of oxen could advance along these new pathways with the bombardments. A city riding the crest of blood and fear that drew the mad, heedless that it never yielded lasting fame or easy money. A city of ephemeral and theatric emperors and lame presidents who were liberals one day and conservatives the next, but always thieves and conspirators. A city of generals enamored of the Kaiser, monocled dipsomaniacs, speculating and landowning priests, a plain town that celebrated its fear in earthquakes, and was brazenly purified by three wars and two revolutions.

Did Villa and Zapata refound the town? Their passage was too fleeting to have purified it. There the Revolution was always a counterrevolution. Zapata's men only fired from a distance on firefighters and their red trucks, symbols of Hades.

8. On the other hand, the result is a city resplendent in the sun, affectionate on rainy afternoons, and friendly in its landscapes. Bordered by mountains and abundant in waters. A refuge for birds that have no other place to go, respite for travelers, flavor of luck.

Do I see it? Did I invent it? Granted, there is much that I divine, remember, and reconstruct in my isolation, but Mexico City is made better by reinvention, though there is no nostalgia for anything.

9. Summer approaches. Calabash flower soup is on the menu.

10. Would my city now return to its malignant origins? The Aztec skulls, the stone craniums with their hollow gaze and portents of absolute horror return from the past. Premonitions. And I am not there to defend the city. It both does and does not belong to me. The observations. The rumors that sustain me. The history which I both know and do not know sustains me.

The sustenance.

The summer.

Calabash flower soup, mushroom soup, tortillas, chicken broth with prickly pears, noodles, corn soup, bean soup.

11. A marriage is blossoming: that of the pre-Colombian skulls with the Nazi cross, the terrible swastika.

4

VENGEANCE

The dead men did indeed leave a trail. They were officially pronounced dead in Tapachula, and that was where the services were held, but the bodies were then boxed up and loaded into an old, beat-up Ford and taken to one of the haciendas for burial. Both were called Hermann and, being dead, seemed harmless enough. There weren't even any speeches at the wake. He couldn't get close enough to La Finca to see the actual burial, but he watched from afar as car after car of armed men in dun-brown uniforms arrived.

At least they had taken with them to the grave the identity of the Chinaman who had gunned them down in their room. His anonymity had been preserved.

This is what had brought Tomás to the region. It wasn't the best of places to start a war. It was too expansive, it had few paved roads and the ones that were paved were full of potholes, and there was little jungle for cover, except for the few pockets that were so thick as to make movement impossible. The hilly terrain was made even more difficult under the tropical sun, and there were too many towns where everyone knew each other. Only the barefoot Indians were invisible to enemy eyes. Damn his tall Chinese frame. A shorter man could have hidden himself more easily, posing as a laundromat worker or shopkeeper, but such roles would limit his mobility.

So Tomás assumed a persona so outlandish that it just might work as a disguise: that of an obtuse, incomprehensible, autistic Chinese curio dealer, which carried with it the added benefit that no one would ever want to speak to him.

Before slipping into character, he went to the Office of Agrarian Affairs and bought a map of the region. With what little money he had left, he bought an old burro, a moth-eaten wide-brimmed felt hat, and ten kilograms of corn flour and beans. He could only hope that this guise would stand up to the precise eye of a foreman or the sharp gaze of a suspicious rancher.

He sat down to eavesdrop in dozens of cantinas, feigning deafness, rationing his few remaining pesos on a beer every two or three hours. He fished for vague rumors and signs of fear. The Germans had quite a presence in this region, he learned; the coffee plantations bore names like La Germania, La Badenia, and Lubeka.

Tomás was also learning that trying to navigate the region's social tapestry was not a simple task. The German plantations were interspersed with the Mexican-owned ones, and many of the old foremen were former partners. Furthermore, the boundaries of the German and Mexican plantations were constantly disputed by Indians claiming ancestral rights to the land.

He was wandering the roads, his duffel on his back, stopping for brief naps in the shade of a bush. He would stop briefly to rest in a hacienda's patio, under the watchful, oblique eyes of silent old men drying coffee beans. He nodded at Indians dressed in white or striped pants that reached just past the knee, palm sombreros, and dusty, buttonless cotton shirts. The Indians, too, looked at him in silence.

But eventually he picked up the trail. Here and there he found its vestiges: the living room of a hacienda vaunting a giant portrait of Hitler, an old abandoned mill where men gathered for target practice, and nocturnal meetings where a previously desolate patio came to life with cars and trucks and horses.

His command of German was limited but functional; it went well beyond the twenty or so phrases of use to a sailor in Rostov or Hamburg. It was a German of the jails and the newspapers, of those who played chess in the solitude of a ship crossing the Sonda, of a novel by Ludwig Renn that had been his only companion on the interminable voyage of a cargo ship that stopped in every damn port on the Mediterranean, of men who frequented Prussian whores. It was a useful German but, in order to actually make use of it, he would have to get even closer still to his target.

It was through a combination of luck and patience that he finally learned that his band of Nazis was going into action. He was in a dilapidated shack set up as a general store, about to barter some sacks of corn flour for a frying pan, when a pair of pink, fleshy men came in and demanded they exchange their shotgun shells for .22-caliber bullets, "for tomorrow."

The next morning dawn broke to find Tomás bivouacked on top of a hillock that gave him a commanding view of the surrounding plantation. He was watching the movements of his three Germans dressed in the same brown uniforms: a foreman and two of the owner's sons. At first light, they mounted their horses and rode off. Tomás tried to judge their route so that he might be able to head them off at some point along the way, but his burro wasn't up to the speed. He tried to force it up a hill via a dried-up streambed, but the burro slipped time and again. A low mist, daughter of the dawn, was rolling in like a wave. Where were they headed? If they made it to the next ranch and got to their trucks, he'd lose them.

But just then, Tomás heard a few scattered shots ring out in the distance, and he knew that his men were headed for a small town called Jacales through which he had once passed. He also realized that his burro would never get him there in time. He led the burro out of the streambed and into the jungle. He dismounted and made his way back to the trail that wound like a ghost through the trees, leaving his pack and his mount behind him, and began to run.

He ran hard but steadily, keeping an eye to the rocky ground, his breathing regular. He tripped and nearly fell on two occasions, crashed through thickets, tearing his face, but he kept on. Half an hour passed, and his lungs were beginning to burn. The jungle began to thin, and he forced his pace harder still. More shots rang out. The town must still be at least a kilometer away, he thought. If he had to run out in the open he would be an easy target. His eyes sought out each tree as he zigzagged his way through the edge of the jungle and on into the outskirts of town. It was little more than two dozen scattered hovels and some thatched-palm huts. In front of the first house he came to, a dead man lay stretched out in the dirt. The firing had stopped. Tomás wheeled around and caught a glimpse of a bloody face in another nearby house. Without hesitation, he strode up to the doorway and looked inside.

The Indian woman was nailed to the wall above a hard old bed, her arms spread wide like a crucifix. They had tied her up too, so that her body weight would not tear the nails out of the weak masonry: a cord hung taut from the center roof beam and was knotted tightly around her neck. Blood covered her torn clothing and dripped, pooling, on the floor.

Tomás's fingers tightened around his pistol grip. He went back out into the street, thirsty for a kill. Down the way, a cloud of dust revealed to him that the Nazis had ridden out of town, heading toward the river. That gave him the advantage. He wiped the sweat from his brow with his kerchief and realized for the first time that he was drenched; sweat was dripping from every one of his pores and his faded blue shirt (the victim of a thousand washings and mendings) was soaked clear through. He dug into his pocket for the salt lick he kept wrapped in a piece of paper, opened it, and, began to suck. Just then, two shotgun blasts ripped through the silent morning air. They had come from behind a half-built chapel, so far just a pair of brick walls. With the salt lick in one hand and his Tokarev in the other, he moved in, using the walls as cover. On the other side, two Nazis were firing at a flock of chickens. Not to kill, but just to harass them. Every time a chicken made a run for the cover of the jungle, a load of buckshot would steer it back into the street. Tomás trained his sights on the closer of the two. He was some twenty meters away, but he took a good, clear shot and it tore a chunk of the man's face clean away. The remaining man, younger and with a pockmarked face, whirled around and fired. The buckshot flew around Tomás, chipping the parapet of a nearby well and grazing his face. He leveled his pistol for a second time just as the young man threw down his spent shotgun and made a dash for the jungle. "Just like the chickens," Tomás thought to himself. But the Chinaman shot to kill, not to turn him back, and his bullet found its mark squarely between the German's shoulder blades. He fell face first in the dust, and a red stain slowly began to spread beneath his drab khaki shirt. Tomás walked slowly over to him and finished him off with a second bullet through the temples.

5

INTERRUPTIONS
AND INVASIONS

3. Argüelles and Casavieja want me to act as an interpreter between the new patient and them. They think he speaks German, though everything that isn't formal Spanish sounds German to them.

He appeared yesterday, standing outside the door with a distant look in his eyes. Casavieja thinks it's from fatigue, and indeed he wears a worn, black leather jacket with a note pinned to the lapel that reads, "This man needs sleep. Please help him."

It's definitely German that he speaks. I'll have to dust off my old student's knowledge.

During the first interview, he told us his name was Herschel, that he was from Vienna, and then tears began to well up in his eyes. Tears, yes, but he does not cry; his is a face without expression. He doesn't mask his emotions in the way that we might; rather, his face itself is a mask. In other words, the mask is what's real; his human face has long since disappeared. It conveys nothing save for a sense of tremendous weariness.

Casavieja prescribes him a heavy dose of soporifics and sends him to my room to sleep. I am gaining quite the reputation as a nocturnal companion. Since I can't take care of my own dreams, I take care of the dreams of others. But if dreams are premonitions of death, then Herschel was as good as dead for those next twelve hours. He lay there unmoving, his arms limp at his sides save for the occasional spasm. His face-mask seems to belong to a frequent visitor to hell, and it frightens me.

4. As I watch from my bed, Herschel produces two books from the folds of his coat, situates himself at my work desk, and reads them periodically, taking notes. I say periodically because, for the most part, although he has his eyes on the page, his mind is clearly somewhere else. I know this absent look; I have lived it.

I am curious. One of the books is Ebeling's *Lexicom Homericum*, published in Leipzig in 1885. The bible of *Iliad* and *Odyssey* scholars.

I make an attempt at conversation: "Do you have a theory on where the Trojan Horse ended up? As I recall, it doesn't appear in the *Iliad*. The *Iliad* ends with Hector's death, but there's no mention anywhere of the Horse . . ."

"You have a point," he says amicably, but without bothering to speculate on the Horse's location.

I press on, though I insist that it's not for want of conversation or the need to seem casual: "Neither does it come up in the *Odyssey*. Sometimes I have to wonder if it ever existed."

"The Horse is part of an independent story. It first appears in the compilations of Homer's oral tradition, in the Alexandrine texts, and in the writings of Higinius and Apolodorus."

"And did Homer exist?"

Herschel decides not to enter into this new polemic.

5. With me acting again as interpreter, Herschel describes to Casavieja his fear of sleep. He flees from it because there, in dreams, terrible and atrocious things that he dares not describe lie in wait. For him, the experience of dreams is terrifying; there is no rest, only so much suffering. If he falters, if he allows sleep to wash over him, he will be trapped forever and subjected to the most brutal pain.

Casavieja does not ask him where these burdens originated, nor does he press further into who he is, where he's from, where he's been, or how he came to end up at our door. Casavieja is a product of those strange, modern medical schools that seem to teach their students that a patient's stories have little to do with his history. I am on the verge of intervening, but it would be in poor taste for the interpreter to dip his oars into the water as well. In fairness, Casavieja is very interested in the nature, if not the origins, of these burdens, but he can't seem to get anything out of Herschel. Nothing concrete, nothing figurative, no images and no metaphors. Only recurring phrases.

The man trembles even at the thought of remembering.

He spends the night standing up in my room, this time refusing his dose of sleeping pills. He stands so as not to fall asleep, sometimes pacing in circles, digging his nails into the palm of his hand, reciting nursery rhymes . . .

6

ENCOUNTERS

The man whom the Poet called Brüning stepped outside his house, a small apartment on Veracruz Avenue that faced a marvelous *jacaranda*, probably the most beautiful tree in all of Mexico City, and spit, first to the east and then to the north. He was always conscious of his geographic orientation, and always spit in that same order. Once, by mistake, he spit toward the south, and a few hours later he caught his leg in a barbed-wire fence and the wounds became infected. This was quite a superstitious man indeed.

In his hand he carried a canary in a birdcage covered with a linen cloth. Carrying the bird and taking great care not to step on his own shadow (and a long one it was, it being six in the evening), he walked down Chapultepec Avenue, crossed over into the Tacubaya neighborhood, and entered a tenement.

The fat woman was waiting for him. She signaled for him to remove his satchel and set the birdcage on the table. In one hand she held a smoldering cigar while with the other she waved a fan. Nothing was said; a middleman had told both to meet here.

The woman began to make passes with the fan over the man's head while puffing thick mouthfuls of smoke from her cigar. There were no words or spells, only gestures and low grunts. The man was infected with a slight curse, and the idea was for this curse to be isolated and then transported into the body of the canary, thus freeing the man. He wasn't new to the office of Doña Amelia; he had visited her on many occasions with varying degrees of success.

The room didn't receive a single ray of sunlight. The doors and windows were shut tight, thickly draped with curtains, and any remaining cracks were chinked up with shelf paper. What little light there was came from the four bronze lamps standing around the room, their bases decorated with figures of horses. They clashed dramatically with the old broom propped up in a corner, the radio console, and the wrinkled skirts heaped on a hard old bed. So much so, in fact, that they seemed to Brüning to be from another planet. He contemplated the scene with curiosity. This was a new ritual, he thought, not much like the ones he had undergone years ago with his survival at stake.

Soon, the woman began sweating profusely. She let the fan and the cigar fall onto the table, took off her shawl, hitched up her skirt, and pulled off the kerchief that had been covering her hair. Then she closed up the fan and, like an orchestra conductor with his baton, tapped the man three times on the head and then once on his stomach. She drew again on her cigar, blew a cloud of smoke at the canary, and tapped it once with the fan. The bird fell dead. The woman let out a deep breath, held out her hand, and said, "That will be twelve pesos."

Brüning counted out some bills and set them on the table. He briefly debated taking the canary and the birdcage with him, but decided it would be better to leave them here in the horse-lamp room.

The woman apparently wanted to conclude her services with an explanation of what had just happened. She brushed a strand of hair out of her eyes and said, "You live in fear of stepping on your own shadow. But other shadows are coming, and soon they will have reached you and yours. You have a very important mission in life, but there are too many things going on right now. They confound themselves . . ." The German nodded, although he hadn't understood much save for the word *shadows*. There certainly were plenty of shadows in the grand design.

Out in the street, the strong midday sun had begun to evaporate, leaving only the uncertain light of dusk's imminent arrival. He walked quickly down toward Chapultepec Park. He was late, but if he walked quickly he could make up a bit of time.

Mexico City is crowned by Chapultepec Castle. Framed spectacularly by the countryside, it was the work of a Spanish viceroy and it housed certain foreign emperors who would later be shot, as well as a few presidents who also died in office. It presides over Reforma Avenue from atop its hill at the foot of which, in the old stable that was later converted into the caretaker's quarters, someone had installed a series of funhouse mirrors. This house of mirrors has become a veritable Mecca for many of Mexico City's children, and it is here, in front of this house of mirrors and at the entrance to the path that leads up to the castle, that the man with the curly blond hair named Kowalski is waiting for him. As Brüning offered his hand, Kowalski snapped his heels smartly together and saluted his superior, but then lapsed into that half-grin which even those who knew it well could never fully interpret.

"Have you taken advantage of the past month to do some sightseeing?" asked Brüning. "Do you like the food here? Have you found the beach, or the island, or whatever they call it? Is the money in a safe place?"

"I was pretty bad back in Havana. Some sickness they call 'shingles' had me laid up in a flea-bag hotel for a week. I had a few problems with the ship that brought us to Veracruz, but don't worry, Captain. Our friends opened an account, and the silver was deposited. We can access the rest whenever we want. You're listed with the Bank of London in Mexico under the name Velez-Müller." Kowalski handed him an envelope, which Brüning placed in his wallet and then in his satchel.

As they began to walk among the enormous *ahuehuetes*, night was falling. Brüning thought of Kowalski as a savage man, as a butcher and a sadist. At the same time, Kowalski thought that Brüning was irrational, unpredictable, and a madman. A bloodthirsty madman, at that. They both, without ever showing it, feared each other. Also in common were the facts that they were both extremely meticulous and practical, and that they both hid things quite well. They were like onions: no matter how much skin you peel away, you never quite reach the heart. They changed names and identities with such ease and regularity that their original selves had been lost and forgotten a long time ago. Somewhere, where not even their superiors had access, there were two tarnished silver boxes where each kept his most profound secrets. This is why, perhaps, as they passed in silence through the trees in an evening already stripped of its light, they stole furtive glances at each other, trying to read one another's mind.

"My assistant is already at the cove. He contacted three Mexicans, and together they opened a small cannery. Bit by bit, we will be expanding the warehouse in accordance with the instructions. Here are the coordinates and a map of the coastline for you to transmit to Berlin. And by the way, what do you know about the disappearance?"

Brüning gripped this new piece of paper and took a moment before answering. He didn't know why he had been asked this. Kowalski and he both held the same rank; only his two extra months of service gave him superiority. Kowalski knew and respected this formality, but would they have given him different orders? He seemed to have been charged with a parallel yet different operation, one Kowalski had no knowledge of. But did Kowalski have his own orders as well . . . ?

"Nicolaus and his men still haven't found it. But from what they told me, they are on the right track. It won't take long to appear . . . Meet with this man on this particular date I'm giving you; he'll supply you with weapons and a car." Brüning passed him a scrap of paper that Kowalski looked at briefly before stowing it in his jacket pocket.

But there was something more: both were upset. Brüning was of average height and had a head of dark, unruly hair that always looked windblown. He dressed meticulously, but with a certain hint of nonchalance. Like a bohemian? An intellectual? A student? Kowalski on the other hand was tall, and he kept his short, curly blond hair neatly combed, as if his barber were also an architect. His starched pants were sharply creased, and his shirt cuffs shone bright white. They didn't like each other. Something in each other's appearance repelled them.

They walked down the hill, draped in shadows. Brüning murmured a "Heil Hitler" which Kowalski answered in a similar whisper. It was the sign of leave-taking.

"I know one thing: I sure as hell don't like Mexican food. Nothing. I hate it all," Kowalski said to himself after they had parted ways.

INTERRUPTIONS

AND INVASIONS

6. The nurses listen over and over again to a song on the radio by Agustín Lara called "Only Once." I've memorized it by now, but it doesn't convince me . . . those unique but nuanceless loves of which he sings are not mine. But what is mine? A gust of wind passes through my mind, creating images. I erase them, evaporate them with a beam of light. I have cultivated the power of forgetting.

I prefer the other song which they also listen to quite frequently: "Prisoner of the Sea" by Luis Alcaraz. It's absurd enough so that it doesn't affect one's sense of reason, especially not someone who is a prisoner in this city, though not of the sea, not even a damn river.

7. Angel de la Calle, the palm tree artist coauthoring a novel about monkeys, orangutans, and gorillas via correspondence with Burroughs, suddenly says to me, "Fuck me in the goat-ass! Hey *amigo*, that guy is Eric Jan Hanussen!"

De la Calle enjoys using expressions he learned, at one time or another, in Madrid. One of my more peaceful neighbors, Erasto the Mute, watches our conversation with interest, totally naked.

"Who are you talking about? Herschel?"

De la Calle nods vigorously. "Yes, yes, the one sleeping in your room."

"And who, pray tell, is Eric Jan Hanussen?"

"It's not who he is, but who he was. He was Hitler's magus. But it's Hanussen, damn it, none other than Hanussen. But he should be dead, worm food, *kaput*. Shit in the milk! That's really too bad. . . ."

DIALOGUE

W e've known each other for thirty years,
Poet. You aren't about to damn me to hell if I tell you a story of Tibet,
Nazis, and the apocalyptic sign of the Beast, are you?"

"I've always taken you for a man burdened by reason, *amigo*. I'm the one
who believes in incredible things. I'll believe anything you say, if you agree
to then listen to my story of a minister and his lover."

"I knew you wrote pornography, Fermín, but I always thought it was
strictly to amuse yourself, not for political reasons."

"I'll just bet that my story is stranger than yours."

They were seated on a bench on Reforma Avenue and had been smoking
and watching the cars go by for a while now. Cobalt Blue, Steel Gray, and
a truly depressing Forest Green. These were funereal colors. Mexicans who
owned cars somehow didn't seem truly Mexican. They spoke about these
and other things, and then told each other their stories.

"Son of a bitch," said the Poet at last, "and I, who thinks I've seen it all
and heard it all before. Well, do you believe them?"

"Yes," said Manterola. "And do you know why I believe them? Because
ever since they told me, I haven't been able to sleep. That, for me, is a
pretty good sign."

"Since I learned about Krüger and the German, I've barely slept as well."

They smoked some more, Manterola with his pipe packed with grotty tobacco that a colleague from the paper had brought him from Nayarit and the Poet with his stinking, filterless Águilas that left the fingers of his one remaining hand stained yellow.

"Have you been inside a church lately?" asked Manterola suddenly.

"For what? They've already banned smoking, so are they now handing something else out?"

"Like all atheists," continued Manterola, ignoring the Poet's sarcasm, "I have a great deal of interest in religion. It's like going to the theater to see the magicians with their differing levels of credulity. Anyway, every time I've gone into a church lately, I've found it to be much more full than usual."

"So the Catholics are beginning to repopulate themselves after the Revolution . . . So what does this all come down to?"

"Nothing. It's just that there, in the church, it occurred to me that my story is the story of the return of the Devil."

"Well then, mine is the damn Mexican version of the story, where the devils all rise to power, *amigo*," said the Poet curtly. "If things keep going the way they are right now, pretty soon Miguel Alemán will be the President."

"Impossible. According to the pendulum theory, whatever follows this current political climate will have to be liberal."

"Pendulum theory, my ass! You don't know the right at all. I can forgive ignorance, but not idiocy. And now you're telling me that you know all about demons?" Fermín Valencia finished with a slap on his friend's back.

9

INTERRUPTIONS
AND INVASIONS

7 . Women's fashion is changing. We see this in the North American and British magazines which feature Avedon's photos of women in pants. With more and more women working in the wartime industries, the style is gaining popularity. The editors of the *Excélsior* are quite concerned about this; they worry that such an antifeminine mode will corrupt our society. I think they ought not to worry so much.

Mexican elementary school teachers read the North American magazines with both caution and fascination, but for now that is all they dare to do. Soon, however, this proletarian style, strengthened by the thousands of women moving into industrial occupations, will rise up like the unrequited desires of the middle class cult.

In any case, if someone wants to start a national crusade against women in pants, they can count me out.

8. President Camacho has relatives in the College of Germany, is president of the German Equestrian Club, enjoys German beer, and admires the martial nature of German parades.

I do not share his tastes, and indeed it has been some time since a president and I saw eye-to-eye. There is a mutual disgust in the manner in which they ignore me and in the way I listen to their speeches or examine their rotogravures. In his vaudevilles, the comedian Roberto Soto described Camacho as "the unknown soldier," an ironic epithet inasmuch as he was Minister of Defense before becoming President. They tell me that Cárdenas wasn't all bad, but in those days I lived a rather distracted life, in such a way as to never form a clear opinion. Those years, both theirs and mine, lie in a misty region of my mind that I haven't the slightest inclination of exploring.

9. De la Calle tells me the story of Hanussen, whom he is sure is my new—and resurrected—neighbor. He says that he saw him acting in Spain, and when I ask him how such a thing happened, he confesses that he has not left Spain these past few years. He doesn't even try to explain to me how it is that, if he hasn't left Spain, we are now conversing on a rainy afternoon in the capital of Mexico.

But are we in Mexico? It is an interesting question, prompting both pure thought and inquisitive thought, both reasonable doubt and doubt without reason. Ever since I lost my sense of certainty and replaced it with skepticism, I have become a fountain of questions, with which my companions are not much help. They have mountains of false and strange certainties; they are full of mysterious truths and ambiguous surprises. But above all, they doubt nothing. It's not extremely important, though it soon will be, but. . . .

I must conclude that we are, in fact, in Mexico. The smell of the rain, the climate, the way the custodians move, and the songs that the patients listen to on the radio both confirm and affirm it.

Moving past this moment of indecision: Hanussen's history does not fit with Hershel's present. I see nothing in the human ruins of my neighbor of the marvelous magician whom De la Calle describes. The only coincidence is that both are (or were) Viennese.

As with all magicians, there are a multitude of stories regarding their beginnings. The one De la Calle tells (and he may very well be right; somehow this young genius knows much about the world) is that he was born in 1889 in Vienna, the son of ruined Danish nobles. His father became a minstrel, a traveling entertainer, and when Hanussen turned twelve, he joined his family's troupe. He worked as a trapeze artist, a lion tamer, the showhorses' stablekeep, and a folk singer. This last role left him with chronic laryngitis, forcing him to speak in a deep, hoarse voice for the rest of his life. I see none of this laryngitis in Herschel, whose voice is very soft and without any hint of a rasp.

Hanussen is said to have traveled halfway across Europe, sailing the length of the Danube and reaching as far as Istanbul. When he returned to Austria, he became a journalist and started an irregularly published newspaper which, rather than printing news, was dedicated to blackmail. He used this rag to publicize rumors and embarrassing situations that social and political figures had gotten themselves into, unless these figures paid him off. Interesting, a paper that thrives on what it doesn't print rather than what it does. Everything looks the same to the Mexican press.

With that fortune in those chaotic times, Hanussen discovered the powers of credulity, hope, and fear. He took in all manner of influences and disciplines: he studied charlatans, learned hypnotism in Vienna, met with Hindu fakirs, learned that the hand is quicker than the eye, practiced the art of suggestion and the domination of other people's will, read astrological cards, and divined false divinations of things to come. All of these attributes are recorded in his record. The name of Eric Jan Hanussen began to echo across spectacular, magical stages, and his birth name was lost forever. But there must have been something to this new persona, because people adored it. He even wrote a pair of books, *The Road to Telepathy: Explication and Practice* and *Reading the Mind*.

But when, exactly, did he begin to associate himself with Nazism? The story is that he had at one time given lessons on diction and expression to a delirious former soldier and amateur painter in Vienna. This opened a network of Nazi connections, and there are tales that Hitler's dramatic gestures, his mastery of speech and rhetoric, are ultimately influenced by Hanussen's magic. Maybe this is true and maybe it's not, but what is certain is that in 1931, in the midst of his social success, the prodigious Hanussen joined the National Socialistic Party, stuck a swastika on the end of his car's radio antenna, took a job editing a pro-Nazi newspaper, and forged strong ties to the hierarchy's newest power: the New Magi.

It is rumored that, in those days, Hanussen would visit his friend Hitler, then suffering from frequent panic attacks. Upon reading his cards, he concluded that someone had buried a metaphysical hatchet in the middle of his chest and, to cure Hitler, he would have to dig up a mandrake from the back garden of a butcher's shop in the Führer's hometown. A mandrake, De la Calle tells me, is a narcotic European plant whose root structure is shaped like a human body and, when it is torn from the ground, it emits a low moaning sound. Hanussen himself made the pilgrimage, and Hitler's mental condition improved. It was then that Hanussen decided to tell him that he would rise to power on January 30th, which, of course, is exactly what would happen.

When I ask De la Calle how he knows all these facts so intimately, he simply smiles commiseratively and says that these are all well-known things, and where have I been all these years?

Later, Hanussen founded the Palace of the Occult, a type of bar/theater decorated with astrological symbols. Here he would listen to music that inspired thought, draw hot swords across his chest, watch three women dressed as nuns perform a striptease, hypnotize himself, or prognosticate the fate of the nation. Such things as these. Nazi officials would come here to seek the aid of their favorite charlatan, who always promised them glory in his deep, husky, laryngitic voice. Entertainment was provided too, in the form of sleight-of-hand, light shows, mirror tricks, apocalyptic speeches, accompanied by prostitutes and champagne.

Some experts say that the structure of the Palace itself was a work of genius, a miracle of light and sound engineering where the tables concealed microphones for recording conversations that would later be used as the basis for suppositions and predictions. The waiters were often generously compensated for repeating the rumors gleaned from their customers' conversations.

Hanussen made millions of marks in addition to the money he made from blackmailing, and added to his many professions that of shylock. One of his debtors was even the chief of the SA in Berlin: Wolf Heinrich Helldorf himself.

On a fateful night in 1933, Eric Jan Hanussen put himself into a trance during one of his shows. The lights came down, a spotlight illuminated his face, and the famous prophet foretold the burning of the Reichstag: "Fire . . . I see flames . . . enormous flames . . . the criminals have burned it down . . . they want to see Germany drown in chaos . . . these worms who resist Hitler's ultimate victory must be crushed." Then he slowly opened his eyes and beheld his audience that, for the first time, was not applauding.

The building burned the very next day.

Hanussen was well aware of the Nazis' intentions to use the fire as a launching pad, and he may even have played a role in it. There were rumors that he had brainwashed the Dutchman who was set up as the culprit.

One way or another, the man was becoming dangerous. A month and a half later, a group of thugs hired by Wolf Helldorf gunned him down in the foyer of his own theater.

De la Calle finishes his story here by commenting that it's a pity that his favorite magician is dead, because it would be just marvelous if Herschel could work some magic out in the patio and make the implacably dripping fountain spring to life.

Then he turns to me and asks, "Why don't you propose it to him?"

SEIZURES

Manterola read over the brief communiqué from the president twice. Following the new mode, important statements were now given only a few lines, while the demagoguery was reserved for hanging curtains of smoke. So he could see that this was serious: The Mexican government, protecting itself with the Treaty of Rio de Janeiro and before the repeated conflicts between various Latin American countries and the Axis powers, had made the decision to seize twelve Italian and German ships docked in Mexican ports.

The formal justification had been the acts of sabotage that Nazi and Fascist sailors had committed in Latin American ports. But this seemed highly dubious. Much more likely was the explanation that finally President Camacho was siding with North American politics.

But whatever the rationale, Mexico has officially taken action against the Fascists, thought Manterola. Was it purely a matter of principle (though the Camacho administration didn't seem to have too many of those)? Or was it that the gringos were putting the pressure on, and the president was searching for a solution that would leave out the oil negotiations, which toughened the situation with the Nazis?

With the director gone, out attending one of those peace conferences he was so enamored of, Manterola rallied his reporters: "Bermúdez, go to the Secretary of the Navy and get a copy of the official order to seize the ships.

Leñero, take our least drunk photographer and get to Veracruz . . . I want pictures of those ships and their captains' reactions. Julita, get our correspondent in Tampico on the phone."

He walked three times around his desk and lit his pipe. Then he picked up the phone and dialed a number. While waiting to be put through, he spoke to the reporter who had come from the president's office: "They're cargo ships, boys, from nine to two hundred tons of cabotage. They were docked in Tampico and Veracruz, and they can't leave the Gulf and head out across the Atlantic because the English have it all locked up."

"So what's the government going to do with them?"

"Probably press them into service transporting raw materials between Mexico and the U.S. They've already been re-christened with Mexican names and a giant Mexican flag."

The reporter took out his notes: "The *Fede* is now the *Poza Rica*; the *Americano* is now the *Tuxpan*; the *Guerrero* is now the *Faja de Oro*; the *Vigor* is now the *Amatlán*, the *Tuscany* is now the *Minatitlán*, and they're calling the *Marina O* the *Tabasco*."

"That's very nationalistic of them. All names of Mexican cities and oil fields."

"It has to be Jara's idea . . . he's the only Cárdenas supporter left in Camacho's cabinet. There's also the *Potrero de Llano*, which used to be called the *Lucifero*, and the *Atlas* became *Las Choapas*. That's the one that the sailors tried to sink."

"And did they?"

"No, boss, just some minor damage."

"Do we have any reporters with serious *cojones* near there?"

"Memo Briseño is there. What do you want him to do?"

"To go to the German and Italian embassies and get their official government reactions," said Manterola, rubbing his hands together.

INTERRUPTIONS

AND INVASIONS

2. My new neighbor is apocalyptic; even during his brief moments of narcotic-induced sleep, he howls like a dog, foaming at the mouth, convulsing like a live wire in his bed. At times he says, in German, things like "I am the master . . . I am the master of Hell." When I was a student, I often remarked that German was a language of grandiloquence, but only after these past few nights of torture am I tempted to believe it.

They say that he was from Vienna and that he was once a tailor. I doubt both things. He can't even sew on a button and sometimes he will recite the names of Berlin's metro stations like a litany. It could be that, at some point, he lived in Vienna, but without a doubt he ought to be treated as a German; as a Berlinite.

"Herschel, are you Jewish?"

Erasto the Mute watches us, silent as always, naked as always, with a glass of water in one hand and scratching contentedly underneath his testicles with the other. Since Herschel has come to share my room, Erasto has taken to visiting us regularly. The doors are always open, and visits are usually allowed unless specifically prohibited. And for some odd reason that I can't even begin to fathom, this false Viennese fascinates him.

Herschel seems to not have heard me. But a bit while later, he nods. Despite the delay, I am sure he has answered my question.

Later that night, I awake with a start. There is a man watching me through the barred window. His face is contorted in the moonlight; a terrible sneer is wrought on his lips, and deep wrinkles run through his cheeks. It is the face of the devil, the face of death.

For a devout atheist like me, it is more than a bit disconcerting to discover that you have, as a neighbor and as a roommate, the devil himself.

THE IGUANA

He's got the spirit of the iguana. The Golden Iguana."

They had barbecued a pig stolen from the hacienda's foreman and the group was finishing off the feast with red salsa and tortillas. Dusk was descending on the jungle clearing. The children, tacos in hand, had gathered around the old man. Very small, barefoot, intelligent children. The old man knew they would listen to a story, but he'd have to make the moral very clear. They weren't blind; they were an important part of the community, and if he didn't tell the story well, they'd get bored and wander off to go throw stones in the river.

"And the Iguana is going to defend us." Here he paused to gauge the reaction of his listeners. They looked fixedly at him. Now they knew that this story was an important one.

"The Golden Iguana is hard, like a rock. His skin is tough and scaly, making him bulletproof and impervious to the spells cast by those of the hooked cross. He's wise and knows the difference between good and evil. He's no ordinary iguana; he has powers, both his own and those we give him through our dreams. But he isn't all-powerful . . . sometimes he is invisible and sometimes he's not, so when he sleeps he has to be careful and hide. He doesn't need a woman, because he's very old and knows that right now a woman would distract him from his mission. He doesn't shave or cut his hair or anything, because he has neither hair nor beard. In his homeland, they call him a Dragon."

The bravest of the children asked, "And where is his homeland?"

"The kingdom of Heaven."

"Where's that?"

"Beyond Sinaloa. Ten times ten times ten days walking and swimming from here." The old man ignored the stupefied looks of the children. He wasn't about to get into the geography of the thing, and so he continued: "He eats slowly, like us, savoring each bite instead of wolfing it down. He dances alone in the jungle, to his own music, while the monkeys and the birds all watch. He sheds his skin to take his morning bath and communicates with us, leaving claw marks in the soft earth of the riverbank. We tell him that they're ruining us, and he says that we're right, and that they're screwing him over too. And for that, he's going to eat them alive, one by one. We tell him that all over the country, and on this very hacienda, are the acolytes of the hooked cross. And he dogs them, hunts them down to a man. At night, he's been known to turn himself into a snake and slit their throats with his fangs."

"What's a fang?"

"Well, the one El Iguana uses is called a *kukhri*, the one the Nepalese used when they fought the British army," said the old man as he traced in the dirt the strange, half-moon shape of the blade and silenced his listeners, who had never seen a *kukhri* nor heard of a Nepalese nor had the remotest idea of the existence of something called the British army.

"And does the Golden Iguana have a pistol?" asked a skinny boy with glassy eyes whose older brother had been murdered by the Nazis.

"Yes, an 8-shot Tokarev 7.62 with .38-caliber compatibility and an adjustable pistol grip. It weighs about two pounds, so you can't carry it if you're a weakling."

Just then, another of the elders stood up and called for silence. The old man had dispelled their fears and torments, but the time for telling stories had passed. The elders were giving instructions:

"We're going to change things just a little bit. No more maize for the gods who are too busy with their own business to concern themselves with us. Starting tomorrow night, everyone will hang a little sack of bullets from his hammock before he goes to sleep. A sack of bullets, some salt, and a few of these damn fine tacos."

"But there aren't any left!"

"Well, then, we're just going to have to steal ourselves another pig," said the old man, and the children laughed.

INTERRUPTIONS
AND INVASIONS

3. Had the Poet found signs of aging when he discovered some twelve white hairs in his beard? Certainly it's as good an indication as any.

What was the Poet's jacket like? Did it have pins to gather up the left-over sleeve? Was the sleeve cut off? Or was it simply folded up and sewn shut?

Did his departed fingers tingle? Did the arm's memory go on after its physical disappearance?

4. Miguel Alemán, our current Minister of the Interior, once said, "In order to truly know somebody, you ought to join him during his favorite pastime." I'll leave it at that, for future reference.

5. We may assume that we have here a malignant trinity: the Jew Herschel (who must be Hitler's insomniac mage), Eric Jan Hanussen, and together they are, of course, the Prince of Darkness. We also assume that the first two of these three personalities must be fleeing something, which is why they have sought refuge among us. But, contrary to Doctor Casavieja's theory, it is not necessarily the third personality from which they flee. Finally, we assume that it hasn't been chance that I've become his roommate and official translator. There must be some intent, some design in all of this.

Here we must address a pair of contradictory elements. In the biography that De la Calle narrated to me, not once did he mention that Hanussen was Jewish. A Jewish Nazi? I think not. And nowhere in that biography did he mention any Hellenic studies. The magi are well-versed in horoscopes and such garbage, but not Homer. These are, without a doubt, contradictory vocations.

I now pose the questions I ought to have posed in the beginning: "Herschel, when did you arrive in Mexico?"

"A few months ago," he tells me.

They have given him a mountain of toothpicks and wooden shoe lasts. Things they don't give to just anyone. Casavieja also has shady dealings with a few of us. I remember when he tried to slip me an extra cube of sugar for my morning coffee, just to make the others angry and jealous. But Herschel builds nothing with these toothpicks; he merely arranges them into geometric designs on my writing desk . . . my writing desk that he has now completely commandeered.

"A few months . . . two? Three? Six? Where did you land? Where did you come from? And why did you come? Who gave you passage through our ports? And who pinned the note to your coat?"

"A woman," he said to me and smiled, as if that one word had answered everything. . . .

BOTTLE-WHIPPED

The Poet wanted to cultivate his memories of Madrid and weed from them his memories of the war in Spain (which he intended eventually to forget completely, or to at least push far enough into a corner of his mind so that he wouldn't unexpectedly run into them). Only his memories of Madrid, and in particular the glory of Cuatro Caminos, which he had first seen on one of the most emotional nights of his long, emotional life. A place where he would later drink literally barrels of Valdepeñas wine and where a woman would try to carry him off to bed even after he had called her a hag.

Those were the memories that Fermín let run.

That night, someone said "we're here," and they got out of the trucks and stepped into the dim splendor of Cuatro Caminos. The 11th Brigade had arrived earlier and paraded down the Gran Vía in the heart of the capital. In the expansive night, it seemed to them a simple, working-class neighborhood, but the darkness had its stealth and magic—born of exhaustion and uncertainty—that were broken by the soft voice of a woman who whispered from a balcony, "The Internationals are here." The whisper was passed from window to window until a man in pajamas and holding a red flag appeared in the doorway of one of the houses. He was lame, and passed sweet rolls around to the soldiers. The quartermaster hadn't fed the men since they left Albacete, and the meager bread was warmly received. Soon, barefoot women began to come out into the cold street with shawls and blankets draped over their nightgowns. A woman with very blond hair who said she was a teacher kissed the Poet on the forehead, and then a butcher embraced him. In his memory (and what a bitch it can be), the Poet was one-armed, but that wasn't the case, for he would lose his arm some months later in Teruel. Some months after that, he would return to Cuatro Caminos and drink his barrels of wine, but that night they simply filed like phantoms toward the Ciudad Universitaria and the front lines.

Along with his memories of Madrid that entered, bit by bit, into his head was a subtle reminder of the fact that he was still after Brüning. Nicolaus had led him to the Hotel Victoria café, and from there he had patiently followed the trail here, to the soccer stadium.

Both pursuer and pursued were heading for the eastern stands where the Spaniards—recognizable by their accent—were concentrated. Maybe that was what prompted his memories of Madrid. Old Spanish émigrés and newly exiled Republicans alike had gathered here for the glory of the game. A great festival was promised, since Hilario "El Moco" López, one of Necaxa's greatest players, was retiring. Already the ramps in the south end of the stadium were swarming with people and, from time to time, Brüning's pearl-gray sombrero popped up amid the crowd. The Poet watched it as it descended the stands, and once again the memories of that distant night assaulted him, brought on by the voices and tones, the gestures and berets of the Spaniards around him. He tried to brush the memories aside by focusing on the game, which had just kicked off. Brüning's gaze was fixed squarely on the center of the field. Did he even know anything about soccer? Was this the first game he'd ever seen? Could he give a damn about any of the twenty-two players or the referee? The Poet smiled at this new discovery. Just then, two men, beers in hand, came up to the German and sat down on either side of him. Brüning greeted them somewhat gruffly, hesitating for a moment before shaking hands.

Were they Spaniards? At least one of them could have been. In his mind, the Poet flipped through pages of photos and files that Mandujano had collected during his investigation into the Falangists in Mexico. Since the beginning of the war, the Falange—the Spanish Fascist party—had set up a network among the old Spanish villages and neighborhoods in Mexico to collect information and above all money and to put pressure on the Cárdenas government. But ultimately it was a network of pawns and puppets, held together more with *chorizo* and red wine than with espionage. A couple of dangerous characters, and many more fat little sinister ones with varying degrees of clout: a thousand and one owners of steam baths, grocery stores, textile factories, hardware shops, mines, brothels, breweries, and cantinas.

But yes, the Poet recognized the man sitting to Brüning's right, whose sing-song voice contrasted sharply with the occasional grunt of approval from the stern-faced German. What was his name, Valdés? Vargas? Valero? That was it, Toño Valero. A real shark of an attorney when it came to labor cases, and one of the Falange's principal financial backers and shake-down artists.

Didn't the Germans have enough money that they didn't have to appeal to the Spanish network? What the hell was going on here? For a brief moment, the Poet wanted to be part of a real secret service like the NKVD. But the whim quickly passed, in part because Asturias had scored a cracker of a goal—a header by the rookie Benavides—but also because the goal prompted a spontaneous chant to well up in the crowd. The Asturias fans, who were vocal supporters of the Fascist military movement, began to shout, "¡Arriba España!" while the exiled Republicans answered with the chant "¡España, mañana, será Republicana!" The Necaxa fans, sensing that tensions were rising, almost felt like applauding the goal against their team, just to show their equanimity and simple love of sport. Someone in the crowd was brandishing his umbrella like a club, while elsewhere the women were heading for the exits. For if there was one thing that the exiled Republican had learned during his brief time in Mexico, it was that sisters and mothers serve as excellent objects of insult.

The riot broke out around Brüning, who seemed to have no idea what was going on. One fan was thrown down the stands while another, after a sharp blow to the nose, began spitting blood.

"These refugees are animals," a woman near the Poet said with the accent of someone who had just gotten off a burro straight from Alcalá de Henares. "If General Cárdenas had heard that old coward, he'd have her cleaning stables in a second," the Poet said to himself: matter-of-factly.

The ruckus had yet to spread from the one end of the stadium, and so now there were two spectacles going on: the game (which was now of secondary interest) and the brawl. Brüning finally realized the danger of the situation and, emphatically negating one last affirmation by Valero, began to look for the nearest exit.

It was then that a deliciously malevolent idea crossed Fermín Valencia's mind. He reached into a random cooler and grabbed a bottle of beer which he quickly dispatched in a single gulp. Brüning had worked his way some fifteen meters up the stairs. In a series of surprisingly quick bounds, the Poet leapt up several stairs, closed his eyes and launched the bottle out on a line straight for the German's head. As the glass turned, happily sparkling in the clear air, the Poet opened his eyes. He hadn't yet forgotten the trap they had set for him in the dance hall, the trap that had cost him a knife in the leg. The bottle flew right between a pair of fighting Spaniards and exploded right on the crown of Brüning's pearl-gray sombrero. It knocked him head-long into a pair of fans who were somehow still watching the game.

The Poet looked around; no one seemed to have identified him as the artist of the cunning attack. But just for the sake of irony, he said, "Savage fucking cowards," and shook his head sadly at the German, who was bleed-ing profusely from a gash in the back of his head. It could be considered unprofessional, he supposed, to go around splitting heads open with bottles, but Fermín Valencia felt absolutely ecstatic as he watched Brüning being escorted out of the stadium by the pair of Falangists and a team of Red Cross stretcher-bearers. Then, with less vehemence, more professionalism, and a wide berth around a Spanish fan wrestling with a Franco supporter, he set himself again to following them.

INTERRUPTIONS
AND INVASIONS

1 . There is a war going on between I.G. Far-
ben, the German pharmaceutical company that produces caffeine tablets
and aspirin, and the North American giants. It has grown particularly intense
in Mexico. The Americans want to force German aspirin out of the market,
no matter how miraculous it is, and have invented a strange new thing called
"Gleaminex." Eavesdropping on the nurses' debates has allowed me to learn
about the virtues of each.

With a free sample of Gleaminex, you get a calendar with the sacred
image of Jesus situated above their slogan, "Gleam . . . Gleaming . . . Gleaminex." It's a strikingly original calendar, unbeatable among headache-fighting
calendars, with its sinister-looking Jesus of Nazareth on the cross, the lance
wound plainly visible. The Association of Publicists, a new company dedicated to convincing us that some things are better than others, informs us
that over the next year and a half, the phrase "Gleam . . . Gleaming . . .
Gleaminex" will be heard 4,700,000 times.

2. Ever since his first conversation with the old rabbi, Pioquinto Manterola hasn't been able to sleep. Naps and daydreams, perhaps, but no sleep.
He who had been a virtual narcoleptic for his entire life has now been
shunned by rest and abandoned by dreams. Where does he try to sleep? In
other words, where does he live? Near the paper, for one, but also in a tiny
closet of a room that he shares with napkins and shiny escalope forks. It sits

atop one of the few four-story buildings in San Rafael, and from the rooftop terrace, he has a commanding view of the neighborhood. But because of his journalist's schedule (no days off, late nights and sleep during the mornings), he has had precious few opportunities to observe this industrious city from the grand perspective that insomnia now permits him. It's a city of working women, and he watches it come to life at his feet: the clothes hung out to dry fluttering in the breeze, the carefully swept patios, and the smells of warm kitchens.

Perhaps, he thinks as he watches the working women (for he is always able to think about one thing while watching two others), this whirlwind of events that blew about him like leaves is the most tentative of tentative invitations to finally write a novel. In the past thirty years, the journalist has started out no fewer than thirteen times, but never has he made it past page five. But it's impossible to be a journalist by day and a novelist by night; to write after having written. One can be a fireman and a novelist or an upholsterer and a novelist, but not a journalist and a novelist. Unless, of course, he were like that young Revueltas, who didn't give a damn about journalism. So this invitation to write must be fictitious. What was certain, however, was that Pioquinto Manterola cannot sleep.

The Poet Fermín Valencia can't sleep well either; he often goes days without sleep. After his discovery of the liaison between Minister Alemán and the actress Krüger and his conversation with Manterola, his mind had become a sort of Gruyère cheese which was, for the most part, made up of holes.

The Chinaman Tomás Wong relaxes in his new hammock which had appeared yesterday, a gift from the invisible communities that offered to aid him in his private war against the Coffee Nazis. But he doesn't sleep either; the world is still too very fragile to take refuge in dreams, and the jungle is full of slinking creatures—on both four and two feet—that wish him nothing well. He knows he is behind enemy lines, and so he sleeps with one eye open, with half his mind alert, uneasily, fitfully, keeping constant vigil.

And I do not sleep. Since the apparition of Herschel, his nocturnal howls have been killing off my dreams. As Don Durito would later write, "I'm returning; prepare the tobacco and the insomnia. . . ."

PART VI

FINCA VIGÍA IN SAN FRANCISCO DE PAULA, A FEW MILES FROM HAVANA

The clock struck twelve, and he put on a pair of shorts. He had been walking naked through the house, avoiding his pile of mail and other household chores. He was considering working on his nonexistent novel, putting a few of his disparate notes into actual prose, but abandoned that idea quickly. But now that he had on his shorts, he went looking for a drink. One can't drink in the nude, after all. Through the open window, he could see Mario in the garden cutting dead palm fronds with his machete.

"Mix up a gin and coconut. Makes for a good morning," he said in Spanish. He continued to think in Spanish, because he knew he needed to work on his noun-article agreement: *la mesa, la cama, un burrito, el gato, la gata.* The last thing Hemingway wanted was for his neighbors to think of him as a dumb gringo.

Mario brought out the halved coconut shell, full of crushed ice and gin, and Hemingway sat down to drink it on the front porch while he contemplated the old ceiba tree. Visitors to the house had often supposed it to be over 150 years old, and he believed them. The mammoth tree was full of the dignity and the grandeur of passing time. That was the way to grow old, he thought. Either that, or preserved in alcohol.

"Alcohol is the only true universal antidote. I've been drinking since I was fifteen, and there aren't many things that have ever . . ." he mused, and let the sentence trail off when he realized that once again he was thinking out loud. "Things that have ever what? Scared me? Alcohol dulls wear and tear; lubricates it."

He got up and walked around the empty pool to the rear of the house with its grand view of the sea. The house was certainly worth what it had cost him. Situated on a small hill overlooking San Francisco de Paula, some twelve miles outside Havana, Finca Vigía had brought him much happiness. He was wrapped up in a bit of money there, too. Money. A writer's mind evolved along the problematic lines of money. Taxes. Leeches. In January he had set aside $85,000, but he wasn't going to be able to avoid dipping into it. You spend your whole life working on a novel and then suddenly it's written and sometimes you get a mountain of money but then those lousy IRS agents, who have never read a book in their lives, who never worried about him when he was scraping by on twenty dollars a story, storm in and make off with nearly everything. *For Whom the Bell Tolls* had sold nearly half a million copies. Not bad.

The sea maintained its usual variations of blue, from the pale blue stripe of the coastal waters to the unmistakable deep blue of the Gulf Stream. The sea set him at ease. The estate was called "*vigía*" because it stood over the sea like a lighthouse, watching over its great dark depths from the crags. It was like the deck of an ocean liner or like the bow of a submarine, and it was a good place. Hemingway had respect for the sea, and having respect was better than feeling affection. Oceans are able to be sailed only because we do so sensibly, we make wise decisions, we abandon the irrationality with which we live life on the land.

He finished his coconut and gin and went back inside. The interior of the house was an unabashed disaster. But life doesn't fix itself, he thought, and this realization brought back memories of her. He frowned with genuine displeasure.

Martha had left—fled, really—after only a year of marriage. And the worst thing about it was that she had left to become the one thing that he had always wanted to be: a war reporter.

Ernest stubbed his toe on a brush that he had left on the floor the previous day. The pain reminded him that he loved her and hated her at the same time. Women make for good friends and terrible enemies. She had always tried to educate him, correct him, half-sanctify him, break him down and build him back up. Had she the chance, Martha could have taken Toulouse-Lautrec out of the bordellos, Van Gogh out of his madness, and Poe from his drunkenness, but she would never have gotten a single portrait nor poem out of any of them. Preachers and artists make poor bedfellows.

His portable Underwood typewriter was sitting on top of his dresser with a blank sheet of paper rolled into the cylinder. Almost mindlessly he typed out a letter to his agent to clear up the issue of Spanish language rights to *The Killers*, specifying that it should be treated as a foreign edition and not a reprint, and that the rights should belong solely to him and not split with his publisher. As a footnote, he gave permission for the story to appear in an anthology being published in the U.S.

A distracted glance at one of the hunting rifles hung on his wall threw him into a mental digression on the State Department's ineptitude in their dealings with Japan. Japan was preparing for war throughout the Pacific, and that included the Philippines and other U.S. territories. They weren't about to permit a "passive observer" to anchor an entire fleet in Hawaii and simply wait for something to happen. Just then a cat entered the room and put an end to the diatribe he was forging. It looked at him indifferently. Hemingway smiled. It was Boise; that look of idle disdain was his alone. Boise was sometimes called Dillinger, depending on his relationship with other neighborhood cats, but at other times—like now—he regained his aristocratic name: Boissy D'Anglais. There were two other cats at La Finca in those days: Tester, a smoky-gray Persian, and a tiny kitten named Willy who couldn't walk very far.

He wandered through the house, steering clear of the bed that was covered in unread mail. Finally he asked Mario to prepare another coconut and gin, and he went out to read in the garden. He collapsed in a Barcelona chair on the pool deck, and realized that he hadn't brought anything to read. It was tough to get good books in Cuba; he missed all the American bookstores, above all the great independent ones like Prairie Lights in Iowa City, and he missed the hours he would spend browsing through their shelves without sense of direction, navigating without the aid of map or compass. It was probably the only thing that bothered him about Cuba.

"I'm going for groceries, Señor Hemingway. Do you want anything in particular?" Mario asked. Hemingway didn't know if he was hungry or not. That's absurd, he thought. If he had to ask himself if he was hungry, he probably wasn't. Hunger is something you know; something you recognize clearly. Nevertheless, he hadn't eaten anything since afternoon of the day before.

"I can make you some *ceviche con sierra fresca*, or some stone bass." Hemingway shook his head. "Turtle soup? We still have that frozen meat from the turtle you caught last week." At this, the writer nodded. Mario would feel bad if he didn't eat something. Still, when he brought out the soup later, he had only a few spoonfuls before he set the bowl down beside the chair.

He went back inside and poured himself a glass of whiskey. The place was sensibly organized enough for reading: an armchair right in the middle of the room with a low table on one side that served as a bar. Scattered over the table were an assortment of notes on the novel he had been working on. In his head, he formed a message for Martha: "You know the vices I can write when I have no one to share them with."

Had she left in order to free herself from him? Or was it something simple; that she wanted to prove herself a better journalist than he, or that she didn't need him to succeed? It was all unfair, but it didn't matter much to him. The writer knew that earlier in his life he had been a real son of a bitch, and that at times he still was. Hemingway smiled at this last thought, and decided to award it to his protagonist as a character trait.

He went to place the glass of whiskey on the table but hesitated, as if unsure that the table could support his notes and the glass at the same time. In the end, he held onto the glass. He knew that whiskey would drown the pages, dissolve them. His notes might well be a disaster, but clarity was always there, hidden, in the midst of madness and darkness. He allowed himself a smirk of self-esteem.

One writes with ideas, with words, with experience, with malevolence. He writes because he has things to say. But was there anything to say? He took no pleasure in struggling with words. One writes out of volition. He didn't enjoy it, but rather did it out of necessity. Discipline was essential; hence his obsession with it: organizing the teacups in the cabinet according to size so that a plane won't crash, writing "I will not return" ten thousand times so that he might eat a piece of cake without getting an upset stomach. It's entropy, disorder's constant inertia, that forces one to be meticulous. Line up three pencils in a row, or else chaos enters into your life. But who the hell needs more than one pencil at a time anyway?

Once she called me "undisciplined, egotistical, and heartless," he thought. Some of my more tactful Cuban neighbors might call me "Señor Wey."

He wrote down the phrase.

She, Martha Gelhorn, had bought the house, but she had done it with his money. It was after Paramount had cut them a check for $100,000 for the film rights to *For Whom the Bell Tolls*. Martha once showed it off in a Havana bar as proof that it is indeed possible to cheat the world and win. The house itself had cost only $18,500, and he had come to think of it in the same way and with the same honesty and affection as one thinks of a boat. And they were similar in many ways. It was like a multicolored reef, looking over instead of lying under the sea. At times, the sea's color was mottled by algae or plankton; the tropics were like that. But it was always there, able to be smelled or divined.

He reread the phrase he had just written, and crossed out the word *might*. He put the pencil down on the table and got up to walk around the room, careful to avoid the scattered books and the treacherous magazine rack. His clothes were irritating him. Whiskey in hand, he went into one of the bedrooms. There were three: one for Martha, one for him, and one for the conjugal bed, which had seldom been used except as a place to throw unread mail.

He stripped naked, lay down on the bed, and began to leaf through the *New York Times*. From inside the library in the next room, the massive head of a cape buffalo looked at him; he had killed it back in '34 while on safari on the Serengeti plains. He liked it well enough, but it wasn't much for conversation.

Just then he noticed a few gray hairs had appeared in his chest hair. They had first cropped up in his beard and mustache and were currently marching through his temples on their way to the better part of his head.

He threw down the paper and sang out in Spanish:

"I don't like your town
And I don't like you
Or your bitch of a mother . . ."

It was a little verse from a song he'd learned from a priest in Spain; the same priest with the sense of humor who always said, "Our troops continue to advance without losing so much as a drummer boy."

He saw Boise pass by the half-open door. It must be time for his daily stroll along the roof beams. Goddamn tightrope-walking cat.

Then came the madness, that general, spinning madness that you can't control unless you chain yourself to the masts of order, of specifics, of premeditated obsessions. He outlined the small space of his madness, gave it order and orders, routines and boundaries that cut off the endless roads of insanity. Or at least that's what he believed. Treading water in that little lagoon precludes sinking in the bottomless sea, drowning in the chaotic ocean.

He put on a new pair of pants and a shirt. It was time to get to work, and you can't work in the nude. Outside the window, dusk was falling. Where had the day gone?

He meticulously prepared a fresh drink. Always the ice before the whiskey, and always pour slowly to a height of four fingers. Four-sevenths of the glass full.

He sat down to write and soon came up with a new opening line, but couldn't advance past it. He x-ed it out and tried another opening, but his mind remained blank. He knew how he wanted the novel to proceed; he just couldn't write it out. He went back to his original line, but again found it impossible to formulate a following one and set it to paper. Two hours later, all he had was a collection of progressively worse, hollow-sounding openings. But he pressed on, though conscious of the fact that he had been dominated by impotence. He smiled at the irony—and at the pages and pages of x-ed out openings—and finally surrendered.

Tomorrow he would confront the page again. Battles have to be fought, but above all they have to be finished, and if he could get past that one damn line, then he wouldn't have to stop again until The End.

It was a night of insomnia. Ernest Hemingway sang songs, told stories to his cats, and drank a lot of whiskey.

PART VII

GUERRILLAS

IT WASN'T MARX

I'd like for you to take a look at this editorial," Vicente Lombardo Toledano, the newspaper's publisher, said to Manterola. Lombardo was a prominent player in Mexican politics, and he usually took great pains to distance himself from the paper he ran. It was in times like these that the publisher, president of the Latin American Workers' Union, and a peaceful Marxist, maintained a tenuous bridge between socialism and the more radical nationalism of Cárdenas.

"Do you want my personal or my professional opinion?" asked the journalist, seated in a rocking chair that seemed a bit out of place in the boss's office.

"Both," answered Lombardo, handing him the two-and-a-half-page article. Manterola read it carefully. It was a denouncement of the fifth Fascist column that was currently operating in Mexico. Most of its heat was directed at the Germans, though it didn't pull any punches with the Spanish Falangists or the Italian Fascists, the smaller local groups funded by their embassies, or the few odd Japanese businessmen who wanted to open a cold storage fish market in Baja California. All in all, Lombardo's assertion was that the government had gradually let intelligence agents from Fascist countries operate unrestrained in Mexico. He concluded with a few comments—making it more of a diatribe than an editorial—alluding to the possibility that "a high-ranking government official" was sleeping with a German spy.

Manterola looked up from the text and contemplated his publisher.

"The part about the certain 'high-ranking government official' doesn't surprise you?" asked Lombardo.

"I know about it too."

Now it was Lombardo's chance to be surprised. He raised one of his eyebrows. "Who, exactly, did you hear about?"

"Miguel Alemán. And the spy is a former German actress by the name of Hilda Krüger." Manterola lit his pipe.

"Why haven't you mentioned this before? You're not the type to sit on inflammatory information or to censor stories. I'd have thought you'd have gone straight to press without any regard for the officials involved or for the danger to you."

"I didn't have any way to confirm it, but you just may have given it to me," said Manterola, and then he shut up before compromising the Poet by letting slip his name.

"And what do you personally think about what we're airing out here so discreetly?"

"Personally, I think that you think (and probably the Cardenista cabinet members do as well) that this man has taken, how shall I put it, a very soft line with the Fascists, and that you want to—forgive the expression—chuck his balls in a vice and twist."

Lombardo smiled. "So I have your support?"

"You do indeed, *señor*. I like what you've done here."

"I think I'll stop before I ask you what you don't like about this paper."

"Thanks," said the journalist, and he left the office. He had just closed the door behind him when he turned around and went back in to say, "Remember . . . golden bits do not a better horse make."

"Is that Marx?"

"No. It's Seneca," said Manterola, smiling mischievously as he went back to his desk in the far corner of the room. From the way that he walked and the way he tapped his pipe's smoldering ash on the desks of certain reporters, the whole room knew that something big was about to happen.

TIE LOVERS

This story you have of the German woman—the mistress or the maid or whatever she is—is it at all true?"

The Poet looked uneasily at his boss. He moved his head in a vague way that he hoped could be interpreted in the affirmative or the negative. Was he really asking him about Miguel Alemán, boss to the both of them? How did he know that he knew? He was treading on thin ice now, skating over a frozen lake of deep shit. That bitch had really screwed things up. He looked over to the window as if wanting to fly away; he searched the room for a rabbit in the hopes that it might share its magic hat with him so that they could disappear.

"Are you still in contact with her?" asked Fagoaga, a bit confused because his garrulous subordinate seemed to have lost his usual powers of speech. Again the Poet shook his head in a display of "yes" and "no" ambiguity. He was on the verge of panic, and so he turned to feign searching for cigarettes on a nearby desk.

"This Quintanilla woman, will she come clean?"

The Poet took a deep breath and sneezed a sneeze of pure relief. They were talking about Nicolaus's spurned lover, and not that Krüger woman. He found a pack of cigarettes in his jacket pocket, shook one out, and accepted the light his boss offered him. The privilege of an amputee.

"That is, if I give you the green light, can you take down the German network?"

The Poet nodded vehemently. He had no doubts. But was this really happening? Were they actually giving him orders to go into action? It was too much for one morning. First having thought that they were about to uncover his furtive investigations into the minister's sex life, and then they order him to stop watching and start moving.

"Get all the evidence together and prepare the arrest warrants. And what evidence it is, eh?"

The Poet nodded again, before the top brass could change his mind. He had just one final question. "Do I really take them down all at once, or just shake them up a bit?"

With a question such as this, the Poet ran the risk of the response that, in Mexico, appearances can deceive, but they can also become truths in the public's eye. But even so, he needed to know the "superior will," or at least the official version-to-be.

"Fuck them."

With his head full of smoke, he went into Cartola's office where they gave him a .45-caliber pistol and fifty rounds of ammunition. Then he went back to his "unofficial" office. In this building, called the Palacio Negro by the opposition, riddled with nooks and crannies, replete with secrets that its deceased owners had abandoned in cups on the counters of closed-up bathrooms, where the dead live in closets and even the most cowardly of office workers keep secrets buried deep in the dustiest of files, the Poet had carved out a secret office within the secret office building. At the end of a long hall and flanked by the Special Services and the Bomb Squad offices was a janitor's closet (to which only the Poet had a key) full of pet cockroaches with big, almost human faces. The only people who ever came by were two old fogies who once in a while would stop by to put in an order for gunpowder.

Among mops, buckets, long-handled feather dusters (used for laying siege to the rafters where spiders had fortified a kingdom of webs), and other cleaning products that had accumulated in such abundance that one might think the maintenance room got a percentage of each purchase it made, the Poet had mapped his investigation into the Abwehr IV network on a wall using notecards and brightly colored thumbtacks. The Abwehr was the only espionage organization worth watching, since Leinz's Gestapo, located next to the embassy, served no purpose other than to watch itself, the ambassador, and his sisters while the intelligence office of the embassy itself was rotting on the vine for want of funding. At the tip of the pyramid was Georg Nicolaus, the chief of the Abwehr's operations in both Mexico and the United States. Under Nicolaus was his deputy, Müller, a man with a wolflike face and chronic allergies who doubled as the embassy's gardener despite the fact that he couldn't tell a red rose from a green tomato. Then there was Schleebrugge, who passed himself off as a businessman, and was in the process of gaining government approval for a radio station in Tampico. He kept the network's transmitters (he had not one, but two) in his house . . . was one a backup? Also the players from Veracruz, whose place in the grand scheme of things had yet to be determined. Players like Macario and Padierna, co-owners of a dairy they bought, doubtlessly, with German money. And the midget messenger, the gray gnome, the man in the hat, the bald Austrian, and "Brüning," the enigmatic Brüning, of whose role he was as yet unsure. And then there was that woman Krüger, keyed in via her governmental "relations."

The Poet lightly traced over the cards with his fingers. The truth was that he didn't know much. He could infer connections between the various players, but to know, to really know something . . . But who the fuck knew anything about anything at all in this country of lies? And what good is espionage in a country of lies anyway? At least he was his own boss, working when he wanted to and without being bothered by anyone. That part of it wasn't all bad.

Ah, yes, and now we have Teresa Quintanilla. A little card tacked off to the side of Nicolaus, only hers is pink. The whims of a poet.

No one could say that Fermín had run into Quintanilla by chance. She was a young secretary in the State Department, an orphan who seemed quite a fan of the pornographic novels he penned on unsuspecting virgin pages. Almost. She was also an equestrian champion, a graduate of the College of Germany, and more of an idiot than a Nazi. She had been Nicolaus's lover for a time, until they parted ways last April, having been convinced that he was leading a double life both in terms of lovers and in terms of his official duties. Although on the surface he appeared to be a simple (if substantial) investor in various industries, she wasn't so obtuse as to ignore the communiqués he was passing via consular reports and U.S. ambassadors' visas.

No, it wasn't luck but rather a job well done that had enabled the Poet to uncover the relationship. Part of this was due to his decision to arm Lola, the barber, as his confidante. The Poet felt so indebted to his subagent and old friend—even with all the convincing she needed and all the time he had to put in as a shoulder for her to cry on after her husband had left her— that she was awarded the "Special Medal," that prize which the Mexican government bestows upon only its "greatest patriots" and which the Poet had bought from a curio dealer in Lagunilla.

The Poet later went to Quintanilla's house where, under the threat of twenty-seven years in prison for the crime of sleeping with the enemy, she cried out every last tear of information. But the Poet's initial sense of success quickly sank in his sense of eternal disillusionment when his boss informed him that the results of this interrogation would be duly archived "somewhere around here."

But thanks to Quintanilla, the wall of his janitor's closet was now quite well laid out. Unless, of course, that son of a bitch Nicolaus was deceiving him . . .

"One, two, three . . . he counted the fingers on his missing hand. But why would that arrogant piece of Nazi shit want to lie to a one-armed poet whom his bosses didn't give a damn about nor a case to? No, he must be telling the truth, that much was clear. And now he was on the verge of finally unraveling the web; of setting off a five-alarm fire. So that they would finally learn good manners and not go around spying on Pancho Villa's land, the yellow-bellied cowards. Come off it. Which reminds me, where is that Chinaman Tomás, anyway?

"You have a phone call," said the cleaning lady Ramira, the true proprietor of the janitor's closet, interrupting his thoughts. She handed him a slip of paper. "He says that it's 'Orson in his best role ever.' "

The Poet walked back to his official office, not at all sure whether he had left his investigation in good hands or not. He picked up the phone.

"Señor Kane. A pleasure."

"I hope that they're going to give you carte blanche tomorrow. Because tomorrow we're going to be clamoring for blood, and I wouldn't make a move unless you had a mattress ready to fall on," said his friend Manterola.

"I already have that. Don't worry; I'll be ready." He hung up the phone and rubbed his hands together.

"Forgive me for asking, but who is 'Orson in his best role ever'?" asked the cleaning lady, who was herself likely a double agent, operating under orders of a common boss.

"Orson Welles, obviously, and his best role was as the sheriff in El Paso in a film called *Touch of Evil*. When it was released in Mexico, they called it *Sed de mal*, like the novel."

"And that's whom you were speaking to?"

"Not quite. But it was the sheriff of El Paso, Texas."

"Well, he spoke very good Spanish."

"He should . . . he was born in Mexico, after all," said the Poet, settling the matter. Verbal deception had become a new art of his.

3

THE SUBTERRANEANS

Manterola received the second official call for his help undermining the Nazi cults in a rather extravagant way: a note, nailed to the door of his rooftop room, that read: "The Doctor wants to see you. Same time, same place, tomorrow."

Ludwig Renn was playing marbles with the child with the toy Spitfire out in front of the hardware store. Manterola watched them quizzically. The German novelist had deadly aim; he never missed a shot.

"Don't you think it was a bit melodramatic to contact me like that?"

"The Doctor has pieced together some new information he thinks might be of use to you. But yes, how did they contact you?"

"They nailed a note to my door . . . must have woke up the whole building."

Renn laughed and shrugged his shoulders. The child, suddenly serious in his role, gathered up his marbles and went inside, possibly to tell the guard they were coming. The two men followed him inside. Out in the patio were two very blond boys who were cleaning an engine and barely glanced at them. Renn's organization, besides the occasional lapse into the sensational, exuded a strange professionalism. In the back room, the usual obscurity reigned. In the shadows, Manterola could make out Doctor Sacal, who was seated on a rickety rocking chair whose seat seemed ready to give way at any moment. He was wrapped in a blanket and topped with his usual wrinkled felt hat.

"He's always cold," said Renn, patting the old man on the shoulder. The rabbi smiled at him.

"Go on and tell him, Renn. We don't have much time."

"I'm sorry, Manterola, that we are again going to lead you into the bog that is the history of Nazism, but it seems that we've uncovered a second connection between Hitler and Mexico. It all goes back to the Great War when Hitler was temporarily blinded by a mustard gas explosion. Remember all the stories of poison gas and trench warfare? Anyway, in the Pasewalk field hospital, someone misdiagnosed the blindness as a symptom of hysteria, and it was for that chaotic assessment that the Berlin psychiatrist Doctor Edmund Forster treated him for a few days. The fact would ordinarily not be of much importance—a soldier, tired and hysterical from battle, being treated by a psychiatrist—but in 1933, when the Nazis definitively rose to power, the Gestapo raided Forster's office, destroyed his files, and the mysterious doctor 'committed suicide.' So we may never fully know what treatment and what relationship existed between Hitler and this otherwise insignificant psychiatrist."

"Tell him about the MI-5," said Doctor Sacal, nodding affirmatively. The old man definitely knew where he wanted the story to go. Renn lit a cigarette.

"We know that the British have been investigating along these lines for years. A division called the Occult Branch was formed within the overall intelligence agency and began collecting information on the subject. We've already mentioned this, right? A group of historians, psychologists and witch doctors work there. With the assistance of a man of great worth, one Walter Johannes Stein—who was a friend of Hitler's during their Vienna days and who was later able to escape Nazism—they were the first to establish that Doctor Forster collaborated frequently with Ludwig Lewin, a German pharmacist who, in 1886, published a study of drugs exceedingly rare in Western Europe and their effects on mental states . . . he called them 'modifiers.' They also connected Hitler to an herbalist in Vienna named Adolf Lodz, who claimed that through the use of a certain drug one can open the door to and even recover elements from his distant past. To put it another way, a man could gain access to who he had been in previous lives. Apparently, Hitler visited Lodz to find out what historical figure had been reincarnated in him. So both Lodz and Forster had that in common—that they both treated Hitler—but they also had something in common with a man we've talked about before. One of the members of the Thule, one of the key players in the rise of Nazism, the man to whom Hitler dedicated *Mein Kampf*: Eckart."

"What was that?" asked Manterola, and he felt truly ready to believe any answer they gave.

"Peyote," said Doctor Sacal.

Renn continued: "Eckart, who later became a heroin junkie and probably died from this addiction, said that peyote enabled him to reach a state of mind where he could converse with his previous self: a man named Bernardo de Barcelona, a Moorish wizard in Spain during the twelfth and thirteenth centuries."

"And Hitler took peyote?"

"The Brits are sure of it."

"But he took so many drugs . . . the last time you told me about all the garbage that quack Doctor Morell prescribed him. What significance could peyote have over any of those others?"

"We're sure that these days, in addition to the usual slew, he's regularly taking two stimulants—Eukodal and Pervitin—that have the side effects of producing disassociate personalities and states of euphoria that border on psychosis. And then there's the peyote . . ."

"Did he smoke marijuana too?" asked Manterola. Ironically, the subject of pharmacology was making him nervous; plus, he was having trouble stomaching the fact that the most powerful country on earth was being run by a dope fiend. If it weren't for Renn's presence and the gravity with which he was describing these things, he'd think it was all a joke.

"No," Renn said seriously. "But what do you know about peyote?"

"Nothing. Is it a root? Whatever it is, it sounds Mexican. . . ."

4

THE RAID

The Poet organized his mediocre forces, all of them on loan from other departments, as if they were real mercenaries hired by a real army. The day had dawned with an extraordinarily blue sky, and the morning papers, which he had read at a Chinese café around the corner from his house, were ablaze with news of his boss's strange behavior the previous day. The stances of Mexican politicians varied from complicitous neutrality and conspiring with the Germans to an aggressive neutrality away from them and toward the Allies. The North Americans had publicized blacklists that named companies (mostly German) which supported Latin American Fascist organizations, and they threatened retaliation. The list specified brewmasters and opticians, metalworkers and millers, machinery and paper exporters, and such glowing examples of the German presence in Mexico as the College of Germany, the Equestrian Club, and the Industrial Club. The German ambassador sent a letter of protest to the State Department, invoking Mexican sovereignty and asking for protection. But this time—and this was driven home in every major paper—President Ávila Camacho responded quite sternly. Staring down the threat of economic blackmail, he cautioned Chancellor Padilla in a very firm tone that "We don't want to lose our commerce with all of Western Europe," and instead severed relations with Germany, withdrawing Mexican diplomats, revoking the German consuls' diplomatic immunity, and officially recognizing the delegates from occupied France and Holland. Not just diplomatic relations, but nearly all relations, the Poet thought to himself as he traced his hand over a table covered in sweet bread crumbs.

At 7:30 on a cloudless, sparkling morning, two squad cars bearing a dozen police officers and six secret service agents roared spectacularly up to Walter Schleebrugge's little house in Mixcoac. They rang the bell and then, without waiting for an answer, fired two rounds into the lock, ripped the door off its hinges, and moved swiftly inside.

At the same time, the Poet, followed by agents Verandas and Agustín Sánchez—a man from Toluca who was widely admired for having broken into the service ranks—entered through the back patio. Always wary of vicissitudes, the Poet proceeded with his pistol drawn, though this prevented him from operating to the extent that two-handed people do; for example, opening the door which he suddenly found in front of him. His partners opened the door and entered first, and made their way to Schleebrugge's bedroom. The German was lying there, tense and straight, on top of his neatly tucked covers. His eyes were open wide and focused up on the ceiling lamp. He didn't twitch a muscle.

"We have a warrant to enter and search the place for a munitions depot," said Verandas, very much into his "good cop" role.

"Fuck you, you Nazi bitch," said Sánchez, the bad cop, as he gaffed and cuffed him.

The Poet said nothing and went about inspecting the house. He had studied the house's blueprints, and knew where the radio transmitters were hidden: a locked room near the patio.

Schleebrugge had asked for a permit to operate a commercial radio station in Mexico. The government, however, had "lost" the papers and later denied that the German had ever filed an application at all. He had tried in the Federal District and later in Tampico, but he was blackballed everywhere. It was all quite a farce. It wasn't too surprising, then, that the German had taken matters into his own hands. But he had no consoles, no floor mics, no mixing boards, no materials for erecting an antenna. Only a pair of shortwave radios.

The Poet looked at them and, unsatisfied, re-searched the room for the codebooks. Perhaps the German bureaucracy had left him a gift. But no matter how hard he looked for false boxes and double walls, he found nothing but dust. What's more, the transmitters were like new, and some parts were still in their original packaging. The equipment had never been used. He felt like pistol-whipping his prisoner. What were these transmitters for? There was one in the embassy, and surely they could have used it. Perhaps this was part of an emergency network, to be used only in the case that

diplomatic relations between Mexico and Germany were cut off. So Schleebrugge wasn't the operator; just the safeguard. So far, their raid hadn't accomplished much.

As he was leaving the house, the Poet saw a few of the officers stealing
a gramophone. Fucking horde. Whose hands are we in? And then, realizing
that he was the one running the show, he called them to attention and belted
out a variation on the old diatribe Guillermo Prieto had delivered in Gua-
dalajara a century ago, except that he replaced the phrase "the valiant ones
do not assassinate" with "cops don't loot." Just at this moment, a pair of
photographers burst in on the scene. The Poet slipped away; he hadn't called
them, someone higher up must have tipped them off. Now it was going to
turn into an exposé; this could hamstring the whole operation.

He quickly loaded the rest of his brigade into a pair of taxis—the squad
cars having left earlier—and thirty minutes later they were at Müller's house
forcing the lock. The gardener with the lupine face didn't try to resist, but
he had a locked box with a pair of Lüger pistols in his dresser. As he was
being led away in handcuffs, looking defiantly at his captors, the photographers appeared again. The Poet, trying to stay calm and composed, continued to rifle through the chests and drawers of Nicolaus's right-hand man,
but he found nothing at all. Just a packet of letters and photos, including
one where Müller appeared next to a fat matron on the steps of the Catedral
Colonia. It wasn't a wedding photo, but Fermín's German wasn't good
enough to decipher the three lines written on the back of the photo or the
scrawled signature.

"Who's directing this operation?"

"Special Agent J. Posadas," said the Poet, jerking his thumb behind him
even though nobody was there.

Nicolaus was not at his house on London Street. The men who had been
on stakeout since the previous night said that the German hadn't come
around there. The house was empty, even of dust. It seemed as if nobody
lived there anymore . . . just a few books, some shaving implements in the
bathroom, and a single, steel-gray suit that hung in a closet. Nothing more.
The Poet ordered the books be taken into evidence.

Fermín stood in the shade of an *ahuehuete* tree while his brigade arrested
the two tough-guy businessmen as they left La Casa Sol, a seafood restaurant
in the downtown area. He followed them like just one more onlooker at-
tracted by the police action, listening as they broke down into a tirade on
the injustice and tyranny that the law had become in Mexico. He noticed
that one was rummaging around in his pocket, as if he were balling something up, and signaled with a wave for Sánchez the *toluqueño* to intervene.
Sánchez got his hands to the prisoner's throat just in time to stop him from

swallowing a wad of paper he had managed to stick in his mouth, and Verandas smashed his nose with the butt of his gun for his audacity.

The operation continued on throughout the morning but Fermín, whose forces were dwindling because gendarmes were constantly leaving to escort the suspects back to the deportation prison in Colonia San Rafael, didn't harbor much hope that things would get better.

After the incident with the bottle, Brüning had been staying at the bald Austrian's house, but the Poet knew that he hadn't been seen around there for a few days. He knew very little about this Austrian, having only glimpsed his passport (which was probably fake) from a distance when he had cashed a check once, but in a rather unprofessional decision, he left verification for later. He didn't seem to be a major player in Nicolaus's network, but the Poet's interest had grown considerably when he had taken in Brüning and his bloody head. The Austrian was a nameless figure who watered the plants in the front yard of his house in the Santa María neighborhood with an enormous watering can, a few blocks from the plaza and the Moor Kiosk. The house had two entrances, the front door and a back one that led into an alley. The Poet hung back in wait while the remaining gendarmes fanned out in a semicircle around the door. The Austrian came out running with a huge suitcase in hand, but the officers quickly stopped him, and the Poet confiscated his suitcase. He liked the looks of it; it was big, well-made, with brass reinforcements, and it bore tags from hotels in the French Riviera and the Plaza de Madrid. A suitcase that certainly didn't seem to belong to this rambling old man.

Fermín amused himself then by examining the gardener's tools in the garage, poking through seeds and insecticides, flowerpots and rakes. It was the perfect place to hide something, he thought. People tend to hide things around other things they use most often. Rummaging around, he finally hit the jackpot: a half-dozen Belgian pistols hidden in a sack of fertilizer.

As he came out from the garage, a car was pulling slowly up to the curb. Fermín felt a rush of adrenaline as he dropped the canvas bag in which he had stowed the pistols and went for his own, which he kept at the small of his back, and as he did so he was struck by the vague and distant impression that he might have forgotten to load it. The car, a dark green Pontiac, didn't stop but rather accelerated, tires squealing as they spun. Brandishing his pistol, Fermín could see, through the window's parted shades, the stunned eyes of the man he called Brüning looking back at him.

He looked for one of his squad cars, but the street was empty. Even his two partners had already left with the prisoners. So he leveled his pistol at the pair of mad eyes inside the car some twenty yards away. He gently squeezed the trigger and winced as he heard the hammer fall on the firing pin with an empty metallic click.

5

THE CHINESE IGUANA

The war waged by the Iguana against the men of the hooked cross seemed to go on in a surreal world, in a fantastic land, in a time extracted from all history. It was a nonexistent war, and it was eternal.

In Tomás Wong's defense, one could say that he didn't start it. The band of brown shirts had moved silently through the coffee-growing region during the past two years, sowing terror. They would burst in on an isolated, unsuspecting community and assassinate an agrarian reform leader, burn down a rural library, or bludgeon a few contract laborers.

Then a strong and beautiful scene would unfold in some of the haciendas: feasts, parades around the granaries, wild fiestas with beer and song.

But not all of the plantation owners were involved. Some would participate directly, along with their children, friends, and employees. Others collaborated only at times, preferring to look away when a farmhand got whipped. The rest kept to themselves off in the margins. And just like a current that doesn't ripple the water's surface, a magical phenomenon had been created, as much in the minds of the pursued as in those of the oppressors. There were many double standards and fears of things real or imagined, because it was easy for the monsters of reason to coexist with the monsters of dream there, at the edge of the world, the ultimate horizon, in isolation, in the absence of roads and trucks, in a land that didn't know if it was jungle or mountain or coast, where everything gauged itself by its ability to strike a path and set off at a good clip.

In the erratic geography a pueblo disappears after a harvest, a river continually alters its course, and the boundaries of haciendas and communities are drawn in the whimsical breezes. And from the outside, from the strange and distant powers of the Republic and the rest of the outside world, silence prevails.

Tomás had waylaid the brown shirts on two more occasions. The first bore no results, for they never came within firing range, and he calmly decided not to risk the safety of his cover to emerge and confront them. The other ambush was more successful; he had cut them off at a pass and was able to wound two of them: one in the gut and one in the leg. He had been aiming low.

He had also burned the home of the fat one who, in the Hacienda la Badenia, acted as foreman and seemed to be one of the leaders of the group. He sprinkled gasoline on the bed, the bookcase, and the armoire containing all his uniforms and armbands emblazoned with the twisted cross, and then sat back to bask in the warmth of the blaze.

But one night they had gotten the drop on him and attacked while he was bivouacked between the roots of two massive trees that a storm or an earthquake had torn down, and if it weren't for the frantic warning calls of the birds and for the quickness of his own feet, he'd have been dead.

Tomás was alone in his war. From time to time he would see *campesinos*, women washing clothes in a stream, children playing, contract laborers on the road at dawn. But the locals regarded him as if he were invisible. They didn't look him in the eye; didn't offer him so much as a single word. They passed him by as if he were immaterial; neither did they succumb to the emotions of fear or enmity. They didn't cross his path, didn't respond to his greetings, didn't agree or disagree with him when he said "It's going to rain" or "have a good day." They had simply declared him to be nonexistent. Or that's what he had thought, but it wasn't quite so.

Anonymous but surprisingly effective allies existed in the communities of silence. One night, the neatly folded hammock mysteriously appeared at the edge of his sleeping area; on another occasion he found in the center of his usual path a little sack of bullets. Another time he entered a ghost town, no more than a dozen or so huts, and he found a suckling pig roasting over a fire. Packets of brown sugar hung from a tree with twine frequently appeared, as once did a battered pewter mug filled with strong black coffee.

His ally—or allies? Could there be more than one?—sent him signals. A broken branch equaled danger. A dead bird, grave danger. These allies became as invisible as he was once the communities had declared his nonexistence. And Tomás understood it. One can't bear witness to the invisible; neither can he testify when he has nothing to say. But he was a suicidal Chinaman, his lungs burned with the heat of his war, and his actions put everyone in danger. Still, he would have liked to get to know these people, to talk for a while and then go to sleep while someone else watched over him. He especially missed the possibility of conversation, the chance to ask them if there wasn't some other way to put a stop to the madness of this little war.

As the days (weeks?) went by, he had come to ritualize this war. He declared himself the Fourth Army of the Chinese Way and he envisioned a green cloth with four small red stars set at an angle as his flag and two quatrains from the poem "Life Is a Dream" as his battle hymn. The poem's author, Calderón de la Barca, had known a Spanish anarchist friend of his in childhood and had spent many upon many hours educating Tomás when he was a ratty urchin living in the streets of the port city of Tampico. He had even given himself the rank of lieutenant (while captain was technically higher, lieutenant was just fine for an army of one) and used for his insignia a braided chain of lizard or chicken bones that his allies had once left him.

Lieutenant Tomás Wong talked to himself, though rarely, just enough to remind himself who he was by the sound of his voice. People would say that he talked to himself because he was going mad, but the truth is that a man's voice—when spoken and not merely thought—accompanies him, sustains him, and therefore was not a sign of madness but rather of his humanity. But above all, he spoke because he had to give orders to his army.

He also shaved and bathed in streams, he ate, he shit, he buried his shit, and he slept lightly. His mind was intact and certainly under great duress, but he always kept part of it focused on these little everyday things while a greater part of it was turned ever toward the past.

You are what you are, but also what you were, thought Tomás Wong, the Chinaman born in Sinaloa, raised in Tampico, and baptized by fire on the Seven Great Seas and the twenty-two lesser ones. And in the solitude of the jungle and the hills, so far from the sea, its smells of saltwater breezes, the bars of the ports, the local members of the Union Steamship and the IWW, the Federation of International Dockworkers and the International Sailors' Union, with their tiny rooms in the back of their offices furbished with only a hard old bed and a bookcase for the captains, the bordellos with his whore friends who had real names and family histories. So far from all of this, in the depths of solitude, you can't help but turn away from your past, your one and only past, because you're being overwhelmed and confounded by the present. You might be startled by the cry of a bird, and for a moment forget where on earth you are. It would take you a moment or two to gather yourself, to locate yourself and determine what had just happened. But just as you do, the age-old head of Fear rears up and returns to join you at your side, like a chronic limp or latent disease. And because of this you begin to sleep with your eyes open, like the dead do. Tomás Wong did, and he dreamed about the old Long March and about these new brown shirts.

6

A COUNTERSPY'S WORK

The yard at the nameless jail on Calle Miguel Shultz, a place of temporary detention for people the Mexican government was waiting to deport, was bordered by high, whitewashed walls. It was an "unofficial" jail, one that didn't comply with legal regulations but, like so many other things in Mexico, it operated under the penumbra of a judicial system that fluttered continuously like a sail in the winds of power.

The walls were nearly as white as the Poet's hair. Everything had turned out well enough, he supposed, if, by well enough, you meant bad. Fermín Valencia smoked his last cigarette and then entered the interrogation room where a secretary was taking dictation on a rusty old Remington typewriter.

He didn't even bother to put on a persona and sat down in the middle of the room, silent, listening to the line of questioning and the verbal diarrhea which the suspect offered in response. In his head he put together a list of questions that he would have one of his partners deliver once the State Department agents had left. Jorge Negrete and Pedro Infante might have been real cowboys as far as cops were concerned, but they knew nothing about espionage.

"Why did you have some twelve—wait, I can't make that out, is that ten?—pistols of Belgian make and model hidden in a flowerpot?"

In response, the prisoner demanded, in German (which drove the stenographer crazy) an interpreter, a lawyer, and the German ambassador. He seemed almost amused by the whole situation, even cracking jokes. "What do you think I am, Belgerman?"

"We know you were born in Veracruz. But why did you turn your coat and go to work for a foreign power?"

The prisoner answered that one was free to have whatever friends he wanted and to strike up talks with anyone, that the constitution guarantees this, and that his relationship with Germany was purely commercial.

"Then why did you have two radio transmitters in your home?"

The prisoner explained that he had applied numerous times for a commercial license to use the transmitters, that they had no military purpose whatsoever, and that since his applications had been denied, he hadn't found anyone who would buy the transmitters off him yet.

"And how do you rationalize having a Lüger pistol?"

The prisoner explained that, as the gardener of the German embassy, he was also charged with watchman's duties, and although he was primarily a gardener, the pistol was necessary for personal protection.

None of this is of the slightest importance, the Poet thought to himself. But this was how the Mexican judicial system worked: the guilty ones talk and talk, explain and justify, and eventually they fuck themselves. They let something slip and then they squirm and stew in it. The only problem was that in some cases, the same thing can happen to the innocent.

The deportation papers were already signed, sealed, and delivered. The press bulletin had been written up before the interrogation even took place by a pencil-pusher who worked directly under the Chief. Everything was kosher. But the Poet couldn't help but wonder if it would all be enough.

When the formalities had been dispensed with, the Poet decided against his earlier idea of letting one of his partners do the questioning and instead found the smallest, dirtiest interrogation room, sat down in a chair, and asked one of the guards to bring in the goon who had seemed the most shaken by the whole ordeal.

"You go by 'Dionicio,' right? That's a fucked-up name; you probably even spell it with a C. You're a yellow-backed coward with a fucked-up name, and you've got bad orthographics on top of it all," he said after the prisoner had entered and he had shown him his seat. "And your mother's name is Eugracia. An even more ridiculous name. 'Disgracia' is more like it. You say that you're a businessman, but I wouldn't hire you to be the lowest of my delivery boys."

"Leave my mother out of this," muttered the goon.

"Your mother isn't shit to me, Señor Dionicio. I just want it to be perfectly clear how stupid you are. The German nationals will just be deported. But you, sir, will end up with a minimum sentence of fifteen years in prison for treason."

The guy had seen it coming. Not even Christ returning as a lawyer could save him now.

"If I were to slip a note into your file, just a little suggestion that you cooperated with our forces, the judge just might consider that a mitigating factor and suspend the sentence. But in order for me to do something like that, I need for you, Señor Dionicio, honestly, to check your balls and your hard ass at the door and cooperate."

The Poet paused to let his proposition take root in the Veracruzano's head. He hadn't done it just for the money; he had really been taken with Fascism. He had been the head of the Veracruz branch of the "Aztec Eagles," the Mexican Fascist party, who fancied themselves members of a superior race, sat down to piss, and wore pearl tie clasps. Please. What a crock of shit.

He sat back in silence, trying to wipe his mind clean, but the odd name of his own mother kept popping in: Aurelia de la Reencarnación. Who did he think he was, making fun of other people's mothers? Aurelia de la Reencarnación, what a horror show. It was for the best that she ran off with a gringo farm-machinery salesman when he was three, leaving his father and him with nothing but a messy house to keep.

Dionicio Torrecillas rubbed the swollen finger on his right hand with his left. The Poet took out a cigarette—just one—from the pocket of his well-worn jacket, placed it between his lips, and struck a match on the sole of his boot. He puffed away contentedly for a moment and then took from his other jacket pocket the little ball of paper that Dionicio had tried to swallow while being arrested.

"It says here, 'Puerto de las Perlas . . . One and a half of fruit.' I can't quite make out the next few lines on account of all your slobber, but then it says, ' . . . see to the tanks of water.' " The Poet paused here to take another drag on his cigarette. "Who is this letter from?"

"It's mine."

There it is, the Poet thought. Once they start to talk, they never know when to stop.

"Where did it come from?"

A new pause, and then the goon began to talk without once looking the Poet in the eyes. Funny, he thought, confessions are always made to the floor and never to a person.

"They told me to buy a fruit stand so I could place wholesale orders, and then every month I was to take a ton and a half of fresh fruit to my hometown of Veracruz. Then I was told to get together a bunch of water tanks—big ones, two hundred liters. And I had to take those to a place outside Veracruz called Puerto de las Perlas."

" 'They told me this, they told me that,' *Who* told you?"

"Nicolaus. He was the boss of the whole operation. He's the one who paid me."

"And you expect me to believe this horseshit? Why were you shipping fruit to Veracruz? It's like shipping sweet potatoes to Puebla. Why not just buy them there?"

"I swear, I'm telling the truth."

"And what was in the middle part of the note?"

"A generator and sixty car batteries. I just had to collect everything they asked for and get it to Veracruz."

"What part of Veracruz? Don't come at me with these generalizations, tough guy. A tough guy who doesn't know his own state is a shame to his country," said the Poet, half seriously and half in jest.

"They were going to tell me this week. It's a port, a small port—just a cove, really—that they call Puerto de las Perlas."

"In the north? Near the city? Near Minatitlán? To the south? Near Poza Rica? Where?"

"They never told me, I swear. Nicolaus never told me, he just said to be ready."

"Why did they want all this fruit, water, and batteries?"

"I don't know. I honestly don't know."

For the next two hours, the Poet grilled his prisoner over these same questions. He got nothing, but took the opportunity to establish Nicolaus's modus operandi. How he liked his coffee, where he held meetings, how the dates were decided upon, what paper he read, where he went when he was done with a meeting, if he wore disguises, which barber he went to, and which tailor.

Up next was Müller, whom he enjoyed interrogating. He was no gardener; evidently he was Nicolaus's number-two man. He was educated, but not in languages, for his Spanish was loathsome, raspy, full of grunts and untrilled R's.

"What's your rank?" asked the Poet. "If you're not an officer, then we'll treat you like a gardener."

"What's yours?" responded the lupine Müller.

"Major in the Special Services. What you might call a commandant," lied the Poet who, in all his years of service with the International Brigades in Spain, had never advanced past sergeant, and he held that rank for only a week. Even during the golden years of his youth, fighting alongside Villa,

he had never commanded anyone other than his horse, and even it diso-
beyed orders frequently.

Müller nodded. It was, at least, a sign of recognition. Something out of
nothing. The Poet looked to exploit this chink in the German's reticence.

"I'm not going to ask you to betray your associates in the network. We
already know everything we need to know about them. I'm also not going
to ask you about your boss, Nicolaus. But what I do want to know about is
a man who doesn't directly pertain to your services, and who is in Mexico
for nonmilitary reasons," ventured the Poet, throwing the dice. "A well-
dressed man of average height, with unkempt hair and an Austrian passport
who goes by the name of Gerhard Brüning."

Müller nodded again. Gamble, the Poet said to himself. Find something
he'll say no to. Brüning was no soldier, wasn't Abwehr, and wasn't one of
Canaris's boys. So he was either Gestapo, an undercover diplomat, or Nazi
SS. And his motives . . . ?

He pressed and pressed, but the chink in Müller's armor had closed up
like a wound. Exasperated, he ordered the guards to return him to his cell.

". . . some beasts . . ." said Müller as they were leading him out. What
was that slip? thought the Poet. His voice had sounded more hoarse than
usual. With a wave, he stopped the guards.

"Who, exactly, are beasts?"

Müller didn't respond. He just hung his head as if to say it was all over
now, that he didn't give a damn about Brüning, and that there was more
than one.

"Who are the others?"

Müller remained silent. Defeated yet proud. The Poet tried one final
time.

"For the last time, *señor*, how many are there?"

Müller lifted his right index finger. One. There was one more. The Poet
nodded and the guards shoved Müller on down the hall.

The Poet stayed behind, alone and angry. He had succeeded, he had
broken through a wall of ice, but it had left him with a million tiny pieces
on his hands.

It took him a moment to gather himself enough to examine the bald
one's suitcase. A change of underwear, three pairs of socks, elastic garters
for the socks, a thick cotton sweater, a pair of boots, a half-dozen hunting
knives, two unopened packs of playing cards, two of Nietzsche's books in
the original German, a dictionary, and a copy of Hemingway's *Across the
River and Into the Trees* in the original English. Eureka! It was the same book
that Hilda Krüger had had in her house. Two German nationals both reading
Hemingway—the same Hemingway—in English? No, this was no coinci-

dence; this was the codebook. He asked the guards what they planned to do with the prisoner.

"The rest we're going to deport, but this guy is Austrian. Where would we ship him to? His country's gone; it no longer exists. Somehow he'll have to stay here in a Mexican prison until Austria magically reappears. Well, you know what they say, this guy used fake papers and now I'm going to give him a good, hard fuck with sand in the Vaseline."

Sweat began to bead up on the Austrian's bald head, despite the fact that a chilly breeze had gusted in through one of the interrogation room's broken windows. The Poet kept his jacket on, both for warmth and so as to hide his missing arm. An interrogator mustn't show weakness. But he shrugged off this axiom with his next argument.

"I lost an arm during the war in Spain, in a bombing run by the Condor Legion. Nothing scares me, *señor*. I can walk through rock. Just the thought of blowing away a battalion of Nazis gives me a hard-on."

He could see that the prisoner was afraid, but not of him. Not of his threats or boasts. Hold on there, tough guy, the Poet said to himself. If he's not afraid of me, then who's he afraid of?

"Tell me what Brüning was doing in your house. Just dropping by for a visit?"

"He had his own room there, which I didn't have a key to. I never knew what was in it, nor did I want to."

"I see you've been reading Hemingway. The fact that you've got the codebook means that you're not just an average fool. To the network you're a very important fool."

"Nothing in that suitcase is mine. You can check that. It all belongs to the man you're looking for."

"To Brüning?"

"I know him as Linz."

"Pull up your pants. I want to see your socks."

The bald Austrian was not wearing garters.

"Take off your shoes." He obeyed again. The Poet compared them to one of the boots from the suitcase. Sure enough, the boots were smaller by two full sizes.

"Tell me what went on in that room."

"I don't know; I was never allowed inside. But there was a blond guy—almost albino, really—who visited him often." The Poet felt a rush of nervous energy. He remembered Müller's raised finger. There were two: Brüning/Linz and this one, the quasi-albino.

It was after nightfall by the time Fermín Valencia, the one-armed Poet, left the jail. He was convinced that the raid had ultimately failed, for two damned reasons. First, Nicolaus and Brüning had both managed to elude them, and the players they had managed to capture were mere pawns. But the second reason bothered him even more: the Germans hadn't been surprised by the raid. It was as if they had been waiting for it. Someone must have blown the whistle. Maybe they didn't say, "They're coming for you at seven o'clock sharp," but they definitely knew that this would eventually happen. They knew that they were going to be arrested, and they were ready for it. They hadn't even been preparing to flee; none of their belongings were packed and ready to go. Had they been left out as bait? Was there another net lying in wait beneath this one?

He walked toward Ribera de San Cosme and found a taxi parked in front of the market. The driver was eating a *pozole* and wasn't very receptive to being pressed into service. The Poet had to convince him that this cab ride was a matter of national security before the driver agreed to take him to the Austrian's house. There, the Poet unlocked the front door (he'd taken the keys to all the houses they had searched that morning) and started searching. He found the door to Brüning's unexamined room at the end of the hall, and then he suddenly realized that it hadn't been a good idea to come alone. What if Brüning returned?

The floor was wet; the prisoner had probably left a faucet running. He felt around on the wall for the light switch. He flipped it on, and what he saw, illuminated by the sad glow of the single naked bulb in the ceiling, left him astonished. There was a solitary bed smack in the middle of the room. No nightstand, no bookcases, no closet. Just the bed. But above it on the wall was the room's only decoration: a series of symbols scrawled in red. Symbols that seemed to be a form of writing. He thought he recognized the S's from the raylike style of the SS, but nothing else. In all, there were close to a dozen of these symbols. And there was something brutal about them. The Poet went up to the wall and, using a penknife, scraped some of the red material into an envelope for analysis. Was it paint? Blood? As he carefully copied the symbols down into his notebook, a deep sense of malaise pervaded him. Horror manifested itself by a dryness in the mouth, an insipidness in the bowels. And it was a sensation that the Poet knew only too well.

What demons was he confronting?

7

CHURCHES

Dawn was breaking. Manterola returned home after closing up at the paper to find his friend Fermín Valencia huddled up in the doorway of his home, deathly cold. This was not normal. The tacit list of modes of decency that had defined their relationship for so many years precluded the Poet from invading his refuge, inquiring as to his economic situation, or commenting on the women he slept with. So something of grave importance must have happened for him to violate the privacy of his friend here. Manterola greeted him with a nod; he was very tired. The vague light from the east was just beginning to silhouette the buildings and, from the perspective of shopkeepers and clotheslines, the Poet was barely able to distinguish the hazy shadow of Chapultepec hill and the castle. With a wave, Manterola invited him in.

"I've only got one chair."

"I'll stand."

"Horses sleep standing up."

The room was desolate, bare, with nothing on the walls save for stains from the humidity. A small, rickety wooden coffee table with a typewriter sitting on it, a chair that seemed like something out of a Van Gogh sketch, and a mattress with no sheets were the only furniture. Manterola collapsed on the bed and folded his arms behind his head.

"I've got some pecans in that tin, but that's all there is for food."

The Poet nodded and reached for the tin, which sat on the table between a dirty spoon and a corkscrew. He took three and offered the rest to the journalist.

Manterola took one and cracked it open, using both hands in a gesture as if he were beginning a speech, and waited for the Poet to tell him what he'd come here to tell. But Fermín resigned himself to his cigarettes, striking a match on his boot and staring silently at the floor.

Manterola was having one of those crises of solitude that frequently drove him mad. The previous day he had nearly strangled a young assistant because he had confused the orders and brought him two beers instead of the black coffee he had ordered. The day's reportage had been chaotic, dedicated almost entirely to covering the raid that the government had executed against the German agents. What was worse was that he knew that the Poet had something to do with it, but he wasn't talking, so the silence remained between them as he watched a spider at work on his web near the room's single ceiling light.

The Poet finished his cigarette and yawned. Manterola was struck by a sudden urge and yawned as well.

Another minute passed in silence.

"Have you been inside a church recently?" the journalist suddenly asked.

"You already asked me that the other day. No, I don't go to church; you can't smoke there, and they ask for alms instead of handing them out, even with all the money the Vatican has. Until that changes, I don't go."

"People don't go out of habit, Fermín. They don't go to ask for rent reductions or better sex with their spouses . . . They go because they're afraid."

"You go to church often then, do you?"

"Some."

"And you see a lot of people when you go?"

"Enough," the journalist said flatly. The sky was getting lighter.

"Don't worry about it so much. A lot of people are going to the cantinas these days, too," ventured the Poet.

The sun was now almost fully up, breaking over the horizon with a grayish light. In one of the room's tiny windows, a pair of pigeons was cooing. The Poet lit another cigarette.

"Tomorrow our paper is going to print this editorial of Lombardo's," said Manterola, taking three folded sheets of paper from his vest and handing them to the Poet. Fermín read them carefully, his eyes widening.

"Holy mother . . . things are really going to heat up at my office when they read this." He then went on to read the crucial paragraph in a loud, clear voice: ". . . and it is now known that a high-ranking member of this government—whose last name is synonymous with his political inclinations—is involved in an ongoing romantic relationship with a woman who has been identified as a German secret agent."

"This will likely cause a few problems, then?"

"I should think so. They'll start looking for the leak to see if it came from our side of things. Alemán's become more cautious about the relationship of late, and Krüger's broken off contact with the network."

"I suppose the Americans told my boss that they want to tighten up on the government, and the left wing must agree with them, because they gave me this note that explicitly states that one particular piece of this government is in love with a Nazi."

The Poet handed back the three sheets of paper as if they were on fire. The rest of the editorial was somewhat less incendiary; identifying a secretary who was on the board of directors of the German Equestrian Club, and claiming that the Treasury minister had been making shady deals with the German-owned breweries in Coahuila.

Silence again fell, this time for a long while. Finally Pioquinto Manterola asked, "Do you know anything about peyote?"

"Perhaps, if you know something about these symbols," replied the Poet as he took out the sketches he had made of the designs in Brüning's room. When it came to enigmatic questions, he was never very far behind his old friend.

8

ENTRY 1:

PEYOTE AND RUNES

P eyote is only a cactus; a *kaktos* if you want to be formal. And it has quite the sonorous scientific name: *Lophophora williamsii*. Those who have seen it in the wild (among whom I cannot count myself) say that it has tuberous flowers and a thick stalk. A doctor once explained to me that it's the alkaloids, narcotics, and hallucinogens in the plant that produce its amazing effects. It's a virtual toxic cocktail that induces temporary madness, or so they say. In Mexico, there are certain indigenous peoples who chew the plant for its effects, and these groups are even related to a religion in the United States that was founded and recognized by the Native American Church.

The peyote mindstate is one where the subject has decided that what is seen is no longer as important as those things which are not there but can still be intuited, divined, or otherwise discerned.

And evidently, the word "pejorative" comes from this plant as well. Consuming massive quantities of peyote can prompt one to slander another without any sort of reason at all.

The runes are just a type of alphabet, one that Germanic and Scandinavian people used at the beginning of the Christian era: twenty-four characters in the former case and sixteen in the latter. We know this because archaeologists have unearthed many well-preserved records marked on wood and stone.

Runes have been analyzed in underground circles for centuries upon centuries, resulting in the theory that they represent a cryptic language used to invoke signs and premonitions. Nazi symbology has adopted the use of runes here and there; the SS have also taken their symbols from ancient runes. There are words in Finnish and Iranian that also recall their rune ancestors, and these words are always marked by connotations of magic or secrecy.

And I'm telling you all of this because life, in all of its marvelous complexity, is becoming a rarer and rarer thing these days, and because sometimes information (which often makes us feel informed rather than actually informing us) is not enough.

9

PUERTO DE LAS PERLAS

The apocryphal Aztec princess inspected the Poet with her sleepy gaze, which was more apocryphal and less princess-like in the mornings and without makeup. She threw the paper down at the foot of the bed and exclaimed, "War's broken out."

"You're two years behind, woman," said the Poet, modestly covering his stump with the sheet and wishing the princess would light him a cigarette.

"No, this is for real. Japan struck the American fleet at a place called Pearl Harbor in Hawaii. They have good pineapples there, don't they?"

The Poet didn't know what to say. The useful part of his brain was busy assessing the fact that the U.S. would now have no choice but to enter the war, while the worthless part was ready to launch into a polemic on the advantages that damned pineapples have over the people of Hawaii.

"They really finished them off . . . They sank a ton of ships; they torpedoed the *Arizona*, the *Nevada*, and the *California*, they dropped bombs right down the smokestacks of the battleships, and they destroyed planes on the ground before they even had a chance to take off. And they came in from long range, too. They brought the aircraft carriers in just close enough and then launched their planes armed with .30-06 machine guns and then, ratatatatat!"

The war had made everyone an expert; men and women who couldn't tell a carrier from a cable car were suddenly able (and if they were flipped around, they would just go on without noticing the difference) to comment on the flank speed of a destroyer or the number of depth charges it carried, and of course everything about a transport's armor plating.

"Well there were thousands—thousands of planes—or maybe not, but there were at least five hundred, and they all came in waves. How dumb could the gringos have been? They weren't ready; they weren't expecting this. The first wave fell on them at dawn and by the time the second wave was returning home, their fleet had become a floating junkyard."

"And they're sure it was the Japanese?" asked the Poet, stalling more for a chance to finish waking up than out of any real curiosity.

"Yes, the Zero pilots were shouting, 'Banzai!' " said the Aztec.

How the hell did she know what they were shouting? But more important, what would happen now? We will be at war now, too, because the Mexican government would surely stand by the gringos, would finally and officially align itself with the Allies.

The Poet pulled the sheet up to his chin and was torn between the happiness in knowing that the war—the war he had wanted—was finally here, and the sad fact that the ass-kissers in the Mexican government had had to wait until the admiral . . .

"What's the Japanese admiral's name again?"

"Ay, baby, Yamamoto. What did you think it was?"

. . . until Admiral Yamamoto saw fit to go ahead and pound the gringos, to force them to take sides. Because that was what was going to happen, right? Or not? They had suffered fewer casualties than the Brits, New Zealanders, and Dutch, who had long since been under bombardment, and they lost fewer ships than the French had at Tolón.

"What was Mexico's response?"

"Nothing yet. What would they say, besides the fact that they're going to wait and consult before making any decisions?"

The Poet moved his good arm out from under the sheets and rummaged around for his pants, which ought to have landed somewhere near the nightstand. His fingers finally closed around his pack of cigarettes and a lighter. When he looked up again, the Aztec princess had stripped, taking off her robe printed with mauve orchids. The Poet couldn't help but wonder where she'd gotten such a kimono, one that left his jaw hanging by a thread.

"Madam Butterfly, that's the style." How was it that war ignited the desires of some and quelled those of others? The woman's nipples were erect, but the Poet wanted nothing of love at the moment. Perhaps it was because he had lived war and when you live it, you grow to detest it. It inspires not love but hate.

Suddenly, as he tried to think of a way to avoid the oncoming sex, he had an epiphany: was Pearl Harbor the significance of Puerto de las Perlas? The Germans had known! They had known a lot of things that led up to this event, and they had played us all for fools. Of course it was that tiny Veracruz port. That was the key to the whole operation. But then why would a dimwit like Dionicio Torrecillas be walking around with the name of the Japanese military objective in the Pacific—the most closely guarded secret of the entire war—fresh on his lips?

INSENSITIVE REACTIONARY BUREAUCRATS

T hree days after the events at Pearl Harbor, on December 10, 1941, Cuba declared war on the Axis powers. It wouldn't have too much importance; it was more a symbolic act, a demonstration of the Cuban government's submission to the North Americans, proof of their acceptance of the imperialist spheres of influence.

Ernest Hemingway had suffered the same shock as the rest of the American public. Perhaps the writer didn't share in the fantastic rumors and paranoia that the sudden attack had loosed upon the population. He didn't check under his bed for Japanese soldiers, and he wasn't waiting on tenterhooks for Zeroes to appear over the Los Angeles suburbs. But he was quite angry indeed. At the end of a long letter to his publisher, he dropped in the following paragraph:

> The myth of our navy's invincibility has evaporated.
> Secretary of the Navy ought to have resigned 24 hrs. after
> the whole Oachu thing. They would have put those
> military bureaucrats in front of the firing squad. It was all
> to be expected, though, partly because I've seen the Japs in
> action in China but above all because I know how Fascism
> moves and thinks. This paragraph is private; for no reason
> whatsoever should you let these opinions be made public.

Strangely, the rage he felt against the U.S. military machine, against the politicians and magazine editors who had never thought to send him anywhere as a war correspondent, seemed to have Cubanized him in a way. As he fixed himself a coconut and gin and sat down to nurse it in the solitude of the most isolated part of the house, the pagoda furthest from the pool, his Cuban half went into action.

The war held no interest for the great majority of Cubans. It was a governmental decision that affected them—to use the old Spanish expression—about as much as the breezes. But the sizeable Spanish colony where the Falangists were active wasn't going to remain quiet for long. They had positions of power in Cuban society; they controlled the newspapers, they had self-contained ranches and money. How would the Germans go about exploiting this? Could the Japanese? He dismissed the idea of a yellow threat.

What would he do if he were in the Canaries? he thought, and then a twisted smile appeared on his lips.

They were going to use the Cuban cays, those hundred-some isolated islands, to assemble a pack of submarines with which to strike the merchant fleets and—more important—the Texas oil tankers that steamed between the Gulf of Mexico and the rest of the Caribbean. Now, what does a submarine need to stay at sea for an extended period of time . . . ? The German's wolf den, where would it be? In Kiel? Was there one somewhere in occupied France? In Brest? What does it take to make it from the North Atlantic to Cuba?

The Brits have suffered all these years. Some of my friends there ought to know something about submarines.

Taking it one step further, he said to himself as he contemplated the empty pool and his emptying coconut, the Germans had to have known about Pearl Harbor in advance. If this operation really existed somewhere out beyond the confines of his pounding head, it would have been months in the making. The submarine base existed. It was somewhere.

What would a submarine need thousands of miles from its base? Fuel. What type? And how much? Can they increase their storage capacities? Can it refuel in mid voyage if it links up with a tanker? It also must have water, nautical charts of the cays, food, quarters for the crew, and an isolated area where it can surface to purge and refill the air tanks.

But where? Somewhere in the house he had a nautical map of the waters around Cuba.

The pool, devoid of water, languid and sad, full of dry leaves and cat shit, seemed oddly like an auditorium. Mario appeared with a fresh coconut and gin. That was one of the things Hemingway liked best about Cuba: that the people there can read your thoughts. Maybe it had to do with the Santería culture. Or maybe it was just common sense.

Submarines, he said to himself later, at the height of his third coconut and gin. Now, those insensitive reactionary bureaucrats who determined the future of the United States were going to find out what life really was like.

BETWEEN BEETHOVEN
AND A FIRST FRUIT

Pioquinto Manterola waited patiently in line to reach the cashier's window so he could collect his Christmas bonus, despite the fact that many of his younger colleagues insisted on offering him their places. What did this bunch of rookies think, that he was some sort of wheelchair journalist? When he reached the window, the cashier handed him his envelope and asked him to count it, but Manterola simply stuffed the money in his wallet and headed back to his desk. He hadn't made it very far when he was accosted by one of the many grifters making his round of collections for the trousers bought on credit by some of the miserable journalists.

"I have something for you, Doctor Manterola."

The journalist had gotten used to cryptic messages of late, and he stopped. "Don't call me 'Doctor,' I'll get a cramp. I merely have the degrees that life has awarded me."

That phrase, heard by one of the editorial assistants, would later pass into the annals of Mexican journalistic lore, would be quoted by generations of ardently anti-academic journalists, and incorporated into *El Popular*'s own little mythology.

"I can get you a great deal on an RCA Victor gramophone, only 647 pesos. Matter of fact, I'll throw in nine LP records of Beethoven's nine symphonies for free."

Manterola had been thinking about saving up for a TV, but the idea of locking himself in his office and listening to all nine symphonies one after the other without coming up for air did seem rather appealing.

He was just about to sign the forms, agreeing to pay it off in small monthly installments over the course of the next year (wherever he might end up), when a secretary began to wave at him from the end of the hallway.

Manterola had made it his policy never to run through the halls and never to answer if someone called him by his given name, since who the hell would want to name a little future anarchist from Pachuca "Pioquinto"? Journalism may well be an art fashioned out of urgency, but he had his dignity as well. He walked calmly over to the lady.

"You have a call from the Minister of the Interior," she said.

"Christ, from the way you were waving, I thought it was important."

And so it was that he was first informed that Mexico had broken off diplomatic relations with the Axis powers and that, in accordance with the Treaty of Rio de Janeiro on Inter-American Solidarity, the attack on Pearl Harbor required this response. Gradually, over the past few weeks, they had served the Germans by officially dissolving the Nazi party in Mexico and by leaving the local ruffians without their operetta.

Manterola went into the office's main room and shut the door behind him, blotting out the sounds of frantic typing and talking. He began to lay out page one. But how would this affect his friend the Poet's hunt? What would the crazed Nazis his German friends and Doctor Sacal had told him about do without diplomatic protection? Were they dangerous? There were clearly other stories running underneath this one.

Just then, Revueltas burst in, desperately searching for tobacco.

"Hey, Pepe, how's that novel of yours coming along?"

ENTRY #2:

A DAIS AND A NOVEL

When he saw his torpedo planes strafing Pearl Harbor, Major Fuchida sent a coded message to the general staff of the Japanese Central Command that contained just one word: "Tiger." It was received by Marshall Sugiyama who, for his part, presented it along with the official report of the air attack to Emperor Hirohito two days later in a formal ceremony. The short and squat Hirohito, in full dress uniform, was standing on a raised dais when he received the message.

Using the typewriter ribbon Manterola loaned him, the novelist Pepe Revueltas, whose real name was José, wrote, on one of the manila sheets that circulated throughout the office, a few lines, more or less thus:

> The turkey vultures know all the secrets of the heart.
> Nevertheless there is always a bond of mutual vigilance
> and hatred between them and man. The vultures are at one
> end of the rope, and man is at the other.

He was some thirty lines from the end of the first draft of his novel.

And I tell you these things because sometimes it seems, when we tell our stories, that history is but a decorated stage; that those who dance in the back line neither live nor die, that they are incorporated merely as elements of color while we, the central players, the protagonists, are destined to move though anecdotes, surrounded by the charm and magic of the scenery. To say it another way, neither Japanese pilots nor emperors on their daises nor vultures nor novelists are part of the grand set design.

THE LONG MARCHES

You have to steer clear of habits, for habit is akin to suicide. You can't create niches or nests, bases or secret hideaways. Nothing is inaccessible. If you got there, then others can too. The best defense is unpredictability, ignorance, erratic behavior. When not even you know where you'll lay your head down to sleep, or whether it will be night or day.

But Tomás was not afraid to contradict this rule, because he loved caves. Tucked away inside his hill, covered by thick undergrowth and replete with water trickling down from some torrent that raged on high, his cave was a wonder of humidity and light that filtered in through natural skylights in the rock. It bore no signs of man or animal, and Tomás had escaped there twice previously as a last resort. Now, however, he had prepared himself to spend two days there, completely hidden and without food, as he had left a dead man hanging in the doorway of the old Kröll hacienda. The man was young, lean, and scarred by eczema, and he had sodomized several local Indian youths in recent months. It hadn't been too difficult for Tomás to snipe him on one of his nighttime raids, and now he was hanging from his wooden doorframe, looking out over the fields with a bullet in his head. The hanging hadn't had anything to do with his death; it was the shot that had done it, and Tomás had strung him up as a symbol, a sign, a mortal challenge set out in plain view like a collection of severed heads. Those who sow terror must also live with it.

And now he buried himself underground while armed posses of men on horseback crisscrossed the land, mad with anger but also with fear. An iguana is at home underground; he is like an ant or a mole in that way. And still he does not eat. To alleviate his boredom, he turns to sound: children's songs, burps, farts, and snorts.

Tomás was one of those Mexicans who could survive on very little food. He was proud of that fact, proud that time and want and poverty had tempered his body and that he could cinch up his stomach at will and sweep the nagging fury of hunger into a corner of his mind and keep it there, isolated, until the times changed. The Long March had done that to him. It had all started when he disembarked in Shanghai, in the country that had given birth to his ancestors, the country that had given him the color of his skin and his last name, and the one country of all the world where he felt the most alone among men. For a sailor, there is no port on earth where he feels completely alien; the global village that Tomás called home was all around him, made up of Chilean barques anchored alongside German sloops and whorehouses where Turkish stevedores, Spanish mechanics, and French cartographers broke bread and shared tables. But in China he felt completely alone, perhaps because he insisted on holding on to the illusion that he was Chinese when fundamentally he was not: he'd been born in Sinaloa and had grown to circle the globe many times over. He was a Mexican with a Chinaman's face. But in China he saw hunger and was afraid. Even for a country whose philosophy and culture were fed by hunger, where starving to death had become just another fatalistically observed accident, the war-induced famine he witnessed in Shanghai was terrible. Thousands of farmers had fled into the cities in search of sustenance only to die, huddled together on streetcorners. Without the will to go and take bread from those who had it. Defeated and despondent. Not even able to look the living in the eyes.

It was early autumn, 1934, and the hunger he saw all around him would soon penetrate his own flesh. Hunger became like a thought, barely dissipated by brief moments of clarity and violence, moments of victory and fear, moments of exhaustion. He had learned many things in China, but above all he had learned to live on the cusp of experience, on the frontier of the self, where actions are only barely produced by the last dregs of the will.

But all that would come later.

He joined the Red Army like so many other things in his life—by chance. A strike broken by gunfire; a game of gunrunning. A desperate escape; Chu Teh's rebel base. The siege by the White Army; the shock of seeing yourself caught in the whirlwind of a civil war where miserable peasants led by student-Communists fought against soldiers who were once miserable peasants themselves now led by the sons of official landowners. In Tomás' mind, the choice was obvious. He enlisted.

Army life was governed by strict rules, but not the sort of rules that Tomás had expected: screw the doors back on their hinges after using them as mattresses and return the straw used as bedding; return everything borrowed from the towns and pay fair price for what you kept, don't bathe in the presence of women, don't rifle through the pockets of prisoners, and always speak cordially.

Now, in the cave, Tomás recalled the sounds of the bugle, the Russian-made machine gun he had manned, and the interminable marches endured in a state of near unconsciousness where you're aware of little more than the fact that left follows right which follows left. He recalled the ever-present battles that were always welcomed, since fighting offered a brief respite from marching. And he recalled the hunger—all the hunger of the world. Unanimous hunger. And discovering strange communities of men with great leather coats and abundant women, and hunger, and the peasants with their conical hats who ate no rice, and hunger, and the moss that covered everything, and the hunger.

Three grains of maize and a pinch of salt to last two days. Less than half a fistful.

And Tomás discovered with a start that his memories wore a veil, a gray patina, a thin gauze of blue cotton. They seemed to be memories of a dream. Memories of death.

To pass the endless army days, he learned the names of many cantons, he learned Mandarin and a little English, and from the Captain of the Internationals (who was alternatively known as Li Teh and Otto Braun) he learned a few words of German. It sounded funny to say, but he always wished he had learned more German while in China. But more than languages, Tomás learned all there is to know about hunger. And now, in the cave, when he felt the walls of his stomach grinding against one another, he could not tell if this hunger was newborn or ancient. But he knew that he could live with it, just as he knew he could live with constant movement from place to place.

These recollections of hunger, coupled with the knowledge that only the irrational is logical, made him uncomfortable. The tranquility of the cave began to bother him. And to calm himself—to escape his memories and understanding—he began to sing his private army's favorite marching song out into the jungle and the night:

I might sleep in peace
If only I had known
Why the heavens permitted
The crime of being born;
What others were committed
In order to punish me?
Others were not born
Or if they were, it seems
That they knew all the privileges
That I'll never see.

THE THIRD INTERVIEW

The journalist crossed the same little patio he always did, but this time the child with the Spitfire was not there. Instead, there was a pair of teenage boys hanging wet laundry up on a clothesline and singing an old Ukrainian song. Manterola recognized it; he'd heard it years ago at a bar in Russia. He greeted them with a wave and received a "*shalom*" in response.

This time it was Egon Kisch who was waiting for him in the back room. He graciously offered the journalist a pinch of pipe tobacco as he walked in.

"We have more things to tell you, *amigo*," said the writer.

Manterola wondered to himself what all this meant. He never acted on the information they gave him, and they didn't ask him to. They weren't using him to manipulate the public's opinion. They just wanted him to know. Why would he tell anyone? Why?

The ancient rabbi wasn't in his usual seat. Just Ludwig Renn, who saluted him with a wave.

"I've taken on the role of translator."

Translator of what, Manterola wondered. But then he saw it. A woman was standing off in the opposite corner of the room, shrouded in shadow.

"Doctor Stern only speaks German, but I'll translate for you as accurately as I can."

The woman, who had been situated in the room's penumbra, unnoticed at first, came forward. She had great, wide eyes, and she wasn't as young as he had thought at first glance. But neither was she old. It was strange—she had a youthful face, but white hair. Moon-white hair.

"Have you ever seen a tank rolling through a city's streets?" The woman's tone was flat, completely without inflexion. Renn translated in the same manner, replicating the icy effect of her words. "It's a cruel machine, inhuman and rumbling. Signs of civilization seem to anger it; it plows through newspaper stands and beds of roses. It's no animal, it's blind steel, iron painted in greens and grays that tears through the whitewashed walls of cottages, its turret rotating to blow each picket fence to pieces, its caterpillar tracks crushing everything that has fallen. Its twin Gatling guns can be blazing simultaneously while every forty seconds it fires a 75mm shell. Fifty-two tons when fully loaded. Dogs go crazy from the thundering and often run themselves right under its treads. It's a rhinoceros with the hooked cross painted in gray, like a crossbones, on the turret, the flanks, and the fuel tank. It might seem like just one more of the absurdities of war that our humanity has sentenced us to, but it's different. Make no mistake about it; this is something different. The Nazis' tank is a golem out of control, a fantastic, monstrous piece of machinery. But it's just a piece—a cog—in a great and terrible scheme. There's nothing human about it."

Why were they telling him this? Was there more to it than war? The war was in Europe, it was distant, aloof . . . but that was just it; they wanted to erase that distance.

"But the tank is not the Nazis' real death machine," said Doctor Stern. "Neither is it the Stukas that sweep in on strafing runs over the cities, the whine of their engines a siren of death. No, the death machine is the train. . Innocent, third-class trains whose old cars were only just saved from the junkyards and put back into service. That is the Nazi death machine. Trains make their rigorously punctual rounds of the concentration camps, sharing the tracks with freight trains transporting howitzers. Trains full of people, sometimes three and four days late, with neither food nor water nor protection from the cold. Three percent of the 'passengers' are dead on arrival. Those are the statistics the Nazi machine offers: 3.2 percent during the winter months; much less in the summer."

"What are you talking about?"

"*Verstehen Sie?*" the woman answered.

"Understand?" Renn translated. Manterola didn't feel obligated to answer. They would tell him what they would, whether he understood or not. But Egon Erwin Kisch intervened, addressing the question.

"We know that it doesn't just have to do with the concentration camps.

We know that besides those who are shot, who suffocate or are crushed to death in the boxcars, who suffer for days without food and water . . . we know that it has to do with slave labor camps and death camps. That this is the final destination of European Jews in Hitler's eye."

"They take us to the camps in order to be done with us. They call it the 'Final Solution,' or 'Night and Fog,' " said Doctor Stern.

"Jews from all over Europe are transported to camps in Germany and Poland where they are systematically executed to the tune of a thousand per day. Men, elders, women, and children. Exterminated. Mowed down with gunfire, gassed in the bathhouses, and buried in mass graves."

"But haven't there been international envoys to inspect these camps? Is there no corresponding with the prisoners?"

"It's all a farce. They have an office with a group of prisoners who send out forged postcards. They've created an immense killing machine, and they only show it to whom they want. Silence quells what goes on behind the barbed wire. But the reality of the situation is that genocide is going on under the guise of military action. Genocide perpetrated against innocent civilians solely for the fact that they are Jewish."

"They think they can kill what, two million people?" asked Manterola in disbelief.

"Five, six, even seven million," responded the doctor, translated by Renn.

"And that figure doesn't even include the Communists, the Socialists, the gypsies, the syndicals, the liberals, the professors, the writers, or the queers," added Kisch.

"Do you have any proof of what you're asserting? It seems absurd to even the most demented logic. Rape them, plunder their towns, enslave them, use them as hostages . . . but genocide? In the name of what? God? Racial purity? What?"

"The good doctor herself is proof of its existence," said Renn. "She escaped."

Manterola looked anew at this woman. She met his eyes, and the journalist could see in her the profundity of the truth. The heavy history of barbarism. The infinite and indefinite dimension of horror.

NICOLAUS

All at once, the Poet, in his office on Bucareli Street, received the results of the three requests he'd filed at the University. The medical school's laboratory had confirmed that the samples taken from Lutz-Brüning's room were indeed the dried traces of human blood. (Brüning's? That of someone he wounded? A human sacrifice? Mother of God! This was not espionage; this was a poker game, but with a pile of shit instead of chips.) A letter from the department of philosophy and letters confirmed that the department of geography had no record of any town with a name at all similar to Puerto de las Perlas anywhere near Veracruz. So his Pearl Harbor theory must be correct. But how the hell were they getting Hawaiian fruit? What did Dionicio's orders have to do with the Japanese objective? And finally, the program in archaeology in the department of history reported that the symbols he had copied and sent were indeed Germanic runes. Further, they corresponded to four modern German words, and therefore couldn't be just a simple copy of an ancient text; in other words, they had used an ancient alphabet to spell out a message in modern German. The four words were, "*Die Tür wurde geoffnet*," which in Spanish meant "The door has been opened."

The Poet felt helpless, felt as if the world were a court and it was being called to "chaos" instead of "order."

Then it was clear.

Nicolaus.

Nicolaus would be trying to contact Krüger. It was improbable but, as Doctor Holmes would have said, it had to be the truth. Nicolaus no longer had the embassy's protection (indeed, the embassy didn't even exist anymore), and so Miguel Alemán's relationship with Krüger made her the only logical contact. The Poet smiled at the Germans' transparency. The problem was that the Poet couldn't count on anyone but himself to stake out that big, two-story house in the Colonia Roma where Alemán paid his lover's rent. There was always the risk that he'd be caught and they'd really bust his balls. But it couldn't hurt to ask his boss. . . .

And at that moment, his boss magically appeared in the doorway. His habit of popping up ever since the note had appeared in the paper was beginning to unnerve the Poet. He had never mentioned the matter, but here he was, between the two, like ice cubes separated in a tray.

"Where is this Nicolaus thing going to end? You say he's the head of the network, right?"

"If you give me two officers, sir, I'll have him within the week."

"I'd give you a dozen, but I'm not as much of an imbecile as you apparently are."

The Poet made a face as if the insult had flattered him. He decided that, in the pornographic novel he was writing (or neglecting to write), he would include a scene where the chief of the Secret Services was caught sucking a leper's cock.

His fingers clamped like a clothespin, he took a cigarette out of his jacket pocket, stuck it in his mouth, took a match out of his other pocket, and struck it on the sole of his boot.

He'd shadow Nicolaus on all of his daily routines. His trips to the bank (since the head of the network would need money regularly). Nicolaus would also need a place to sleep, and since several houses were recently made unavailable, as it were, that left Krüger's. To hell with the pair of officers. He'd go back to running his own show.

He scratched his head. Why so much dissatisfaction? Why this itch? This hunger? This bitter taste in the mouth? Because Nicolaus wasn't worth shit, that's why. He was on the other side of the street from Brüning and the other man mentioned in passing during the interrogation. Completely apart. And invisible.

Before giving instructions and heading to Krüger's house for a night of spying, he decided to stop off at the old house on Veracruz Avenue, the one he had followed Brüning to after the soccer game.

TO GROW AND GROW RICH

And what did you find?"

"The same. A room in a monastery. No papers, just the same runes painted on the wall in blood that read, 'The door has been opened.' "

The journalist dunked a biscuit in his coffee. It was his way of thinking while feigning a lack of interest. The Poet looked at him sharply, on the verge on indignation, but fortunately Manterola asked,

"And at Krüger's house?"

"Nothing yesterday. Not even that usual surprise visit from the boss."

"Have you ever seen him up close? Actually spoken with him? And I don't mean that time you ran into him at the house."

The Poet realized that he was talking about Miguel Alemán and not Brüning.

"No. In our office, the minister always keeps his distance."

The journalist chewed his biscuit in thought.

"It's a new thing in the government, something born of the Revolution. He's no general; he's a lawyer. The son of a general, yes, but with a law degree instead of an officer's rank. He's part of a new caste. A brief campaign, then the senator's office, then three years as governor of Veracruz. Without leaving so much as a fingerprint on the office. And now it seems as if he's teamed up with the president according to that damned pendulum theory: Cárdenas's government swung to the left—*damas* and *caballeros* and good consciences undisturbed—but now it must return to the right. I always thought that siding with the gringos was his idea, but that history soon turned and spun off to the Germans. The cabinet is always talking about a 'return to normalcy,' taking advantage of the war and with no intentions of returning the oil. A return to normalcy. Bah. On the one hand, Germany was (or seemed to be) safely pro-Cárdenas, supporting the Isthmus Socialist Party and other such things, but when Alemán became a lawyer for the Board of Conciliation in Mexico City, he defended workers and bosses alike. Lawyers who don't make such distinctions get on my nerves in the worst way. Along with Ramos Millán, he's a member of that giant real estate company, Development Mexico, which buys property and builds apartment complexes on the outskirts of the city. They began in Cuernavaca, then they bought the old Morales hacienda, and now they've made off with a piece of the Chapultepec jungle, the part they call Rincón del Bosque. If he were to see Nezahualcoyotl, the entire wooded homeland would be fucked. It's business, plain and simple, and I don't like it. Land is relegated to the realm of politics. Ávila Camacho himself even got land in Cuernavaca. If they can dictate the way the city expands, they can revalue their holdings in astronomical amounts. It's just a matter of putting the state at the service of big business. I get the feeling that they think the time has arrived for the Revolution to bring economic justice to the puppies of those who killed it off. Fucking pendulums."

The Poet knew pieces of this story, but he was oblivious to the gravity of the matter.

Manterola continued: "Don't you feel a new sort of reverberation in the air? During and perhaps because of this war? More than one man is sharpening his teeth; the biblical call has been heard by many: they're growing and growing rich. The government moves from the right to the servile right. It's all on the books, everyone with a relative has a contact, and the gears just keep on turning."

"And all this has something to do with the Germans?" asked the Poet.

"I can't prove it, but I'm willing to bet that when you investigate the minister's relationship with the Germans, you won't be able to miss his business dealings. And don't tell me you're not going to get involved; I know you better than that."

For a moment, no one said a thing. Dusk had fallen. Outside their little Chinese café on Donceles Street, a group of waiters who had gone out for bread came running, fleeing the rain. A schmaltzy song by Agustín Lara was blaring over the radio. Always Lara, it would seem. The journalist was first to muster speech.

"The country is full of rumors, of vagaries and clouds. It's all fucked up. Mexico, which used to have the bluest of skies, now looks like London. Lake Chapultepec has become more like an estuary of the Thames. The *sinarquistas* are spreading the rumor that conscripts are going to clash with the foreigners, and obligatory military service gives added weight to the rumor. A reciprocity signed by the Americans stated that nearly ten thousand Mexicans were drafted into the gringo's army, but not one American has enlisted in Mexico."

"It's for the better. They'd probably end up with chilblain and shoot themselves in the feet."

"However impossible they said it would be, Mexico is at war. But with whom? For what? In effect, the gringos already have everything they want— Mexican oil, raw materials, their asses are covered in Baja California, and we're at work tearing down the Nazi network before it spills over the border into their country. War for what?"

"For nothing. Nothing at all. It's war for war's sake," said the Poet, interrupting his friend's diatribe.

"Do you have any idea what condition the Mexican army is in?"

"I'd say it's generally fucked, but I suppose you'll tell me in more specific terms, eh?"

"We have forty-two thousand poorly trained soldiers, armed with muskets. Their artillery is obsolete. Their cavalry is nineteenth century, and though it's heavy, look what happened in Poland when their heavy cavalry went up against an armored tank division."

The Poet nodded. It did seem bad, but he wasn't overly concerned. As one who had ridden with Villa, he wasn't about to speak ill of the cavalry, at least no worse than the riders or the generals.

"There is no armor and no transports. The generals are all old, decrepit descendants of Obregón, drunk and potbellied. The navy is next to nonexistent. The quartermaster corps is a den of thieves. If the Japanese landed a beachhead in Baja California, they'd be knocking on the door of the capital within a week."

"And just why would the Japanese land in Baja California? How would they get there if their closest base is in New Guinea? And even if they did land in Baja California, wouldn't they rather march on up to Hollywood to see all those damned movie stars?"

The journalist laughed. There was no arguing with his friend's logic. Maybe he'd even use that argument in an article to quash the rumors circling about such an invasion.

The Poet hadn't eaten; he hadn't touched his *café con leche* nor made a dent in his sweet bread. Manterola was concerned; in their last few meetings, he hadn't seen his friend eat so much as a cracker. But he'd been a glutton his whole life. What was wrong?

"You don't give a fuck about the Japs, do you?"

"I will. Thanks to my German friends, I seem to have lost my mind."

"I hear that. The same thing happened to me; I stopped listening to my friends a while ago," said the journalist, and he began to bring his friend up to speed on his meetings with Uhse and Doctor Sacal and the white-haired woman and Ludwig Renn and Egon Kisch.

Halfway through the story the Poet, his eyes wide with shock, began frantically to take notes.

THEORETICAL SUBMARINES

Ernest Hemingway hadn't written a line of his novel in months, just a few rambling notes, but he had learned quite a bit about submarines and rumors.

In Cuba, the kingdom of truth was ruled by rumors. Truth was generally less rich, less colorful, than rumor. Rumors gave it substance; made the truth believable.

The facts—as opposed to the Cuban truths—were these: the Germans had submarines in the North Atlantic. U-boats of 740 tons, models 9B, 7C, and 9C, with a six-week operational window. It would take fixfteen days to reach Cuba from Lorient in occupied France, fifteen more to return, giving them twelve days of functionality in the zone in question. A mere twelve days; that is, unless they found a way to take on additional fuel and supplies.

There were rumored sightings off the North American and Cuban coasts, but aside from these tales of periscopes and German captains disembarking to buy fuel at isolated, rural gas stations, there was nothing concrete.

But on the other hand, Hemingway had identified the perfect place for situating a base: the cays to the north of Camagüey and Las Villas. It couldn't be in Pinar del Rio, off the Yucatán peninsula, where General Batista had ceded an air base and harbor installations to the Americans, since that zone was heavily patrolled by the U.S. Navy and Coast Guard. No, it had to be in the cays north of Camagüey, protected by virtue of their isolation but still not far from all the powerful rural landowners, many of them old Spanish nationals and Fascist sympathizers. Román Cay, Paredón Grande, Frances Cay. That was where to look.

He had recently had a few *mojitos* with a naval attaché from the U.S. who had warned him of the possibility that Franco had provided the Germans with a base in the Canary Islands, on the way to America. But Hemingway shook off the idea. Franco, the old vulture, would not be mixed up in that right now. Not yet. No, it would have to be in Cuba, and it would have to be a very limited operation.

The Camagüey cays. Obviously.

He was thinking like Admiral Dönitz, like Canaris. But only a writer could think like that and actually pull it off.

THE FOURTH INTERVIEW

What are you saying here? What does it mean?"

"They're ancient Germanic runes. But the spelling isn't correct; they're ancient characters that form words in modern German. And it's no coincidence. It reads 'The door has been opened.' "

"I already knew that. But what does it actually mean?"

"In the language of esotericism, it can mean only one thing . . . that a door—the door—has been opened into a new dimension. Physical or spiritual. Real or metaphorical. Where did you find this inscription?"

"It was written in blood on a bedroom wall of a Nazi I'm counterspying on," said the Poet.

Manterola, who had set up this meeting after much badgering from his friend, looked at the ceiling. This was the moment of revelation. Why was it that every time he ran into Valencia, their histories had to conflate? He, who didn't believe in anything, a skeptic even of the impossibility of organized thought, was on the verge of succumbing to fate, the mother of all science, in a chance meeting set up by the god of atheists and his godmother, the deity Destiny.

"Describe your man to me."

"He's around forty, has wild, curly, unkempt hair, like mine but without the gray. He's well dressed, average height but not very strong, with a beard, a sharp nose, and fine features."

"Could it be this man, plus ten years?"

The rabbi took out the photo of Otto Rahn in the Ornolac caverns. The well-worn antiproof of life or death.

The Poet peered at it, examining it carefully. He tried to dress the blurry spelunker in the guise of Brüning.

"It could be. But it's tough to be sure. It could also be me, before I lost my arm and with a little more than ten years tacked on."

DEATH AT THE RIVER

They found him as he was hiking through a stream to hide his tracks and began to fire on him from the hillocks. At that moment, they couldn't have known if this was the man who had been hunting them or if he was just a nameless *campesino*, which they wouldn't have minded killing either. But as they continued to press their advantage, they assumed with good reason that they were dealing with the same phantom guerrilla who had stolen into Finca la Estrella and burned a stockpile of arms, munitions, and copies of *Mein Kampf* in a work of tremendous arson. But he had committed the error of attacking in the waning hours of the night, and now the dawn had caught him in his retreat.

The Chinaman tried to take cover beneath a tree that had fallen across the river, casting its rotting bark into the current. But the longer he stayed put, the tighter the noose closed around him. Now there were only three or four, but more would soon be coming.

He jumped up and stood over the stones and the eddying water, thinking that this would be a cowardly way to die, not the least of reasons being the fact that his attackers weren't even in uniform. Just then he felt something impinge upon his back, and he pitched forward onto the jungle floor as if someone had checked him hard from behind. As he dragged himself toward a tree, his face was cut by flying flakes of stone as bullets ripped into the river rocks around him. He heard his pursuers shouting in triumph as they started down the hill to finish him off. He braced the butt of his Tokarev on a stump, using it like a tripod, took careful aim, and fired. The nearest of the three caught it in the hip and fell, tumbling down the slope. The other two dove for cover. Tomás brought his left hand up to his back, but there was no need to verify it: a burning sensation was beginning to spread down into his leg, and the water around him had taken on a surge of crimson. A new shot impacted near his feet. He was not well covered; it was only a matter of time before they made the killing shot. Tomás fired twice more but hit nothing, managing only to keep them at bay.

The last thing he noticed before losing consciousness was that it had suddenly grown very quiet.

He dreamed about toucans and parrots and cockatoos and about feathers falling like snow amid the crossfire.

Sometime later he opened his eyes and realized that his arm supporting the pistol had gone numb. The two Germans were cautiously sidestepping their way down the slope, using a line of *pirul* trees for cover as they made their way toward the riverbed. Tomás could see them clearly now. One was dressed in blue overalls and sprouted a tuft of very blond hair. He looked quite young; the other could well be his father. He decided, for what it was worth, that they were in fact father and son, and that they both were named Karl, or Carlos, like Marx or Carlos Martell. He had only one chance at this, he thought as he let them close in on him. He set his weapon to automatic. The elder man, now some twenty paces away, brought his rifle up to his shoulder and fired. The Chinaman felt the bullet pierce the flesh of his leg, tearing it to the side, away, toward nothingness. He gritted his teeth and fired a burst. The elder man caught it full in the chest and broke down, coming apart like a doll or like a shadow in the firelight. The younger man turned and ran. To clamber through the slippery mud he cast off his rifle and grabbed at one of the *pirul*'s lower branches. Tomás took aim and fired, and the young man's head erupted in a cloud of blood.

Tomás smiled and began to die. It wasn't such a bad way to go out after all, he thought, having won your last battle, awash in your own blood at the bank of a river at the absolute end of the earth. The parrots and cockatoos took to wing in silence, shedding feathers into a firefight whose echoing shots could no longer be heard. A firefight of feathers. And of silence.

A SHOT IN THE OTHER LEG

The Poet put on the wire-rimmed glasses he used to give the illusion of better sight and contemplated the night as if it were his kingdom. A vampire-poet. A wolf-poet. The pistol strapped to his leg was annoying him. The house in the Colonia Roma remained in near-total darkness. Just one little stain of light, probably from a bedside lamp in Hilda Krüger's bedroom. Huddled in a doorway across the street, he felt the icy assault of February's winds. He couldn't smoke. He sucked on an aniseed candy.

The worst thing about nocturnal stakeouts was the uncertainty. To think that he could occupy himself for an entire night replete with nothingness deeply disturbed him. He could be reading in his room without the wicked interruptions of the Aztec princess who, in the end, seemed to him little more than a horny character from one of his own pornographic novels. He could be writing. He could be dozing in the upper balcony of a theater.

A pair of cars passed each other several blocks down Alvaro Obregón Avenue. When the sounds of their engines had faded, he heard the muffled "tok-tok-tok" of approaching steps. High heels meant a woman, not a man. As she came nearer to the Poet's stakeout, she passed beneath a streetlight that illuminated her face and the Poet seized up with shock. It was the African woman, the beauty from Senegal whom he had met at his Aztec princess's party. What was she doing here? Visiting Krüger?

The woman paused, sniffed the air, and changed her direction, heading directly for the door where the agent-poet was hidden. The Poet stepped out to grab her arm and pull her into the shadows.

"What are you doing here?"

"Looking for you."

"How did you know where to find me?"

"I was having dinner nearby, and I suddenly got the feeling that you were out for a bit of nighttime hunting. I thought I'd better help you. Although . . ." The woman paused, trying to read his face amid the shadows of the doorway. "Although I see you're not after what I thought you were."

"And what is it that you do think?" whispered the Poet.

"You're just after a henchman. You don't need me for that. You're enough on your own here."

And with that, she kissed the Poet on the cheek, stepped out into the street, and continued on her way down past Krüger's house. She left a wisp of perfume lingering behind her; something tropical. Fermín broke out into a cold sweat. He could direct everything but the uncontrollable. He could confront everything but the metaphysical. It was absurd that poetry was the only realm that was denied him. He tried to recover the woman's face, to fix her image in his mind. How was she dressed? She'd been wearing a dark gabardine coat and something around her neck. A scarf? A shawl? And she had those brilliant eyes, set above the high cheekbones of her face. Supremely beautiful.

His mind was on these things when a new character appeared on the block, walking slowly, looking shiftily. Even under the streetlight, his face was still half-shadowed by his felt hat, but there could be no mistaking it. Nicolaus. I've got you now, you punk. The Poet drew his pistol, trying not to hitch the front sight on his underwear. He counted to ten, calculating the German's footsteps, and stepped out into the street.

"Freeze, Nicolaus. Hands up," he called with the gun cocked and steady. And he grinned, because he couldn't help but think that if their situations were reversed, Nicolaus would have to say, "Hand up" instead, which struck him as quite ridiculous indeed.

The chief of the Abwehr in Mexico stepped back and drew a pistol from his jacket pocket. They fired at nearly the same time. The German's gun sounded with a pop and a muzzle flash, and the shot winged the Poet's hat. Fermín's shot, however, sounded dry. Less thundering than he would have hoped but, in the end, it was much more effective. Nicolaus fell to the ground, clutching at his knee, blood streaming through his pantleg. The Poet approached him and took his pistol, a Lüger, brilliant in its blackness. He tucked it in his belt. Had he really been aiming for the knee? He took off his hat, holding it by the remaining piece of the brim, the other half singed and smoking. He looked up, hoping to see lights coming on in the neighboring houses. Nothing. It would seem as if people walking the streets at night and blasting away at each other was a common occurrence in this neighborhood. There was only the muted light coming from Hilda Krüger's bedroom window.

The German moaned softly.

"It's over, Nicolaus. Finished. *No más México*. You're going away for a long time, plenty of time to fuck with other people's hats, especially tyrolean hats, but you'll have to make the holes in them with your teeth from now on."

"I'm just a businessman; it's the others you should be worrying about. The madmen," said Nicolaus in perfect Spanish.

And then, by virtue of hate or of symmetry or of simple vile vengeance, the Poet fired a second round into the boss of the Wermacht Secret Service's other leg. Then he grabbed the German by the lapels of his jacket and, with a good deal of difficulty, dragged him half a block to the corner of Alvaro Obregón Avenue. He didn't want to have to explain why the shootout had taken place right outside Krüger's house. As far as he was concerned, that house didn't exist. Not yet.

He went to find a phone with which to call a squad car and an ambulance. While they were on their way, he searched the German thoroughly. He found nothing besides a worn copy of Hemingway's *Across the River and Into the Trees*, which he tucked into his pocket, and a well-stuffed wallet from which he took two hundred pesos so that he could go to Tardán the next day and buy himself a brand-new black wide-brimmed hat.

PART | VIII

THE END OF THE WORLD

PREFACE

An explanatory note on madness:

Madness is not much fun. And when you live in its company, it's even less so.

Each moment of madness manifests itself as a single impenetrable world. If something isn't social, then it's demented. First paradox: what you all call madness is really a perverted alphabet, a Tower of Babel designed to bring down the heavens, a series of poisoned messages.

Madness is the great constructor of the contrary. Along with the mechanisms we instinctively use to connect ourselves with others, madness uses communication to confound people and those around them. It is the great witch of supreme lies.

Madness is deception and dementia is solitude. Are we?

Each case of madness closes in on itself and constitutes a terrible spectacle for those who bear witness to it, if there are people in this world who can perceive it at all. Some eat earth, others cry silently and uncontrollably, others search for things in the landscape that no more exist there than they do in the most recondite corners of their minds. They're nothing but façades and mirages. The horrible truth isn't as visible; it's a man fighting against a demon, personal and (as they say on cashier's checks) nontransferable, a demon that defeats him bit by bit and day by day. Madness can be clear, happy, exotic, innocent, bloody, or terrible like tidal waves devouring everything in their path, full of pain and spouting violence.

And these demons can, at times, be contagious.

Madness is hell.

I know, because I have lived both with it and within it. With myself and with others.

One holds on tight to confirm himself in the opinions of others, tries to live his own, intelligent life. But what happens when these others reflect new deformities like a mirror? Reason does not always permit you to be like the others, to understand the others, to see yourself in their eyes. You emerge from the mist. From the nothingness. And nothingness in a thick nighttime sea, where memory is of no help. Who was I yesterday? What was I doing? What did I call myself? Why am I so captivated by the humidity stains on the washroom walls, trying to extract meaning from them? What do I fear? The horror of panic brought on by fear? I try to swim. My mind swims, elegant and graceful, through the mist. And you have to cling to your will to float, because although you hurt, it is this pain that prevents abandonment, prevents you from letting yourself drift into the depths, staves off the temptation to fail, the permission to concede and sink into the chaos of free associations, manias, obsessions, and freedom.

Clarity is a prison replete with rules, regulations, and sacrifices. With pain. But killing the monsters does halt the descent into hell.

Clarity is the antithesis of liberty, but it is failure even more. Calderón de la Barca was wrong even in his immense genius. I recite here, for the simple pleasures of evoking the verse's sounds:

> I might sleep in peace
> If only I had known
> Why the heavens permitted
> The crime of being born
> What others were committed
> In order to punish me?
> Others were not born
> Or if they were, it seems
> That they knew all the privileges
> That I'll never see.

The dreamer Calderón and his innocent god. There was no malignant election. Calderón's god has nothing to do with any of this. Madness is human, it's a personal choice one makes when faced with the inability to live with oneself, it is earthly, it is infernal.

Clarity is the only paradise.

Alberto Verdugo, Esq. Summer 1941–42

A NOVEL

Proposed title: "The Sexual Adventures of a Mexican Politician."

And the subtitle, in lowercase letters, just for the purpose of stating the names, to read: "A work in which, for the first and only time, León Vaspatrás and Doctor Leandro Voyivengo meet each other."

Cover: in the foreground, a fortyish lawyer with a youthful countenance stands in front of a green Oldsmobile, smoking, unaware of what's about to happen. Behind him, in the background, a man in a chauffeur's uniform with his pants down is pleasuring an elegant woman with her skirt hiked up and her lilac-colored panties down around her knees.

Summary: the dirty world of high Mexican police officials revealed. Private bordellos in the Colonia San Rafael, where Oriental graces are performed. Wives being delightfully fondled by their handsome chauffeurs who were armed farmers in our past Revolution. Murky business deals in white slavery. Persecutions of innocent servants and priests who were once agrarian reformers. The power of money with regard to the sodomizing of adolescents. The descent into sexual hell. Desperate farmers forming never-ending bureaucratic lines outside the waiting rooms of the Office of Agrarian Reform, in whose bathrooms embarrassing comparisons of cock length are held. The vices of Onan and the masturbation competitions in the magnificent offices of the highest politicians. The switching and sharing of lovers and spouses. Jealousy, envy, and being limited by the size of one's testicles. The mysterious results of an orchitis epidemic. The secret archive of Doctor Fernández Tomás, an expert in the treatment of venereal diseases. All this and more.

Advance payable to the author: two thousand pesos.

INTERRUPTIONS
AND INVASIONS

6. At what exact moment did Hitler say, "Mexico ought to become more German . . . Mexico is a country that needs to be governed by competent men, but with its current system, it finds itself on the verge of meltdown. Germany would be great and powerful if it possessed Mexico's natural resources. Why do we not dedicate ourselves to this task?"

Should we treat it as private discourse or a public statement? Was it said during a meeting with his closest circle of advisors?

But whatever the context, those are his words, he said them, he conceived of them, he believed in them.

And what a depressing honor it is to find ourselves part of the grand design and objectives of the Third Reich!

7. Pioquinto Manterola has decided to cease being Mark Twain. Now he wants to be Jewish. It's not a religious issue; he wants to be Jewish but to go on being an atheist as well. He also wants to be a Negro. A frustrated, suicidal journalist from Pachuca wanted his second opportunity on earth to be as a Negro Jew. And upon being reborn as such he would call himself Solomon Manterola Shamba. "S. Manterola S.," he'd sign his articles. It was his first wholly transcendental decision, made here, on the cusp of his sixtieth birthday, while listening to Kleber's direction of the Berlin Symphony

performing Beethoven's Third. In the grandeur of the human spirit, he feels he has to do something to counteract Nazi barbarism, and thus the decision to add one more Jew against their plan to wipe them from the face of the earth.

If Ludwig Renn and Egon Erwin Kisch and Bodo Uhse had been there at the time, in that little rooftop room just before dawn, overwhelmed by the music that had been created by the genius of that old deaf man who has been listened to more than any other man in history, they would have observed that this recording of the Berlin Symphony had been done before the orchestra was purged and half of its members expelled, deported, incarcerated, or shot. An orchestra whose greatest musicians today are forced to live in exile or play in a concentration camp for the crime of being Jewish and, for some of them, the double whammy of being a Communist besides.

Without knowing it, Pioquinto Manterola has selected just the right music for making his decision.

8. Hemingway takes his notes on submarines on his portable Underwood typewriter that stands on a bookcase in his bedroom. The machine rests on a thick book to raise it up to just the right height. Hemingway always writes standing up, usually in a T-shirt and shorts. This is generally thought of as being a private act, something like shitting or masturbating. Writing is perhaps one of the most intimate acts that exist. And he probably writes standing up at his typewriter simply because tables and chairs annoy him. Or did he suffer from piles, like Marx and Saint Thomas Aquinas once did?

9. The Poet stows the royalties from his pornographic novels under the thin mattress that covered his day bed. He's been thinking of donating this money to a doctor who works treating lepers at a hospital in Africa, or perhaps using it to commission a grand statue of Pancho Villa on horseback for Parral. But the wounds of *Villismo* still fester in Mexico, and the war makes it difficult to get financial support to a leper colony in Africa. War kills faster than leprosy, and it disrupts the flow of men and money, and so he's also been thinking of using the money for personal enjoyment. But he has no ideas of what to do or where to go, and he's never learned how to play chess. What's more, thanks to his *sui generis* ethics, he feels that it's money that doesn't truly belong to him. From time to time he counts this loot, if for no other reason than to assure himself that his Aztec princess hasn't found his stash. Yesterday he had to count it by candlelight because his lover and landlord had cut off his electricity, arguing that he always comes home so late that it isn't worth the effort to light up the room at night. All told, the money hidden in his mattress is six times his annual

salary as an intelligence agent. In other words, he'll be able to finance a six-year espionage operation, paying his own salary—as his own boss—if they happen to fire him.

9a. Nicolaus is drinking a cup of chicken broth in the Miguel Schultz jail, awaiting his deportation. The Poet has tried on numerous occasions to interview him, but the chief of the German Secret Services has no intention of talking to "that damned one-armed midget who filled my legs up with lead," and he shuts up like a trap whenever the Poet enters the prison.

10. During the war in Spain, Hemingway acquired a tic that appears whenever he brings a pair of field glasses up to his face or goes to light a cigar. The Pacos, Franco's North African snipers who fought in Tercio during the siege of Madrid and in the trenches near the University and the Casa de Campo, would fire on the slightest of whims, at the glint of the sun on a lens or the flame of a match in the night. It's from this buried memory, this learned reaction, that Hemingway takes his nervousness. With the tic comes a dryness in the mouth and a raspiness in the throat. In the end, when he would wear his binoculars around his neck, this dry rasp became chronic. He thinks that this is one of the reasons he came to drink as much as he does.

11. We are organizing a festival for Epiphany. The pudgy little woman in the white cap insists on putting little wooden dolls into the large, donut-shaped cakes. Casavieja refuses to eat; he's convinced that we're going to swallow the figurines unwittingly and never know who's won. Herschel declines to help in the trimming of the Christmas tree, and does not know how to sing *olerulis and olerilis* and the Austrian songs sung by men in tyrolean hats that echo throughout the snow-capped mountains. On the other hand, Erasto the Mute has painted his face as well as his more noble parts black in order to look like Balthazar, the only king of any interest around here, the Negro King. The festivities attract some friends of Argüelles and Casavieja, who show up profoundly drunk and reeking of alcohol. They give off fumes like body heat on a cool August afternoon. Nearly all of them are zombies from Jalisco, Sahuayo, Zapotlán, and Sayula, where raw pulque is distilled. We are surrounded by these human heaters, these man-shaped chimneys that sweat vapors and stinking clouds of ethyl.

I write, and that is my gift. De la Calle insists on learning stenography, the secretary's art of speed writing. He'd like to teach me someday because to him, velocity is everything. He says that his novel on monkeys' sons (or some such thing) that he's coauthoring with his British friend Edgar Rice Burroughs would be going better if he knew stenography.

Still, I decide not to go into action. Reflection, rather, has come to please me more. To see from afar, to have the ability to alter reality. Which reality you ask? Ah, how easy it is to play God!

12. The war rages on there in the distance. The Ajusco mountains that border Mexico City to the south prevent us from seeing it. The radio reports it, mixing the roar of the tanks with the songs of the Los Pachos trio. The Stafford Crips mission, Bialystock's bag, the Inugi battleship, the Dauntless planes, General Eremenko. The war that's reported is a creation of neologisms, of ephemeral characters, unusual geography; like the sickly sweet songs of the *corridos*. But it is somehow not concentrated in these banalities. Its ominous shadow persists, buried beneath the radiophonic trivialities.

We Mexicans respect this war, which is a strange attitude to take. We will not enter from the front because we were too busy making our own Revolution that cost us a million lives. It seems that, because we can perceive this war with our slew of information, we have become spectators, spectators with the ability to equate it with stupidity. After Pearl Harbor, to be an Asian child in the Federal District has become a nightmare.

Where will Tomás go?

There is no doubt that a killing machine has been set in motion, one that will make previous machines pale in comparison. We try not to see the horror, so that the game may remain.

3

FUNERALS FOR EL IGUANA

It was the children who did nearly all the work. From their hiding places inside a tin boat and in the hollowed-out trunk of a tree they took armadillo bones, snake fangs, and even a tooth from an old jaguar who had come here to die many years ago. They put together papaya and mamay seeds, old rock-hard limes that looked almost petrified, a little mound of coffee beans, pages from a hydrology field manual they had found in a satchel abandoned along a trail, a pound of silver, and a photograph of Emiliano Zapata's drunk, ill-at-ease brother Eufemio, who dropped it while on his way to visit his mistress in Oaxaca. They loaded all of this onto a makeshift altar to the dead, along with a gold-painted iguana. They sat in front of the altar for several days, always at dusk, and they repeated the stories told to them by their elders, as well as stories of their own invention.

That was all cult and symbol and ritual, but soon thereafter they went into action. They stole four cans of paint from the Hacienda Lubecka and with them they painted stylized, six-legged golden iguanas on every available surface: on the trunks of trees, the doors of houses, on the whitewashed walls of company stores, on the stone and wood fences and on telegraph poles. Their golden iguanas reached even to the rocking-and-rolling cantinas near the port of Tapachula, the bathrooms of its bordellos, and the sides of its tractor trailers. Within a month, better than half of all of Soconusco had been decorated. Between the conscious perpetrators and their unknowing imitators, they filled the earth with their little golden iguanas. Soon, red and green varieties began to appear, provoking claims of heresy. These new iguanas often had exaggerated teeth shaped like a Saracen's sword and those that were painted by more skilled hands often sported a pistol in a low-slung holster.

A drunk once said that a new brand of beer was trying to make a name for itself, while his partner in wine tried to convince him that it all had to do with the war, that it was a Japanese symbol, meaning that the damned yellow threat was going to invade there, near Chiapas. And yet a third man, one-eyed, older, and more sober, interpreted it as a sign that class war was returning to Mexico.

4

TO RUIN AN ARMCHAIR

The Poet collapsed in his favorite seat back at the Aztec princess's apartment, propping his muddy boots up on the cobalt-blue satin and making a general mess of the upholstery. He took out the first of three folders he had brought from the office: official records of the investigations conducted by the Minister of the Interior. Official, that is, save for the fact that Fermín had neglected to request permission from anyone before taking them. New directions in his life.

One was labeled "Veracruz," the second read "Chiapas," and the third was "Immigrants." All three were thick and bound with twine.

When you search for something, you do so in an erratic manner. There's no science of detection; there's only intuition, the bells that go off when you come across the odd fact. In "Veracruz," the Poet searched for traces of Nicolaus's network over the past few months. He also scanned for references to fruit, bottled water, car batteries, and bits and pieces of rumors that might somehow fit together. "Chiapas," on the other hand, was unfamiliar territory. He had promised Múgica that he'd keep an eye out for stories of Nazis harassing Soconusco communities, but had left that promise in the drawer of forgetfulness, his priorities dominated by the malignant network of Brüning and Nicolaus. In "Immigrants" he looked for evidence of the second German, the man with the ash-blond hair whom Müller and the bald Austrian had mentioned during their interrogations: the aide to Brüning-Linz-mythical-Otto Rahn. He also kept an eye out for second-hand Austrian passports dated before the annexation of Austria had occurred. The Germans had, in terms of espionage, all the power in the world, all the necessary rigor when it came to mounting an operation, but Nazism was still a bureaucratic ritual.

He took advantage of the fact that he was alone in the house to raid the pantry, coming away with a half a case of beer. He started quaffing the beer down, smoking, and spilling all over the armchair that was beginning to look more like a dishrag. Such sweet vengeance against his landlord.

If "Veracruz" and "Immigrants" didn't proffer more than a few cold crumbs, then "Chiapas" left him astonished. It was rife with alarming reports of abuses committed against communities by "those of the hooked cross." There were all manner of rumors, however credible: rumors of a armed and uniformed group who had killed a farmhand, rumors of a woman hung from a tree with her guts torn out, rumors of Germans marching in torch-lit parades like he'd seen on television (the SS? Brownshirts? Didn't all those disappear in the thirties?). Nazis in the coffee-growing region of Soconusco? And the worst was that the employees of the minister in Chiapas often began their reports with a dismissive "apparently false rumors" that tainted even the most plausible of cases with doubt. The Soconusco region was the base of operations for a Nazi faction, probably made up of German immigrants or second-generation German-Mexicans. And then there was the story of La Iguana, a hunter of Nazis who, if one was to believe the report issued by the Mayor of Tapachula, was a secret service agent from the same office as the Poet. So what the hell am I supposed to think, he asked himself. According to some reports there are no Nazis, but according to others, this guy is going around killing them? Copies of drawings of the six-legged golden iguana were also in the folder. What kind of iguana carries a pistol with a stock like those Russian models, the Makarov or the Tokarev? Did the Soviets have an anti-Nazi agent operating in Chiapas? He tore the drawing out of the folder, thinking he'd hang it over his bed.

What was really happening here? The information he had was vague and diffuse at best, on account of the region's isolation and the vast distance separating it from the capital. What was he to make of the communiqués from the governor of Tuxtla, the reports typed out by a semiliterate office worker from San Cristobal de las Casas, or the other vague rumors that linked Nazi activity to the coffee-growing region of Soconusco? Did it have something to do with Brüning's operation and with Veracruz?

"Veracruz" didn't prove very useful to him. The only meaty scrap was the report of a meeting between Dionicio and his fruit spies with a group of suspected Falangist Spaniards who worked in the construction industry.

What would a collusion of that sort do? Build a fruit stand that also sold bottled water and car batteries? He made a note on a scrap of paper to ask his prisoners about it in the morning, and stuck it in his boot.

In "Immigrants" he found a record of sixteen Austrians who had entered Mexico in the past few months. Besides Brüning, there were two other men whom he knew and detested like a plague. They had both disembarked at Veracruz. One of them, a worthy seaman named Kowalski, was, from what he could tell of his photo (a shitty one at that, full of staples, since they always saved the best treatment for the immigrant's papers and the absolute worst for everything else), anywhere from thirty-five to sixty-five years old. But even through the blurred image he could see his clear, cold eyes and light gray hair. Was he albino? Was this the man aiding Brüning? The other character who caught his attention was an elegant doctor named Salomón Leonard Herschel. He didn't seem to have anything in common with the near-albino man (this being the only trait he could count on to identify Brüning's cohort). In fact, this Herschel, who was allegedly on his way to Monterrey to work in a private hospital by the name of El Reforma, was very tall, with dark hair encircling a prominent bald spot, and wearing scholarly looking glasses that lit up a look of awe in his eyes. Whether it was from surprise or fear, the Poet could not tell.

But what linked them? And then, I'm a genius, the agent-poet (or was that redundant?) thought to himself, for it was then, halfway through his sixth beer, that he had found a common denominator between the Austrian passports. All three characters, Brüning included, had been born on April 20th—albeit in different years—and all had been born in either Vienna or Linz, or Budapest when it had been part of the Austro-Hungarian empire. But the same day, the exact same day of the exact same month. A coincidence? Son of a bitch! Coincidences are the results of study.

The Poet fumbled for the phone and dialed the number for *El Popular*. He asked for Manterola and when he got him on the line he veritably leapt out of the ruined armchair.

"Guess what sons of bitches were all born on April 20th?"

"Um, I don't know. Miguel de Cervantes was though, right?"

The Poet hung up, exasperated. What would Cervantes have to do with Nazis? His friend wasn't always the best counsel.

Herschel was heading for Monterrey, and Brüning was off and running somewhere in Mexico, perhaps with a new cast of characters. And Kowalski? The documents from the Office of Emmigration had a record of him leaving on board a fishing vessel bound for Havana.

Fermín wrote out a pair of telegrams which he would send from the office that afternoon. One was addressed to the Nuevo León Department of Public Security, asking them to discreetly check on the status of one Salomón Leonard Herschel in Monterrey. The other he addressed to the Veracruz Immigration Department, ordering an immediate arrest of Kowalski if and when he returned from Cuba.

But to whom could he send a telegram to check on Brüning? He took off his boots as he pondered, alternating heel pushes and toe tugs. A one-armed man has to be well-versed in such skills. His socks were frayed and dirty. Where could Brüning be?

If you ask bad questions, you'll get bad answers, he thought. It didn't matter where he was, but rather what he was doing there. What door had been opened, and where did it lead? It was obvious that Krüger was taking advantage of her relationship with the minister. But was Alemán getting something from the Nazis? He contemplated the drawing of the pistol-packing golden iguana. Chiapas? Veracruz? Mexico City? He'd better get moving, hadn't he?

5

INTERRUPTIONS

AND INVASIONS

1. Hitler's birthday is April 20th.

2. He was born at six-thirty in the morning at Braunau del Inn in Austria in 1889, according to the first page of the report issued by the British Special Branch. This team, made up of writers, former childhood friends of Hitler, anti-Fascist astrologers like Ludwig Leon Wohl, better known by his pen-name Lois de Wohl, library rats, and tabloid journalists who earn the same salary as a first lieutenant in the Royal Air Force, is conducting top secret investigations into delerium tremens, commonly known as senile delerium.

3. Why does this report, dated just a few months ago, languish in the office of an obscure Spanish-Mexican alienist like Emilio Casavieja y Rodarte, left just so, on a chair, so that whoever comes in for a *café con leche* might chance upon it? Who sent it from London? The answer is that I decline to ask. I turn a blind eye to the strange papers that have come to dominate the office.

4. The report concentrates on Hitler's purported Jewish heritage. It opens with a little scandal that came up a decade ago when a group of reporters for the British *Daily Mirror* found a tombstone bearing the name Adolf Hitler marking the ninth grave in the eighteenth row of the Jewish cemetery in Bucharest. According to the archives, the man had been buried thanks to the generosity of the Jewish group "Philanthrope." This claim is not worth much; first, the fact that a Jewish society buried our homonymous

man in a Jewish cemetery does not necessarily make him Jewish, and sec-
ondly because his recorded age makes him five years older than Alois, the
sinister customs officer who was Hitler's father. There is no official register
of such a clan. Other sources situate the Hitler surname among the Jews of
Sosnowiec in Poland, but neither can this theory be attributed to anything
more than coincidence.

Much more plausible is the speculation that Hitler's paternal grand-
mother, Maria Anna Schicklgruber, while serving as a cook in the home of
a Graz Jew named Frankenberger, who worked in the wine industry, became
pregnant and went to her hometown to give birth to Alois. We're talking
around 1837. It's believed that the father could be either this Frankenberger
or his nineteen-year-old son. Maria Anna declined to ever reveal the father's
identity, and Alois Hitler's birth certificate lists him as the son of a single
parent. This history has not been confirmed to the satisfaction of the British,
but there are interesting hints that Nazi leaders, including Hitler's own legal
advisor, have been sticking their noses into the matter for the past ten years,
perhaps at Hitler's own request, perhaps to cover it up, or perhaps even to
have it for use as blackmail. There are also rumors that Alois received childhood support from a Frankenberger until his fourteenth birthday, but there
are unfortunately no records of such a person having lived in Graz, of there
having been a winery, or of Maria Anna ever having worked there. Alois,
Adolf's father, could just as easily be the son of a wealthy farmer, Nepomuk
Heuttler, or his brother Georg, with the surname gradually evolving into
Hitler in the county register.

Regarding this latter case it's worth it to note that in the Jewish tradition
ethnicity is transmitted through the maternal side of the family and not the
paternal side as in our patriarchal cultures (that's if there is something besides gonorrhea, delusions of grandeur, and castles in Spain that are transmitted). The interesting thing, stress the British, is not whether this history
is true, but rather whether Hitler believed it to be true. If he believed himself to be the bastard grandchild of a Jew who couldn't even recognize his
own father, then this belief could easily have culminated in a delirium that
gave birth to his official policy of anti-Semitism. Oh, for purity of blood!
Nonsense.

These readings compel me to revisit the Marxism that I never truly read
in the first place. It's all an economic conspiracy designed to disenfranchise
the middle class in order to finance the new imperialism draped in ideolog-
ical paraphernalia. Raw flesh for the carnivorous multitudes. The problem
rests in both the hide of the wolf and in the wolf itself. At what moment
did the Nazis begin to believe in their own deliriums?

5. Among Casavieja's papers, I read some notes that Anna Freud sent

him during her father's last days in Vienna. There is one anecdote in particular that stands out. On one Anschluss evening, some Fascist hoodlums
were forcing an elderly Jewish woman to lick the street. Two or three little
bourgeois passersby stopped to look and then applauded. The essence of the
horror here lies not in the aggressors but in the observers who rejoiced in
the humiliation of another human being.

6. What am I to make, then, of this limited report from the British
intelligence services on Casavieja's desk? Since when did he have a rapport
with Freud's daughter?

7. I used to correspond frequently with the Hungarian journalist and
novelist. I presume it was recently, though I admit my memory here is rather
nebulous. Arthur Koestler was my assignment: a photograph, a few signa-
tures at the bottom of typewritten notes, all part of a campaign asking for
his liberation from Franco's jails that resulted in a report from a group of
international lawyers. Was it thus, or did I merely read a few of his articles
and listen to someone tell me his story? If we do not know ourselves, then
why, after his exile in London, did I receive (and who sent it to me if I
haven't so much as seen a mailman in years? What are mailmen like these
days? Do they still wear those cute, jaunty caps?) a clear yet strange case
study on Kazaros, the town in Eastern Europe where the Jews—the eastern
European Jews—originated? In this study it says that Jews did not descend
from the tribes of the Palestinian desert, but rather in the Caucasus region.
They converted to Judaism in the eighth century and then made a mass
exodus from Eastern Europe some two centuries later.

This much is certain: that the Fascist anti-Semitism not only sustains
itself with cowardice and fundamental barbarism but also with the fallacy
that Jews are not an Aryan race. The Kazaros people of Caucass were Aryan.
To go on existing, Aryanism would have to reconcile itself with the fact that
one of its constituent parts is Jewish.

Erasto the Mute has a friend whom I have never managed to see, though
apparently he comes around to pass out papers. Normally they are simple
recipes or headlines copied out of the newspapers, while at other times they
are mathematical equations. A short while ago he brought me one that says,
in spidery handwriting, "Even if one goes back to the original nomadic tribes
and descends the length of the human scale, it is mathematically impossible
to find a single, racially pure man. We are all *mestizos*. Don't be an asshole."
He signed it, "Professor Estragón."

8. In the enormous garden the evergreens, fed by the cold, have lifted
their scent. Wind gives them their rhythm. The last thing left surviving from
this obsession.

9. The festival for Epiphany was a disaster. We ran it by the letter of the law, *de rigueur*, surrounded by experts on Casavieja's friends' alcoholic tendencies. One of them, a hopeless case, stole a liter of wood alcohol from who knows where and, in the deep hours of the night, secretly drank himself to death. It was an agonizing death, full of vomited blood and screams clamoring for a mother who was not there. I was curious to see the dead man's face. There was not a hint of placidity on it. De la Calle sketched out his portrait. Erasto placed a pair of horns at his temples just as the mortician was snapping his photo.

10. De la Calle enters our room and loudly asks me, or himself, or nobody at all, "Did Hitler not ban astrology after 1933? Yes, man, there is a law on the books drafted by the Chancellor himself that prohibits tarot cards, dream interpretation (including Freud's canon of theories), and chiromancy or palm-reading. He stopped just short of banning the lottery and horse racing. But why ban it if he himself was a true follower? Why mask it with reason, and the State's reason at that?"

He asks all these questions in a loud voice to provoke (or at least convince himself he's provoking) Herschel, who is stretched out on his cot completely silent, his eyes glassy and fixed on the ceiling.

"Horoscopes can go fuck themselves. Astral cards, the confluence of Venus with Mars, the hour of your birth, and the place Neptune occupies in the firmament? Har, har."

He dances through our room in a T-shirt and boxer shorts. I take it as an act of sociability, of amiability toward us. I down a glass of water in a single gulp. Herschel does not hear him, that much is clear. And even if he did, he doesn't speak a word of Spanish. He hasn't just buried himself within us, but within himself as well. He is not here; he is nowhere.

"Saturn's rings, the filthy canals on Mars full of garbage, the ellipse and Mercury's heliocoidal orbit. Trivialities and scarecrows. As you well know, even if you don't admit it, it's crap."

Herschel seems calm in his reticence. He spends several more days with nary a word. He withdraws into himself as a result of a few words he hears me say to Erasto, whom I sometimes use as a confessor on account of his muteness (since he can't answer questions that need no answers). I tell him about Hitler's birthday and about his alleged Jewish heritage, and Herschel begins to tremble uncontrollably. He lapses into a hysterical crisis of babbling and screaming that alternates with a state of calm introspection like the current one. Does he speak Spanish? With Erasto, I obviously don't speak any German.

"Zodiac cards my ass," says De la Calle triumphantly. "If Hitler were the only lout on earth who still believed in them, why would he ban them?"

A voice from the cot—though it could well have been from beyond the grave—answers in a guttural and clipped Spanish:

"He banned them in order to hide their sources, to bury their wisdom. In order to take the charlatans off the shelves and leave us to ourselves in the shadows of his power. He banned astrology in order to protect his seers from the masses. But not everyone saw it that way."

Amazed, I contemplate this Austrian who, in his days of auto-isolation, has grown a monstrous-looking beard, as have I. I recite his freshly spoken sentences, his strange confession, in my mind. He still has not come out of his immobile state, his erratic gaze, but there is a certain peacefulness in his hoarse voice. He seems, somehow, a different man.

"You see? I fucking told you! It's Hanussen! It's dead fucking Hanussen!" Angel de la Calle cheered even more triumphantly this time. . . .

6

THE M.A. (LOWERCASE) DOSSIER

I want to begin by saying that the notes collected herein assimilate risk with pleasure. I have taken them down as such so that they may remain constant in the case that life takes a sudden turn or twist, or I become warped myself.

Before the disappearance of B., I concentrated on the visible things—Minister Miguel Alemán, to be precise—though as discreetly as possible.

I myself have never managed to achieve such a level of invisibility. But I did put all my knowledge and resources toward obtaining this information unnoticed. Here is a sampling of what I found:

The minister is only forty-four years old, and his career with the financial company has been relatively short. His real estate dealings in Mexico City blow to stern. An informant tells me that these are not the cleanest of deals, but that he cannot be directly linked to anything but the straight and narrow. My informant also tells me that they have thus far earned millions, and that they expect to earn even more in the future. The latest acquisitions are some scruffy plains to the northwest of the city that aren't worth much now, notwithstanding the fact that a road to Querétaro will soon be running through the region, causing the city to expand in that direction. They're using a term borrowed from the Americans, calling it a "satellite city."

They have also initiated an orange grove buying operation in Veracruz (again it's Veracruz, and therefore Puerto de las Perlas . . . ?) in a region through which a federal highway will soon run.

They have many deceitful middlemen, but the Angulo brothers, whose offices are in the National Lottery building, stand out among them.

There is also a mysterious bank account that connects the minister with the Germans. Called the "reptile fund," this accounts is set up in the Bank of London and Mexico. I have not been able to determine the account number or in whose name it is listed.

Miguel Alemán has offered the German businessmen protection. Protection consisting of what? I do not know. What did it cost in exchange? That I do not know either. Is there something else that has been worked out? Again, I simply do not know.

FROM THE DIARY OF
LÁZARO CÁRDENAS, FORMER
PRESIDENT OF THE REPUBLIC

End of April, 1942

In port, reorganizing the Pacific military installations.

I have just received a long, confidential telegram from the journalist Pioquinto Manterola. The story he tells is quite disconcerting, and the depth of the charges he asserts goes beyond what I would have thought possible. We do not know how these Nazi interests became involved in Mexico. Several functionaries of the current government are also implicated, one beyond a shadow of a doubt. In my response to him, I suggested he speak with Múgica.

AMONG THE STATUES

What do you know, General, about the real estate speculation being done by our current Minister of the Interior?"

"I can assume your paper is going to be reporting on this matter, Señor Manterola?" the general responded with a question.

"I don't know yet."

"Then to what do I owe your curiosity?"

"General Cárdenas asked that I bring it up with you, in particular the allegations that the minister has some very suspicious connections with German businessmen and secret service agents."

"And what does Lázaro suppose I do with this information? I'm just a poor governor of the most isolated and sparsely populated state in the country."

"That you will have to ask him yourself."

Manterola and Múgica laughed openly. Lázaro Cárdenas was famous both for his discretion and for his hermit-like personality. To get anywhere with him, one often had to become a fortune-teller.

Manterola had his theory. The Cardenistas, both within and outside of the government, were concerned about the swing to the right, and somehow Múgica had been made Minister of Information without being given a file on Nicolaus's network. That was the problem: for two years, every cog in the governmental machine was pro-Cardenas; now, however, there were very few left, not because they had been forced out but because they had simply turned their coats with the turning of the times.

"Is this to be an information exchange?" the general asked.

Manterola, who had censored himself and did not smoke out of deference to the diminutive general, could bear it no longer and took out his pipe. The conversation had rolled out like a carpet as they passed on down the central alameda, skirting the horrible Porfirian statues of naked women that the journalist had once baptized as "Monuments to Drag," "The Lost Wallet," and "Morning Breath."

"Not necessarily. Just listen to me, and perhaps then you'll want to contemplate my story."

9

A SIGH

I have a very delicate mission for you."

The office of the chief of the National Secret Service was patriotically adorned with flags and the official seal of Mexico. The man had placed three of the Belgian pistols seized from the Germans on a panoply.

The Poet, knowing that the office had been decorated by many of his successes, felt tacit permission to take out a filterless cigarette, stick it between his teeth, and strike a match on the sole of his boot. The gesture, something he did every day, made him feel at home. He sat down in a chair to smoke and wait.

"*El señor* minister thinks he's being followed. He can't be sure, but he's asked me that this office, given the international tensions that exist, take charge of the matter. Personally I think that it's got to be some damned foreigner, since what Mexican son of a bitch would have the audacity to stalk our Minister of the Interior?"

A heavy silence filled the room.

"The President?" offered the Poet in a stroke of wit and cold sweat.

"Goddamn it," said the Chief. He paced around the room with his hands interlaced behind his back. He seemed more like a caricature than a man. The Poet wiped his forehead with the back of his hand and then dried it on the seat's upholstery.

"I was going to suggest that you take charge of this situation, but you're right. Better to dig up a bit more background information before jumping right in. And there is to be absolute silence here, Valencia. You're dismissed."

The Poet got up, saluted in the military style, and exited the room. When he heard the door click shut, he let out a deep sigh.

PREFACE TO 10.
ANOTHER EXPLANATORY
NOTE ON MADNESS

Second paradox: if the world is dominated by limitless, borderless dementia, dementia created by the skill and sophistication of the modern überstate, then what importance can minor madness have?

What weight do my deliriums have, my absurd panics and worries, the absurdity of my reality, when compared to the shooting of hostages in Prague or the bombing into rubble of an Abyssinian village?

I have two choices: to defend personal madness as a form of resistance against the greater madness of the world, or appeal to clarity in order to try and at least partially defeat my own madness, therefore allowing me to see myself, immersed and defenseless, in the *mare magnum*.

It's no easy choice.

Once again,

Alberto Verdugo, Summer 1942

THE *PASE DE PECHO*

As he was leaving the Hotel Plaza, Hemingway, who was telling Martha a Pollack joke, passed a Mexican general with a handlebar mustache and a sour look on his face. He didn't recognize this man, but for some reason the face looked familiar. He kept his gaze on this stranger a moment longer than usual. On the other side of the mirror, General Múgica seemed to recognize the man looking at him. Was it from the photos on the jackets of his books, probably from *To Have and Have Not?* In the end he decided that his mind was playing tricks on him, that he had simply confused a wealthy gringo with one of the world's most admired novelists.

Ernest Hemingway was in Mexico at the invitation of his friend Nathan Bill Davis, a Californian and brother-in-law and heir to Connolly, the literary critic. They were there for a few days of vacation that included a running of the bulls. That was a far better pretext for being in Mexico than vacationing with his wife. Things between them were not going to get any better, but at least the festival looked promising.

Hemingway looked at bulls and bullfighting with a mixture of respect and scientific curiosity: he thought that even the truest *aficionado* could not understand the festival from the matador's point of view, but rather it was his place to focus on the complicated dance, in the symbiosis between matador and bull. Only an opponent of the mode would look at the brave, fierce festival as art. For him, everything had to do with balls and teaching. The valor of the matador and the education of the beast. Technique and talent, yes, but above all *cojones*. He knew, or thought, that this issue of the balls was no small matter; that valor, bravery, and courage were among the most complex human conditions, confusing emotions that emerge inexplicably at times out of nothingness and at other times out of the strangest of fears, such as the fear of cowardice or ridicule.

On this particular occasion he was also very preoccupied by the rumors that he'd been hearing that they were now "shaving" the bulls' horns. He thought that, of the several thousand *aficionados* filing into the El Toreo plaza in the outskirts of Mexico City on that soft spring afternoon, only a few knew anything about bulls and even fewer were worried about the horn-shaving controversy that threatened to kill the spirit of the whole festival. Deep down in his heart he was convinced that only a select group of people had the secret keys to that which was about to transpire here this afternoon while the faceless masses who were renting seat cushions, eating tacos, and pouring cold beers from kegs into waxed-paper cups would be simply happy and oblivious in their sins and sun.

The theory of shaving was that, by reducing the size of the horns, the bull loses his depth perception and thus greatly reduces the chance of a goring. This shameful idea had been founded by matadors and managers alike, in accordance with some corrupt stockbreeders, and consisted in a careful reshaping of the horns, which were "shaved," filed, and polished with motor oil. The "shaved" bull not only lost his sense of distance but he also now had overly sensitive horns, and after a few collisions with a barrier or with a picador's horse, he tended to shy away from contact. He became a hesitant, awkward beast.

Hemingway decided to watch the bulls bred from a certain Zacatecas ranch in particular, ready to lash out in his writings against cowardly matadors, unscrupulous businessmen, and general blowhards who think they know everything.

But on the other hand, a young matador named Manolete was fighting in Mexico that day. He had been born in Córdoba, the son and grandson of matadors, and he was preceded by the enormous reputation he'd acquired in Spain. The critics there were spellbound by his seriousness, his sobriety, and his tragic sense. Hemingway had yet to see him fight, but after reading a pair of reviews sent to him by friends in Spain, he'd already decided that Manolete's clerical style, as if he were a poor man's monk, was not to his liking, and he was here today ready to confirm it. Because if there was something that the American writer had respect for, it was his own manias and irrationality.

The majority of the public shared Ernest's prejudices. Just because some-one had made it big in Spain did not mean that he could come triumph in Mexico without having to spill a bit of his own blood on their ground first. The time of Spanish viceroyalty had ended a long time ago, and Franco now ruled in Spain surrounded by Galician shopkeepers, slicked-over Falangists, and lazy generals. People like that were not going to tell the Mexican people how to act.

Manolete faced more enemies initially that afternoon than he had in all his previous fights. With a look of exquisite boredom wrought on his tragic actor's face, with the look of a sad child who didn't know why life had stuck him here, he set about conquering the Mexicans' affection pass by pass. And as he did, so did his own coldness warm. From the solitude of the center of the ring, his air of vulnerability and the tepid smoothness of his classic fight-ing technique were capturing the crowd. But still Hemingway was resolute. If he were unwavering in anything it was in his phobias, and he couldn't help but offer a pair of gestures of displeasure.

Immutable and erect, Manolete sighted the first bull from afar and slowly approached it. But the animal did not charge; it was as if they had a pact with one another. Finally, as if in slow motion, he unfurled his piece of scarlet serge and the bull came to investigate.

Manolete garnered an ear from the first bull and both the ear and the tail from the second. But more than that, he was waging an emotional *tour de force* with the public, gaining their love inch by inch, conquering both the bull and the crowd. In the end, both were his, though with the exception of a few obstinate men like Ernest Hemingway.

If the public had known that the American writer continued to despise Manolete despite what he had seen, they likely would have buried him under a hail of seat cushions. But Hemingway continued to spurn him, couldn't come to appreciate his air of sad aloofness. He didn't like the way he choreographed the bull. And finally, in some unfair way, he held him responsible for the shaved horns and the racketeers who had invaded the honorable world of *el toreo*.

But despite his stubborn opinions, the writer did harbor an inkling of admission that there was something more than just myth here. But it was just an inkling, and Hemingway continued to begrudge the slim young man from Córdoba.

As he was leaving the plaza with his wife and friends, a man capped in a mariachi's sombrero handed the writer a note. The man was evidently naked underneath his long Saltillo sarape embroidered in blue with an eagle capturing a snake. Hemingway read the message through twice. The man in the sombrero looked around, embarrassed, waiting for a response, and the sudden appearance of a pair of police officers off in the crowd unnerved him exceedingly. Davis offered him a few centavos, which the man refused with a wave.

"¿Habla inglés?"

The bizarre character nodded, which caused the brim of his sombrero to flap like the wings of some giant bird. Hemingway would take that as a yes.

"I go to see him. Tonight I go to see him," said Hemingway in an awkward Spanish.

The character extended his hand ceremoniously to the writer while, in a simultaneous act, produced from beneath his sarape (a move which confirmed that underneath he was wearing nothing but a belt) a copy of *A Farewell to Arms*. The book had a fountain pen stuck between its pages.

"He'd like for you to sign it," a woman—perhaps the man's wife—said to Hemingway.

"Want me to sign it?" asked Hemingway, again in his awkward Spanish. The man in the sarape nodded vigorously.

"Your name?" asked the writer, who had by now caught the man's paranoia, from time to time scanning the crowd for police.

The man in the sarape shrugged his shoulders.

"*Para señor Mudo*. With great pleasure. Ernest Hemingway," he wrote, pronouncing the syllables.

The strange man beamed, took back the book, and, flashing his pubic hair once again, vanished into the evening.

"What was all that about, Ernest?" asked Martha.

"You all go back to the hotel. I have to go see the friend who sent me this note. I have to reach him at once," said the writer, and disappeared himself into the crowd.

ENTRY #3:

CULTS AND BULLS

The great José Belmonte often said that it wasn't valor that allowed him to pass so closely to a bull's horns but knowledge and understanding. He took this theory to the extreme when he once declared to an *aficionado* that indeed no bull could gore him, that at the peak of his career he had acquired a professional skill in which there was no room for error. A few weeks later he was on his deathbed; a bull had hooked him in the thigh and tossed him spectacularly skyward. When the *aficionado*, visiting him in the hospital, asked, "Maestro, I though that to err was impossible," Belmonte nodded with a smile. "Yes," he replied, "but it wasn't I who erred . . . it was the bull."

During the war, a British commando base on one of the south Pacific islands gave birth to a strange religion.

For centuries, no one had disturbed the natives' isolation, but as soon as the British soldiers disembarked they set up a base, built a radio tower, and crates of supplies began to rain in on parachutes. After a period of reflection, the natives fabricated imitation antennas out of bamboo, replica radio transmitters out of cardboard boxes, clotheshangers, and lengths of copper pipe discarded by the British, and even made out a notebook to resemble a codebook. They would sit down at their radio-boxes and clearly enumerate their lists of requests to the gods. They were just as human as the British, they argued, so they prayed for the giant birds flying overhead to shit out cans of Spam, packets of dehydrated potatoes, jars of marmalade, rubber skiffs with outboard motors, hammocks, shotguns, fishing rods, and all other manner of blessings that the British were receiving. But the liturgy was a frustrating one, since it seemed to work for the foreigners but not the islanders. Unjust religions are the worst ones of all. As time went on, this religion became known as "The Cult of Cargo," but it would not last.

I tell this story because when one gambles with life it doesn't much matter whether it's the bull or the matador, whether it's one man or the next who doesn't follow the script, or whether or not there are any lines drawn out beneath our lives leading us to destiny.

I tell this story because however our history plays itself out, it matters not whether it's we or the Nazis who remain in Mexico after the Poet's raids, since we're all just sending our prayers on up to the God of Cargo.

There's always tragedy, *hermano*.

FALSE LEADS

W e found these allusions to Mexico in one of Linz's texts that never saw the light of day. We don't think that it has to do with Otto Rahn and all that's happening, but perhaps . . . perhaps we ought not to ignore anything," said Ludwig Renn.

Manterola was again attending the usual meeting in the usual back room guarded by the usual hardware store out front. Coming here to sit and listen to strange tales was evidently becoming something of a habit for him.

Doctor Sacal took charge of the conversation. He seemed cold, just as he always did, but this time it was with good reason, for a chill was in the air and an icy breeze scudded in through a broken window.

"Linz, Hitler's master occultist, argued in an unpublished manuscript that whoever reunited the three symbols of true power would attain that very power. These three symbols are the Lance of Antioch, the Scepter of Charlemagne, and the Headdress of Montezuma. I have no idea why he chose these three artifacts from among the many symbols of power that populate Europe's museums; perhaps it is just because of their proximity to each other."

Renn cut in to elaborate. "Charlemagne's scepter was in Aquisgrán, and Antioch's lance was in Vienna, as was the headdress. Hitler now has all three."

"What is Antioch's lance, exactly?" asked Manterola.

"In the Christian tradition, a Roman centurion called Longimanus pierced Jesus's torso while he was on the cross. Many years later, when the Crusades were in full swing, the Christians, in a crisis of morale, ordered a fanatical priest to feign a revelation that the sacred lance could be found in the Cathedral of Antioch, buried beneath the altar. They found the lance there, where it had probably been planted the day before. It doesn't matter how the soldiers would know if it really was the lance belonging to an obscure Roman legionary; things will be what you want them to be. And they got it. Later it would pass through the hands of Raymundo de Tolosa and centuries later it became part of the Hapsburg treasure, eventually ending up in a display case lined with rose-colored satin in the Schazkammer of Vienna."

"Hitler had what can only be described as a religious epiphany when he first laid eyes on it. He describes the experience in *Mein Kampf*," said Renn, taking a wrinkled copy of Hitler's autobiography from his pocket and translating: " 'How could a symbol—and an apparently Christian one at that—provoke such emotion in me?' Apparently Hitler, who was a great painter (it's said he could do an entire apartment in one afternoon . . . two coats!), was painting the exterior of the museum when it began to rain. He ducked inside to avoid getting wet, saw the famous lance, and was smitten."

"All three artifacts have recently disappeared from the museums that were displaying them. The lance was taken from Vienna to Nuremburg in 1938 by a group of Gestapo shock troops. Around the same time, a squad of SS agents took Charlemagne's scepter from the museum in Aquisgrán, in Renania, and yet a third armed group confiscated Montezuma's headdress 'for reasons of national security' from the Vienna Museum of Ethnohistory," said Doctor Sacal.

Manterola broke out his pipe. These conspiracy theories were becoming somewhat less maddening. He was beginning to think in terms of metaphysics and conspiracy himself; beginning to feel slightly at home in delirium.

"I don't really know about the scepter, but it seems obvious to me that the lance is a fake, just like so many other fraudulent relics. But I do know a good deal about the headdress because I spent a few years reporting on the matter. It's thought that Maximiliano, back in the days of the empire, received it as a gift from a group of notable Mexican conservatives. Then, for unknown reasons, Carlota took it with him on his travels into Europe to ask for help that ended in madness. So it either is or at least was in Vienna. Well now. Was it really Montezuma's headdress? Was it a replica based on old descriptions? Was it simply a fake? We can be sure that the headdress came from no Mexican museum; it didn't belong to the collections of any of the conquistadors' ancestors. It was simply accepted as Montezuma's headdress and clearly, if there were one headdress in a Mexican museum and another in the Vienna Museum of World History, then the latter one must be the original. But then again, perhaps Montezuma had more than one headdress. He must have kept extras somewhere. Knowing the hoard that Cortés made off with, they may well have stripped the headdresses of their lapis lazuli and their gold and silver twists and wiped their asses with the quetzal plumes. This scepter of Charlemagne is probably just as full of shit."

Renn laughed loudly. "It keeps you sane to look at things skeptically once in a while. But remember that reality has little to do with reason. What interests us here are beliefs. If Hitler believed that these three symbols were the source of immense power, then that's what's important."

"But what does this have to do with Mexico? He already has the artifacts, right? Taken from Germany and Austria? He wouldn't send anyone to Mexico to look for them."

"You're right," said Renn.

"Yes, it's probably just a false lead," said Sacal, and he exhaled despondently.

NONEXISTENT SUBMARINES

U pon returning from their Mexican vacation, Martha disappeared and Ernest went back to his daily routines.

What had he found out about German submarines in Cuba over the past few weeks?

Only rumors of water and fruit. Someone had told him that the president and general Fulgencio Batista had been engaged in business dealings with the Germans. But later that same informant told him that no, that wasn't it just yet, but that's how it would be if Batista dealt too much with the Americans. Some folks had reported that the submarines were off Pinar del Río, at the extreme western tip of the island, but Hemingway dismissed them. The wolf's den wouldn't be so close to American vigilance—to seaplanes, coast guard cutters, and naval bases—no, Camagüey was it. A drunk told him that the black market still operated unchecked in Cuba, and that the chief of police, a man named Benítez, who ran shady deals and hustles for the general, could be his contact. There were campesinos' tales of drunk Germans passed out on the beaches and the usual old-timers' legends. The most imaginative of his informants even told him about a plan to sell fuel, water, and fruit to the Germans directly, going behind both Benítez' and Batista's backs. These rumors were quite vague and thin indeed.

In the meantime and on account of the state of war, Germans and Italians were rounded up and detained in internment camps at the Finca Torres, in

Castillo del Príncipe, and on Isla de Pinos. Bastista seemed to be playing everything by the rules.

Hemingway put on his best khaki shirt, made a pair of phone calls, and asked his driver to pull the car out of the garage. They drove on down the winding road to Havana.

The chief of the U.S. embassy's FBI office had a small, neatly trimmed moustache, mud-flap sideburns, and he spoke with a southern accent. Hemingway disliked him at once. As far as he was concerned, men like this were responsible for having started the Civil War and even now they still hadn't lain the ghosts of their ancestors to rest. He gave Hemingway one more reason to begrudge him when he said, before he had heard a single one of Hemingway's carefully articulated theories, "Why don't you leave this to the authorities?"

"Because you know that the Fascists are gaining strength, yet you continue to insist on turning the other cheek. You stationed half your fleet in Hawaii, in plain view of the Japanese, who had no choice but to attack. No, don't give me that crap. This war isn't for the 'authorities.' Just listen to me for a minute."

"I'd be more than happy to pass your concerns along to my superiors. But I can assure you that this office has thoroughly investigated each and every rumor and has found nothing to substantiate any of them," said the chief in reply to the arguments which he still had not yet heard.

On the road back home, Hemingway stopped in Floridita for a couple of daiquiris and ended up staying for nine. But not even that could temper his anger.

Back at home, he paced in solitude through the rooms of Finca Vigía. Martha had disappeared again; gone to England. I should have known better than to discuss such things with a woman, he thought, and also, above all, I should have known better than to ever have gotten married again.

He set himself about his daily routines: chasing down ants on his porch armed with a can of insecticide and lying down on his bed with his eyes wide open to think about nothing at all. He wanted to read . . . just read until he drifted off into the land of dreams, but still Hemingway read nothing at all.

INTERRUPTIONS

AND INVASIONS

3. He says, "Did you know that Hitler only had one testicle? One nut, the guy had. It's amazing what happened: the mess a guy with only one nut can make."

He swings his arms around like a helicopter with blades spanning the width of the earth. I don't quite see the point of this information, but it seems promising. I'm always trying to find out where De la Calle pulls these stories from. Perhaps from his conversations with the Galician Bastián, whom I haven't seen in months, though I know that he does come around here to visit, and that he was a metro conductor in Paris after the war in Spain ended. And he likely has dual motives for telling them to me: both to educate me and to make the Austrian nervous enough so that he goes out into the patio to "work his magic." He succeeds. Herschel puts down volume three of the Encyclopædia Universitas and looks up. He acts as though he hasn't heard us, but he's been captivated by evil. Information is the only Eve's Apple.

"It's the left one that's missing," says De la Calle.

"It's probably a case of cryptoorquism, when the testicle remains lodged in the abdomen and doesn't descend into the scrotum. It's rare, but it happens," injects Doctor Casavieja, who has come in with Herschel's dose of pain killers and tranquilizers.

"No, it's nothing like that. He lost it when he was wounded in 1916. Shrapnel from a mortar shell hit him in the groin," asserts De la Calle, who presents himself as the resident expert on this sort of esoteric information.

Herschel turns around and stares at the wall.

4. The Poet keeps his notes on Miguel Alemán in what has recently come to be known as "The m.a. (lowercase) Dossier," painstakingly typed out on an old Remington with the index finger of his one remaining hand. He suffers just about every conceivable mechanical error, and it takes him quite a bit of time. Out of sheer exhaustion and in favor of economy, he leaves out much information.

5. Doña Estela goes around trying to convince us to sign up for basket-weaving classes. She's managed to convince a few of the more simpleminded ones. I, however, am convinced it's a ploy by her to sell them to governmental offices on the outside for use as wastebaskets.

As one very healthy reaction to my time here, my companions (including Doctor Casavieja) and I have all let our beards grow. Wild and unkempt, in an informal style. And we weave no heavenly whore. We go on writing, reading, and conspiring. In other words, surviving.

6. The perverted paradise, the fool's hell in which we live, has collapsed. They came in.

With pistols drawn they went toward Casavieja's tiny office and as they passed by our door they saw Herschel stretched out on his cot. He cried out something in German, and I came running out of the bathroom. The men rushed in and plucked him right out from between Erasto and De la Calle, who were playing checkers.

They dragged him by his feet down the stairs while he howled, his head banging against each step. Several shots rang out.

It ended tragically. They shot Simón, the doorman, an ugly and ill-tempered man, like a dog. Erasto is sprawled out on the floor, screaming in pain, his kneecap crushed. Blood streams from Angel de la Calle's nose, his cheekbone shattered by a pistol butt. Casavieja, being the doctor that he is, tries to stop the flow. Our room is full of blood and screams of pain, of broken glasses and books and my writings strewn about the floor.

Though a godless man, I now bury myself in the chapel. I have broken the one vow that sustains me here, on the edge of the human kind. I have returned to violence. In the midst of the struggle I bit the arm of the man who seemed to be directing the raid, the one with the icy stare. I still have the taste of his blood and tweed jacket on my lips. If I'd had a revolver in my hand, I would have killed him. If I'd had a hammer in hand (for example, if I had been hanging a painting on the wall when all this happened), I would have bashed his skull into smithereens. But for better or for worse, it's been years since I've seen hammers or nails or paintings around here. Just blank walls.

My palms are bleeding. "Stigmata," Doctor Pola, a young and frightened medic, tells me. It's as if I had drilled a pair of holes in my hands. The stain of the mystics. The syndrome of Santa Teresa de Jesús. The marks of the nails. The body must produce the wounds by and on itself, because I do not remember any point during the fight where knives or daggers were drawn. Toledo blades: The finest steel in the world. Razors of the soul. The body, in a mystical trance, reproduces the original crucifixion.

Stigmata, stains, and scars. The mind in knots, sending incomprehensible signals. An atheist with a Christian affliction. Or worse, an atheist with mysterious Christian deliriums.

There were four men, all with guns. Or was it three? There was the one who shot Simón Malacara in the foyer, and then there were the two Germans: the more violent one with the very blond—almost albino—hair, and the one with the cold glare and the hat whom I bit. They had a car waiting outside, which they loaded Herschel into. He was screaming something in German as they took him away. What was it?

I reconstruct what I can with my rusty student's German: "There he is." "It's him." "Rainer, shoot." Orders like incomplete paintings, which were finished with gestures: "Take." "Leave." "Fire."

After a bit, Casavieja appears in the chapel, which is just a regular room set aside for speaking to the gods. Nothing more. A chapel sans religious images, a refuge for pious men and heathen men and madmen alike.

"Your body does the strangest things, Alberto Verdugo," he tells me, contemplating the wounds in my hands. He treats me with mercury chromide and cotton swabs.

"Seems like not even here are we able to escape the war," I tell him.

"I don't think I'm going to call the police. The whole world could be on a hair trigger right now. A real fine edge. No, I'm not going to call just yet. So they took the mad Austrian. The police will come and ask their thousand annoying questions. As if we have any answers! They just came and took him! I hadn't even opened a file on him yet. I just don't think it's worth the pain, do you?"

I go out to ruminate in the garden.

Will normalcy return? Irineo is digging up worms and eating them. I set up my telescope; perhaps, in the dawn, I will be able to contemplate my mythical woman. I search meticulously for the spent shell casings. I heard nine shots. I find six casings. My memory has been multiplied by 150 percent. They are Smith & Wesson .38-caliber rounds. I line them up along the windowsill where I keep my telescope. Normalcy is pleasing. I decide to save the casings for when I see Herschel again.

I go back to bed. Most of the others are already asleep. Somewhere in the distance, a radio is playing.

But there is no such thing; there are but mere apparitions. My beard is full of gray hairs and blood. . . .

THE CLUES

Both had received the same envelope, identically labeled "To the journalist and the poet," but, as they discovered when they met later that afternoon at the offices of *El Popular*, they contained different messages.

The journalist's read:

a. 13 VySM A14S23
b. The studio of unicorns, oriental whores, and lions. The north wall, between the cows and the skulls.
c. Where the tiger killed.

The Poet's read:

a. To whom Doctor Guillotine gave work.
b. Verne, the final light.
c. In the water pitcher.

Poet and journalist looked at each other. The journalist considered himself too old for enigmas, crossword puzzles, and brain teasers. The Poet thought that his life was too complicated these days to warrant stories like this coming into play. They simply looked blankly at one another, neither wanting to say what was on his mind. Thinking required too much of an effort, and if someone wanted to toy with their lives, he wouldn't have much to toy with, since they were both physically, mentally, and emotionally exhausted. The Poet shrugged his shoulders.

"Do you know someone who doesn't want us as his friends?" he asked, turning a bit in the office desk chair in which he was seated. The journalist took out his pipe. If he had to think, he'd have to smoke, too.

"What the hell is 13 VySM A14S23 supposed to mean?" he asked in a loud voice. The young novelist José Revueltas, who was drifting like a ghost ship through the halls of the office, looked up at the question, wondering if Manterola was being serious. The journalist handed him the paper.

Revueltas helped himself to a pinch of Manterola's tobacco, packed and lit his pipe, and then pondered the clue.

"It's easy, it's a card catalog number from the National Library. The second group of letters gives it away: *A* for aisle 14 and *S* for shelf 23. It's the old system. The first few letters are the book code. Go to the library and you'll see."

"And you know this because . . . ?" asked Fermín, not quite ready to believe him.

"Because when I'm cold and broke, I spend a lot of time in there. It's warm, I read what I want, and I doze off from time to time. And the people-watching opportunities are endless. It's the Mount Parnassus to us poor scholars."

And indeed it was warm when Manterola and the Poet arrived, with the sun shining in through the stained-glass windows above the great reading room off Carmen Street. A man in a gray workcoat showed them to the book: Alberto Verdugo and Sáenz de Miera. Professional Thesis. "The International Treaties Affecting Trans-Oceanic Channels." Jointly Published by the National Autonomous University of Mexico and the University of Berlin.

The Poet and the journalist looked hard at one another. This was a message from beyond the grave.

" 'To whom Doctor Guillotine gave work.' It's him! Prisoners condemned to death gave Verdugo quite a bit of work," repeated the journalist.

"So the first clue in both of our messages points to Verdugo. Our old lawyer Verdugo. But resurging out of oblivion after some twenty years . . . ?"

The Poet scratched his head, the tips of his fingers dancing over his curly, gray cranium like ballerinas. Did he used to do that with his left hand before the accident? Twenty years ago he might have used his left hand, but now it had to be his right. Either that, or neither hand, he said to himself.

"So it's clearly a message from Verdugo. He wants to speak with us, wants us to come and find him. Or is it that someone wants to keep the three of us apart?"

"Do you remember him? I mean really remember our old friend Alberto Verdugo?" asked the journalist. "He made a career out of defending whores in court, just to bring suffering to his family. He frequented whores himself, because he saw a frankness and openness in them which he saw nowhere else in Mexico. He had an impeccable, implacable morality, I'd say, although few people would ever subscribe to his definition of it. Malignant in his rhetoric. Proud of his surname. Do you know what I mean? For several years, I didn't even know his first name was Alberto. It was only Verdugo. El Verdugo. Him and his many whores. Husband to a whore, even, whom he murdered for you know what."

"Told that way, Manterola, it's a litany of lawyers, doctors, academics, prostitutes, pimps, and whores. And I know a bit about prostitutes myself, mind you, because I've always been a bitch when it comes to the beds in which I sleep and the doubts and fears and food of love. So let's cut to the chase."

"If Verdugo wants to emerge from the shadows, why doesn't he just call us?"

"Maybe he doesn't have a phone. Maybe he just doesn't like phones. But if it's really him, then there's no question, is there? We go."

"We do, at the very least out of faithfulness to Alexandre Dumas. You know, the old and rickety musketeers reuniting after twenty years and all."

"Manterola, that's a hell of a way to put it. We owe our lives to one another."

"That's not much of a debt. Poker debts, yes, I'll grant you that, but not life. Whoever said I wanted mine, anyway?"

"Fine. The next time our asses are getting shot at, I'm just going to walk away and go have a beer. Far enough away so that I don't get your damn blood splattered all over me."

"You don't say!" the journalist said, laughing. "I knew I could always count on you to get out of the messes I get us into!"

They sat and thought in the warmth of the library's reading room. A pair of young students were flirting over a book of Da Vinci's etchings. Elsewhere, an old man was reading Vasconcelos while another was nodding off over an Azuela novel.

"What's the next clue?" Fermín asked, his secret agent's spirit being frustrated by his secret agent work. "In my note, it says 'Verne, the final light.' What's yours say?"

" 'The studio of unicorns, oriental whores, and lions. The north wall, between the cows and the skulls.' "

"What kind of a studio is that?"

"Maybe one that belongs to an architect, a sculptor or a painter. A studio full of unicorns, lions and odalisques."

"And mine . . . Jules Verne, obviously, but what's this about a final light?"

The journalist got up and walked over to the card catalog. He walked two laps around the stacks of drawers before finding the one that he wanted. After a minute of flipping through the cards, he looked up at the Poet and smiled.

"*The Lighthouse at the End of the World*. One of Verne's novels."

"Beautiful. A true people's poet. The final light, *The Lighthouse at the End of the World*."

"One of Verne's nineteenth-century novels, published in Spain by Sopena in 1931, the last year of the Republic."

Poet and journalist shook hands.

"Verdugo's in the lighthouse at the end of the world; that is, unless we find something to the contrary in the artist's studio or from his Egyptian whores."

"But where?"

" 'Where the tiger killed.' 'In the water pitcher.' "

"Now I'm really lost. We need another scholar like Revueltas."

"The tiger could be the one from the Chapultepec zoo that escaped about ten years ago. Is Verdugo in some lighthouse there?"

"What about the Tiger of Santa Julia, that robber who Porfirio's men caught on the shitter?"

"It could also be the Tiger of Tacubaya," offered the old man, who had woken up over his Azuela novel. "Pardon me for eavesdropping, but I'm an expert in crossword puzzles. Remember Leonardo Márquez, the conservative general who fought Juárez in the War of the Cripples? They called him the Tiger because of his savagery, and the Tacubaya massacre is famous too because that's where he slaughtered a mass of liberal doctors during the War of Reform because they wouldn't euthanize the wounded."

The old man who had been immersed in Reyes looked up from his book to get in on the intellectual action.

"They didn't catch the Tiger of Santa Julia shitting behind a thicket of prickly pear trees; they caught him in his mistress's bed in the old Puerto Pinto neighborhood."

"Excuse me, but the gentleman didn't ask where they caught him but rather where he did his killing. And in that regard, it was Tacubaya."

"The Tiger's name was Jesús Negrete and he always carried a Colt .45

and a jute satchel with a hundred rounds of ammunition. And when I say that about the cops catching him with his pants down, I say because I know."

"How?"

"I was watching."

"What about this part referring to a pitcher of water?" asked the Poet.

"Tacubaya," asserted the first old man. "That's what I said, in the Tacubaya neighborhood. Before being a neighborhood in a conquistador's city, of *tenochcas*, Tacubaya is a Spanish corruption of *atlacuihuayan*, which means precisely that: a water pitcher."

"I'm afraid you're mistaken," interjected the man reading Reyes, who wasn't about to remain on the sidelines of this intellectual decathlon. "Tacubaya comes from *atlacocuaya*, which itself originally comes from *atlatl*, that instrument of wood and cord used for throwing small spears."

"And what do you know about a studio full of unicorns, odalisques, and lions?" asked the Poet.

"Nothing about that, I'm afraid. But . . ."

"Is there a lighthouse in Tacubaya?"

"There's not even a river, much less a sea that would warrant a lighthouse."

The Poet took Manterola by the arm and literally pulled him out of the scholarly polemic. With a cry of "Let's have a smoke," he dragged him out the library's front doors. They lit their respective pipe and cigarette and exhaled. A guy hustling three-card monte tried fruitlessly to convince them to play.

Verdugo was emerging from the shadows at a very strange time indeed.

PART IX

THE OTHERS

THE OTHERS

For the purposes of understanding, I have to point out that there is a certain "we" that exists; "we" are those who will, in the future, become the poker players. It should be obvious that there is an intermediary zone to this "we" which encompasses the Rabbi Sacal, the German writers, the forgotten caretaker of the German embassy, General Múgica, the Poet's disconcerting African visionary, and the Tzeltzal elders and children who looked after the Iguana. And it should also be clear that there are "others" as well. But "others" requires a more precise definition. It implies more than one thing. It's many, I think. On the one hand there is the man with the ash-blond hair called Kowalski, and then there is the one called Brüning, who may actually be a dead man by the name of Otto Rahn. Will we again see Herschel, the mysterious Austrian who they say is the resurrected mage Eric Jan Hanussen? And then there is our Minister of the Interior, the melodramatic man from Veracruz named Miguel Alemán, and his mistress Hilda Krüger.

Perhaps we ought to spend a bit of time here on them.

As it happens, it was raining everywhere.

It was a tedious downpour, one of those early summer showers that starts to come down just as the afternoon light is escaping into the oncoming evening, falling with a tenaciousness, a sense of persistency, unexaggerated but obstinate, emptying the streets of people and leaving tiny puddles and rivulets in their place. At the offices of Renato and Rosendo Angulo, in the recently inaugurated El Moro wing of the National Lottery Building, at the top of Paseo de la Reforma, the rain rang out happily against the glass of that glorious new example of national architecture.

It was coming down in torrents, waves of water whipping through the air, a furious tropical storm, when the Board gathered at 7:15 in the unlisted room 116 of the Hotel Luna in Tapachula. The electric lights were flickering on and off, and they had brought several candles and a pair of kerosene lamps up to light the room.

It was also raining violently in La Marquesa, on the outskirts of Mexico City. An enormous electrical storm, which would later descend on the city itself, was brewing. They had set up shop in the great hall of the hacienda, which had seen its better days and which once had been a dairy farm and now served as both the *casa grande* and a stable, both well dilapidated. There was an enormous oak table, used in its day for kneading dough, a few old armchairs with the springs bursting from the seatcushions and dancing freely, a pair of suitcases open on the floor, a nightstand upon which rested three grenades and four pistols, and three cots, one of which held the man called Herschel, deep in a drug-induced sleep. In front of a great standing mirror with a washbasin at its side, Kowalski was angrily dying his hair black. He had always seen his ash-blond hair as a challenge to the world, as a display of his own immortality. He had gone hatless in Kiev when the Russian snipers wreaked havoc among the German officers. He had kept it blond on missions where discretion forced one into bland, unassuming appearances. It just wasn't right that now he had to divest it of its color (or lack thereof) on account of four second-rate Mexican cops.

Brüning worked at the codebook. Lit up by a kerosene lamp that threw dancing shadows across the whitewashed walls and the occasional flash of lightning, he laboriously went about the work of breaking the groups of codes down and deciphering each block. He had already decoded half of Executive Order #170m and he heard the captain's grumblings.

Although it was noon, seven hours behind the Mexican mesa, it was raining in Obersalzberg in Bavaria as well. It was an unusual storm for this time of year, with an icy wind that made the rain feel more like sleet. This rain was delaying the meeting that was to take place, because Hitler was distracted, watching it drum against the windowpane.

Obersalzberg had been a "field house," not much more than a wooden observation deck covered by a tarp, when it was bought in 1928. But in 1935 and with Hitler as the Chancellor, this field house was converted into a strange architectural monster. Following the Führer's instructions, Martin Borman began to buy up all the farms in a ten-kilometer radius, from the heights of Mount Kehlstein on down into the valleys below. Many of the farmers happily bought into this unexpected boom which filled their pockets in exchange for hard-to-cultivate land, while others, for reasons of family tradition or simple business, declined. But both parties soon saw that this was no benevolent operation, but rather that the shadow of the State's totalitarian power had suddenly been cast over them. The farmer Jager and the innkeeper of Zum Tuerken ended up being arrested by the SS and locked away in the concentration camp at Dachau, their property expropriated with a smile as they were branded "Enemies of the State." Their families, too, soon began to disappear.

This little shack gradually became a small palace with over thirty rooms, marble columns, and stained-glass windows. Below ground there was a pantry, garages, a bowling alley, an extensive network of halls and tunnels, and over fourteen kilometers of internal circuitry. The whole thing was surrounded by a double fence with electrified gates. Barracks were raised for the SS guards, a smallish hotel—the Plattehof—was established to accommodate guests, and a pavilion was built for the Führer's frequent walks. They started a farm that included some eighty cows and over a hundred pigs, the meat and milk of these creatures were among the most expensive in Europe, and they built a posh teahouse near the peak of Mount Kehlstein. Everything was inaugurated in September of 1938 during the Sudeten crisis.

Obersalzberg soon fell into disuse. It seemed to bore its new owners. Hitler hadn't used it in years, preferring instead to meet in the State Department in Berlin or in Berchtesgarden, but on the recommendations of Doctor Morell had spent the weekend in the mountains to rid himself of a pernicious flu that could have permanent consequences. Morell had decided to take him off the cocktail injections he had devised, and he also kept no records of the strange side effects that it had been producing in the German dictator's left side: a continuous stream of tears that ran from his eye and a partial paralysis of the thigh that would later spread to his hand. Morell was now administering a new treatment to his patient, something based on Doctor Koester's antigas pills, which Hitler popped like candy and which contained a stomach-calming antiflatulence agent, but which also contained trace amounts of strychnine and belladonna, producing a slight yet systemic intoxication.

Which is why Hitler was a bit stoned and euphoric as he watched it rain from inside the grand, thirty-meter hall made up to look like the cabin of a trans-Atlantic ship which formed the center of the Obersalzberg complex.

There were to be only two other people in attendance at this meeting: two rather obscure people in terms of the Reich's command structure and who, according to the traditional lines of hierarchy in Nazi Germany, would ordinarily not have participated in such a meeting without the presence of their superiors, Heinrich Himmler, supreme chief of the SS and Admiral Karl Dönitz, head of the Navy. But this meeting was of a singular importance.

These two assistants were SS Colonel Wolfram Von Sievers, director of the Ahnenerbe, the Society for the Study of Ancestral Heritage, and Richard Schulz, captain of the attack submarine U231, one of the seven submarines which, in twenty-four hours, would depart for the Gulf of Mexico and the Caribbean on a mission of ambushing the Allied merchant fleet. Captain Schulz had been practically kidnapped in Paris where he was enjoying a twenty-four hour shore leave pass and was flown directly back to Bavaria for this meeting. An accidental yet third participant in the meeting was a shadowy hitman, assigned to the Obersalzberg staff as a beekeeper but actually a companion of Hitler since the 1920s as a sort of combination steward-bodyguard. He was rumored to sleep wearing a muzzle so that he couldn't murmur the Chancellor's secrets as he slept. Behind his back he was known as Der Bluthund: "the Bloodhound."

These three characters, who had waited for over an hour, were finally ushered into the great hall where the Führer was ready to receive them.

Under the candlelight, in Tapachula, thousands of kilometers from Bavaria, the Board had begun its meeting whose purpose was simply to receive orders and execute them. There were five present: the cupola of the Nazi party among the coffee ranchers.

A frumpish character who, being the network's primary operator and cryptographer who regularly relayed instructions from Germany, took the initiative. The loss of communication with Mexico City had left the group's directives in limbo, and now a new message had arrived directly from Germany, altering their priorities.

"We have been instructed to send a portion of the network into secrecy. It is possible that the rupturing of relations between the German and Mexican governments runs even deeper than we thought, and although headquarters doesn't think it will affect the German citizens' assets and doesn't plan on shipping us off to the internment camps just yet, things could get hairy. Beyond the procedures under which they have been operating, procedures regarding the 'person in question,' this could paralyze us. There are very precise orders to start stockpiling arms, establish a secret base in the Chiapas jungle outside Tabasco, and forge papers to settle six of us in the south of Veracruz and in Tuxtla Gutiérrez. We also have to guarantee a route of delivery through Guatemala of at least a ton of coffee per month, and use a Mexican intermediary. But headquarters places particular emphasis on the Führer's desire to locate the pyramid. Have we found it?"

In Mexico City, Miguel Alemán entered the Angulo brothers' office and tossed his hat on a desk.

"Everything is ready, Señor Minister," said Renato Angulo. His brother Rosendo went over to a bar set up in the corner of the office and broke out a bottle of Spanish wine.

Alemán approached the desk and began to leaf through the notebook pages that summed up his conversations with the Germans. He made a couple of notes on a card which he stuck in his pocket, and began slowly and deliberately to shred the pages.

In Tapachula they were busy discussing the pyramid, but one of the younger ones, who bore a scar on his cheek, the product of a recent bullet grazing, felt obliged to ask: "I've been hearing more of these idiotic rumors of this golden iguana. Are they at all founded? Is it possible that the man who has been hunting us is still alive?"

In Obersalzberg, Hitler took charge immediately, sinking into a black leather chair and without even offering his guests a seat: "There is a mission that has been developing in recent months; a mission in which you are involved and which is of the utmost importance to the Reich. I have asked you here tonight so that I may give you your final instructions personally, such that there is no room for error."

At La Marquesa, Brüning finished the first block of code and discovered that an incomprehensible string of gibberish followed. A second block of the message became the key within the key. He smiled. It was the type of intellectual challenge he had been passionate about his whole life. He grouped the ciphers together and contemplated them. They reminded him of the puzzles they used to give to agents in his cryptography courses back at Nuremburg. This was no traditional code. But nevertheless the positions of the groups of letters described a certain geometry, and hinted at a geometric resolution.

He reordered them and sat back to look at the result. A smile again played across his lips: it was a variation on the old Rosacruz Code, a veritable alphabet soup basic enough for even first year students to solve.

Executive Order #170, the first of a series of orders that bore this number and that carried different levels of restriction (Canaris's groups had no idea that they were being transmitted across the Abwehr network many times over, and the chiefs of the national sections didn't know what the orders dealt with), had been an open order. It said, in effect, that it was in the particular interests of the Führer's particular interests that the Mexican coffee grown in Soconusco continue flowing into Germany, that a secondary Nazi network must be formed among the German nationals in the region but linked only to the Abwehr and not the official party and which should have at its disposal a social and commercial structure as well as Chilean and Guatemalan vessels to ship the goods.

The second executive order, 170b, instructed SS Captain Rainer Kowalski to withdraw one million marks in silver bars that had been plundered from Ukrainian banks in Kiev, Jarkov, and Krivoi Rog. He was to get them from the front's auditor and then transport the eighty-three ingots by train to the French town of Lorient on the coast of Bretagne, where he would await new orders.

The third order, 170c, laid out the plans for the Abwehr and the admiralship to establish a covert submarine supply base on the Mexican coast outside of Veracruz. It included a very precise list of what the base would have to stock, including potable water, fresh fruit, spare electronics, a large supply of fuel, and detailed maps of the littoral. The base would be given the Spanish code name of Puerto de las Perlas. There was nothing specifying the precise geographic location of the proposed base, though there were indications that it would not be near any regular routes, military or commercial, naval or aerial.

Curiously different from the meticulousness of the previous Nazi communiqués, the fourth message had nothing to do with coffee, silver, or supplies and was focused instead on alerting the networks in Mexico and Cuba that a pair of *sturmführers* (a rank equivalent to an SS captain) called Brüning and Kowalski would be passing through their countries and should receive complete cooperation.

The place in the archive where the fifth executive order should have been was instead occupied by a single sheet of paper that read, "Transmitted verbally, destroyed."

The sixth exectutive order, 170f, ordered the Heidelberg Gestapo to locate and destroy all documents, notes, manuscripts, and personal papers that had belonged to one Rudolf Glauer, also known as Baron Von Sebottendorff. Particular emphasis was placed on those papers or documents that could have been hidden in his library before his death or smuggled sheet by sheet into the house in which he spent his final years. Thus the retirement of all of Von Sebottendorff's works from all the libraries in the occupied countries was ordered.

After that order, seven more would follow, the only reference to which is that they had been transmitted to the *sturmführers* Brüning and Kowalski. There are no copies of them in the archive.

3

In 1940, one year before the executive orders began to circulate, on the 20th of April to be precise, a man accompanied by a brief escort and draped in a leather coat and scarf entered the Olwicz prison in occupied Poland, much to the guards' distress.

Olwicz exists on no map; it's a hamlet of no more than three hundred people some thirty-five kilometers east of Varsovia. Its only two-story building housed a small textile industry which was abandoned by workers and patrons alike in 1939. The SS converted it into a prison, turning the six rooms where the bolts of cloth had been stored into cells. They were spacious as far as cells go, and with high ceilings but no windows. The first five were always empty. Only the sixth held a pair of prisoners. In a very real way, the entire prison, its warden, the eleven guards, the cook, and a youth who was in charge of the cleaning and laundry, existed just for those two men whose faces had never been seen.

They had arrived wearing hoods and since then, every time their cell was opened they had to put their hoods back on before the guards could bring them their food, hose them down, or change their waste bucket. The singular rule which bound both prisoners and guards was simple: if the prisoners took off their hoods in the guards' presence, they would be shot. Any guard who happened to see a prisoner's face would be summarily shot as well.

None of the guards had ever read *The Man in the Iron Mask* by Dumas, but the two prisoners had read the book earlier in their lives and knew it only too well. They lived on their memories of books, since for years not a single book, magazine, newspaper, or ray of sun had found its way into their cell.

With a wave of his hand, as if swatting away a fly, the man in the black coat ordered the warden to open the prison's only occupied cell. He had a mechanical manner which was often hard to interpret, and he rarely gave explanations or even very clear orders. He simply waved, and legions of men assumed.

A solitary lightbulb covered by a wire grille hung from the ceiling and barely illuminated the cell's two cots. One of the masked men was huddled in a corner of the room; the other was busy doing pushups on the floor. They were dressed in the odd combination of T-shirts, boxer shorts, and their eternal hoods which covered their faces save for two small eye holes and one for the nose and mouth.

The warden called, "*Actüng*" and then left the room. The man who was on the floor reacted with a swiftness, snapping to attention in the military style, while the other simply turned his head to look at their new visitor from behind his mask.

"Herschel Steinschneider, also known as Hanussen, son and grandson of Jews; Otto Rahn, descended from Jews on the maternal side. Remove your masks."

"My Führer," murmured Rahn, as he elevated his right hand to an upward diagonal, his palm open and down. Hanussen raised his arm slightly less rigidly and remembered one of the first pieces of advice he ever gave to this man full of tics, whose movements seemed dictated by a puppet-master's strings, many years ago: "The illusion of the supernatural must enrapture the eyes of your audience, making them a thousand times more manageable. With success, confidence grows, and with the confidence, so does the power of persuasion."

4

We've followed the original indications, but they're all worthless. As you know, the region is a virtually impenetrable jungle that only starts to open up in the vicinity of the Usumacinta River. There are no references and the dates of the march from the journal we found abandoned along the river are all relative. There are no paths or directions, only vague indications of the northeast route that the first expedition followed. All of the data we have come from 1923. We have nothing else to go by. There are no indigenous communities nearby. There have been no other archaeological expeditions in the area. If the pyramid really was here once and isn't just a myth, then the jungle has long since swallowed it up," the man coordinating the search in Tapachula said.

"The operation ought to be covered by silver or jewelry, not by the money that could be dredged up. That's our opinion," said Miguel Alemán.

"You will both be brought back to life," the man in the black coat said to the two men as they removed their hoods to reveal their pallid, thickly bearded faces. There was no rhetoric in what the man had said; he simply held the powers of life and death in his hands. He could snap his fingers and make them disappear, vanish into a puff of smoke, dissolve into nothingness like so many other Jews.

"You will be brought back to life, although you have no right to live. You are traitors. Traitors to the party and to your country. But as you have already died, you have already paid for your crimes. Anyone who reads the papers knows that. If new life shall be . . ." and here he lapsed into suspense, noting that what he had in his hands was not the gift of death, which he had borne for quite some time, but something new: the gift of resurrection.

"We are operating under the guise of a group of Canadian prospectors searching for copper deposits, but . . ."

"Silver would be preferable," said Miguel Alemán, Mexico's Minister of the Interior.

"Everything is possible . . . That man they call the Iguana was without a doubt gravely wounded by Heinz and his father, but the body disappeared. When we searched the ravine we saw traces of blood, but we also found signs that the body had been dragged downstream. Personally, I think that he's dead and that they dragged him off to bury him. It's nothing more than those things which are so common in Mexico today: rumors," said the chairman of the Nazi board in Soconusco.

"If you bring us back to life, it will be a miracle," suggested Hanussen, but the joke was lost without an echo because the man in black had no discernible sense of humor.

"I'm reviving you to take on an immense task, something essential to the future of the Reich," said the man, his hands fluttering as if coaxing something to grow inside of his stomach. "You will rise like the Phoenix to complete a grandiose task."

"Our fidelity is absolute, Führer. Our mindset is resolute," said Otto Rahn. Hanussen remained silent.

"Oh, I am going to ask much more of you than that," said Adolf Hitler.

PART	X

THE WAY OF THE
LIONS AND UNICORNS

1

THE FURIOUS POET

When he left his office at the Ministry of the Interior, the Poet stopped to buy a selection of mangoes fresh from Manila while he set himself about re-elaborating his strategy. This was risky business. At such heights they could pretty much cast out the theory that it was the president who was tailing his own Minister of the Interior, and so he would have to send his boss and his boss' boss after a new wild goose. If he said that it was the Nazis, Alemán could easily check and then he would know that he was lying. He could say—or better yet, merely suggest—that it was the gringos, and alert the ministry as such. But the minister was already aware of that. Perhaps it wasn't such a bad idea to blame the American embassy's amateurs and set Alemán on edge that way. It was all rather like throwing at a dartboard in his mind.

He began mentally to draw up his report while he filled his jacket pockets with mangoes, keeping the juiciest one to eat while on the road. As dusk fell, and with his mango in hand, he headed east on Bucarelli when, suddenly, he bumped into the woman who had engaged his dreams of late.

"No, I'm not going to listen to a single word until you tell me your name," he said, offering the sucked mango to the Negro woman who resembled Veronica Lake.

"You can call me Veronique," she said, accepting the mango, "and I'm not going to say anything; I'm going to ask that you come with me. There's something that you really ought to see, something that will surprise you."

The woman was wearing an apple-green dress with a matching kerchief covering her head. They went down Victoria Street, toward the downtown area. She forced the pace while the Poet was in no hurry. He was enjoying the day's last few rays of light, the woman, the city, and his mango. The woman took him by his arm, urging him to walk faster. He could smell magnolias. Just before reaching López and next to a cheap electronics shop, they entered a neighborhood tenement. The woman greeted neighbors doing their wash, a cobbler, and a group of children who played at soccer with a bottlecap. It seemed to be part of the ambience of being at home. Upon reaching a blue painted door bearing the number 5, she took out her keys and went inside. The Poet waited for an invitation. If she was going to seduce him, he was going to act like a reserved gentleman.

"Hurry, it's about to begin. And no, I'm not going to seduce you. At least not now."

Fermín blushed. He had forgotten that the woman had the ability to read minds. What was one to do in such circumstances? Stop thinking? Wipe your mind clean? Perhaps he could think only the most obscene thoughts, so that the woman would have no choice but to shut off her mind.

"Neither of those first two ideas will work, *señor*," she said, but offered no assessment of the third theory, and with that, the Poet resigned himself to following her into the apartment. The first room, bare save for a dining table and a pair of chairs, gave way via a curtain to a second room where, strangely enough, there was no bed but only a pair of giant closets. The woman opened the first and took out two black cloaks.

"Don't move; just listen. You have to hear it before you can act," said the woman, smoothly pulling her dress over her head and replacing it with the cloak. She helped the Poet into his cloak after having taken his jacket and hat and hanging them in the closet. The Poet had been a bit disarmed by the speed and ease with which the woman had undressed, and he wanted to preserve the fleeting image of her body in his mind. The cloaks were capped with monastic hoods and bore, in the center of the chest (as the Poet was only now discovering) an enormous black swastika emblazoned on a red circle. It reminded him of the cloak a childhood friend of his had worn when she dressed up as the Mad Monk. They were very similar, save for the swastika.

The woman opened the second closet and took out a lantern that had been hanging on a nail and, as she activated some unseen mechanism, the back wall of the closet retreated into the shadows to reveal a corridor and a set of descending stairs. The Poet followed her down without question or hesitation, not worrying about traps. But he did sense a sort of ubiquitous danger. Somehow he had come to the conclusion that if this woman was to be his guide into hell, then he would at least make the most out of the tour.

From the look of the passageway, Fermín had thought that it would be cold, but on the contrary it was muggy and hot, as if they were passing through a factory's boiler room. But he couldn't remember ever having seen a central heating system in Mexico; that was a European phenomenon. Still, though, the heat intensified, as if they were descending toward Avernus. But hell doesn't exist. Only purgatory. And with the certainty of that knowledge, the Poet continued on down, led by the shadow of the woman and the tenuous thread of light cast by the lantern she bore in front of her.

Around a bend the passage came to an end, stopping at a spiral staircase whose wooden steps were almost completely rotten and worm-eaten. They descended some twenty feet and found themselves at the mouth of a tunnel dug into the earth. It was just tall enough for the Poet to stand, but it forced the woman from Senegal to stoop slightly. Again, the Poet found himself thinking about the woman beneath that cloak and about what he had seen during that ephemeral moment between when she had removed her green dress and replaced it with the black cloak.

"You're not afraid? The only thing you're worried about is seeing me naked?" asked the woman.

Now that you mention it, the Poet thought, I'm really not afraid. Just full of sweat and curiosity. And my pistol. Did I bring it?

"Yes, but you forgot to load it again."

Fermín smiled.

The woman lifted up her lantern to illuminate a large door straight ahead.

"Silence, please."

The Poet nodded.

"Cover your face as best you can. Keep behind me, and repeat the gestures of the others. And don't jerk that empty pistol of yours, or they'll kill us both."

"Could I get a kiss before we go on in?" the Poet asked hesitantly.

"No, we're about to enter the second level of hell."

2

INTERRUPTIONS
AND INVASIONS

1. Of course the fact was not made public. That is why Servando Peñaloza is listed in the military records only as having been "killed in the line of duty," without mentioning what sort of duty it was or how he happened to be killed while doing it. Nor did it say who it was that had killed him nor why. Nevertheless, one of his widows, the "legal" one, receives a pension from the Ministry of Defense.

2. I've discovered that the book Angel de la Calle is coauthoring with his American friend Edgar Rice Burroughs by correspondence has in fact already been written and was published nearly thirty years ago under Burroughs' name and with the title *Tarzan of the Apes*. One of the nurses, who has read it many times over, tells me about it in great detail. She has even seen the film version. Where was I when all this happened, she asks me. I thank her for the information, and she proceeds to tell me about two more Mexican films. Worth its waste, information is power. I take advantage of the window to disturb De la Calle, who is having his broken jaw reset, and tell him all about this story that he's "writing."

Burroughs first got the idea from a story a drunkard told him. It is set toward the end of the past century and has to do with an English lord and his wife, a mutiny on a ship, and the couple being abandoned in some wild part of east Africa. Unable to survive, the couple dies, orphaning their infant son who was taken in and raised by a tribe of apes. Something here doesn't seem clear to me: if the pleasures and habits of this child were constructed during his life among the apes, then how is it possible that he would fall in love with this Jane woman instead of one of his female ape friends? Wouldn't Jane seem a bit too hairless and her teeth too small and weak to someone with Tarzan's tastes?

"Damn!" slurs De la Calle, who can't speak very clearly with his busted jaw. "We haven't gotten to that part yet, but you already know all about it. All that time you spent with Hanussen must have turned you into a wizard yourself. Why don't you go out and work some magic on that fountain?"

To my surprise, he does not seem very affected; rather, he simply limps over to his desk and retrieves a few letters in which Burroughs asks for his advice on characterization and descriptions of tropical climes, sketches of mandrills, palm trees, boa constrictors and, of course, orangutans.

The memory of Herschel-Hanussen's kidnapping disturbs me deeply. It draws on a vein of mine which I have tried to bury and forget and of which I am very afraid. It's not that I am a terrible man, it's simply that I am pathetic. But dangerously so. To the others? Probably not.

3. Corporal Servando Peñaloza died in the following way:

General Múgica arrived in Mexico City by train, come from Guatemala to meet with the Minister of Defense on the need to send an army division to fortify the coastal territories. He got off at the Buenavista station carrying a smallish suitcase, elongated like a trumpet case. Inside it was a Thompson submachine gun that some customs officer in Baja California had confiscated and sent to the governor's office. The Thompson was a fairly common weapon in those days, and the standard used by U.S. marines. But this was not one of the contemporary models; rather, it was a 1919 original, the old tommy gun with the drumlike magazine and not the 1928 model with the vertical clip. It was the gun that had been in all the papers during the 1920s on account of its popularity among Chicago bootleggers and gangsters. Though it was some twenty-three years old, the gun, which weighed a hefty 4.5 kilograms, was in excellent condition, and the case also contained a fifty round magazine of .45-caliber rounds.

As he got off the train his assistant, Corporal Peñaloza, took the case from his hands and accompanied him in a taxi. They went straight to the Hotel Alameda, just as they always did. Múgica went immediately up to the room they had reserved to bathe while Peñaloza went to the café to order a chocolate and a few slices of toast with marmalade for his boss. He knew that his boss would not eat all of them, and ordinarily he would not have helped himself, but it seemed such a sin to waste food. Plus, the previous night's bout of drinking and revelry had left him a bit hung over and craving sugar.

He was just dusting a few crumbs of toast from his shirt when he broke out into a cold sweat, and a wrenching pain in his stomach threw him to the floor. Múgica bolted out of the bathroom, alerted by the screams down in the café. When the medics arrived at the hotel and confirmed that this was far more serious than the usual stomach colic, the general ordered them to take him to the Hospital Colonia. Peñaloza was dead on arrival.

When, at the general's request, the hospital analyzed the remaining pieces of toast, they found that the marmalade contained enough strychnine to kill a rhinoceros. Múgica, after asking the doctors for complete secrecy in the matter, took out a small notebook and started to make a list of who might want him dead.

4. Normalcy doesn't return to these parts. The whole world seems deeply disturbed by the intrusion of the German thugs into our lives. The tortillas served with pork and beans are burnt. We eat without complaining, as if an act of penitence.

3

THE OPEN DOOR

They went through the door and entered an enormous room lit up by torches fixed to the earthen floor. It had to be the basement of one of the old colonial buildings in the area. At one end of the room a makeshift altar stood beneath a giant swastika hung on the wall, and a table nearby was sinisterly adorned with a pair of skulls. A dozen or so cloaked figures stood in a semicircle around the table. The Poet hung back, as far from the altar as possible, trying to hide his empty sleeve behind a column.

One figure, of average height, whose cloak bore not one but two swastikas, raised his voice in the recital of an all too familiar rhetoric: the world has turned against the Jews and their allies the Bolsheviks; Fascism has been born in Spain, Italy, Hungary, Romania, Germany, and Japan; it is the new mode . . . He had a monotone voice, inflectionless, as if he were a schoolboy reciting a poem. Nevertheless, there was something subtly disquieting—almost hypnotic—in the cadence of his speech.

The heat, the torches, the damp basement, and the cloaks. The Poet felt a nagging dryness in his throat and thought longingly of the mangoes in the pockets of his jacket hung up in the closet above.

"And now, something new is happening, and it is here, in Mexico, our beloved land, where this dawn must break. The door has been opened. The long-awaited door that rationalism and materialism have kept barred now opens."

The Poet felt the hairs on the back of his neck stand on end, and his absent arm wanted to spring to life and stretch out. It wasn't the first time he had felt this; a Czech medic with the international brigades had once explained it to him. The arm was no longer there, but its sensation was, and the brain pointed it out as if it wanted to shoot itself. It was like this damn door that insisted on opening. The damn door written about in blood on the walls of houses where Brüning had lived, and now, these fools, these small town Nazis, were bringing it up again. What were they talking about?

"And through the opening door he comes. He comes!"

For a man who had renounced religion at the tender age of eight, the Poet was well-versed in such fits of mysticism. He saw them with a mix of curiosity and disdain. Who was coming? Surely this was vital, since the cloaked congregation reverberated with the message, standing as though nailed to the floor, like feverish turkey vultures possessed by an airy truth.

"He comes . . . He comes . . ." the congregation softly repeated.

The Poet was thinking that the right wing had no sense of the ridiculous, had no sense of decency or restraint, and that that was one of its advantages, when the cloaked man leading the chant took one of the torches from the floor and held it to a pyre which the Poet had not noticed until now. It must have been presoaked in gasoline, because the entire thing burst furiously into flame. A bonfire of books and photographs. The Poet approached the pyre with curiosity and saw, surprisingly enough, a copy of one of his early pornographic novels with the rather vulgar title of *Tears from My Tube* among the collection. It burned (what an honor!) alongside poems by Brecht, the *Communist Manifesto*, one of Leon Feuchtwager's novels, the *Collected Speeches of Lorenzo Cárdenas*, the *History of the Fifth Regiment*, Howard Fast's *Infancy in New York*, *The Complete History of the Great Revolution of Kropotkin*, *All Quiet on the Western Front* by Remarque, poems by the young Italian communist Cesare Pavese, Hemingway's *The Killers*, and *Walls of Water*, José Revueltas's first novel. He'd have to tell Manterola to tell his fellow journalist and friend. It was quite a selection indeed.

"The session is over," said the leader, his eyes reflecting the firelight from within the recesses of his hood. "Each of you may now ask a question of the Grand Master."

The Poet raised his hand. "It's not necessarily a question," he said in a thunderous voice, "but rather an incontrovertible axiom. The German Chancellor, little Adolf Hitler, sucks General Pancho Villa's cock, you bunch of assholes."

He said it smoothly and without pride as he reached into the flames to rescue his slimy porno novel and a copy of Freud's *Interpretation of Dreams*. With the burning books in hand, he seemed vaguely like a raging archangel.

"Treason!" shouted the Grand Master, and he drew a silvery dagger from the altar.

The Poet thought that an unloaded pistol was better than no pistol at all, but in order to draw it he'd have to drop the books, lift up his cloak, and reach around to the small of his back. An unloaded pistol wasn't worth all that. His eyes searched the room for the marvelous, bewitching Negro woman who had introduced him to all this madness and who was now responsible for saving him, but this woman, who had been at his side at the beginning of the ceremony, was now nowhere to be found. He planned a prudent but impossible retreat. The books were beginning to singe his one remaining hand.

"You're all under arrest!" he shouted, just for the sake of saying something.

4

INTERRUPTIONS
AND INVASIONS

1. and only: Where can Manterola and the Poet be? What is taking them so long? In what labyrinths of this infinite city and impossible history are they lost? What other emergencies are claiming them? What are those sons of bitches dreaming about? Bloody hell. To reminisce over them, to go around in search of them conjures certain ghosts from my past that don't necessarily have to do with them but rather with my own personal history. I feel like I'm losing control, like I'm fleeing myself.

The worst thing is that I know all the answers, I understand and recognize them like faces. I know only to run toward the nothingness, toward oblivion. I have slipped dangerously back into silence.

5	

BLOOD AND SMOKE

Back up against the wall! Hands behind your heads!" shouted the Poet.

The Grand Master edged toward him, brandishing his silver dagger and flanked by two other men with revolvers drawn.

"I was fucked as it was," the Poet said to himself as he retreated back up against a wall. There was a subtle honor in dying with your ass backed into a corner. He still held the burning books in his hand. "Poet flambé," he thought. Not bad.

One of the cloaked figures misjudged the distance between himself and the Poet who, with his cowboy boots, planted a solid kick right where he figured the man's balls must have been hanging underneath the cloak. The man staggered backward, gurgling in pain, but the two armed men were now between him and the escape passage. The Grand Master continued to inch toward him, dagger poised to strike, screeching the word traitor over and over again like a litany.

"God protects cripples, cowards, and careless folk," the author of pornographic novels, poet, and secret service agent would think many years later as he recalled that time—that one moment—when the two cloaked gunmen committed their own treason against their master and, without so much as a flicker of hesitation, emptied their pistols into the Grand Master's back. Chaos erupted. In the confines of the basement the gunshots sounded like dynamite multiplied by a thousand echoes. The man dropped like a bag of concrete, blood jetting from his back in streams, soaking his cloak which, by some magic, then began to burn. The rest of the cloaked masses began to run every which way, searching for the exit. The Poet threw his burning books at one of them, who similarly burst into flame, all the while shouting, "You're all under arrest! Hands up, you chicken shits!" Strangely enough, one of the gunmen chimed in on the first of his two exhortations.

The cloaked figures continued to run through the enormous basement without any apparent intent or purpose. His two faceless allies had managed to isolate one from the crowd and now were holding him up against a wall at gunpoint. The Poet made his way over to them, more out of curiosity than any real desire to help them or the one who was now rolling around on the ground, trying to extinguish his flaming cloak. One of the gunmen pulled back his hood and looked at the Poet.

"Saved your skin there, huh boss?"

The Poet shot his savior a look of thanks. It was the guy from Toluca, Agustín Sánchez.

"Put this guy out just enough so that we can interrogate him later. What the hell are you doing here anyway?"

Sánchez took off his cloak and began to pat out the prisoner's flames with it.

"Overtime, boss. If you can't give me the hours, then I'll make them myself."

"Overtime? On whose account?" demanded the Poet.

Sánchez signaled to the other cloaked gunman, who held their other captive spread-eagled up against the damp, fungus-covered wall. He nodded in salutation.

"Take off your damn hood! Don't you know it's illegal for Mexican agents to take second salaries?"

The stranger pulled off his hood to reveal a sharp though friendly face, some thirty years old, with a melancholic look in his eyes, a lightly pink nose, probably due to alcohol, and a black beard yellowed around the lips, probably due to nicotine.

"Graham Greene," he said in Spanish laced with a strong British accent.

"Fermín Valencia. Are you Graham Greene the novelist? Because if you are, you are the most fucked-up, reactionary novelist I've ever read," said the Poet, who had read *The Power and the Glory*.

"I'm afraid I don't know what you're talking about," said the Englishman wisely; wisely because his name was not Graham Greene, it was a voluntary pseudonym; wisely because it was a pseudonym sans literary art, and wisely because he was, in fact, the novelist who had written *The Power and the*

Glory, a novel which was widely rebuked in Mexico for its defense of Catholics persecuted during the Crusades and because it attacked the modern secular state of the generals. As such, he was here in Mexico under the pendulum of Article 133, which provided for the deportation of undesirable aliens. He had also written *Lawless Roads*, a book even more vehement in its criticism of General Cárdenas, but the Poet had not read this one. In a country of rumors, he who whispers first is king, but in the end he just wasn't in the mood to fire up a debate with a Catholic gringo who had just saved his life.

"What's your rank, my ephemeral ally?"

"Captain."

"Then salute, soldier. You're looking at a major," lied the Poet.

Greene quite ceremoniously brought his right hand up to his hairline in a starched military salute.

"What should I do with this burned guy, sir?"

"Uncover him . . . that goes for the both of you, too," the Poet ordered. Then he walked over to the fallen body of the Grand Master. The man was awash in blood, and a wisp of smoke rose from the wounds. Was it cold? Was his black habit burned? Was the man himself burning from within, and this was the smoke that escaped? He put two fingers to the man's neck and felt no pulse. He was good and dead. They stripped off his cloak and examined the sickly pale face of Telésforo Morón, the former lifetime president of the Knights of the Aztec Eagles.

The burned man was wheezing softly. The Poet didn't recognize him. The third, who looked fixedly at the British agent's pistol, didn't look familiar either.

He pulled a charred book out of the pyre: Remarque's *All Quiet on the Western Front*, a novel that had always brought tears to his eyes. He strode over to the man whom the Englishman had jammed up against the wall and held the book up to his face. His soot-smeared face sat behind a pair of wire-rimmed glasses, and he broke out into a sweat, either from the heat or from the panic that the Poet stirred inside him.

"What the fuck kind of a meeting was this?"

"We didn't break any laws . . . it was just a regular meeting of the Aztec Eagles . . . and you just shot up our Grand Master!"

"Sure it wasn't an illegal assembly. Sure it's not illegal to go around sucking the cocks of Hitler and Franco and those other Fascist bastards. But burning books is illegal, and the penal code classifies it as a Class A Felony under Articles 69 and 69a. And that, my friend, gives my partners and I the right—and the duty—to turn your man into a loaf of lead-poisoned hamburger."

The Poet really enjoyed that little lie, but it didn't seem to have the desired impact on the man with the glasses, so he decided to try his luck with the burned one instead.

"Who are you and what's your affiliation?"

"Somebody get me a doctor . . ." the burned man gasped.

"You full name and affiliation," insisted the Poet, ignoring the man's charred face and blistered arms.

"Lucas de la Garza Ochoa . . . I'm a conservative studies major at the National University."

"And you're not ashamed to be going around like this? Fascism is the ideology of Spaniards and washed-up bureaucrats, not conservative students! You ought to be reading Rousseau, Tom Paine and Benito Juárez. And who is it who's arriving? Who's going to come through this open door?" And then, turning to Sánchez and the Brit, "Get a cord to tie these two up, and something we can carry the dead one on."

The mini-brigade, formed of the man from Toluca and his recently acquired purveyor of overtime hours, had apparently decided that this operation which had just gone down in an old colonial basement somewhere in downtown Mexico City was the Poet's domain, because they went immediately into action without so much as a question.

"So, Lucas, who is it? Who's coming through that door?"

Greene and Sánchez had found a length of rope somewhere and were busy tying up the man in the glasses.

"Do you know a way out?" the Poet asked them, not wanting to reveal the passage that his Black Witch of Senegal had shown him. He'd just have to get a new jacket and fill its pockets with mangoes all over again. Greene nodded.

"Well, then, De la Garza, who are we waiting for? Who's coming to our glorious capital city? Who's going to pass through the door into this city of palaces? Who are you Nazi bitches waiting for with such expectation? Tell me!"

"The Führer. Adolf Hitler is coming to Mexico."

"You're shitting me," said the Poet.

6

INTERRUPTIONS

AND INVASIONS

1. Blood and smoke. My dreams are dominated by this strange combination. The warmth and sweet thickness of blood and a frail thread of smoke ascending in happy spirals, as from a cigarette. I haven't smoked in quite some time; in here smoking is forbidden, on account of the risk of fire. Blood alone will have to be enough.

2. Palm fronds and palm trees. De la Calle is truly consumed by his art. The walls of my room are completely filled. He has managed to obtain some oil paints; now his palms are not simple sketchings or drawings but rather grand murals.

I ask: "And you never tire of your subject matter?"

He replies: "'In the old age black was not counted fair / Or, if it were, it bore not beauty's name.' Shakespeare, sonnet 127, from the only anthology I have. And further, there are some sixteen hundred varieties of palms, and if it has cost me this much work to commit them to memory, then it will cost me even more still to bring them back into life. Cohune palms, royal palms, date palms, yucca palms, coconut palms . . ."

3. The Poet has, without a doubt, a true sense of the stage, and eyes will later light up and shine when he tells how he drove his two prisoners, Mexican Nazis stripped to their underwear, at gunpoint down Victoria Street toward his office at the Ministry of the Interior, to the surprise and cheers of people out for their evening stroll. A few meters back, the *tolu-*

queño Sánchez pushes a gurney they have borrowed from an orthopedic supply store which bears the dead body of Telésforo, ex-Grand Master of the Knights of the Aztec Eagle. The British agent has disappeared.

The Poet misses his mangoes dearly and still he has before him a prisoner to interrogate and a partner who has somehow gotten involved with a British auxiliary which, after all, is not necessarily a bad idea, depending on where Sánchez's ultimate fidelities lie. And the Poet would go appeal to the entire country, which was known to have him well moored on their side.

4. I agree, the Poet is doing very important things. But Manterola? Why does he not come?

5. Pioquinto Manterola can be doing one of two things. One, he has gone home, back up to his rooftop room in Colonia San Rafael, and sat down for a spell of Beethoven. The rooftop servants seem to flock to his magic call. Or perhaps he is in some empty, phantasmagoric drafting room, trying to find a phone number for Diego Rivera.

6. Tomás Wong cannot come; I fear he has indeed died along the bank of a river in Chiapas. . . .

7

THE PAINTER-CANNIBAL

It was Diego Rivera, the author of some of the loveliest essays on cannibalism ever written, whom Pioquinto Manterola had chosen to help him resolve the final clue.

In an impressive, provocative attack on the bastards, Rivera had claimed that he had been a cannibal himself once, that all Communists in fact ate their children, and an amused Manterola had walked right into the trap. Only just as the interview was ending did it occur to him to take out the slip of paper he had in his pocket and ask,

"Maestro, would you by any chance happen to know where this is?"

"The studio of 'unicorns, oriental whores, and lions . . .' Well God damn, with references like that it can only be Joaquín Clausell's studio. Only Clausell would be capable of combining such themes. Odalisques, lions, unicorns, strikes, and abundant sex. Clausell was a genius, though he never dared to prove it on paper. In secret, in that studio of his, was where his madness ran rampant. Pure oneiromancy and orientalism combined with the best Mexican impressionism ever done. I used to visit him in his studio some twenty years ago. It's in the attic of Count Calimaya's palace on Pino Suárez Street. He lived there, too. Married one of the heiresses. Him, a fierce Republican and a veritable magician with paints, ended his life in a palace of the oligarchy. It's a fascinating studio, really, but I haven't heard much of it lately. Not since Clausell killed himself, that is. Nowadays, scarcely anybody remembers him. Not only does this country have no memory, it has no shame, either."

Pioquinto Manterola stopped his frantic scribbling and shut his notebook.

"And now that you've cleared up one of my mysteries, do you think you could tell me something about a lighthouse in Mexico City?"

"Manterola, you ask the strangest questions I've ever heard. Couldn't you behave like a normal journalist and just ask me the usual drivel?"

8

INTERRUPTIONS

AND INVASIONS

1. Hemingway shuffles his way down the smooth grass slope, cocktail shaker in hand and the sun overhead, toward the empty swimming pool. How many daiquiris has he had? Innumerable. Other "I" words indicative of his daiquiri count come to mind as well: immense, interminable, incredible. And as to the origins of his love of the drink: immemorial. Almost. Haze and clouds. The pool empty and dry, save for a dusting of leaves and dead insects. He lies down on top of them. Closes his eyes, blotting out the fierce sun, holds onto the shaker with his right hand. Although he has filled it with ice, it is dissolving rapidly in this heat. Surely he will fall victim to sunstroke. He stretches his arms out in the shape of a cross and breathes deeply.

2. Do the British have some sort of spy network set up in the Federal District? Since breaking off diplomatic relations over oil controversies, the British have stayed on as veritable half-orphans in Mexico. Doubtless they are interested in maintaining contacts with people inside the Mexican spheres of influence. But it doesn't come easily; there are many Germanophiles in the cabinet. Those who look to the future do so under the penumbra of the gringo flag and the Cardenistas don't sympathize with the British Empire. Not at all. The British companies were the most belligerent during the oil embargoes, and the conservative Catholics have been a constant annoyance, no small amount of which is due to the novels of Graham Greene,

who ought to go on writing those spy novels that he does so well.

3. Múgica pares his list of possible assassins down along four lines: Germans who believe him to be the Mexican government's point man; Americans who think that he could pressure the Mexican government into ending its "collaboration" and, worse, offering them land in Baja California; someone in the cabinet who thinks that agents still faithful to Cárdenas are operating and reporting to him; and finally someone who just plain hated Peñaloza.

Each of the four theories are equally absurd. They offer nothing.

He reviews them one by one. The government is pressuring the Germans into ingratiating themselves with the Americans. He is not going to get involved, not going to jump in and put a stop to anything. The gringos are on an international crusade against Fascism, the lesser of two evils and a bit of the same. If he can prevent them from getting a military hold on Baja California he will, but his job is to collaborate with them while at the same time keeping them at arm's length. Sovereignty is a very delicate thing when the Americans are involved. They are easily invited in for tea, but then it's impossible to get them to leave. Their intentions are well-known throughout the government; this fact is no great mystery. So much for the value of knowledge. The rumors circulating about Miguel Alemán, those strange stories the Poet tells, don't seem to justify much. Múgica knows tales of corruption that would shake the country to its core. In recent times, the moral fiber of his former revolutionary compadres has deteriorated substantially. They used to say that "the Revolution will bring justice," and they thought that it was economic justice that they were talking about. Favors were called in, pockets were lined, other ways were looked, and the channels of power were used for personal gain. Why the silence? What corporate lasso has united the generals and the new generation of scholars who all have fallen silent? What unwritten laws say that dog does not eat dog, even though the dogs have tasted human flesh? Shaking his head in disgust, he returns to the matter at hand. The matter of Peñaloza's death. Someone wanted Peñaloza dead? Clearly he had wanted to kill him himself at times, but . . . no. Nobody would actually kill Peñaloza.

He decides to do two things: one, send the tommy gun to a friend, and two, write a note to Lázaro Cárdenas, who is currently in Baja California preparing a move to occupy certain positions in a nearly deserted region around Magdalena and the salt marshes, thus establishing a military zone there before the Americans can move in and claim to be preparing to defend against a Japanese west coast attack. After telling him what has happened and offering his speculations of things to come, he warns that the gringos, though they could be a strong anti-Fascist ally, are not to be trusted. He ends with, "If you let them enter as allies, you will soon see that the only way to get them out is as enemies."

4. The Poet does four things in rapid sucession. He tries to squeeze his two homegrown Nazis like lemons, but he is unable to get anything out of them. He puts his file on Graham Greene on his table. He intensely questions the *toluqueño* Sánchez. And he goes to the house of the dead man, Telésforo, Grand Master of the Knights of the Aztec Eagle.

5. I find a letter from the British Prime Minister Winston Churchill on Casavieja's desk, in which he thanks our misplaced Spaniard for his suggestion of *boldo* tea as a muscle relaxant, and says that he recognizes the incredible virtues of *gordolobo* tea for the afflictions and irritations of the throat, and expresses gratitude for the packages of native Mexican herbs that were sent.

Something of a stupor sweeps over me. Does the British premier have nothing better to do with his time than correspond with an obscure Mexican doctor? Is there some secret message hidden between the lines which I do not see at first glance? Who was Emilio Casavieja before he founded this place? Does he do some war-related work for the British? But when and with whom, if he never leaves the sanitarium?

I will have to carefully review the list of inpatients and Casavieja's friends who sometimes come by here to rid themselves of impenitent alcoholism and to play bezique with a Spanish deck. No matter how hard I try to reconstruct the past few years, my memory is like a dark, bottomless pool laced with interstices. I am unable to find anything significant that links Doctor Casavieja to the perfidious Albion, land of King Arthur and, in better times, to Shakespeare, to Dick Turpin, and to that benevolent bandit Robin Hood.

THE STUDIO OF THE
ORIENTAL WHORES

R ivera said something about having to go up
the stairs to the attic," said Manterola. The Poet used his one arm to point
to the sky.

They were in the middle of a great colonial patio dotted with parked
handcarts and wheelbarrows, giving the sensation that the grandeur of the
old palace had been overcome by filthy industry. Vestiges of the recent rain
were everywhere: the metallic shine of puddles and windows.

They had bribed the night watchman who, for fifty pesos, not only confirmed the studio's existence but also offered to act as their tour guide.

"They say that unconsecrated graves lie on the four sides of this patio.
In 1928, when they remodeled the palace, during Señor Clausell's life, the
masons found some very strange bones indeed buried in these walls. Some
did not even appear to be human; they were more like one of those," he
said, pointing out one of the gargoyles which adorned the central staircase
that ascended to the top floor.

They went up to the first landing, but not before the Poet had taken a
good look at the gargoyle's face. He surveyed the perimeter of the great
patio, searching for any other stairways. The railings were rusty, but in the
light of the moon the ancient stones revealed their strength and majesty.
The palace was divided in a highly unusual way into living quarters, storage

rooms, workshops, and who knows what else. It was as if the plumbing had burst, for water was dripping everywhere.

In one corner of what they thought was the top floor, a second staircase, much smaller and tighter than the first, permitted them to continue on up.

"If my memory serves me, I think that it was here," said the watchman, showing them a large wooden door set deep into the stone.

The door finally gave way after the sixth pry with the short crowbar.

"It used to be a storeroom for old textiles, but nobody's used it in quite some time," said the watchman.

The Poet lit his lantern. Sure enough, the space was chaotically yet completely filled with bolts of cloth. They sorted their way through, on into the center of the room. There, the lanternlight suddenly fell on waves of brilliant color covering one of the walls. Manterola and Fermín began to clear away a broken shutter and some roofing materials.

"Shine it here, over in this corner," said the journalist.

What they saw was difficult to describe; the entire wall was covered in paintings, organized like hundreds of individual portraits that spilled over into one another without regard for personal distinction. They slowly panned with the light and saw that the paintings covered the entire wall, floor to ceiling. It was a mural teeming with intricate narratives. With the combined eyes of a poet and a journalist, the two friends surveyed the scenes.

The stories on the wall had a certain force, a capacity to evoke, to relate, to suggest. The lantern passed from story to story: Eve dancing with a serpent, a winged politician, brooding landscapes, forests of fairies traced in greens, golds, and blues. Fermín and Manterola were dumbstruck in front of the spectacle revealed by the lantern's light.

"I've never seen such a thing," Manterola finally said.

There were landscapes done in an almost purely impressionistic style, scenes full of suggestion and things only hinted at. But more than that, it was a work of dream and illusion, a narrative technique that no Mexican painter had ever explored. It was much softer and more smooth than the work of the great muralists, much less precise, without rhetoric. Everything was more ethereal, more diffuse.

"Once in El Prado I saw some of El Bosco's works. They couldn't hold a candle to this, but this reminds me of them. I don't know why," said Fermín.

"It's the sheer number of stories that's captivating, that's overwhelming. It's as if you open a door and walk in on the totality of one man's dreams and fears," said Manterola in astonishment.

They rearranged the bolts and bundles of cloth, moving them to the center of the room in order to open up more space near the wall. The mural had been damaged in places with peeling paint, though sometimes the effects of humidity and mildew seemed to add even more vigor to a scene. The Poet recognized his mother in one very beautiful portrait, standing alongside something that seemed like a slave revolt. It was situated next to a seaside landscape that seemed the exact picture of how his father had described Greece to him many years ago when the elder Valencia had read to him from the *Iliad* and the *Odyssey*.

Had Clausell painted this for him? For someone who would come knocking ten years after his death just to poke around in his studio?

The sheer variety of stories wrought in marvelous geometry was astonishing, as was the intricate narrative woven behind them. Classical busts, studies of sculptors, amoebas, and volcanoes, a woman dancing an Aragonese *jota*, and lions—many lions—gifted with a singular humanity. Sad lions and impatient horses. And evocations of sex: female imagery, both explicit and suggested, both clothed and nude, was everywhere. And fascinating, leafless trees and gilded skies.

The Poet's past, his days with the cavalry, was also stirred by this sudden reencounter with so many horses.

Manterola wanted to gather it all in, to scan the walls and unravel the histories. He discovered several of his most intimate and beloved nightmares on the walls: the woman with the white plaits who points (at him?) and asks for stories, the man who laughs at unfinished works, characters out of our ridiculous destiny; and forests, odalisques, one of Goya's whims, unrequited love, green and orange clouds, burning lands; a woman who once belonged to Modigliani after having been painted by Van Gogh, a figure emerging from hell.

The Poet, on the other hand, wanted to focus on a particular scene before relating its matter to another, parallel history. He wanted to know what horses and naked women had to do with a barque heading to seaward, or with a brigade of firefighters who, with their rainbow jets of water, formed an arch over a man preparing to take his own life.

That was the key, these parallel histories: the hunters, the dancing strongmen, the green man of the marsh, the ship's anchor, the red feces, the crucified man, the rich ambiguity; green swathes, a wounded animal in a yellowy world, the purity of sex, brushstrokes that swept across the wall while a winged man, unmistakably Mexican despite the vagary, fished for an eagle or an anonymous vulture.

"What do you know about this man Clausell?"

"Only what Rivera told me, plus a bit more I scraped up in the newspaper archives. Joaquín Clausell, of Catalán ancestry, liberal student, opposed Porfirio Díaz's dictatorship at the end of the century, went into self-imposed exile to study painting in Paris. Have you ever heard of him before all this? He laid down his brush for years at a time, at least publically, but in private he must have been painting this room. He killed himself in Lagunas de Cempoala about seven years ago."

"I'm as Mexican as you are, and I never knew that we had such a genius as this right under our noses."

Manterola and the Poet sank into contemplation. But after a minute or so, the Poet suddenly realized that they had just spent a quarter of an hour being captivated by the walls without regard for the original purpose of their visit.

"The north wall, between the cows and skulls."

"Here," said Manterola, pointing to a part of the wall that had been blocked from view by a roll of cloth. To the right, a pair of skulls, cows grazing on a meadow above them, a bull watching from below, another pair of cows in a pasture to the left, and in the center a stretch of orange and yellow sky where, in the middle of a field, the hulk of a hacienda could be seen, dominated by a tower crowned with a . . .

"That tower, it looks like a lighthouse."

"That's it, that's what they call the asylum, the Lighthouse. That's why Clausell painted it; he was afraid that one day they were going to haul him off to there forever," said the watchman.

"Where is this place? Is there a lighthouse somewhere in Mexico City that doubles as an insane asylum?" demanded the Poet, grabbing the watchman by the lapels.

"Is that what you're looking for? A lighthouse converted into an asylum? You should have just asked me that earlier. Sure there's one, chief, in Tacubaya, near the Chapultepec jungle. Nowadays they call them "homes" or "hospitals" and they give them elegant names like 'The Lighthouse.' I had my father committed there for a time; not for madness but rather for drunkenness," the watchman offered.

"Christ," said Manterola. "Of course."

"Tacubaya, Lighthouse, Asylum, and Verdugo," the Poet summed up.

INTERRUPTIONS
AND INVASIONS

3. We meet in the library to watch a film. The projector is old and chatters away incessantly. The film is old as well, with several burned-out frames. It's a British war picture.

The theater does not seem to overly impress the group. They don't accept it as reality. Don't perceive it as information coming in from the outside world. It doesn't incorporate illusion or fantasy. It's accepted merely as the obsessions of an alienist. What do they want me to think, to gather from this film? Why do they show it to me? It's like going to school and suffering through an endlessly boring class. But I disagree with my collected companions. Film is real. This theatrical world is real. It wouldn't be worth it to make films otherwise. And even if film were not, in fact, real, it would deserve to be so.

But I must admit that in some personal way they do receive this outside information (despite the fact that we have many newspapers saved up) and interpret it. I say this because they applaud the children and they boo the pilots.

4. The Poet receives a note together with an elongated case that looks like it might carry a trumpet. The note reads:

"They have killed my assistant with a poison which was probably intended for me. I suspect that this is related to your investigations, but the perpetrators think that I'm behind them. Keep me informed as to what you find out; keep me up to date. I'm enclosing this gift which may prove useful.—M."

The Poet opens up the case and discovers the Thompson. His mind is ablaze with all these things when Manterola comes to pick him up.

A PAIR OF TWOS THAT WAS

A THREE OF A KIND

It was the longest bender of his life. He remembered that Martha was off working as a war reporter somewhere in the Pacific or in England under the rain of German bombs or taking in the sun in Malta while the Stukas attacked, screaming, in droves. Or something like that. The fact was that she probably would never return. It frightened him. He was a "precocious anti-Fascist," as was said of some of the boys from the Lincoln Brigade who had fought in Spain but now were not wanted for the army. He was a "precocious anti-Fascist writer and journalist." And so, with that idea rooted firmly in his head, very proud of having been "precocious" but full of anger because they wouldn't let him fight his battles, he recalled that he had begun his Thursday at 12:40 p.m. with a daiquiri in front of him, a pale blue sky beyond the window, and a humid, muggy heat all around. He had followed that path down to the empty swimming pool outside Finca Vigía with a cocktail shaker in hand and ice cubes clinking. Now, his head droning amid that certain brand of irreality that is produced only in nightmares, he was here. But where was that?

Ernest Hemingway asked for the next card face up.

"Hit me."

The Mute, standing reservedly though naked, dealt him a card. An ace of hearts.

"Hit me again," he asked his opponent.

They were playing in a padded room, with no doors or windows, with a ridiculous sewing table in the center flanked by two chairs and a quartet of characters seated on the floor next to a small table holding a pitcher of lemonade and glasses.

"What day is it, what time is it, and where are we?" asked Hemingway in English of his opponent, who hinted that the pair of twos he showed was actually a three of a kind in disguise.

It had all the qualities of a nightmare without actually being one. The sensation of unreality was pervasive. Only unreality is real. Or if not, it at least seems very real while being just as absurd.

"Sunday night, I think. They haven't let me wear a watch in quite some time," his opponent answered in good English, though with just a bit of a stiff accent. The English of a Latin American scholar. "And we're in Mexico, I believe. It's been a long time since I stuck my head out a window. Metaphorically speaking, of course."

"And how did I get here?"

"In quite a bad state indeed. Drunk, doubtlessly. I suppose they remembered you from your last visit here."

"And they let me in just like that? I remember the last time they put a mountain of paperwork in front of me."

"This place admits drunks at any time of day or night. Fumigating and drying them out is the official mission. There's another thing, too . . . the one who received you, the director Doctor Casavieja, is a longtime admirer of yours. He's got all your books in the library."

He asked for another card, face up. An ace of hearts showing, two fours, and an ace of spades face down. He was dealt a five of clubs. His opponent was showing a pair of twos, a six, and a jack.

"But how did I get to Mexico? The last thing I remember is being by the pool at my home outside Havana . . ."

"De la Calle thinks you were dropped off near Veracruz by a German submarine," replied the lawyer Alberto Verdugo.

"Bullshit," said Hemingway.

"I have a few theories," said De la Calle, pouring a pair of lemonades. "But first, forgive me, we haven't been properly introduced."

PART	XI

THINGS NOT
NECESSARILY TRUE

THE PYRAMID

The Germans found the pyramid purely by chance. It was not simply a pyramid but also a burial mound, and it didn't rise powerfully above the forest canopy, dominating the jungle like those at Uxmal or Chichen Itzá. This pyramid was set into the base of a hill, more sunk into the earth than soaring over it, making it very difficult to find. It had eluded explorers along the Ruta Maya for roughly a century, from Stephens to Maudsley to Charnay. It was situated several kilometers to the east of the Usumacinta River, in a region that was no more Mexico than it was Guatemala or Belize. Lost for 1250 years. The mausoleum housed the remains of an obscure prince who, in life, was called Conejo-Pez and whose son, Conejo-Venado, succeeded him and built it to house his remains and memory. The place had no name; it was more than fifty kilometers from the nearest village, and so Rudolf Glauer had dubbed it Die Tür, "the Door," perhaps moved to awe by the supremely beautiful figure that presided over the entrance to the pyramid. It was a warrior-priest, something rare in Mayan lore, looking at once east and west. The face that looked east wore a mask of death.

After taking a few photographs, he went in alone into the interior and emerged two days later, feverish and dehydrated, trembling, his eyes glassed over. For two more days he didn't breathe a word and did nothing but sleep fitfully in the camp they had struck at the river's edge. His guide, who had refused to enter the pyramid with him ("because it was a place for the dead, and the dead ought to be left to rest"), took the German's condition as further proof that one shouldn't meddle with the past, and urged him to leave the region at once. But on the third day, Rudolf decided to go back inside. When he faced again the figure of the warrior-priest, he had a change of conscience and, with the help of his guide, he covered both his find and his footprints with dead palm fronds. Something that was perhaps a bit unnecessary, for the jungle would reclaim its territory within days.

The guide, whose name was Manfredo Uk, was never seen by his family again. Perhaps it was because the Germans killed him to ensure his silence, perhaps because Rudolf took him back to Turkey with him as a manservant where he would die years later of syphilis, perhaps because Manfredo went to Veracruz and became a merchant and married a new woman and had new children and later went to work as a haulage contractor in the Federal District and never again returned to Chiapas.

But the pyramid's discovery didn't just afflict Manfredo. It's rumored that from then on, Rudolf was never again able to sleep, became an insomniac, stopped using the ridiculous safari hat and monocle that had made him almost a caricature of Prussian nobility, though perhaps that was because he was a tinhorn nobleman in the first place. And he never told a soul about what he saw inside that pyramid save for his friend and disciple, a young, mediocre Viennese painter named Adolf Hitler Poelzl, who was rapidly moving upward in the circles of nationalism and esoterica the postwar period. Whatever it was that he told him, Hitler noted it down on a slip of paper and hid it carefully in the hollow leg of his office desk.

THE THEORIES

How did Ernest Hemingway arrive in Mexico?
   Given that the American writer was never able to offer a coherent explanation to that effect, I will venture a few theories of my own.
   The First Theory (chaos):
   During his drunken binge by the empty pool at Finca Vigía, Hemingway began to obsess about the submarine base off Camagüey to such an extent that, in a moment of relative physical stability, he stumbled into his room, hung his field glasses around his neck, and started on down the road toward San Francisco de Paula. The local ice truck, driven by a mulatto named Germán, picked him up and eventually dropped him off in Cojímar where he continued to drink, this time a highly infamous brand of home-distilled rum known as *chispatren*, or "engine fire" to the unacquainted, with a group of sailors and fishermen who knew him well. Before night fell the Cubans deposited him on the deck of a small argosy being held in port for technical reasons and which, say those who chartered it, was on its way to Mexico with its cargo of El Gaitero-brand Spanish hard cider which the crew had delivered to Cuba by mistake. But this cannot be entirely correct, because in those days there was a Mexican embargo against products from Franco's Spain, although perhaps this was a way of passing the cider off as Cuban rather than Spanish. And besides, who the hell would want to drink hard,

frothy cider during the summer? But whatever the case may be, Hemingway slept for a full day on the deck of the ship, awaking with sunstroke and a hangover in the Veracruz port, still sprawled across the crates of cider which the docksmen were already beginning to unload. The theory falls apart again, however, since what argosy could ever have docked at Cojímar, which is little more than a fishing village? And what vessel of that size could have crossed the gulf in twenty-four hours?

To confirm this hypothesis we would have to (a) find one Germán the ice truck driver; (b) find out if a Cuban cargo vessel unloaded two hundred cases of Spanish cider and one drunk gringo in Veracruz; and (c) check to see if he ended up traveling with the cider to the freight station where he was loaded into a boxcar for the long ride to Mexico City. Even with all of these coincidences intact, it still doesn't seem plausible.

The Second Theory (fantasy):

Being drunk, Hemingway had forgotten that he had asked his driver to prepare an exploratory trip to Camagüey, and so it did not surprise his driver in the least when he showed up, stumbling and stammering, binoculars in hand, got in the car, and immediately passed out. The driver, following his previously laid out instructions, drove on to Matanzas before finally coming to a stop out in front of a big, rambling old house whose address Hemingway had given to him.

What happened next may even be beyond the definition of fantasy, but the theory is that Hemingway was captured by the crew of a German submarine, tossed in the back of a pickup truck, and driven to the Camagüey coast where a rubber skiff awaited to row them through the mangrove swamp and out into a lagoon where U164 was waiting for them. Surrounded by mist, Hemingway heard a bearded Captain Dietrich barking out orders in German. A swift crossing of the gulf and a surfacing off the coast of Veracruz, and Hemingway was left to be picked up by an ambulance which delivered him to a train station in the highlands near Perote, where a pair of Spanish monks mercifully helped him to board the train to Mexico City. However you look at it, seventy-two hours after lapsing into a drunken stupor in his pool outside Havana, Hemingway arrived, dazed and confused, at Mexico City's Buenavista Station.

In order to confirm this theory, we would have to check if Hemingway's Plymouth and his driver Juan were still waiting for him in Camagüey, and if one of the subs in the German fleet was manned by a Captain Dietrich. But above all, we must ask ourselves this: what possible interest could the Germans have in ferrying Ernest Hemingway across the goddamned Gulf of Mexico?

The Third Theory (aerial):

Hemingway went stumbling from the pool into his room where he took $600 and his passport from his writing desk along with his ready-packed satchel, which contained a pair of socks (Hemingway never wore underwear), a spare nylon comb, a bottle of aspirin, quinine pills to combat malaria, a softcover notebook, and two pencils. He called a taxi, went to the airport, got on the next plane leaving: one bound for Los Angeles with a stopover in Mexico City.

He slept for the duration of the flight.

This hypothesis is half-solid, because Hemingway himself well knew that drunkenness is an excuse to do any sort of thing at all, but he doubts very much that the frightful experience of passing through customs would not have registered in his mind.

We would, of course, have to confirm that such a flight existed, since many commercial flights have been suspended on account of the war, and we would have to check and see if the immigration records bear the name of our writer.

In summary:

Given the inconsistencies in each of these three theories, we have no choice but to conclude that Hemingway never came to Mexico.

We have shuffled these and other explanations around, always arriving at the same conclusion, which is something of a nuisance, because if we are not, in fact, in Mexico, then why, from the tower which dominates both our abode and the surrounding terrain and which they let us go up into once a year, do we see the Chapultepec Palace instead of the old Morro fort?

This is, indeed, a bit of a problem.

THE RESURRECTION

The rumor that the Iguana was still alive began, very slowly at first, to spread, though it wasn't just one single rumor but rather several highly dubious and contradictory ones.

A massive bonfire raged to one side of the company store of the Hacienda Walkirias; a bonfire which had been no accident, for two empty four-liter gasoline cans were found near the entrance to the hacienda that hadn't been there before.

Most rumors spoke of the return of the Iguana, but there were others circulating too that said that he had been reincarnated as a Golden Badger, much younger than the Iguana had been and who carried only a hunting knife and not a Nepalese *kukhri* as before.

Other rumors told of how the Iguana, full of lead but losing blood, had been found by a group of children who bandaged his wounds and carried him deep into the jungle, somewhere outside Tabasco, and hung him in a hammock high in a tree to rest until he recovered.

Proponents of reason say that this is impossible, joking about "how many children does it take to hang an iguana in a tree" and things of that nature.

"Many," replied the spreading rumors. "Many, many children."

And there was one final rumor that contended that the Iguana had been seen at the bar of the Hotel Excélsior, sipping a mescal as if nothing were wrong, and that later, on the bathroom wall, a picture of a golden, six-legged iguana had appeared . . . but that this time, for the first time in all iguana iconography, the iguana was smoking a cigarette.

PART	XII

SHORT STORIES

THE PADDED ROOM

"**C**ome in! You're slower than I remember," he said as he opened the door to the padded cell. The walls were covered in a puffy white fabric, though in a morbid way, as if a great, off-white, buttoned quilt had enveloped them, even the floor, save for the high ceiling where a single naked bulb hung from a dirty black cord.

There is something about families reuniting after long periods of separation which allows discomfort to dominate pleasure. A certain prudish tenderness, perhaps, or a strong dose of timidity. What can a group of people who have not seen each other in years say when what unites them is merely vague recollections of things best left unremembered? What can you ask and what is forbidden?

To the eyes of the lawyer Verdugo, the Poet had deteriorated. He seemed shorter and slightly askew, listing like a sinking ship on account of the missing arm whose absence was marked by the empty sleeve of his jacket which floated there at his side. Manterola, in turn, seemed older, more myopic, more bald, more sad.

To the eyes of the Poet and the journalist, Verdugo had been profoundly transformed. The shadow of still other shadows. His hair was cut very short, like a soldier's or a prisoner's, nearly shaved and full of grayish swatches, a sparse, uneven beard, with a gaze lost in the hollows of his eyesockets. He had grown quite thin in these past sixteen or seventeen years since they had seen him last. Only his voice remained unchanged: cold, raspy, with a touch of irony and masked by a half-grin.

"Come in, I said! How slow can you have gotten?" Verdugo said to Pio-quinto Manterola and Fermín Valencia as he opened the door to his padded cell.

To get this far the two friends had had to negotiate a series of quite odd situations indeed. A cab driver had refused to drive up to the asylum door because it had once admitted a friend of his but never released him, and then a paved path running up to the Lighthouse materialized in front of them, as in Clausell's painting, and then the ugly doorman who blocked the way, saying "Visitors are only allowed on Thursdays," and then a small doctor in a white coat who waved them through with the cryptic phrase, "Let them through, Jacinto, they've come for poker," followed by a walk through in-terminable gardens under the aggressive gaze of a collection of strange hu-man beings who wove baskets hunched over like assembly line workers and watched them as if they had no right to exist, and all of it culminating with the final trip led by a lame nurse who directed them down into the basement and to a room whose door would be personally opened by Alberto Verdugo, who greeted them with,

"Come in! You're slower than I remember!"

2

SUBMARINES

Admiral Karl Dönitz had established certain explicit regulations governing the German submarines that were operating in the Gulf of Mexico: maintain absolute radio silence during the crossing from France, do not engage the enemy or attack merchant vessels unless the prey is in excess of nineteen tons, and under no circumstances sink ships flying under the Mexican flag. Dönitz felt that, as Mexico was not a belligerent nation, this last regulation was a bit much, but he knew that errors were committed with an alarming frequency in submarine combat and that during a war, especially operating under the cover of night, many unfortunate incidents could be produced. Canaris, the Abwehr chief, had made this fact particularly clear.

The operational zone had been laid out in a grid, and the emphasis had been placed on attacking fuel or crude oil tankers passing between the Texas refineries, the Gulf ports of Venezuela, the British Caribbean islands, and the Florida canal.

But a single attack sub, U231, under the command of Captain Richard Schulz, had received more specific orders, and it abandoned the grid to which it had been assigned and nosed its way into the Gulf and Mexican territorial waters. At the very modest speed of nine knots, it made its way to a place whose existence was known only by a select few men, a place by the name of Puerto de las Perlas.

HE WAS SPEAKING IN CHINESE

When Tomás Wong opened his eyes, an ancient Indian man with a wizened, leathery, face spoke without waiting for him to accustom himself to this new reality. The Chinaman had always thought that death was nothingness, which seemed like it would have been enough. But this nothingness was ringing with speech.

"A bit of your magic is true magic, but the majority of it is just power and money. If only it were magic, then we could fuck them. Ours against theirs, and we break them, we finish them," the Indian said in Spanish, and then continued on in another language.

Tomás decided that he was dead, and that death was this softness where the pain of fatal wounds was now perceived as merely an echo, where everything was shrouded in great banks of glowing mist, and where you found yourself in front of an old man speaking an unknown tongue while a faint, musical murmur of falling water dominated it all.

"I don't believe in God; you can take your damn speech and shove it."

But his words came out in Chinese.

"What did he say?" asked a child who had walked in at that moment with a dead armadillo for making soup.

"He was speaking in Chinese," the old Indian said, renouncing his Tzotzil and smiling a broad, bat-winged smile, his one remaining tooth shining brightly.

THE PRACTICAL WRITER

Ernest Hemingway liked to think of himself as a man of action, which is why he was able to occupy himself by retracing the strange paths that had brought him from an empty pool outside Havana to an insane asylum in Mexico City. He concentrated on the details. Where was his missing shoe? How had Verdugo managed to bluff him into believing that he was holding a pair of aces? What did this brochure say, the one written in Spanish that Doctor Casavieja had very generously given him just a couple of minutes ago and which was ostentatiously entitled *"Parámetros de Desintozicazión por Evaporación de Efluvios"*? Was it destiny that had brought him here? They had given him a room with a view of the garden and on top of the dresser there was a washbasin, an Olivetti, and a ream of blank white paper. He had been up the better part of the night working on his impossible novel. Finally his alter ego, Thomas Hudson, had been able to get past the first few lines and was now locked in an interminable conversation with his ex-wife—or his wife on the verge of being his ex—at a Florida bar only to be interrupted by a group of drunks and casual acquaintances. The tension of these words, which apparently said nothing at all, was strong, successful, and lifelike as ever. This was good, hard, terse prose and he knew it. It was also charged with autobiography, autoindulgence, autodisdain, and premonitions colored by what had been his relationship with Martha and what he knew it would be. In the end, this all seemed fair.

A writer needs good material, and what better material than his own life and his own contradictory disputes? The important thing was that he was writing. But in an insane asylum? Perhaps fate had finally brought him to his proper place. If you accept madness, others will take care of you, prevent you from harming yourself, and then you can dedicate yourself to writing without reservation. He would even have to check and see what the Internal Revenue Service—the pernicious IRS—had to say about collecting taxes from a madman.

He made two apparently contradictory decisions: try this "detoxification by the evaporation of emanations" that Casavieja had suggested, and in the meantime search the entirety of this new universe of his for a place that made a decent daiquiri.

GOD WAS A WOMAN

God was a woman. This confirmed every suspicion which he had never before dared, in his pragmatic logic and his vital and rational mentality, to admit to himself. But here God was, high in the branches of a tree, and she said, quite ceremoniously to him,

"I am going to give you, Golden Iguana, an army of ants the color of coffee to see if together you can defeat the brown shirts."

"Give me what you will, but I'm not going back. Because, for one thing, I don't believe in God," said Tomás Wong, and suddenly his entire body burned with pain. Evidently, God had decided to revive him.

It was the single worst ordeal he had ever suffered in his life.

He decided to sleep. He wasn't strong enough yet to think about such complicated things. As he descended into dream he began to prepare a list of questions that he wanted to ask of God: Do angels have wings? Do they serve beer in heaven? Why were the Jews of Palestine the chosen people instead of the Zulus or the Cubans? Is God an atheist? Knowing the nature of Romans, why make the Vatican the seat of all Catholicism? Was she really—no, I mean really—against divorce? And if she likes Mexicans so much, why did she drive them out of the place that later became Hollywood in the war of 1847? Is it true that Saint Peter accepts bribes?

Tomás slept with a sardonic smile on his lips. The female God interpreted this as a sign of goodwill, and she let herself down out of the tree, mild, placid, divine.

6	

DETOXIFICATION

The way the emanation treatment worked is this: the doctor gave you a spade, an ordinary steel spade with a wood handle, a complicitous smile, and then he locked you in the basement to shovel coal into the furnace which heated the water for the entire asylum. Dig in, shovel out, and the furnace door devoured the coal as if it were the boiler on the Titanic.

After a quarter of an hour your back began to ache, but more important, you were expelling vapors and sweating like a hog as the alcohol that had accumulated in your body worked its way out. Hemingway put down the shovel, having decided that no lunatic ever complains about the temperature of his water, and set himself to a more important matter: finding a decent daiquiri.

He made his way back to the padded room to ask the lawyer Verdugo.

AN HOMAGE TO QUEVEDO

Tomás Wong viewed the classic writings from Spain's Golden Age in a skeptical light. The fact that they had been dubbed "classics" was what made him the most uncomfortable. The term was a disease that could blight good literature, could condemn it to the realm of scholarship and erudition. Literature was something that had to happen without premeditations and prejudices, without middlemen shuttling between reader and text, both acting in a state of solitude. Nevertheless, raised in a world of athenaeums and clandestine libraries, he had to remember that any well-formed anarchy must include the liberating monologue of Calderón de la Barca, the satirical poetry of Góngora, the love poems of Lope de Vega, and, above all, the sonnets of Quevedo, those devastating verses that shine across the centuries like beams of light illuminating the consciousness. Or could it be that, despite the nature of rebellion, the classics were also savored by the anarchists? Tomás pondered over this question because a magestral line from old Pancho Quevedo, which he had first read on one of his long-ago voyages, returned to memory: "God dresses himself." What else could have dressed God? It was a brilliantly simple phrase that defied all explication.

He reorganized his thoughts. A true atheist would not permit God to so easily stick his or her nose into his life; therefore, this female god was not in fact God but was probably a minor deity assigned to work with atheists. Now that the initial shock had worn off, he could see it all very clearly.

He timidly half-opened one eye and this simple act awoke in him an avalanche of fears and pains. He tried to adjust himself to the light. Was he high in a tree or deep in some cave? He tried to place each possibility in the context of his new reality.

It was neither one nor the other. It was . . .

8

THE REASONS FOR POKER

C an I smoke here?" asked the Poet, breaking the awkward silence that had settled in after the initial shock of recognition.

"No, I'm afraid it's the only known restriction," replied Verdugo, ushering them into the padded room and directing them toward the makeshift card table, the chairs, and the lemonade.

"And to what do we owe this unexpected reunion after so many years?" asked Manterola, sinking heavily into his seat.

"I've organized a game of stud poker."

"Have we given up on dominoes?" asked the Poet, taking off his hat and tossing it into the air in a magnificent flight that ended as it came to rest in a corner of the room.

To ask questions or not . . . that is the question. To delve into that uncomfortable twenty-year gap. How is it that one of us is now a madman? When did another lose his arm? Is it true, journalist, that you attempted suicide a few years ago? How do you, Poet, tie your shoes with only one hand? Is it true that you killed your wife, Verdugo? Are you still single, Poet?

The return bears powers and potencies, but it also brings hesitancy.

"Why decks and not bones? I get the impression that breaking such a tradition requires some very important motives," Manterola both asked and answered.

"Because a new player has come to join the old group. He's not familiar with dominoes, even though he lives in Cuba. I was playing with him just yesterday, in fact."

"Verdugo! Where can I get my hands on a decent daiquiri?" asked Hemingway as he entered the room.

"Motherfucker! It's Ernest Hemingway!" exclaimed the Poet, who had seen him once before, during the war in Spain. He was a bit paunchier now, a bit grayer, the tension in his gaze had thickened, his cheeks had rounded, and he seemed to have just emerged from a week's worth of insomnia.

"How was your detoxification?" asked Verdugo.

"*Muy buena*. So *buena*, in fact, that I need a reintoxication. Where can I get a decent daiquiri in this dungeon?"

Verdugo handled the introductions:

"The Poet and, as I understand, secret agent, Fermín Valencia, who is also like you a veteran of the war in Spain . . . the renowned journalist Pioquinto Manterola . . . and the novelist Ernesto Hemingway."

9

THE CHILD

While Otto Rahn, known in Mexico as Brü-ning, scrawled the words "The door has been opened" on the dining room wall in his strange and bloody runistic calligraphy under the peaceful gaze of the dead man who contemplated him with impossibly wide-open eyes, as if he couldn't believe what had just happened, Rainer Kowalski poked through a little bookshelf in the bedroom. The dead man was apparently not much of a reader: a few magazines, a cookbook, a half-dozen porno-graphic novels published by Alegría, a copy of the Mexican constitution, and a copy of the Transportation Union's collective contract. And strangely at odds with this collection was a book on Mayan archaeological treasures. Although he couldn't read Spanish, Kowalski decided to take a look, first flipping through the pages and then the look became a more and more meticulous one. Perhaps there would be a sign, some sort of mark.

"Captain, I may have found something over here."

Rahn was a wreck. The violence had gotten him a bit unhinged and although he hadn't taken part in the actual torture, letting Kowalski's natural sense of brutality take charge of that situation, his eyes were bloodshot and his pulse was racing. He came into the room feverish and mad, his hands swathed in blood and his hair disheveled.

Kowalski shot him a look of disdain. He didn't like this little psychopath who had been assigned to be his partner. He held out the book to him and as he did, a pair of photographs slipped out from between the pages.

"What's this?" asked Rahn as he picked up the pictures, getting bloody fingerprints all over then and then smearing them worse when he tried to wipe them off with the cuff of his sleeve.

They were faded and blurry with a sepia hue. Perhaps twenty years old. They showed a clearing in the jungle and a Mayan statue which seemed to guard the entrance to a pyramid half hidden beneath the thick vegetation. They were the same photo taken from two different angles, but with one alteration: the first showed a younger version of the dead man, dressed in shorts and a loose-fitting shirt, standing in front of the stela, while the second one featured a European man with a safari hat looking haughtily at the camera like a landowner.

"It's Rudolf Glauer, Von Sebottendorff! It's the pyramid! Where did you get these?"

"They were in the book," said Kowalski, annoyed by his clumsiness. Then, as he went to hand the book to Rahn a second time, he saw that a young child was watching him. They hadn't noticed him until now; he had probably been hiding in the bedroom for the full two hours that they had spent torturing Manfredo Uk. He was perhaps ten years old, wearing shorts and a stained white shirt. He had wedged—almost embedded—himself between the bed and an armoire. Rahn, following Kowalski's gaze, was dumbstruck.

"Get rid of him, *sturmführer*," he said, leaving the room.

Kowalski walked slowly toward the child, who sank himself even further between the two pieces of furniture and covered his face with his hands.

Kowalski drew his Lüger from his belt. He reached out his hand toward the child, motioning for him to come out as he began to make his way toward the other room. If he was going to kill this kid, he wanted Rahn to see it. Backing away and with his hand outstretched, he began to talk softly to the child. The sound of his voice, coupled with the effect of the pistol, exerted a terrible force on the child, who eased his way out and began to follow him.

"Come on now. Look. It's your father, right? He's fucked. Come on. That's it. He's fucked because I am the devil, and I've come to take him to hell with me. Come on now. You can't get away. You've got nowhere to go. The door is here, behind me, and I've got the gun. Come on, that's it. Closer. Look at him. Look at the way the blood runs down his head. But you can't run . . . not from the devil. You know that, right? You've got nowhere to go, but you want it to all be over. Come on, closer. Look at the pistol. It's scary, right? Stick the barrel right down your throat. That's it. It hurts now, doesn't it? Now close your eyes. You're about to go off with your father. Close them . . ."

But the child, his eyes tremendously open, understood nothing of Kowalski's German and simply sat down hopelessly at his dead father's side.

And then Kowalski fired.

CURRENCY

The money collected on the table was a mish-mash. There were Hemingway's dollars, the Poet and Manterola threw down pesos, Verdugo contributed beans (because no money circulated in the Lighthouse), De la Calle had declined to play but lent out his collection of old Spanish doubloons, and Erasto offered kernels of maize. All of this was equated in a complex table which held that six beans were worth one peso, three pesos were worth a dollar, three dollars to a doubloon, and one doubloon to fifty kernels of maize.

The Poet won the first round with three eights.

GOD WAS CHINESE

He was inside a pyramid. A Mayan pyramid. The stelas on the walls described Chac, who looked to be the god of rain. They had found many such likenesses during the construction of the Pan-American Highway. The Maya evidently placed a singular importance on rain.

He lay on a camp cot looking up at the natural vault of a cave covered by trickling water and thick vegetation. How, then, did he know that he was inside a Mayan pyramid? All around the cot there were lit ocote wood torches fixed to the floor. Was someone holding a wake over him? Two rabbits sat at the foot of the cot, watching him attentively. No one had ever said anything about there being rabbits. Not even the most devout Franciscan would have dared to promote such a theory. It had to be that

a. God didn't exist,
b. God was a woman,
c. Heaven was full of rabbits, or
d. He was dead and they had left him inside a Mayan pyramid.

A fine end for a former naval mechanic and domino player, just under two meters in height, who had survived the Long March of Chu Teh.

Tomás Wong began to laugh. He tried to hoist himself up out of bed, but an intense pain and dizziness obliged him to lie back down. When the world stopped spinning like a galaxy inside his head, he surveyed the walls as far as the meager torch light would permit. Stelas and drawings described a city torn by conflicting forces: the plumed priests and the warriors. Just then he noticed one of the characters who seemed to be revered by the others. He looked closely at him. His face, though not his hands, was painted yellow.

Tomás Wong laughed again. It was all clear to him now. God was Chinese.

THINGS KNOWN

AND UNKNOWN

He showed up at our door with a note pinned to his jacket that read, 'This man needs sleep. Please help him.' He was crying. The guy intrigued me. I've always had an interest in (an affinity toward?) people possessed by the devil. He howled in his sleep, told us to call him Herschel and that he was from Vienna . . ." Verdugo reconstructed the history.

They spoke, alternating Spanish and English, out of deference to Hemingway, who had difficulty following the story and the uniquely Mexican idioms.

"And De la Calle is convinced that he was Hanussen, Hitler's mage."

"But Hanussen died; his assassination was a conspiracy and quite big news," said Manterola, who had read about it in his own paper years ago.

"Well, he's sticking to his story," said Verdugo with a shrug toward a silent Angel de la Calle who was seated on the floor in a corner of the padded room, working on a new series of palm drawings. He nodded vigorously.

"How is it that your Herschel could be Hitler's Hanussen?" asked the Poet. And without waiting for a response, he replied, "Tall enough, dark-haired, a tendency toward grand entrances, and wire-rimmed glasses like the intellectuals wear."

"Face down," said Hemingway, asking for another card and showing a six accompanied by a five of diamonds.

"And he was wearing an enormous coat, much too big for him, and he had books on the *Iliad* in his pockets . . . It's my turn, hit me with one face up," affirmed Verdugo.

The Poet deftly dealt out the cards with his one hand.

Manterola was showing a pair of sixes and asked for one face down, readying with his hand the grains of maize he was prepared to bet, whatever card might fall on the table.

"This Herschel is one of those men carrying an Austrian passport that you told us about. The group of Germans who infiltrated the country a few months ago and who so obtusely all carried passports bearing the same date of birth: April 20th."

"*¡Ay, carajo!* That's Hitler's birthday," exclaimed Hemingway.

"Describe the kidnappers. One was blond—almost albino—and the other was small in stature and he had very curly hair, no?" the Poet both asked and answered Verdugo once again.

"The coat! His coat ought to still be around here somewhere. He wasn't wearing it when they carried him off . . . But yes, they were exactly as you described."

Erasto the Mute reacted to the suggestion like a bolt of lightning and ran out of the room like a naked soul being hounded by the devil.

"I'll bet six kernels," said Manterola.

"I'll see you six kernels, and raise you a dollar," said Hemingway.

"You see, that's the problem, because there are six and a half kernels to a dollar, and if we start cutting these things in half . . ." protested Manterola as Verdugo and the Poet threw down their cards.

"Then I'll just take your six kernels. *Está bueno*," Hemingway said condescendingly.

Five card stud is a game for intelligent folk. Chance plays a role in the short term, the ability to calculate becomes important in the later stages of the game, but a talent for bluffing is necessary for ultimate victory.

The journalist was dealt a two; Hemingway had a low straight: five-six-seven.

Hemingway bluffed too often, the journalist was cursed with a tendency to hesitate, the Poet was completely irrational, and only the new Verdugo seemed to be able to successfully combine luck, counting, and farce in such a way as to gradually collect the majority of the doubloons, kernels, beans, pesos, and dollars in front of him.

Another six kernels and the pot grew again.

"One up for me," asked the writer. He was dealt a four of diamonds. If he was sitting on an eight, his straight was complete.

"One down for me," said the journalist, revealing that his two sixes were accompanied by two twos.

But just then Erasto burst in with Hanussen's long, dark, and worn overcoat, and the duel of the deck was put on hold.

Verdugo rifled through the pockets, which held some loose change and a Spanish language copy of *Across the River and Into the Trees*, which Hemingway looked at in shock.

"It's the network's codebook," explained the Poet. "Each member has a copy."

"That's quite an honor," the writer said in Spanish.

The Poet leafed through the book page by page. The cover had been doctored. A tiny slit had been cut into the edge of the laminated cardboard as with a razor, and something was stuck inside. Fermín, in an act of dexterity which was next to impossible for a one-armed man, coaxed it out. It was a piece of silk.

"You truly are a genius among agents," said Manterola.

"Keep it up and I'll kiss your shiny bald head," grinned the Poet as he unfolded the scrap.

AN AUTOGRAPHED PHOTO

At one side of the greater altar at the temple of Jesús Nazareno, on Pino Suárez Street in the historic center of Mexico City, there were a series of deep recesses in the wall used as tombs. There, on the top half of the third headstone from the bottom, a cross and the name of Clemente Díaz Canesco are etched in the grayish marble. Pressing the four E's in the deceased's name activates a mechanism that causes the stone covering the niche to slide smoothly outward while a lower part of the wall opens to show a tunnel running for a hundred meters or so down into the basement of the old palace of Saturnino Heredia, which today is in a sad, crumbling state on the verge of collapse.

"I would like to thank you for your cooperation and also to present you—in the name of our great leader—this photo which he has signed," said Otto Rahn in German.

The depleted remnants of the Aztec Knights nodded emphatically and smiled underneath their hoods.

Rahn made the formal presentation of Hitler's autographed portrait to the new Grand Master, who placed it on top of a trestle table covered in black velvet where there was already located an etching of the Virgin of Guadalupe and a photo of General Saturnino Cedillo.

SLIGHT CERTAINTIES

So what's on that mysterious little scrap?" asked Hemingway.

"Some instructions, in German I think. Who here can read German? Verdugo, of course. Forgive me," said the Poet, handing him the piece of silk. Verdugo unfolded it carefully and began to read falteringly:

"The objective has to seem suspended in the air, with no apparent connection to the things surrounding it. The key is to blur the supporting elements into the background while at the same time creating a visual distraction. It is very important for it to appear fixed in space to observers, its motion hidden from them through some sort of coincidental filter. Light will be the key. The act must take very little time so that there is no time for reflection after the initial shock."

"And . . . ? That's it?" asked Manterola.

"That's it."

"It sounds like the definition of an act of optical illusion. Something a magician would keep in his notebook: 'The ABC's of the Apparition of the Virgen de Fátima in Your Own Living Room' or something."

"All right, newsman, how much are your sixes worth?" demanded the American writer.

Poker is a game whose fundamental essence is to lose as little as possible when you can't win and to win as much as possible when you can. Both defensive and offensive, poker requires time. Time for unraveling your opponent's strategy and for neutralizing the factor of chance. The silence of the night and the padded room lent themselves well to it. But there were too many distractions. Stud poker does not work well in an excess of information.

Dawn was already approaching by the time everyone had finished telling their tales of Nazis, Puerto de las Perlas, Miguel Alemán and his mistress, submarine bases nestled in the cayes off Camagüey, the prevalence of esoterica in the origins of national socialist movements, rabbis rescued in Veracruz, brownshirts patrolling the Soconusco jungle and being hunted by a golden iguana, exiled German intellectuals meeting in the back room of a hardware shop, a mysterious African woman who reads minds, a British agent called Graham Greene, and so on and so on. The stories cast a spell over the game, since no rational endeavor could proceed normally through such dense chaos. Finally, as the first rays of light filtered in through the outer windows and gradually crept into the padded room through the half-opened door, a long silence came to roost.

Erasto the Mute had curled up on the floor to sleep, and De la Calle had discovered that by soaking his pens in lemon juice, he could draw on the fabric covering the walls.

"I suggest we review what we know for sure, then move on to examine the rumors, and leave some time at the end for more speculations," said the Poet. Manterola was surprised; he rarely saw this rational side to his friend.

Verdugo asked for his next card face up. A second four appeared to accompany the first, along with a jack and the covered card.

"But what do we know for sure?" asked Hemingway. "I sure as hell don't know. I was dozing in my pool outside Havana and the next thing I know, I'm here in this asylum. Everything about my presence here is absurd."

The Poet, being something of an expert in enigmas, offered a summary:

"I think we should concentrate on the players themselves: Minister of the Interior, Miguel Alemán, his mistress Hilda Krüger, the mysterious Otto Rahn (alias Linz, alias Brüning), Hanussen (alias Herschel), and the man with the ash-blond hair. Now we move on to the places: Veracruz, Puerto de las Perlas, and Chiapas? This part isn't very clear. What do these brownshirts and this golden iguana have to do with the rest of it all? I've received reports of Nazi groups operating among the German community in Torreón. So why Chiapas and not there? And then there is this backdrop of esoterica: all the stories Manterola has heard, the Aztec Knights chanting "He comes" while Otto Rahn's messages read "The door has been opened," and the fact that the cast is made up of both Jews and Nazis . . . that office which Manterola's friends talk about of the Ahnenerbe in Stuttgart. It's all so perfectly clear."

The poker players laughed. But was a forced laugh, like that of a school-boy caught looking up his teacher's skirt.

"I don't know why, but I think that it'll end up being important that these two Nazis, Rahn and Herschel, are actually Jewish," said Hemingway. "That can't be just a coincidence."

"We're not just blindly accepting the fact that these two men are alive, are we? I mean, they are officially dead," protested Manterola.

"Let's take it step by step. Information can't be controlled if the overall landscape isn't taken into consideration," replied Verdugo.

"Christ, I thought I was the poet here."

"Actually, now that you mention it, I've been calling you 'the Poet' for the past twenty-two years, and I've yet to hear a single one of your poems," said Manterola.

"If you promise not to laugh."

"It would be impossible."

"Well then . . .

> I grew out of poetry,
> But when I arrived at the advent of glory
> I found that days of infamy
> Had grown under the soles of our feet
> I am what I am,
> The Other,
> He who could have been
> Had he ever reached the stage.

Verdugo patiently translated it, line by line, into English. Hemingway showed no emotion but nodded energetically.

A short while later, the Poet finished them off with a full house, queens high. After a wave of yawns, they decided to end the meeting.

They walked out the large exterior door of the Lighthouse, under the sleepy gaze of the lame doorman. The Poet struck a match on his boot and lit a cigarette, Manterola broke out his pipe, and Hemingway felt sad because he didn't smoke. Dawn was breaking dirty and gray, nothing was clear, and the valley was replete with dense fog.

"I know a place in the Mixcoac market not far from here where they sell a chicken soup with rice and garbanzo beans that's absolutely marvelous," offered the Poet.

"Let's do it," confirmed Manterola. Again, Hemingway merely nodded, partly because he had no idea what garbanzo beans were and partly because he had only just now soberly realized that he had gone several hours— days?—without eating.

"We can head toward civilization and maybe a taxi too, leaving this urban ranch behind us."

They found a road that ran down toward the well-heeled town of Tacubaya, but the cobblestones were poorly set and treacherous. There would have to be an easier way into town. In the distance, a paperboy and a milkman challenged each other for the right of way on the road which had been deserted just a few moments before.

Upon reaching Tacubaya, they were accosted by a child who emerged from a doorway where he must have been waiting for quite some time, judging from the sleepy look in his eyes. Manterola recognized him immediately; it was the boy from the hardware store, the one who had been playing with the Spitfire.

"Looks like we have a message from Ludwig Renn and Doctor Sacal."

The boy handed Manterola a slip of paper and left, without waiting for a response, like a soul bearing the devil.

"What does it say?"

"That there are three Germans living in a house on La Marquesa, a little way up," said Manterola, handing the note to the Poet.

WHAT THE HELL KIND
OF AN ARMY IS THIS?

An hour and a half later the Poet, together with a squad of officers armed with old Mausers, raided the house on La Marquesa only to find it deserted. Three beds, a bloody shirt tossed in a corner, food decaying on plates. It must have been abandoned two or three days ago. Arriving after the fact seemed to be becoming a habit.

"What's that?" the Poet asked the *toluqueño* Sánchez, who had found some sort of rosette and was toying with it.

"It's one of those pieces of crap that soldiers wear on their shoulders to show their rank, though from the size of this I'd say it was worn on the collar," the man from Toluca said to his boss, tossing him the thing without a second thought. But the Poet was not about to dismiss it as easily as that, and he peered intently at it, turning it over in his hand.

"What the hell kind of army would wear something like this?"

"Beats the hell out of me, boss. Technically I wasn't even a soldier when I got my first assignment."

The Poet continued to look it over. It was a sort of fern leaf on a black and silver pin.

"With two thousand armies marching all over the globe, it could be anything. What do you think . . . could it belong to a captain of Nazi auxiliary forces in Croatia? An officer of the Iron Guard in Romania?"

Just then he noticed a motorcyclist was waiting for him at the door.

"*Compañero* Valencia, the chief wants to you to get to this address quick. He says they found some more dead men in a house there with more of those strange drawings on the walls."

MIRRORS

Hemingway wanted to shave, but the asylum didn't seem to have a single mirror, razor blade (which was understandable), or bar of soap. During his labyrinthine search, though, he did have the chance to strike up brief conversations with some odd and unique individuals. These friendships didn't last long, though, because as soon as Erasto the Mute saw him speaking to one of the inpatients, he came at once to rescue him.

"I understand the lack of razors," Hemingway would later say to Verdugo. "But soap?"

"A while back we had one Don Remedios here who ate soap. But that was a long time ago. I suppose it's something more vulgar and miserly; that since the raid and our strike of the beards, someone decided we could do without soap."

"And the mirrors?"

"I guess they don't want us to be able to see ourselves," replied Verdugo, who had wondered about the matter before himself.

A DEAD DRIVER

The Poet's sensibilities had been dulled, and a light dusting of cynicism had settled over his emotions. He had seen too much death, too many friends sharing a wineskin destroyed by bombs, too many disemboweled horses neighing in the night, too many widows and orphans. But even so, he tore helplessly at his hair, roiling with rage. Espionage was one thing; going around killing innocent people and leaving bloody messages scrawled on walls was quite another.

"Fucking Nazis. I want you to get photos of all this, everything, the most horrible and cowardly," he ordered Sánchez. "Call that photographer from *La Prensa*, the one who made a name for himself photographing images of depravity. What's his name, Castañeda, Castañón, Alfonso, Adolfo, Armando, whatever that son of a bitch's name is, and have him make a set of prints for me. And don't pay him anything."

A quick canvassing of the neighbors revealed that this man, Manfredo Uk, was a truck driver who worked out of the Merced market. He was a widower and father of two young sons, but only one had been murdered here. Where could the other be? It was Sunday; he couldn't be in school. Why had they killed a truck driver? Was he transporting something? Did they want to prevent him from transporting something? Was he silenced because he had somehow come across the location of the mythical Puerto de las Perlas?

He contemplated the dead man, half expecting to receive a response. He was tied up in a chair, full of knife wounds to his chest and arms, with a look of horror that not even death had been able to wipe from his face. Then he looked at the body of his child, still clutching at the rigid, lifeless arm of his father with rigid, lifeless fingers.

"Boss, what are we going to do when we find these guys? Tell me, please . . ."

"We're going to saw off their scrotums," he replied.

A SEARCH FOR THE IGUANA,
WHO IS EVERYWHERE

Verdugo, you have a phone call," called a nurse as she passed by the invariably open door.

This was something unexpected. He tried to conceal his dismay. He hadn't so much as touched a phone in years. The unwritten rules of the Lighthouse did not permit the use of this magical apparatus. Not to make or to receive calls. So when had they abolished it? What were phones like nowadays? He choked down his concern and confusion and walked into Casavieja's office.

The phone was black, and Casavieja smiled at him as he handed him the receiver.

"Verdugo, is that you?"

He responded with silence, not knowing what to say. There was quite a bit of static on the line.

"Can I speak with the lawyer Alberto Verdugo?" said the voice. "Tell him it's his old friend Tomás Wong calling from Chiapas."

The voice was his. By some magic, Tomás Wong had been conjured back into existence. But something was different: he had lost his Chinese accent, replacing it with something undistinguishable that surged through the trills of static. A harsh, gravelly voice.

"Verdugo, is that you? I'm calling to tell you I know how hard it is to be a revenant archangel flying solo. This resurrection business is no walk in the park."

"I know," he managed, his voice faint and yet thick with emotions he couldn't control.

"If they ever let you out of there, come and find me. I could use your sense of humor. Just look for the Golden Iguana . . . he's everywhere around here."

A slight smile.

More static.

"Stay alive, Tomás. Reinforcements are on the way."

Verdugo returned the receiver to Casavieja without waiting for a "goodbye" to end the conversation. That black box frightened him. It seemed to be part of that other reality which he refused to accede to.

PART | XIII

THE BURNING SEA

1

SEA BREEZES

The sea was there; there could be no doubt whatsoever about that. You could smell it, taste its smooth salting on your tongue, hear its low roar in the offing. But it wasn't alone; it was accompanied by the smells of coffee and juice squeezed from freshly picked oranges, by the rumble of streetcars and the putrefaction of coconuts and sweat.

The sea was an eternal referent in the lives of both men. One of them, the writer, had found the Gulf of Mexico to be a place to live that stirred and motivated passions. The other, the poet, held on to childhood obsessions which remained like the vague murmur of waves in the ears. Despite having been born in Chihuahua and spending the better part of his life on the Mesa (two places that don't have so much as a river running through them, much less a sea), he maintained a sonorous nostalgia which, at times, invaded his dreams.

Which is perhaps why he had decided that the next stage of the investigation would be Veracruz, the water depot, the batteries, the shipments of fruit, and the writer who had united them all.

Ernest Hemingway and Fermín Valencia were in good spirits, lounging in deck chairs on the terrace of the rugged port's Hotel Diligencias, sipping coffee and listening to marimbas being played in the street below. Neither had spoken in a long while, as both were of the opinion that a hot and humid climate such as this was not propitious to adventures and heroic deeds but rather simple contemplation.

The Poet and professional spy kept a keen eye trained on Fulgencio Rivas y Reyes, the Spanish Falangist who had been identified as being the link with Nicolaus's network and was now standing just over Hemingway's shoulder. He was well-versed in seeing without being seen himself. And although missing an arm and having Ernest Hemingway sitting next to him weren't exactly factors which lent themselves to invisibility, he was hoping that the Germans had not circulated his description this far from the capital. In any case, his coffee was full, and between so much clapping of dominos on tables, waiters passing from customer to customer, booming voices, and dirty jokes, the four-table distance they were keeping was enough to remain unnoticed.

Down the street in front of the hotel passed a group of musicians preparing for the Veracruz carnival. They were clad in bathing trunks and banging on drums, tin cans, miniature clavicords, cymbals, triangles, pots, pans, vases, bottles, and old coffee cans with sticks. They were painted black.

"Have you noticed that even the black men paint themselves black for this?" asked Hemingway in English.

"What are you, racist?" answered the Poet in Spanish, having only half heard the question.

"God, no."

Just then Fulgencio paid for his coffee and got up, adjusting his vest and jacket. He was sweating profusely in the damp heat, but refused to so much as loosen his tie. This confirmed it: this was their man.

While Hemingway paid the check, the Poet picked up Múgica's gift— the trumpet case or trombone or clarinet case or whatever it was—and slipped off through the archways, hiding himself behind a newsstand. The Spaniard was heading east.

The two kept a half-block distance. The streets of this port town were bustling with traveling salesmen, sailors, businessmen, bureaucrats escaping the confines of their offices for a quick bite, and beggars and whores getting a jump on their night's work ahead.

Fulgencio stopped in front of a shop on whose door hung a faded sign which read, "Vigo's Imports." In front of the door was parked an old Ford farm truck and full of pineapples.

"There it is, the infamous fruit," said the Poet.

INTERRUPTIONS
AND INVASIONS

6. There are those who think that the novel has to explain everything. That novels ought to be the reparations of life and its inconsistencies. But was life ever once coherent? Some, too, think that the writer exists in a central place in space and time for giving beginnings and ends to stories and histories (though are there any examples of either which have such an end, a true conclusion, a final act?), for connecting, filling holes once they've been dug, dissolving nebulae, melting clouds, explaining characters' motives and performances.

There are those who think that the novel has an informative pedagogical function. Nothing could be further from the truth. The novel is not a tool for giving order to chaos. Novels aren't for giving order to shit. Novels are not born to satisfy our desires and whims. They are for relaxing within the frantic vertigo of modern life. They are for creating chaos, for stirring it up and enjoying it.

The novel must not be considered a response to questions but rather as the bearer of new and more lively or worrying ones.

The novel, like reality, like the histories we all know and those that always befall us, is full of parentheses, pitfalls, ellipses that dance and that jump from side to side with no desire to settle down or to explain themselves.

I feel that I have emerged from the illusion that when life becomes profoundly incoherent, the novel comes to repair it.

Though, on the other hand, we ought not to be overly cynical. The novel is, without a doubt, the one-eyed man in this expansive Mexican desert where blind men abound.

7. I first met Ernest H. in Milan in 1918. I was eating a light ravioli with a nice tomato sauce, on my way to Genoa, where a ship left monthly for Venezuela (though I had heard that for $150 I could disembark in Havana or Veracruz), when a mutual friend, after confirming that I was indeed a lawyer (though I neglected to tell him that my degree was granted by a university in Germany, a country which was, at the time, at war with Italy), asked that I see a mad gringo in his room at the North American Red Cross Hospital.

I did two things for Ernest H.: smuggle a pint of whiskey into his room and draw up his will and testament. In those days H. was a simple, romantic American who walked with a limp on account of shrapnel from a trench mortar shell that had wounded him when he was an ambulance driver on the Piave front. Today there is nothing left of his will; neither he nor I remember what we put in it. But I do remember that the nurses were kind and had no serious objections to the whiskey, and that we spent the afternoon discussing the current cinema. H. asked me what a Mexican was doing in Italy when there was a Revolution going on in my country. I told him that it wasn't mine to fight, and we simply left it at that.

8. A trunk that weighs eighty-one kilos, being too bulky and heavy to travel inside the passenger car, has to be charged extra and loaded into the merchandise car, located somewhere before the boxcars when counting up from the caboose.

Eighty-one kilos is the weight of a large, well-built man. It took two porters, under Kowalski's watchful gaze, to load it.

Sterling is not a silversmith's last name; it is just a legal adjective applied to pure, genuine silver. Not that faux silver made from an alloy of nickel, zinc, and copper, which a German by the name of Alader Pacz invented by chance and is called "nickel" or "German silver" and is used for making the forks that my mother used to hide from her well-heeled dinner guests.

9. The rosette that the Poet has tucked into his pocket bears a silver laurel leaf inclined from left to right and is the symbol identifying an SS colonel. Strangely, it does not correspond to Rahn's and Kowalski's rank of captain; they had left their insignias in Germany: three vertical bars and three pins squared across the back.

3

SWEATY PALMS

Hemingway looked with respect out of the corner of his eye at the Poet while their taxi drove them down something that, with a good deal of generosity, could be called a road but was more aptly described as a rough dirt track that the vegetation threatened to devour.

What had this little, one-armed man done to find out where the fruit-laden truck was headed? It was quite a mystery. He had whispered with a couple of the drivers, passed a few bills, visited a few bordellos where they were received by the open arms of prostitutes who called them Juan and Pedro and brought them tall glasses filled with ice, mango juice, and generous splashes of rum, and he spoke with a lottery ticket vendor who couldn't have possibly seen anything on account of his being blind. From all that, the Poet had determined that what they needed was a taxi driver *con cojones*. Hemingway understood that expression perfectly, for he had heard it many times in Spain. It often bothered the American that the Poet's quick, clipped accent was so different from the Spanish and Cuban accents that he had grown accustomed to. He was learning that he had even less of a command of the language than he had thought.

Their ballsy driver turned out to be a mulatto who shivered as though he had malaria, and his car was a dilapidated Ford straight out of the 1930s that bounced and trounced its way down the path, shedding nuts and bolts all the way. It was getting dark, and the novelist was beginning to nod off, with all the rocking and bouncing of the car. The Poet held the trombone case at his feet, and he wiped his hand on his pantleg from time to time. Hemingway had seen this often during the war in Spain: sweaty palms just before going into action.

"This is it here, *compadre*," said the driver.

The Poet took out a notebook from his pocket and scribbled something in the dark. "To be delivered tomorrow morning. You're not going to leave me hanging here, are you?"

"I stick to my word," said the driver.

They got out in the thick night and when the red glow of the taxi's taillights had vanished, Hemingway looked for some comfort to the moon, which mockingly hid itself behind the clouds. They were in the middle of nowhere.

Just then he heard the sea.

ARTHRITIS

our condition is completely normal for your age," said the young doctor, prompting a furious look from Manterola. "Rheumatism—arthritis—is common and not at all serious. Granted, it's degenerative and annoyingly painful, but . . . aspirin and this new drug called 'Gleaminex' taken daily, coupled with a move to a less rainy city, should do the trick."

"I like this city," said Manterola dryly, flexing the fingers of his painful left hand.

"I could recommend a diet for you, but it's been my experience that patients don't often listen to me."

"Well, you can add me to that list."

"It's also been my experience that patients of your age often blame me for their conditions."

"And how old are you, doctor?"

"I'm twenty-four."

"And that doesn't embarrass you?"

PUERTO DE LAS PERLAS

Puerto de las Perlas was something of an ironic code, because after sucking down thousands of oysters caught along the coast, the brutish locals had yet to find a single pearl. Either that, or it was christened by someone who had never been to the place.

It lay some fifty kilometers from Veracruz and was comprised of a hidden beach isolated by an inlet of the sea, two hills thick with palms, a thatched hut, a few cots and hammocks, tanks of water, a corrugated zinc building over which projected a large antenna, and a wooden storehouse full of fuel and food.

Seen at night, lit up by a bonfire and the few Coleman lanterns which hung from the joists of the thatched hut, it didn't seem like much.

The Poet slipped from the natural parapet toward the relative security of a thicket of reeds. Hemingway followed, slithering on his stomach.

"What the hell is this?" asked the little cripple.

"A refueling base for submarines operating in the gulf. Here they can stock up on water, fresh fruits and vegetables, food they couldn't afford to carry with them, electronic equipment for making repairs, and above all fuel," said Hemingway. Yes, it was hell, but it was in Veracruz and not Pinar del Rio. The big American smiled inwardly at his insight.

"And where are the submarines?"

Hemingway waved to the offing, toward the open sea.

"They have to stop at the mouth of the inlet because they . . . *cómo se dice?*"

"*Calar.*"

"*Sí, calar.* They draw too much water so they stop out there and the Germans row out to meet them in launches. See? There, at the edge of the dunes."

"Yes, two. Just down the beach," said the Poet.

"Just like that. See? *Se lo dije.*"

"What's a submarine look like?"

"Long, thirty or forty meters, but almost invisible. Even when it's at the surface, only the periscope and conning tower can be seen."

"And where are Rahn and Hanussen and the one with the silvery hair? What do they have to do with this?"

Hemingway shook his head. The Poet lit a cigarette, cupping his hand around it to mask the glow. Hemingway looked up at the night sky; a long arm of the milky way stretched overhead, shining majestically.

"How many are there? *Cuántos hay?*"

The Poet crushed out his cigarette in the sand and opened the trombone case. He locked in the magazine and clicked off the safety.

"Over a thousand. One thousand and twenty-two, actually," said the Poet in English, because it was the Lexington Avenue address of a cousin of his who lived in New York.

Hemingway smiled. "Got one for me?" he asked, nodding at the case.

"Sorry."

The Poet got to his feet and started off toward the crest of the dune. Hemingway hung back for a moment, stifled a sigh, and followed.

6

CONFIRMATION

If Pioquinto Manterola had not been worried about Hemingway's and the Poet's luck, and if he had not regretted not accompanying them to Veracruz;

If his friend Pepe Revueltas had not noticed his anxious state, seeing him pace around the office scattering pipe ash every which way, and if he had not convinced him to come along to cover a dance competition for the paper;

If he had not sat in the first row at the Salón Colonial;

If none of that had happened, Pioquinto Manterola would never have known that the Faustino who, together with Encarnación Perea, gracefully won the XEQ-sponsored dance contest was the same man who, one long year ago, had wiped the spit from the plaque that adorned the gates of the German embassy that he himself had spat the night before.

But just to be sure, Manterola, who had been well aware of the tremendous tension of the final round, of the precise movement through brief space, the efficient cutting that meshed perfectly with the sound of the trumpet, and the magical revolutions of the three couples vying for the right to take home the thousand-peso prize, had to listen in on the questions Revueltas was asking of the winners, all smiles and sweat.

"Don Faustino, Doña Encarnación, what do you do when you're not dancing?"

"The señorita is an operator with the phone company, and I am unemployed as of recently. I used to be a custodian over at the German embassy, but since they broke off diplomatic relations, I was laid off."

Manterola looked up from the double tequila that was being forced on him to the face of the victor, and the man with the broad-lapelled suit and the necktie pulled slightly to the side gradually metamorphosed into the man in the gray overalls who had painstakingly wiped away his gobs of spit.

"What's your opinion of the Nazi party?" Manterola cut in.

"To me, the dance is the one thing I love most in life," exclaimed Perea.

"The Nazis are a bunch of tight-fisted bastards," said Faustino. "They don't pay overtime."

"But you no longer work for them, right?" pressed Manterola.

"Well I do work, but not in the same capacity. They did kick me out into the streets when they closed the embassy, but the minister's aide, a Mexican named Alonso, offered me work. Just yesterday I went to buy him some train tickets to Veracruz."

"The best dancers in the world flock to Veracruz," said Perea.

"How many tickets? For what train?" demanded Manterola.

"Three, for the overnight express. Leaving right about now."

7

THE ATTACK

In the light of the moon, the Poet crept out of the shadows of the palm grove like a character in a musical comedy, with the tommy gun held out front and Hemingway two steps behind, the trombone case his only weapon.

"In the name of the Mexican government, you are under arrest! Throw up your hands and . . ."

Here the tirade was cut short as a blond man came running out of the thatched hut, his pistol blazing. One of the shots pierced the loose sleeve of the Poet's missing arm.

Three more men came running out of the depository. One carried a rifle. The Poet unleashed a burst and two men fell. He turned and aimed at the space of darkness where he had seen muzzle flashes and fired again. The depository erupted with a deafening boom. Hemingway felt his eyelashes curl from the heat. The Poet fired a third burst at the man with the pistol, who had uselessly taken shelter behind a hammock and turned to run.

At his back, Hemingway emerged from the shadows just in time to land an overhand right to the jaw of a giant Aryan dressed in a sailor's blue uniform who was rushing at them with a hatchet in hand, ready to hack the Poet in two.

Two more shots rang out from behind the water tanks. The Poet wheeled to face them, his weapon ready, but the trigger didn't respond to pressure.

"We're out of ammo!" he yelled to Hemingway, waving the spent weapon in the night air. The American waved to the sea, to the launches, and began to run.

In the light of the blaze, the Poet watched as a man got on the radio, barking out phrases in German. He felt like an ass. As he ran he went over in his mind the worst insults he knew. A sublime fool he was, not having brought an extra clip, or a dozen fully loaded pistols.

They reached the boats and Hemingway furiously pushed one into the water. Helpless to assist, the Poet simply followed him in. More shots rang out. The shouting was getting closer.

They rowed desperately out toward the open sea.

8

INTERRUPTIONS

AND INVASIONS

4. Manterola reaches Veracruz just as the dawn does, having taken the midnight express. According to what he gathers from the porters and mango sellers in the station, his three Germans and their trunk arrived just a bit before him. He loses a few hours following a false lead that brings him to the Hotel Emporio where he finds three gringos (not Germans) with a trunk full of women's underwear (not silver). He curses his investigative abilities.

5. There is quite a commotion here, as the winning ticket to the national lottery ends in 666. Hanussen scrawls it on the wall of our room, and all the other inpatients are betting on this number. I do not know if they gamble thanks to the complicity of the nurses or the complicity of their deliriums. But for all practical purposes, it is the same either way: there is a feeling of triumph around here.

6. I have been dreaming about a burning sea.

9

BE CAREFUL, FOR THERE ARE SHARKS IN THESE WATERS

The Poet could do little to help besides offer shouts of encouragement while shots hissed into the waves around the launch. Hemingway was rowing at a good clip, but the boat was unbalanced, having been designed for only one person. As they made it past the break-water, they could make out the running lights of a ship approaching them at mid-clip. A midsized ship, perhaps sixty meters in length and lit up like a Christmas tree.

Shots continued to ring out from the launch which was following them, one of which lodged itself in the wood of the rudder. The approaching ship seemed to have cut its engines and was drifting toward them on inertia alone. It was an oil tanker, and Hemingway maneuvered the launch up alongside its bow. They could clearly see a broad Mexican flag painted on the hull.

"Motherfucker! Save us already!" shouted the Poet.

"Come to and we'll weigh you aboard!" they shouted back.

From the deck of the tanker a dozen or so sailors watched the scene being played out beneath them in fascination, as if it were a western film. They tossed down a rope ladder; the Poet stowed his tommy gun in its case and began with great difficulty to climb.

"If it wasn't for the shooting, we would never have seen you," said the captain, offering his hand to the Poet, who was supporting himself with his stump while using his one hand to pass over the case.

"Are you all Mexicans?"

"You're on board the *Tampico Hermoso*, of the Mexican oil fleet. I'm Captain Hernández."

Hemingway, whose eyes were still locked on the sea and their pursuers, interrupted the introductions.

"They've stopped. They're heading back to the beach."

"Let's turn the screws, Chucho. Back on course," called the captain to his engineer, and almost immediately the low churning of the engines resumed.

The exhausted men leaned heavily on the gunwales. In the distance they watched the splendor of the fuel depot burning in the distance.

"Goddamned Nazis. Fuck 'em. Let them get their petrol from their bitch mothers back in Germany," said the Poet as he wiped away a tear. Hemingway gave him a slap on the back that nearly sent him flying overboard.

"I'm hungry. *Comida*. Let's go," he said, and went off to explore the ship.

The Poet stayed behind, his chin resting on the railing, watching the distant blaze and trying to forget what had just happened. He felt strangely cold in this tropical night. His teeth chattered, and he started to shiver. His hand shook.

"That hand of yours," remarked Hemingway when he returned, empty-handed, from this explorations.

"Yes, it's my hand. What are you talking about?"

"Strange things happen to it; it sweats, it shakes . . ." Hemingway explained in Spanish.

"No, my dear novelist, you don't understand. The things that happen to the other one—the one that's missing—are worse. This one sweats and shakes and swings on its own. But the other one swings here, in my head," said the Poet, raising a finger to his temple. "But I can't move it any more than in my dreams, and because of that, the good one, the real one, the one that remains, drives me mad."

Fortunately, just then the captain emerged from his cabin, coming to the rescue with a bottle of tequila. He poured each man a generous ration.

"Pardon me for asking, but who were those guys shooting at you on the beach?"

"A band of crazed Nazis. This here is Doctor Einstein," said the Poet, nodding at Hemingway "and I am Captain Palancearte of the Ministry of the Interior—Secret Services," he finished, using for his own pseudonym one of the characters from his pornographic novels. The ship's captain looked at them with newfound respect.

It was moments like this that gave the Poet enormous cravings to smoke. Hemingway rubbed his right hand; he may have dislocated a finger when he laid out the man with the hatchet. The tequila was warm and pleasant in their bellies.

"Captain, we need you to take us to Veracruz," said the Poet.

"Those lights there are Veracruz," said the captain, waving at a band of hazy light, low and flat against the sea.

"Perfect."

"But I'm afraid I can't enter the port. I have very specific orders to be in Havana at dawn. The best I can do is drop you off near the coast."

Three hours later, with the first light of dawn, the Poet prepared himself to jump into the sea with a kapok life vest and his trumpet case. He didn't bring everything with him, because although he was only a ten-minute swim from the Mocambo beach, and if he couldn't swim with just one arm the tide was going in and would carry him to land. They had sent him off with a cry of "Be careful, for there are sharks in these waters. Not always, but they have been seen cruising off the beaches."

Hemingway embraced him and stood watching as the Poet, who had not bothered to take off either his hat or his boots, leapt into the gray sea. The limping tanker slowly inched away toward the rising sun and Cuba. Hemingway lay down with a coil of rope for a pillow and immediately fell asleep, lulled into dream by the sailors who broke out their guitars and chased away the echoes of the recent gunfight with a round of "If a dove comes to your window . . ."

INTERRUPTIONS

AND INVASIONS

3. A messenger on a motorbike rides up to the Lighthouse door to leave me a dossier tied with a piece of twine and sent by the Poet. I wonder aloud how he manages to use his department's resources without paying for them, and the messenger (his name is Lorenzo) gives me a clue: he owes the Poet a bit of money, because our good friend once gave him a loan so that his mother could place a bet on the traveling lottery.

This dossier deals with the Graham Greene investigation. I skim it through. Born in 1906. Came to Mexico in 1938 as a reporter for a conservative British daily. Relations with England have been rather tense for the past three years on account of the echoes of petroleum expropriation. The report suggests that he was acting "as an agent of the Vatican." As a by-product of his trip, he wrote a travelogue which was published the following year in England as *Lawless Roads* and in the U.S. as *Another Mexico*. There is a note here that calls the book "degrading to Mexico" and another from the Minister of the Interior that prohibits Greene entering the country, labeling him an "undesirable alien."

There is also a more personal commentary on both the author and his book: "On every page the author confesses that through his travels he learned to hate Mexico, that the food is shit, mosquitos are everywhere, everything stinks, the cars break down, and that the roads are nothing more than endless stretches of potholes. He looks down on the language and his only concerns have to do with those regions of the country where the churches are falling into disrepair. This negative vision of the country and of the southeastern states in particular did not, however, prevent him from taking advantage of our liquor and our prostitutes, which seem, in his eyes, to be our only redeeming qualities."

What follows next is a review of his novel *The Power and the Glory*, written a bit later with part of the material and observations that he realized on this trip and which seems situated in an earlier time, in the days of the Red Shirts of Tabasco and the shabby antireligious persecution by Governor Garrido Canabal. It gives me the feeling that whoever wrote the review hadn't read the book.

One final note in the dossier, from the Mexico City hotel where Greene stayed, points out that he spoke not a single word of Spanish.

4. I imagine it thus: nine agents from the Ministry of the Interior drive up in dilapidated vans to the place formerly known as Puerto de las Perlas eleven hours after the Poet's reckless attack. They find nothing but a shed full of overripe fruit, a truck with a half-disassembled engine, a thatched-roof hut and three hammocks, and a pair of smoldering tanks which must be the remains of a fuel depot. The sand around them is blackened and melted. Not so much as a footprint remains. They ask every person they find within a ten-kilometer radius, but no one has any idea who has been living there or who it was who had led this massive raid. They don't even know that this place was once known as Puerto de las Perlas.

Through some lack of competence, the agents do not notice the four shallow graves dug some two hundred meters away down the beach.

The German submarine base in the Gulf of Mexico is no more. Not even the local brutes, rather likeable characters who can dance like nobody else and who are given to gossip, rumor, and rhetoric, can invent a decent story to explain those miserable smoking ruins.

THE *POTRERO DE LLANO*

In the early hours of the night of May 13th, the *Potrero de Llano*, which was formerly known as *Lucifer* and was one of the ships which the Mexican government had seized from Italy the previous year, made its way through the waters off the coast of Florida to Miami with 46,000 barrels of oil on board. Captain Gabriel Cruz was nervous because during the past few weeks German submarines had been dancing across the Caribbean, ducking in and out of British colonial ports and sinking merchant vessels. Still, though, he had decided to sail, his lights running at night so that the Mexican flag, painted broadly on both the port and starboard sides of the prow, could be clearly seen.

Five minutes before midnight, Lieutenant Richard Suhren, at the helm of U564, saw that same Mexican flag through his periscope and proceeded with the orders he had received seventeen hours earlier from Puerto de las Perlas: fire at will. These new orders, which had been confirmed by Berlin, annulled all previous directives with regard to the neutrality of ships flying under the Mexican flag, particularly one in the waters northeast of Veracruz, possibly on its way to a U.S. port. Four submarines operating in this quadrant of the Gulf, Walter's U237, the U511, Pfef's U171, and the U126 under the command of Captain Ernst Bauer were all on the same page as the U564.

Suhren waited, grinding his teeth and holding his breath, as if his stillness could steady the torpedo's course. And then a single explosion, dead in the center of the tanker's hull. Fire ripped out, killing several sailors instantly. The ship broke in two but did not sink immediately, allowing the fire to move up and consume the deck. A sailor trying to launch a lifeboat was killed by a second explosion, and several more succumbed to the flames that had then spread from the deck to the surface of the sea, now slicked with oil. It seemed as if the entire crew would burn alive, but by some miracle a portion of the crew was able to escape the floating torch on lifejackets and bits of flotsam alone. In all, fourteen of the ship's thirty-six crewmen died in those few short moments.

The sea continued to burn for hours. U564 cruised out of the quadrant at a moderate depth.

Hours later, the shipwrecked Mexicans were rescued by U.S. naval units and taken to Miami. The radio beat out a rapid-fire news bulletin, "Mexican ship sunk by German sub," and the Mexican press picked up on it immediately, dubbing the shot "The Pernicious Torpedo." The streets of Mexico City, normally reverberating with slander and rumor, now took on a patriotic fervor, condemning the damned German sub and the son-of-a-bitch captain who had fired on an unarmed Mexican ship, as well as those malicious conservatives who claimed that it was actually an American sub that had attacked: a Yankee ploy, they claimed, to draw the Mexicans into the war on the side of the Allies.

INTERRUPTIONS
AND INVASIONS

1. Casavieja comes to take my temperature. He is dressed up as a real doctor, in a short white coat, a neatly trimmed beard, and with a pair of tongue depressors protruding from his shirt pocket. It's the first time he's taken my temperature in years. I think. I suspect. I follow his lead. If he wants to play at being a doctor, then he can interact with us. As a start, he offers a bit of news:

"The Germans have torpedoed a Mexican ship. Everything is on fire. The Minister of Foreign Relations is on the radio now reporting."

I don't get there in time to hear the government's official statement, but I do catch the ship's name: the tanker *Potrero de Llano*. The stations are all playing patriotic marches.

2. I imagine it thus: Manterola picks back up on his trail at the train station. A boy hawking papers shows him the taxi in which the three Germans and their trunk left the station. "They went in that," he says, and points to a driver leaning back against the door and dozing, obviously in no mood to help this Mexico City journalist who has come to disturb him.

3. The 10th of May, Mother's Day, passes without note. With a few exceptions, those of us shut away in here have no mothers. Or if we do, they don't want us. It's interesting to note which festivals and holidays we celebrate here in the Lighthouse and which we coldly ignore. In here we don't give a damn about the Virgin of Guadalupe but we love the Three Wise Men.

4. I imagine it thus: Miguel Alemán is out horseback riding on his ranch on the outskirts of Veracruz. He usually does this when he returns to his home state. A taxi pulls up the local access road to the hacienda. A wooden gate blocks its path. A barefoot man armed with a shotgun is standing guard and calls the taxi to a halt. He sends his young assistant to give warning and after a minute or two, he waves the taxi on into the heart of the ranch. Alemán watches the car pull up from astride his horse, and rides on. One of the Angulo brothers comes out to greet the arrivals. The horse snorts and sweats. Alemán pats him on the neck, calming him.

5. They show us a film whose title I forget just moments after it has flashed upon the screen. It is another British war picture; here, a pilot—an officer—is in love with his best friend's wife who, halfway through the film, finds herself a widow. When we get to the part where the German Stukas appear in the sky, their engines whining as they begin their strafing attacks, the crowd begins to throw things at the screen, memories of the submarine attack fresh in our minds. They stop the movie there, in the middle of the attack and the agitated spirits.

6. I cannot even begin to imagine what the Angulo brother talks about with the Germans. They have brought the trunk, but when they leave they take it with them. Where is the silver? Is it not in the trunk? Have they kept part of it?

Miguel Alemán rides up to the car as the Germans are reloading the trunk into the car. He greets them with a nod of the head; perhaps he murmurs "*Buenas tardes*," or some such thing. And neither he, nor they, nor the shotgun-packing guard, sees Pioquinto Manterola hidden behind an orange tree, surrounded by the fresh smell of orange blossoms, asking the same questions that I ask myself here.

7. De la Calle's latest painting is a grove of burning palms. It must be the subconscious influence of my dreams.

8. I imagine: the Germans depart the ranch. Manterola returns to his own taxi, hidden in the orange grove, and rustles up his driver, who is again dozing in what seems to be his eternal custom of the siesta. When they reach the junction with the main highway, they can find no trace of the Germans. Logically, Manterola thinks to himself, the port is to the north. And they had taken a taxi from the Veracruz port when they had started to follow them. So that has to be the way. But a half hour of highway later, they come to the conclusion that they have erred. Manterola stops the taxi and gets out to smoke and piss. He smokes with his right hand and holds his cock with his left. Surely, though, the Poet has a more inventive way of combining these two activities.

I WON A THOUSAND DOLLARS
AND SANK ONE SUBMARINE

E rnest Hemingway woke up with a tremendous pain in his temples that throbbed angrily in time with his pulse and, shading his eyes from the sun, he contemplated the soft green sides of an empty swimming pool. He was stretched out near the drainpipe, the paint was slightly chipped and peeling, and the entire bottom of the pool was caked in mud and the familiar dead, dried leaves. There was no mistaking it. It was his house at Finca Vigía; it was his pool.

He got up, walked a few steps to a shaded part of the pool, and lay down again. The sun was on its way down; it was early afternoon. Who had called for the pool to be emptied? Was it him? Why hadn't he ordered it to be cleaned as well?

The writer had always thought that he lived an out-of-control life, that he always seemed to be on the edge of the abyss, and frequently collapsed into it. But he also knew that he was himself solely responsible for this, that they were his weaknesses and—though he scoffed at the thought—the causes of his sins. Because everything was dissolute, and it pleased him to see it as such. He had a soul sequestered deep within his being, and he was certainly guilty of being a Christian-Lutheran-Anabaptist-and-remotely-Jewish man. But this time, his life had fallen into new levels of chaos. It was as if waking up from a Mexican fiesta where the only thing that had outnumbered the tequila was marijuana.

With that memory of tequila, its flavor having left caustic footprints down the back of his throat, he got up and walked toward the house. Boise appeared and, as if happily surprised to see him, rubbed up against his leg.

"I spent a week in Mexico," he said. "We played poker and I won a thousand dollars. I bought a painting from a madman and listened to marimbas and sipped coffee in Veracruz. Then we went after a band of Hitler's men, and ended up sinking a submarine."

The cat didn't seem to ascribe too much importance to the matter. Hemingway opened the refrigerator and began to fix himself a sandwich of raw onions, ham, and thinly sliced tomatoes.

The hand which he had thumped the German with was still throbbing, and his knuckles were skinned. Armed with his sandwich, he went into the bedroom he used as his mail depository to look for an American newspaper. He couldn't say why, but he had no faith in the dates on Cuban papers, and somehow the whole nightmare had been conducted in Spanish. The Miami papers usually arrived a day late, so whatever the top piece of mail was in that stack of correspondence, stories, magazines, and announcements, it would give yesterday's date.

May 13th; therefore today was the 14th. One week exactly. Incredible. But Hemingway decided to put it out of his mind for the time being, and went out on the porch to get some fresh air.

INTERRUPTIONS
AND INVASIONS

3. Why does Kowalski have those strange scars on his hands? What caused them? They are like tiny threads that radiate out from the middle of his fist, at least three each to the left and right. They do not seem to be the result of a wound from a cutting weapon or a burn.

4. Casavieja has brought another odd character to the Lighthouse. He calls himself Graham Greene, and fits the description that the Poet gave me of the man who saved him while he was infiltrating the Aztec Knights' subterranean rituals. He arrives in a deplorable state indeed, covered in vomit, blubbering and whimpering. He speaks only English, but his drunkenness does not prevent him from insulting a pair of nurses and declaring, when they tie him up in the boiler room for his disintoxication, that the Mexican climate is shit.

I go down to see him. He looks blankly at me; I do not register. But he says:

"When it comes to human relations, a good lie is worth a thousand truths."

Hours later find me writing at Casavieja's desk as if nothing had happened. Focused and concentrated, as if lost in another universe, I fill page after page with a thick fountain pen.

5. I hear on the radio: "Only your fatal shadow, your shadow of evil,

follows me everywhere with the obstinacy of cancer." The phrases come, as always, as a preface to a tale of unrequited love. The youngest son of composers, a twenty-year-old *ranchero* singer named Cuco Sánchez, sings it in his convincing yet disturbing voice, boyish and yet raspy as if his throat has been scarred.

I wonder: has the ether been populated by messages directed at me?

PART	XIV

THE PYRAMID
AND THE WAR

<table>
<tr><td>1</td><td></td></tr>
</table>

FRIENDS OF SPARTACUS

In his return from death, Tomás Wong was able to recover things he had thought were lost. In some way he had been born anew: he had a more refined sense of humor and his myopia had improved. He still needed glasses to read, but his sight had improved noticeably. Now, for example, he could discern with great clarity and vividness the color of a man's pants at a hundred meters, and the movements of a monkey stirring in the highest reaches of a tree.

He lifted his hand and stretched out two fingers. In the jungle at his back, the smallest of the tiny ants, elevated to the rank of Copper Iguana, crept forward in silence, scarcely stirring a blade of grass; or better yet, masking his movements with the sounds of the jungle. The jungle can be quite noisy at times, laced with creaks and sighs. A gusting breeze can produce marvels.

There were more new changes in the Chinaman as well. A streak of white hair had appeared where before it had been coal black; he had seen it reflected in a stream. He la-la-la'ed the tune to "Lili Marlene," the song the Germans sang in the trenches during the Great War and, by an unconscious act of balance, combined it with "The Army of Ebro *rúmbala rúmbala rumba ba,* one night they crossed the river," one of the most famous Republican songs from the war in Spain.

He descended from the tree to discover that his military cortège was there waiting for him. He breathed deeply. This jungle was not foreign to him. Returning from death had its virtues.

"There are three, just like Caesar said. We'll let them pass; we'll hear them tonight. Marcus Curtius, get on their tail."

The boy in question peeled off from the group and vanished among the trees.

"The brothers Gracchus and Cicero will come with me. Eugenius, you're the forward observer. Wait for us at the black pool."

The boy brought his fist up to his chest and, in silence, took to the path from which they had come. The mini-iguanas now had call signs. They had opted to Romanize themselves, imparting a strangely imposing military effect, and Tomás had also culled from his memory a few fictitious names from Raffaello Giovagnoli's novel. All in all, they had themselves a fine mix of gladiators, poets, historians, and emperors.

TWO APPROXIMATIONS
OF THE PYRAMID

The woman appeared in his dreams. Since returning from Veracruz, he had abandoned the Aztec princess's apartment, returning only once to pack up his scant wardrobe and some money he had hidden. One doesn't escape death just to go back to sleeping with a woman he doesn't love. He had moved into a flea bag hotel at the corner of Palma and Cinco de Mayo, near the Zócalo, the central plaza of his loves and his city.

"I have news for you," said Veronique.

The Poet was not surprised; he had been expecting the visit. He reached over to the nightstand for his pack of cigarettes and lay back to smoke. He never knew the luxury of letting questions and surprises pass without concern. But how did she always seem to find him?

In the lamplight, the woman seemed more beautiful than ever. Her black cheeks shone, her gaze was penetrating. She smelled of jasmine.

"Are you awake?"

"No, I smoke in my sleep. I love it."

The woman smiled. She moved over to the chair that held the Poet's clothes, tossed them on the floor, and sat down.

"May I help myself to one of your fine cigarettes?"

The Poet offered her the pack.

"The men you're after are looking for a pyramid, somewhere on the Ruta

Maya. There are too many rumors and unanswered questions; it can be no other thing."

"So what do they want a damned pyramid for?"

"For a rite of black magic," replied the woman, releasing a lungful of smoke in a series of voluptuous rings which floated on out of the small circle of light cast by the lamp.

"Is this thing working?" asked the Poet, looking quizzically at his cigarette after trying and failing to blow a smoke ring of his own.

"I don't know. I both believe and disbelieve in magic, but what's certain is that those who do fully believe in it can do terrible things with it. I have seen a man, dying of consumption, who believed himself to be cursed, and I have seen rain fall on a town where the people thought they could make it rain with ceremonial dances. Sometimes I can read people's minds, and sometimes I can sense an evil presence as if I were surrounded by the stench of shit. I know how to make teas that relieve menstrual colic and tonics that make men forget their ill-fated loves. If I stare hard into the fire I can see the shadows of futures that sometimes come to pass and sometimes do not. However you look at it, I am hardly a fountain of truths."

The Poet was on the verge of drooling; the woman had him absolutely captivated. The grace with which she moved the hand that held her cigarette, her sly look, like a gypsy's, her eyes like the tide, the slightest of smiles ever on her lips, her air of sadness and energy.

"I'm afraid of the Nazis. I'm afraid of the pyramid and what they're seeking there."

"Where, exactly, is this mythical pyramid?"

"Near Palenque, on the border between Chiapas and Tabasco, I think."

"You can't be more specific? There are thousands of square kilometers of jungle there, and little else."

The Poet turned from the woman to look for his ashtray, and took advantage of the impersonal nature of the situation to broach a question.

"Now that you've come here to wake me up, what do you think of sharing my bed for a while?"

But there was no response. The Poet, his ashtray—a dried, hollowed-out half of a pumpkin—in hand, turned around to discover that the woman was gone.

He sat up, smoking, until dawn. Finally he reloaded his tommy gun, pulled on a pair of pants and a T-shirt, and went down to the reception desk to call the journalist. The connection took a good while to be made. Manterola's office fielded the call in their lobby, and Manterola had to come all the way down to take it. When the Poet finally heard his friend panting like an asthmatic dog on the other end of the line, he dropped a bomb on him.

"Listen, keyhack, a very reliable source of mine tells me that the Nazis we're after are hunting for a Mayan pyramid. Do your friends know anything about that?"

"I can ask them," Manterola replied. Several seconds of silence passed over the line. "Yes, and we ought to check with Verdugo and see what the food is like there at the Lighthouse."

The Poet smiled. Yes, they and their story were indeed fodder for insane asylums. "And if the laundry service is decent and if the mattresses are any good and what the library is like," he added. Prime candidates they were becoming.

"There are just two things preventing me from going there to spend the rest of my days: the lack of women there, and that whole electroshock therapy I keep hearing about. I don't like the sound of that one bit."

"What a coincidence," said the Poet.

PLUNDER

Iguana Grande, permission to speak?"

Tomás nodded.

"They have some sort of depository there. They bring in coffee from our land on mules and store it there."

"How many guards?"

"Three armed guards, and then there are the laborers who work for them and a Spanish foreman. The Germans call themselves One, Two, and Three. Original bunch, these Nazis are, eh?"

Tomás smiled. He got up from his place at the bonfire to go over to Crixo and tousle his hair.

"Well done, *muchacho*."

The little iguana was resplendent with joy.

"Will we attack?"

Tomás nodded, and tension ran like a current through the faces around the campfire. Tension and excitement.

"All night long you can hear the Germans fart and snore in their sleep. Night's the time to do it," said a thin young man whose birthname was Flavio José and who had lost an eye on account of a lashing he had endured while working on one of the coffee plantations. "Yessir. Night's the time to do it."

Far from their base, here in the coffee-growing region of Soconuso, the

Germans were much more vulnerable. First Tomás and his band had raided a munitions depot to stock up on arms and ammunition. Then they had been following the movements of two groups to the south and east and a third which had gone off in the direction of Veracruz and the Gulf. Finally, they had discovered this coffee warehouse. Why would they possibly want to store their coffee here, hundreds of kilometers from the place of production?

"Let's go to war, boys. Flavio José, advise the communities around here that tomorrow, at first light, they will have all the free coffee they can carry. Tell everyone from the townspeople we saw across the hill to the charcoal-makers and the brush-clearers," said Tomás as he slung his rifle across his back. Ten of the eleven young iguanas followed; the one remained to put out the fire and break camp before spreading the news.

They slipped into silence in the moonless night, barely able to see the shoulders of the one in front of him. Tomás was nervous. He had to take care of his army. No longer did he have the luxury of only one potential casualty. He was immortal, but these little iguanas followed in the shadow of his protection.

For two hours they crept through the jungle. The little ones were indefatiguable, serious, resolved, disciplined, and gravely proud adolescents. Some were malnourished to the point where their stolen rifles hung from shoulders thin as broomsticks. Suddenly the forward observer stopped. He raised his left hand, and then extended three fingers: "Enemy ahead." Tomás crept forward to join him at the point position.

Ganicco pointed toward a weakly lit storehouse. To the left was a shed; to the right was a slightly less rustic wooden house.

"There are no guards; the Germans are asleep. There was a guard posted by the workers' quarters, there, but it's my aunt's cousin, and I told her to tell him that the Iguana had ordered him to return home."

"And he left?" whispered Tomás.

"No, he said that for once, he was going to stick around for the prize. He just went to piss down by the river," whispered the boy in reply.

Tomás made the sign of the spider—two arms coming together as if clutching something—and then signaled toward the house.

Like slowly moving shadows, Tomás situated two of them with rifles at a window and three more at the door. Then he himself slipped over to the other window—this one half open—with his moon-knife in his hand and the rest of the iguanas at his back.

"Now," ordered the Golden Iguana. Flavio José lit the torch he was carrying, revealing the three Germans asleep on military cots. One of them, blinded by the sudden light, fumbled under his pillow for his pistol, but was hit twice by shots from the boys, his body convulsing from the impacts. Tomás fell upon another, a fat, ginger-haired man, and put the long knife to his throat. Momentarily struck by the terror in the man's eyes, the Chinaman hesitated before dealing the killing blow, allowing the third German the chance to leap out of bed. But he immediately tripped over his own footlocker and tumbled to the floor where Cicero, a young Tojolabal dressed in loose-fitting pants and shirt and with his boots hanging around his neck because he had not yet grown into them, put the barrel of his rifle to his chest.

"This is the one who got my eye," he said.

"Hog-tie them. Get all their papers together and lay them out on the table there," ordered Tomás, and his troops went into action.

Dawn came. In its light and in the light of a lantern, Tomás had been studying the German's belongings. Nothing made sense. Coffee receipts and payments. Something about a shipment to be made via Guatemala next month. Nazi propaganda written in Spanish and printed in Havana. A dun-brown shirt in a suitcase. A photograph of some twenty healthy, salutary, and well-armed young men in Nazi uniforms standing around a hanged *campesino*. Their fat redhead was among them.

He went out on the porch. Three of his iguanas were asleep on the ground. Four more had commandeered a hammock. Another was keeping watch at the edge of the clearing. Tomás scanned the rim of the jungle for his other sentinel. He had to be somewhere where he could cross his fire with that of the first. He had to be . . . of course. Perched up in a tree. He had trained them well.

First came the warning from Marcus Curtius, who was at the mouth of the path. A bird call and his right thumb raised in the air: "Friends ahead."

And suddenly, out of the uncertain light that ushered in the dawn, men and women, grandparents and children, appeared in the clearing which had been deserted only moments before. Tomás opened the doors of the storehouse and the 150 or so Indians began to help themselves to the coffee. Loading a sack on his back and using his belt as a trumpline, a man could carry a forty-pound sack for forty miles.

The entire operation was conducted in silence and without any great displays of jubilation; just the freshly awakened iguanas who saluted with their rifles on high to each man and woman who disappeared back into the jungle with their share.

In less than an hour, all the coffee had vanished. Tomás regrouped his forces and set fire to the house and store. They stripped one of the Germans naked and lashed him to a tree and shot the other—the fat redhead from the photo—and disappeared into the bush.

4	

A PYRAMID?

This time the meeting was not in the mysterious back room of the hardware store. Like innocent friends, they were out for a walk on the outskirts of Bellas Artes after a symphony. Doctor Sacal sought out the sun, Manterola the shade, and Ludwig Renn walked between them and found himself the path of perfect compromise as they walked down the tree-lined avenue.

"The immigration office is getting tougher to crack. Those puny bureaucrats are afraid to deal with the Nazis. With whom in the government can we speak? Alemán won't meet with us, and the president just ignores any exiled anti-Fascists like us . . ." said Renn.

"Perhaps we should speak with Lombardo. He carries some weight in these matters."

A farmhand, a pork rind vendor, and a lottery ticket salesman seated on the iron railing tried fruitlessly to lure in the three men.

"I have to ask you an important question . . . The Nazis that my friend the Poet has been following, who are presumably Otto Rahn and Eric Jan Hanussen, look to be searching for a certain pyramid along the Ruta Maya. Do you have any idea of what pyramid it could be or why they would be searching for it?"

"A pyramid?" asked Doctor Sacal.

Manterola nodded. "A Mayan pyramid. Or, as the Poet said, a 'damned pyramid.' "

"The only thing I know is that the Nazis have long since been interested in the pre-Columbian world, especially when you consider their explorations in Tihuanaco searching for Atlantis. But until now, the Nazi investigations or those of the esoteric groups that preceeded them, were never directed at pyramids or Mayas."

"Damn it."

"A question for you: your friend, the one who has access to the government archives . . ."

"The Ministry of the Interior," specified Renn.

". . . your friend, has he tried to find out what the Mexican government knows, or knew, about the trip Von Sebottendorff took to Mexico in the 1920s? Remember he could have traveled under his peerage name or his real name, Rudolf Glauer. Perhaps there's something there."

"If you need any help, my friends and I . . . There are a few of us who have fought, either with the war in Spain or against the Nazis in the streets . . ." said Renn.

"I'm grateful for the offer. I'll keep you informed," replied Manterola, and after warmly shaking each man's hand, he went of down the alameda toward his office. From there he would phone the Poet.

5

THE *FAJA DE ORO*

Manterola . . . this just in . . . they've sunk another Mexican ship."

The journalist went up to the teletypewriter and read the text as it came off the machine; behind him, several editors held their breath. It was a cable from the AP office in Mexico which had translated a press release from Miami.

On May 20th, toward 8:15 in the evening, the oil tanker *Faja de Oro*, originally the *Genoan* before being seized from Italy, was returning to Tampico after having unloaded its tanks of oil in Delaware. Captain Ramón Sánchez had been worried; over the past few days he had personally seen several U.S. ships sunk and he had even participated in the rescue of a crew of North American sailors whose ship had sunk a German submarine.

The torpedo had struck the *Faja de Oro*, but not fatally. The German captain then ordered the submarine to surface and finish her off with deck guns. Nine sailors were killed; the other twenty-eight (including the captain) managed to escape in life rafts. After drifting for two days, they were picked up by a U.S. PBY-5A Catalina.

There was no doubt as to the identity of the attacking submarine. The sailors, as they sat in their life rafts, could even hear the Germans singing victory marches from within the steel hull of their craft.

"What's going to happen now, boss?" asked the man covering the cables.

"Looks like it'll be war. Take this to the director," replied Manterola matter-of-factly.

6

THE DECLARATION OF WAR

The ministerial cabinet met in the official residence of Los Pinos by special order of the president at 6:45 on the afternoon of the 22nd of May.

Ávila Camacho, square of face and awkward in speech, gave a summary of what everyone already knew: German submarines had sunk two Mexican ships, killing twenty-three sailors. The German government had not even responded to the first declaration of protest issued after the first sinking. Then he put before his cabinet his request to declare war on the Axis powers.

The meeting lasted three hours.

In the end, he would have to overcome the objections of two ministers who, strangely enough, were on opposite ends of the political spectrum. Heriberto Jara, Secretary of the Navy and a good friend of Lázaro Cárdenas on the left, and the Minister of the Interior, one of the most conservative members of the government, Miguel Alemán, on the right. Jara's argument was twofold: declaring war would put Mexico in a subordinate position with respect to the United States, because Mexico had very little it could contribute in a military sense to this war between powers, but the Mexican merchant marines would still be bearing the brunt of the war's disasterous effects. In only a brief span of time, all of Mexico's merchant fleet would be sunk. There was just no way to protect them. Jara argued that they should involve themselves by offering economic support, petrol reserves, raw industrial materials, and diplomatic support to the Allies, but stop short of actually declaring war. Wars are not waged solely with guns and bombs, he cautioned.

And Minister Alemán? What were his arguments?

He spoke of Mexico's weak armed forces and the economic damages that war could cause. None of it was clear to anyone.

But Ávila Camacho stuck to his guns, making only one concession to Jara: he named Lázaro Cárdenas the Secretary of War. The rationale for the move was obvious; in the eternal balancing act that characterizes Mexican presidencies, the subordinate rapprochement with the U.S. and the entry—however symbolic it might be—into the war had to be counterbalanced by the reemergence of the most anti-American of the former Mexican presidents. It was clear that Cárdenas would make only the bare minimum of military concessions to the U.S. and would never permit or even consider allowing them to establish military bases on Mexican soil.

The president then passed around a draft of the declaration of war, which would be sent to congress for its approval.

7

YES, A PYRAMID

I'm leaving for Chiapas," the Poet said suc-
cinctly to Manterola as they sat in their usual Chinese café on Bucarelli.

The streets were ablaze with news of the war. The war? It was a strange
concept for Mexico. War against the Nazis and the Italian Fascists and the
Japanese military machine? And who knows against what else next, Hungary
and Romania?

"If you wait half an hour, I'll go with you. I just want to get a camera
from my office," replied Manterola.

"Officially I'm going in order to verify the detention and internment of
certain German nationals. But of course I'm really going there to look for
this pyramid. Look . . ." he handed the journalist a worn and yellowed folder.
It contained a single sheet of paper marked with a few scant notes. The file
on Rudolf Glauer, a German nobleman who, in June of 1923, had come
from New York and landed in Mexico at Veracruz. In November of that
same year, he departed Veracruz, bound for New York on the second half
of his round-trip ticket.

A memo, probably originating from some municipal office, told of how
the German had been conducting archaeological expeditions along the Ruta
Maya. In those days, the Minister of the Interior had sent out a communiqué
ordering that all foreign archaeologists be kept under close scrutiny, which
was intended to prevent the looting of ruins. And so because of this, the

Poet's anonymous informants had begun to record the movements of Rudolf Glauer.

Toward the end, the report described a town by the name of Tenosique which had sprung up around a sawmill on the border between Tabasco and Chiapas and where Von Sebottendorff had chartered a local guide called Manfredo Uk.

Manfredo Uk? Wasn't that the name of the father they had just found tortured and killed? Manterola looked up. The Poet nodded.

"Tortured and killed along with his son, and the words 'The door has been opened' painted in his own blood on the wall. We're getting close."

"How does one get to Tenosique?"

"In a puddlejumper from . . ."

8

SCHOOL

They moved, following the signs that Craso had left for them: a yellow swatch on a treetrunk, a single fish bone left in the middle of the jungle, a little mound of earth here or there.

Tomás took advantage of their time in camp to provide schooling. His student-soldiers belonged to just about every Maya ethnic group in the region, and there were even a couple of Nahuatl children who had been driven by the ranchers from the central mesa ever deeper into the jungle. There were Tojolabales and Choles and Mijes and Mopans and maybe even a Lacandón. Curiously Tomás, who had originally thought that he was going to have to learn Mayan, had since learned that the Maya speak a myriad of tongues and that his rudimentary Castillian Spanish was actually what they had in common. His troop was comprised of eleven boys and two girls and they ranged in age from thirteen to eighteen years. They had sought the counsel of their community elders, both out of curiosity and desperation, because some were orphans and there were no parents to cry for them because they had already cried for their parents. And they were intelligent; indeed, they knew the jungle better than the Chinaman knew the seas. They bore the scars of misery and abuse at the hands of the ranchers: Flavio José with his missing eye; Julius Caesar, his back scarred by having been flogged with a belt; Cicero so malnourished that his belly was distended and his mouth full of raw pustules; and the rest suffering from acne, skin infections, and fever. In the early days of their adventures, Tomás had encouraged hunting. Once they had acquired rifles, the meat fell readily at their feet, but soon the entire army was sick with diarrhea. Now he made sure to vary their diet; they stole fruit from orchards and groves, they ate sweet potatoes and wild tubers, and had become enamored of bird stock soup. They boiled their water and chewed the bark of the *cinchona* tree because it contained quinine. They dug out ticks and botfly larvae and held campfire festivals of burning bugs, and each carried his or her own ration of salt, dried meat, beans, and maize.

They had never been this far to the southeast, and the terrain was unfamiliar, but the legend of the Iguana seemed to have transcended Soconusco.

At night they struck camp at a ford in the river. The iguanas built a fire and sat basking in its glow. School was open. Their teacher had broken the lesson plan down into three areas: reading, history, and just a bit of geography. He hadn't been able to explain very well what there was to the south of the Soviet Union and to the east of the Mediterranean. And neither did he have a good handle on how to relate England and Palestine and Afghanistan.

History was more clear; they began with Spartacus and his slave rebellion, which they had spent nearly a month on, because the little iguanas had wanted details and specific names, wanted to know everything about swords, chest plates, shields, and Sicilian wheat. Now they were on to Chapter Two, which Tomás had decided would be the peasant uprisings of Lutheran Reform-era Germany. That was another history he knew well.

He was trying to explain the difference between the Lutheran rebels and the Utopia of the Anabaptists, the Munzer rebellion and the egalitarians. It was turning out to be a bit tougher than he had expected.

9

HEAVEN AND HELL

They flew under an impossibly blue sky over an interminable mass of trees, a seamless green sea of a jungle, a leafy green tapestry blanketing the ground beneath. Heaven above and hell below. Many years ago, Pioquinto Manterola had been in Milan during a brief train layover, and he had taken the opportunity to visit the Sforza castle. There, in a completely unfurnished room, Leonardo had painted one of his most unique murals. The room's entire ceiling was taken up by a grand forest, a thick mass of tree trunks that stretched to all four walls. Once you recover from the shock of seeing it for the first time, its image will remain forever in your mind's eye. It was the most subversive work of art that he had ever seen, for in a time when the ceilings of palaces and chapels were filled with biblical scenes and images of angels, Leonardo had wanted to take them down and paint a forest in their place. Heaven is a forest, he seemed to be saying, it is earth.

Over the roar of the engines, the Poet was trying to ask him something. He tried to concentrate.

"When we got together twenty years ago in that strange domino club, I think it was you who said that we were 'the shadow of a shadow,' right?"

"Yes, I remember, we were talking about the feeling we lived with in those days, the feeling of being eternally pursued and how there seemed to be a strange shadow hanging over us. But if my memory serves me correctly, it was you who came up with the metaphor."

"No, I'm sure it wasn't me. I would remember; for being a poet, I don't come up with such colorful metaphors too often. It was either you, or Tomás."

"To what do I owe this memory of the shadow?"

"To the fact that I now have the distinct feeling that we are returning as shadows, as pallid shadows of our former selves. We've been reunited yet again, or nearly so, but we are no longer what we once were."

"I'm wiser," offered Manterola.

"I'm more of a bastard, more stubborn, more determined, and slightly less complete," said Fermín Valencia, shrugging his stump.

"Returning as shadows," said the journalist, savoring the phrase. "I like it. And next time, after another twenty years, I'm going to remember it was you who said it."

1 0

THE GREAT ONE-ARMED
IGUANA CHIEF

They were going down the Usumacinta in a canoe when they heard the shots. They couldn't tell if they were nearby or distant; it was not easy to keep your bearings in that jungle that closed in like curtains draped over the river's winding course.

The Poet grabbed his suitcase and jumped into the water, splashing his way toward the shore where he burst out running. Manterola, slower of reflex, paddled over to a sandbar, got out of the canoe, and began to clamber up a hill. But the fates were against him, as he tripped and fell helplessly to the ground.

When Manterola, dusting himself off and patting himself down for matches with which to light his pipe, finally looked up, he discovered, standing before him and smiling a broad, toothy grin, the Chinaman Tomás Wong, dressed in the dirty white clothes of the local *campesinos*.

"Where the hell have you been?" he managed finally.

Tomás exhaled in a low whistle. "I was in China and then I came back and then I was building a highway and then I ran into some Nazis and I killed them and then they killed me and then I was reborn as the Iguana. And you?" said Tomás, laughing at his own incoherence.

"I was in my office minding my own business when three German writers and a rabbi explained to me that Hitler's rise to power was the result of an esoteric conspiracy and Verdugo, who's been in an insane asylum, summoned us from beyond the grave to come and play poker with Ernest Hemingway. . . ." replied the journalist, offering his own litany of nonsense.

"They told me you were coming down the river. . . ."

"And where's your accent?"

"I suppose I was never a true Chinaman. I figured that if I could speak Cantonese, I might as well learn to talk like a Mexican too," said Tomás.

Just then a group of indigenous boys armed with Mausers came running down the path.

"Iguana reporting, *señor*," a boy with one eye said to Tomás. The Chinaman nodded.

"When you started shooting the two who were on guard got scared and threw down their rifles and ran off into the jungle. And the one we were guarding, the one with his hands tied, just walked away. Then a lopsided little guy showed up with a cannon."

"No, *señor*," interjected a girl. "He just means that the guy had only one arm, and I saw him go into the pyramid. But yes, he did have a really big gun."

"Is there a cripple with you?" Tomás asked, turning to Manterola.

"It's the Poet, Tomás. He lost an arm during the war in Spain."

"Shit, I'd forgotten. I saw him years ago in New York. But what's this about a cannon?"

"A Thompson machine gun."

"The one-armed man is with us," the Iguana said to his troops. "He is the Great, One-Armed Iguana Chief. Watch out for him."

"Marcus Curtius went off into the jungle after the man in the coat."

"Valeria, go after Marcus, and between the two of you, stop him, but don't do anything else . . . How many are there inside the pyramid?"

"Marcus Curtius said only two, the chiefs."

"Who are they, Manterola?"

"The last two heads of the Nazi network. A pair of dangerous, psychotic assassins. Rahn and the man with the ash-blond hair."

"Let's go," said Tomás to Manterola and his troop.

DON'T PAINT THAT SHIT
IN MAYAN PYRAMIDS

It was terribly humid. Vegetation grew up from the floor, climbing the walls, but it also crept down them. The air was heavy and close with the smells of fungus, loose earth, and dead insects. It was a smell that reminded the Poet of his childhood in Chihuahua; after his mother had left his father and him, the smell of rot had invaded their home.

"They just don't clean pyramids like they used to," he said in a low voice.

Light filtered in through cracks in the ceiling. On one of the walls a mural narrated a clash between priests and warriors, lances and arrows, lightning and floods.

"And you, what right do you think you have to paint this shit in a Mayan pyramid?"

The Poet heard the voice, which seemed to be coming from the darkness ahead, and if he had had two hands, he would have rubbed them together. He quickened his pace. Was it Tomás Wong? A Tomás without his Chinese accent? Perhaps he had acquired a Mexican brother. But how had he reached this remote corner of the country before him? He set the trumpet case on the ground in order to better wield his weapon. He would come back for it later; no one would notice if he temporarily littered in a pyramid.

He moved cautiously, trying to keep out of the center of the passage. Shots rang out like thunder in the tomblike vault. He turned a corner to discover the body of the man with the ash-blond hair, whom he had never seen in person until now. He had taken a single round in the forehead. The wound was clean and did not bleed.

Two more shots echoed through the darkness. The Poet quickened his pace again, and soon found himself at the entrance to a wide hall lined with columns. A whisper off to his right alerted him:

"Poet, your German is behind those columns. But don't go shooting at anyone else; the boys are with me. I am Tomás Wong."

"I know, *compadre*," he whispered back, looking out of the corner of his eye at his old friend who was crouched a few meters away, gripping his pistol with both hands.

The room was duskily lit by the sunlight that wound its way through the cracks in the vaulted ceiling and by a series of torches fixed to the ground. On the far wall, he could make out the words *"Die Tür wurde geoffnet."*

Rahn was saying something in German. Reciting, droning. Then his voice rose in a crescendo and he began to howl. Horrifying, staggering screams. And then, suddenly, he emerged from behind the columns, his twin pistols blazing. The Poet emerged from his own refuge and pressed down on the Thompson's trigger, loosing a rain—a river—of lead. The Chinaman simply stood up and squeezed off a single round from his Tokarev.

SS Captain Otto Rahn hung there, midscream, in the air, as if levitating for an instant, and then fell, shattered, to the floor.

From nooks and crannies in the walls emerged several young Mayas armed with rifles. The Poet walked forward, stepped over Rahn's crumpled body, over toward the columns along the far wall. The infamous trunk was there, at the foot of one of the columns, as was the lifeless body of a stabbed *campesino*.

"Well, here's where he got the blood for his one final painting," said the Poet.

"Who was he?" asked Tomás, kicking the German's corpse.

"A man they called Brüning, whom I've been chasing for over a year now. A man returned from the dead. An SS officer who went by the alias of Otto Rahn, who never paid his hotel bills, and who murdered children," said the Poet, giving the corpse a swift kick of his own.

PHOTOS

I don't think it'll do you much good, now that they're going to confiscate the ranches and detain the Germans at Perote, but who knows what the future may bring," said the Poet, and on the trumpet or coronet or saxophone or trombone case he wrote: "To Whom it May Concern: Señor Tomás Wong . . ."

"Tomás, what's your full last name?"

"I don't know," he replied, never having known his mother.

". . . Señor Tomás Wong Martínez, for services rendered to this Office. Signed: Special Agent Fermín Valencia.' " He signed it with a flourish.

"You won't get in trouble for this?"

The Poet shrugged his shoulders.

Manterola had lit his pipe to scare off the mosquitoes. "And what about the third man, Hanussen, the one they kidnapped? Somehow he was with them in the beginning, and then he escaped to Verdugo's asylum for a time before being taken back."

"If he's alive in this jungle, we will find him," said Tomás and, raising his rifle, gave the iguanas the signal to fall out.

"You're right, Tomás. If the pattern continues, the next time we all see each other, we'll be seventy," said the Poet, lapsing into a farewell mode.

"It's a good age for philosophizing. We'll take care of the pyramid until then," he replied, and disappeared off into the jungle after his men.

Sweat or tears were welling up in Manterola's eyes. He wiped off his brow and pulled his camera out of his satchel. He took several photos of the bodies of Kowalski and Rahn at the foot of the statue of the warrior-priest. They seemed somehow like better people in death than they had been in life.

Whatever, thought Manterola. If I can't use these photos with a story in the paper, I can always just mail them off to Hitler.

PART	XV

PERIPHERIES

INTERRUPTIONS

AND INVASIONS

1. I am out on the patio giving a lecture on international rights versus the laws governing insane asylums to three colleagues while they weave their baskets. I am told that two men are here to see me; that they are waiting for me at the front door. Curious, I walk through the garden and back inside.

I find Tomás Wong dressed up as a southern *campesino*, in a low-slung straw sombrero, huaraches, and a machete hanging from his belt. He is just as I have imagined him, with his eyes a bit more almond-shaped, a bit less golden, a bit more closed by the sun. At his side is Eric Jan Hanussen, with the timid look of a deer in his eyes and wearing his long black coat in the middle of a splendorous summer afternoon.

"My German friend here isn't quite right in the head, but I understand he wants to be brought here. Perhaps you can take care of him?"

I nod. Hanussen goes inside, hands in his pockets, and walks off down the hall behind me. Tomás embraces me. We stay locked for a long while, saying nothing. Then he breaks away, turns, and walks off into that urban jungle which I can only just intuit from my side of the window, in here. That city which I love so much and which I can feel; that country which I describe through the eyes of others, through the eyes of imagination and memory.

HANUSSEN'S MONOLOGUE

Heard in whispers of German in the middle of the night and translated the following morning by Verdugo:

"The labyrinth is accessible from three points; each represents one of the three symbolic centers of power. Once they are found, something happens. And if nothing happens? Then we have found ourselves at the wrong labyrinth, the three symbols are mystifications, are fallacious. We are not the proper bearers. Do we not know the language? Perhaps we haven't put the symbols in order? Perhaps we are not really bearers at all. How have we arrived here? The guardians tell histories of annihilation. Each star in a cloudless night sky marks a death. There are millions. We three have died along the way. The voyage began long ago . . . The little man called to us from hundreds of miles away, called us to murderous dementia, and we followed him voluntarily, singing hymns and telling lies. The little man of afflicted manners, who didn't speak clearly and swallowed his vowels, the little man who didn't know when to pause, set us in motion, set us on the road. The little man who hides an abomination inside of him. A throne, a dominion, a legal authority? Those spirits of second intensity whom St. Paul knew . . . The labyrinth must be entered simultaneously. Does he have to enter the labyrinth? If the answer is yes, how are they going to get the three symbols there? Only one can be carried at a time. I fled from all this, but I cannot flee from myself. The stars are being extinguished; they tire of so much hanging death. And as they wink out, a coldness arrives. Not Horbiger's cold, but the cold of hell. The icy throes of the inferno. Cold is final."

INTERRUPTIONS
AND INVASIONS

2. We have returned to writing. A welcome creative fervor sweeps over us. The Poet has sent me several reams of typing paper that he stole from his office. I write on paper bearing the letterhead of the Ministry of the Interior, Department of Investigation. I have a few of Hemingway's dollars left from poker as well. I write messages on them. Letters printed on paper that no one will destroy, paper that passes through the membranes of this asylum, notes that may find those who need them most. Reaching across the gates of eternity.

The afternoons are soft; the spring seems to be taking on summer's splendor. The garden fills with flowers. Roses and marigolds abound. At one end, near the gate, a lush mat of arum has sprung up.

De la Calle has again taken up the novel he is writing via correspondence with Señor Burroughs. He informs me that one of the apes will play a key role in the second part, even becoming a sort of co-protagonist, and that there is a strong possibility of recovering the lost cities of King Solomon and therefore a part of his erotic wisdom.

Even Erasto is writing something. Rumor has it that it deals with the true history of Montezuma II, one of the wizard-kings. He has yet to show it to any of us.

I do not put my prose on display either. I carefully collect my materials night after night and place them underneath my mattress. It's nothing more than the first-time narrator's fear of outside interference.

I believe that what I'm writing here both is and is not faithful to the events of the past year. I also believe that no one will be overly concerned with this faithfulness.

The padded room has not seen another game of poker. For the past several days, it has held a disturbed man who broke an arm during one of his violent rages.

3. Casavieja pulls a car out of the garage, a freshly waxed apple-green Alfa Romeo. He is meticulously groomed as well. It is an event, a *cause célèbre*, for the car has been penned up for several years. But how many? It is in things such as this that my memory fails me. This past hits me with another which I don't think I want to remember. But memory is a broad blotter; if you want to erase something, you will erase its immediate family as well.

Some of the inpatients meet at the gate to bid farewell to Doctor Casavieja. They salute him, waving their kerchiefs in hand. He takes the apocryphal Graham Greene with him, who is also extremely well groomed.

4. I mail to Hemingway the pages of the novel he was working on during his brief stay with us. I receive a note from him in return. He thinks that the submarines that were operating out of Puerto de las Perlas have moved to another base in Cuba, somewhere near the Camagüey cays. I receive his observations on the marvels that are the Mexican people like gifts, including the virtues of tequila over the daiquiri (though this could well be a diplomatic falsehood). He also appoints me his permanent attorney, clarifying that if there is one thing which he has distrusted all his life it is lawyers, "a clan of miserable bloodsuckers." He also encloses a stack of autographed cards so that any inpatient who wants one can have a personally signed copy of *To Have and Have Not* just by affixing the card to the first page of their book. He asks that I have Angel de la Calle forge an old Mexican painting for him, promising to hang it in his bedroom. He ends his letter with the phrase, "*Nos vemos en el infierno*, Ernesto." See you in hell. It doesn't seem likely. Hell has to be replete with inhabitants by now, saturated and overpopulated. One likely can't walk down the street without bumping into someone at every step. It's going to be very difficult to find any one person in particular.

5. Hanussen agrees to "work magic" out by the fountain. He pulls a pigeon out of a hat and ties a dozen colored handkerchiefs together in midair. The patients look up from their baskets and applaud. He goes on well

into the night. At times, I come out and sit by his side and take his hands in mine.

He asks me in German, "Why are you here?" I have yet to answer this question. I cannot explain it. I don't remember it well enough. Perhaps I don't want to remember it well. Or poorly, for that matter. I smile. Could I be in some other place. . . . ?

4

EL PILAR

In 1934, the magazine *Esquire* paid Hemingway an advance of $3300 for the right to publish a series of short stories. Hemingway used the money to make a down payment to the Wheeler shipyards in Brooklyn so they could begin construction on a yacht for him. A short while later, when the impressive forty-two-footer powered by twin outboard diesel motors was finished, he piloted it to Key West where he was living in those days. He christened her *El Pilar*, perhaps in remembrance of his tour of duty in Spain; perhaps also because Pilar was his pet name for Pauline, his wife at the time.

When he first moved to Cuba, *El Pilar* was anchored in Havana, and when he made Finca Vigía his permanent residence on the island, he brought her to anchor at the nearby little fishing village of Cojímar.

For years she (and her well-endowed bar) were used strictly for fishing expeditions, but in the summer of 1942 she underwent a strange transformation. The bottles of whiskey and gin and demijohns of chianti stowed in the hold had been replaced by grenades, bazookas, and machine guns.

Following Hemingway's instructions, Gregorio Fuentes, the ship's cook and skipper, had taken her to the shipyards at the Cuban naval base at Casablanca where they made a series of customizations, although one major change, situating a pair of .88-caliber air-cooled Brownings on the foredeck, could not be accomplished because the internal structure of the smallish boat wouldn't support them.

A pair of carefully lettered signs that read "American Museum of Natural History" provided the final pieces of camouflage.

Hemingway recruited a motley crew for *El Pilar*'s missions, which were undertaken with the tacit complicity of the U.S. embassy's Naval Department: Americans, Cubans, and Basque Republican friends of his who spent their afternoons playing jai-ali in the streets of Havana.

"Operation Friendless," named in honor of one of his cats, began. For the next several months, *El Pilar* patrolled the Camagüey cays, waiting for a German submarine to appear or to run across a secret supply base.

It has to be said that during those months spent fishing for subs, Hemingway and his crew didn't catch so much as a nibble, though they were convinced that they had come close to the U176 on a pair of occasions.

5

INTERRUPTIONS

AND INVASIONS

1. The woman has come back to water the hydrangeas on her balcony. I have recently installed my telescope on the Lighthouse's tower. Her home is nearly a kilometer from here, an isolated house on the outskirts of Tacubaya. Her routine is impeccable. The woman, strolling through her house, appears briefly at the kitchen window; her silhouette, the echoes of her movements, fills the window; she passes swiftly into the living room, removes her blouse, and goes out onto the balcony to water her plants, her breasts bared to the morning air. Solitary woman; white, abundant breasts. But I cannot remember her face from one day to the next.

2. A drawn and haggard Poet and a trembling Manterola return from Chiapas. Casavieja, while passing through on his rounds, examines the journalist and determines that he has contracted a touch of malaria. He puts him on a regimen of quinine.

We organize a poker party. They show me photographs of the pyramid and of the bodies of Otto Rahn and Kowalski stretched out and bloated under the sun. The trunk filled with silver bars. A closeup of one of the ingots shows that they are stamped with Cyrillic markings. What did the Russians have to do with all this?

Bah. There are many questions. But we sit down for poker with resolve and concentration, going after the beans and kernels of maize piled up on the table with a fervor. Bit by bit, they begin to collect in my favor. Night falls. The patio fills with the smells of jasmine and *flor de la noche*. We allow ourselves one question apiece. As a farewell.

"You, who knows everything, tell me where I can find Veronique. I think I'm madly in love with that woman," the Poet says to me.

"I'm sorry, but I haven't the foggiest."

"Are you going to leave this place someday, *amigo*?" asks Manterola.

I choose not to answer, though by doing so, I forfeit the chance to ask my question: what did they do with the silver . . . ?

6

SUBMARINES

I n the days that followed, other Mexican ships were sunk by German submarines: on June 26, Captain Hans Witt ordered the torpedoing of the tanker *Tuxpan* near the mouth of Tecolutla, one day after the same sub had sunk *Las Choapas* near Tampico. A small tragedy is coupled with this sinking: a woman by the name of Liliana Díaz Villela was stowed away below decks. She was injured in the attack and died a short while later.

The *Juan Casiano* would be sunk as well, but the captain's logs of the German subs who were operating in the region do not register that attack. A shady deal to defraud the insurance companies? An accident? A tragic mistake by the Americans? A storm? Indeed, a minor mystery.

The Germans continued to attack, sinking the *Oaxaca* and then the *Amatlán* (which was known as the *Vigor* before being commandeered from the Italians) sixty-two miles off the coast of Tampico on its way home from Havana.

Minister Jara's prophecy was proving true. On the other hand, the Japanese had not moved toward Baja California at all.

INTERRUPTIONS
AND INVASIONS

1. They gunned down the Poet at his office door. He was on his way back from buying a pair of slipper-like shoes—moccasins, they call them—from the El Borceguí store when two men, standing a few meters away from the building's back entrance, drew their revolvers and unloaded on him.

It's rumored that the men who tried to kill him worked for that very office, the Ministry of the Interior . . . that they were government agents.

The newspaper reports tell little more. Is he dead? Injured? Kidnapped? It seems more likely to me that he turned the tables, left his assailants draining in the streets, and then vanished.

2. Miguel Alemán seizes and dismantles the Chiapas plantations, but does not nationalize them. Why? Those days have passed. The men he sends there are held in confidence by the local government, the Germans, and the *caciques*. In the end, the land will return to the same old owners.

3. Doctor Sacal comes to see me. Until now, we have only heard of each other. We talk of interbellum Berlin and of gardening. He is a profoundly sad old man. I suppose that he hasn't come just to see me. Surely enough, he shuts himself in my room with Hanussen, interrogating him, taking notes, and at times managing to break his spell of silence. On his way out, he blesses me. I tell him I appreciate the thought, but that I am an atheist. He tells me that in times such as these, it's a wise decision. We don't speak of

what has happened; we don't read into the presence of Otto Rahn and his group in Mexico. Each of us will draw his own conclusions.

4. Strangely enough, I am full of questions. Which arm is the Poet missing? I do not remember. What would Erasto the Mute say if he knew how to speak? Why does Doctor Casavieja keep among his clinical reports a few pages stolen from the novel which I am writing? I have not given it a title, but he has dubbed it *Verdugo and His Companions*. What would this terrible, ongoing war have come to if Hitler had indeed been able to come to Mexico? But did he really intend to do so in the middle of such a war? To go to Mexico and leave the war in Himmler's hands or Goering's? Where will the real Graham Greene go? Probably to that brothel in the Colonia Roma where the girls amuse the clients, as they say, "orientally," and where Rahn and Kowalski had spent some time during a part of the story which I've neglected to tell. Which of Beethoven's symphonies was Manterola's favorite as he and the servants sat in his rooftop abode to listen to them?

5. The Nazis will win the war. The world will fall. All the reports that reach my corner of the corner of the world point to this conclusion. As I write, the Germans have reached as far as the Volga, looking down on Stalingrad from atop their ominous tanks. Haffa is wreaking havoc in north Africa, and Rommel seems invincible. Continental Europe is caught in the throes of Fascism. Dissidents are being shot in France and Holland. The Americans are pinned down on the Solomon Islands, fighting a war of shadows and fancies with the Japanese navy, who control most of Asia and the Pacific.

6. Where do Hitler's phials of caffeine come from now that the Chiapas networks have been dismantled? I imagine a bit of good news: the supreme German chancellor wakes up in the mornings, drenched in sweat, his hands trembling, stuttering and stammering. His new brand of caffeine does not have the same effect. It is not the Mexican caffeine he knew and loved. It is Ethiopian, sent to him by Mussolini.

De la Calle contends that these are the sorts of things that can turn the tide of a war. I disagree.

7. I have lost many things along the way. I have lost and found myself time and time again. I could end it thus: sharply, suddenly, in the middle of a phrase, one final interruption and invasion.

But I conclude with the word without hope, the damned word, the mortal word, the interminable word, the initial word: "End."

EPILOGUES

OF MADNESS AND NOVELS

Ernest Hemingway returns to his home at Finca Vigía after yet another of *El Pilar*'s fruitless missions, to change clothes and meet with the U.S. ambassador, and he finds a small pile of clean shirts stacked neatly on his bed. On top was the white guava which he had woken up with in the swimming pool after the longest stretch of drunkenness in his life. The guava he had brought home with him from Mexico. Under the guava was a note, written in his own handwriting, which someone must have pulled from the pocket of one of his shirts before washing it. It read, "Is the Mexican lawyer Alberto Verdugo truly demented? Or is madness a form of clarity? Was madness simply a literary recourse enabling him to relate things which he never saw or otherwise knew of? Can that novel of his ever be written?"

ALBERTO VERDUGO'S
FINAL NOTE

I suppose that not even Hemingway would attempt to construct a novel with materials such as these. They are simply too fantastic, too delirious, too disconnected, too outlandish, too bizarre, too absurd. But in Mexico, reality has always had this quality of the absurd. And on those rare occasions when it doesn't, we have to assume the worst, the deceitful curtain of words, the false language of the system. The justification for power's injustice.

However relatable (or not) they may be, the things that I have described here did more or less happen. Those left alive or dead or wounded can attest to it all.

We go back to eating calabash soup with dinner. Fortunately, they also give us wheat flour tortillas, *a la norteña.*

It seems evident that with the conclusion of this history comes the conclusion of my second life. The bells herald the end.

The woman has not returned to the balcony. De la Calle hesitantly asks if she doesn't remind me of my wife. I have no answer, though he may well be right.

In all ways, today's dawns are not what they once were.

ERNEST HEMINGWAY'S
FINAL NOTE

I received a letter from the Lighthouse, from Doctor Casavieja, written just after he had finished speaking with the law-yer's roommate. From what he gathered, Verdugo finished the manuscript on which he had been working for the past several months, spent a few hours looking through his telescope at the countryside, and then took a pistol he had somehow managed to obtain and keep hidden from the guards and fired a single shot through his palette and out the back of his head.

Along with this news, Casavieja enclosed a copy of Verdugo's manu-script. It is in Spanish, though I can read it with a bit of difficulty. It inter-sects in certain ways with something I have myself been trying to write for some time.

THE POET'S FINAL NOTE
(FROM A LETTER HE SENT TO
H. SEVERAL YEARS LATER)

If I may be permitted, and in my omniscient state in the style of Verdugo, I have a few questions that remain to be answered:

Why, at the end of the war, did the Doctor Emilio Casavieja, proprietor and director of a mental hospital in Mexico City referred to as the Lighthouse, travel to London to receive a commendation from the British Intelligence Services which was pinned to his chest by Winston Churchill himself?

Why did I—also known as the Poet—leave the ranks of the Mexican secret service, change my name and my citizenship, and dedicate myself fully to a clandestine life of resistance and pornographic literature?

Why is it that the Hollywood film starring the woman from Senegal (alternatingly known as Veronique and as Estrella Soares) and Humphrey Bogart and based on an obscure Raymond Chandler story was never screened, leaving that enchanting Black woman to disappear forever after her ephemeral presence on the silver screen? Where is she now?

How did a package of Mexican coffee bearing a rough stamp that read "Soconusco Coffee. Cooperativa El Iguana" slip through countless blockades to reach the mountain base of the Red Army in Yenan and the hands of Chuh Teh and Tse Tung?

Perhaps the only thing that remains to be said is that Miguel Alemán became president of Mexico the following term further entrenching the ruling party's swing to the right. His policies of pillaging the state set the stage for the tradition of robbery that has come to dominate Mexican politics. The Americans overlooked his Naziphilic views and Truman, who had read the various reports himself, received him with great fanfare in May of 1947. They offered him all the regalia of a circus: he addressed Congress, he received a worthless honorary doctorate from Columbia, and was given a good old-fashioned New York City ticker-tape parade.

As you might have expected, he had returned the coffee plantations in Soconusco to landowners of German descent the year before.

Mexico will be a long time in maturing. I am glad that I am not there to see it. The vultures will sweep in over the land and plunder it. It will live under the reverse of Midas's touch: in trying to make gold, everything they touch will turn to shit. Welcome to Age of Robbery.

Still, though, I will return.

I love that damned shitty country.

PIOQUINTO MANTEROLA'S
FINAL NOTE

Nineteen years later, at his home in Ketchum, Idaho, Ernest Hemingway also killed himself, eating both barrels of a Boss shotgun over a breakfast of eggs and orange juice. He left a series of papers in the strongbox at Scribner's editorial offices in New York City, among which was a manuscript, authored either by Verdugo's hand or his or both, which tells our story from the winter of 1941 to the summer of 1942. His family has requested my presence, as per a note which he left in which he revealed to me the existence of another, half-finished manuscript on his adventures with the submarines off the coast of Cuba. He is not entirely enamored of that one.

I have shut myself away in my rooftop abode described herein, with only Beethoven's nine symphonies to accompany me, to read this manuscript, in order, starting at the beginning. I will take as long as I need, for I am in no hurry. I retired from journalism long ago. There is nothing left to tell that's worth the pain.

AUTHOR'S NOTE

TO END THE NOVEL

The boundaries in this novel between reality and fiction are not well defined, not even to the author's eyes. It would not be a stretch to say that the historical information has been generously retouched. Perhaps the greatest manipulation of the novel's historic backdrop is how things which, in reality, occurred several years apart are here compressed into one succinct period of time: the summer of 1941 through the summer of 1942.

On the other hand, who today can say or remember what Hemingway did or did not do during that one fateful week, which even his most conscientious biographers such as Carlos Baker have recorded as an empty hollow, a blank page, a blurry photograph, a void?

And there is more than a bit of proof that, in 1942, Hemingway turned *El Pilar* into a privateer and dedicated himself for several fruitless months to hunting German submarines along the Cuban littoral.

Hemingway as a character himself presents us with great curtains of smoke. Being able to brush them aside and move past them makes his novels that much more exhilarating, especially those which have to do with the Caribbean and which were published posthumously and carry a strong autobiographical tone: *To Have and Have Not, The Garden of Eden, Islands in the Stream, True at First Light,* his observations on bullfighting in *The Dangerous Summer,* and *Fiesta.* Revealing, too, are the biographies by Burgess,

Carlos Baker, Denis Brian, and Kenneth S. Lynn, and *Selected Letters: 1917–1961*, edited by Baker. The *Cubano* Hemingway is deftly portrayed by Norberto Fuentes, Mary Cruz, and Uri Paparov.

Hemingway's language herein was constructed from reading his correspondence, his journalism, and from the manners of speech and thought of his many alter egos: Thomas Hudson (*Islands in the Stream*), David Bourne (*The Garden of Eden*), and Captain Henry Morgan (*To Have and Have Not*), both in the original English and in translations by Marta Isabel Gustavino, Pilar Giralt, Héctor Quesada, and León Ignacio.

I visited Finca Vigía a half-dozen times and, thanks to the kindness of the museum directors, I was able to peruse in detail the Cuban Hemingway's working environment. When my memory failed me, the *Museo Hemingway* guide, written by Máximo Gómez, was a great resource.

Hemingway did, in fact, write standing up and probably suffered from piles, but I cannot specify if it was in 1942 or thereafter. His typewriter and bookcase can still be seen, as I have described them, in Finca Vigía.

It would have been, of course, impossible for Hemingway to have seen the matador Manolete fight in Mexico in 1941; Manuel Rodríguez did not fight there until the winter of 1945–46, when he earned his stripes in the Toreo de Cuatro Caminos and realized a season that bore him triumphantly through the country.

It also would have been impossible for any of the German agents to have been reading *Across the River and Into the Trees*, which would be written seven years later and published in 1950.

I could not locate the documents in which Diego Rivera confessed to cannibalism, and so I must cite them from memory. I believe, however, that the statements were made after 1942.

In terms of other things that could not have been, the German embassy was not, in fact, located at the corner of Hamburgo and Insurgentes streets, but it pleases me to imagine it there.

And the Poet could not have seen Orson Welles's *Touch of Evil* which, though it is set in the 1940s, was not made until 1959. On the other hand, though, the journalist could indeed have claimed to have seen *Citizen Kane*, filmed in 1941.

And it is unlikely that the Spanish soccer fans would have been chanting "*España, mañana, será Republicana*" since the slogan was not actually born until the 1960s during the anti-Franco student movements.

Graham Greene was indeed in Mexico working for British Intelligence in 1939, but by 1941 his assignments had taken him to Freetown and Sierra Leone after having been part of the civil defense in London during the Nazi blitz. Therefore, the ephemeral character who bears his name here must be an imposter. The magnificent biography by Norman Sherry pays close and detailed attention to this stage of the real Greene's life.

The history of the Naziphilic coffee growers in Chiapas is well documented by, among others, my friend Daniela Spenser, and a differing version of the chaotic and harried A39 reports described here can be found somewhere in the National General Archive of Mexico (I know this, because that's where I found them). We also know that Mexican ships were, in fact, torpedoed by German submarines, and that a very meticulous chronicling of the sinkings and the U-boats who perpetrated them can be found in Mario Moya Palencia's book *Mexicanos al grito de guerra*.

We may also assume that the Doctor Atl described herein did indeed act in this peculiar way; the research conducted by my friend Armando Castellanos in various national archives supports this.

Furthermore, the streets, government officials, and landscapes both are and are not as I have described them.

Georg Nicolaus was arrested in February of 1942 by Mexican secret service agents and subsequently extradited to the United States. However, he was not, during his detention, shot in both legs.

And although Verdugo could easily have heard Cuco Sánchez's songs on the radio (since that was around the time when he was breaking out), I doubt that he heard *"Tú sólo tú"* by F. Valdés Leal, which I believe was recorded subsequently.

And after all, the Poet, when he prefaced his own reports, could not have known that the Palacio Negro de Lecumberri would, years later, become the head office of the National Archives.

Tomás Wong's experiences during the Long March have been pieced together from Dick Wilson's book *The Long March* and from the testimonials of actual participants in the Cuban edition, *La larga marcha*.

The Nazi esoterica, the secret societies, the racist deliriums of the Thule society, the Hitlerian occultism, and the stories of Rahn and Hanussen are amply, if chaotically, documented in works by Pauwels and Bergier, Jean Michel Angebert, Dusty Sklar, Wolf Schwarzwäller, André Brissaud, René Alleau, William Bramley, Jeffrey Steinberg, Bernard Schreiber, Frank Smyth, Peter Levenda, Nicholas Goodrich-Clarke, Leigh Baigent, Pamela M. Potter, Jackson Spielvogel, Walter Johannes Stein, Francis King, and Ravenscroft and Robert Ambelain. If I may be accused of anything, it's of cutting this list too short.

If the Lance of Antioch truly exists, and Montezuma's Headdress is in a Vienna museum (though if it's a fake we demand that it be returned to Mexico), the Scepter of Charlemagne is my own invention. My fraud is no more sinful than the other two.

The poem by Albert Haushoffer, which is part of a collection of eighty sonnets, was written in 1944 in the Moabit prison, shortly before his execution for opposing Nazism. That makes it difficult to have been cited by a rabbi in 1941, but it didn't seem right to me to leave it out.

The story of the relationship between Miguel Alemán and Hilda Krüger is documented in the FBI's archives, which is where I chanced upon it. A profound veil of silence has been draped over this and other similar subjects in my country, although the social history of Alemán's white-collar robbery is part of the collective memory of thousands of Mexicans.

The United States had a profound lack of confidence in the Mexican Minister of the Interior. According to State Department documents, the gringo ambassador Messersmith had a pessimistic opinion of Alemán, describing him as "unscrupulous," which perhaps hints at the fact that he had dealings with Nazi Germany, serving as a sort of "front man."

Curiously, and demonstrating the gap in imperial politics in terms of memory and morality, and despite the warnings that the government received from the FBI and Donovan's SS, and as the Poet makes clear in his Epilogue, in May of 1947, Miguel Alemán, then President, made an official visit to the U.S. where he was received with much honor and acclaim.

It is true that Hilda Krüger became a writer in Mexico and, though she used a pseudonym, she wrote a biography of La Malinche. Salvador Novo makes a vague reference to it in his diaries.

The poem which Pedro Garfias recites to cast off his alcoholic albatross still did not exist in 1942; it would not be published until 1948 in *De soledad y otros pesares*, and it is therefore improbable—although possible—that a Spanish poet would have recited it in his sleep.

Clausell's studio can be seen as it is described here in the Museo de la Ciudad de México. It is a unique, marvelous, unforgettable room.

Nevertheless, there are corners in this novel that do not exist, impossibly formed by parallel streets, events such as the poison attack on Múgica which never occurred, and dialogues that historical figures most likely never had. Miguel de Cervantes was not born on April 20; rather it is thought to be September 29 or thereabouts, the only reliable fact being that his certificate of baptism is dated October 9, 1547. José Revueltas could, with a bit of effort, have completed his treatise on turkey vultures before December of 1941, understanding that he would complete *Human Mourning* some months later in August of 1942. Arthur Koestler could not have sent Verdugo his investigations on Kazaros in 1942, since he collected them during the early 1970s and published them in 1976 under the title *The Thirteenth Tribe*. And it would have been very difficult indeed for Miguel Alemán to